Praise for Ali Hazelwood

"A literary breakthrough. . . . *The Love Hypothesis* is a self-assured debut, and we hypothesize it's just the first bit of greatness we'll see from an author who somehow has the audacity to be both an academic powerhouse and [a] divinely talented novelist."

—*Entertainment Weekly*

"Contemporary romance's unicorn: the elusive marriage of deeply brainy and delightfully escapist. . . . *The Love Hypothesis* has wild commercial appeal, but the quieter secret is that there is a specific audience, made up of all of the Olives in the world, who have deeply, ardently waited for this exact book."

—*New York Times* bestselling author Christina Lauren

"With her sophomore novel, Ali Hazelwood proves that she is the perfect writer to show that science is sexy as hell, and that love can 'STEM' from the most unlikely places. She's my newest must-buy author."   —#1 *New York Times* bestselling author Jodi Picoult

"Funny, sexy, and smart. Ali Hazelwood did a terrific job with *The Love Hypothesis.*"

—*New York Times* bestselling author Mariana Zapata

"Gloriously nerdy and sexy, with on-point commentary about women in STEM."

—*New York Times* bestselling author Helen Hoang

"STEMinists, assemble. Your world is about to be rocked."

—*New York Times* bestselling author Elena Armas

"This tackles one of my favorite tropes—Grumpy meets Sunshine—in a fun and utterly endearing way. . . . I loved the nods toward fandom and romance novels, and I couldn't put it down. Highly recommended!"

—*New York Times* bestselling author Jessica Clare

"Pure slow-burning gold with lots of chemistry."   —PopSugar

"A beautifully written romantic comedy with a heroine you will instantly fall in love with, *The Love Hypothesis* is destined to earn a place on your keeper shelf."

—Elizabeth Everett, author of *A Lady's Formula for Love*

"Smart, witty dialogue and a diverse cast of likable secondary characters. . . . A realistic, amusing novel that readers won't be able to put down."   —*Library Journal* (starred review)

"Hilarious and heartwarming, *The Love Hypothesis* is romantic comedy at its best. . . . A perfect amalgamation of sex and science, sure to appeal to readers of Christina Lauren or Abby Jimenez."

—Shelf Awareness

"With whip-smart and endearing characters, snappy prose, and a quirky take on a favorite trope, Hazelwood convincingly navigates the fraught shoals of academia."   —*Publishers Weekly*

TITLES BY ALI HAZELWOOD

• • • •

The Love Hypothesis
Love on the Brain

LOATHE TO LOVE YOU

Under One Roof
Stuck with You
Below Zero

Loathe to
Love You

ALI HAZELWOOD

BERKLEY

New York

BERKLEY
An imprint of Penguin Random House LLC
penguinrandomhouse.com

Copyright © 2023 by Ali Hazelwood
Under One Roof, *Stuck with You*, and *Below Zero* copyright © 2022 by Ali Hazelwood
Penguin Random House supports copyright. Copyright fuels creativity, encourages diverse
voices, promotes free speech, and creates a vibrant culture. Thank you for buying an authorized
edition of this book and for complying with copyright laws by not reproducing, scanning, or
distributing any part of it in any form without permission. You are supporting writers and
allowing Penguin Random House to continue to publish books for every reader.

BERKLEY and the BERKLEY & B colophon are registered trademarks of
Penguin Random House LLC.

ISBN: 9780593638835

The Library of Congress has cataloged the Berkley Romance
trade paperback edition of this book as follows:

Names: Hazelwood, Ali, author.
Title: Loathe to love you / Ali Hazelwood.
Description: First edition. | New York: Berkley Romance, 2023.
Identifiers: LCCN 2022021252 | ISBN 9780593437803 (trade paperback)
Subjects: LCGFT: Romance fiction. | Novellas.
Classification: LCC PS3608.A98845 L63 2023 | DDC 813/.6—dc23/eng/20220502
LC record available at https://lccn.loc.gov/2022021252

Under One Roof, *Stuck with You*, and *Below Zero* were originally published separately as audio
editions, February, March, and April 2022 respectively, and then as ebook editions, May, June,
and July 2022 respectively, by Jove, an imprint of Penguin Random House LLC.

Printed in the United States of America
1st Printing

Book design by Daniel Brount

Contents

Loathe to
Love You

Under
One Roof

For Becca, who is the best and had the best prompt

Prologue ⚙

look at the pile of dishes in the sink and reach a painful realization: I've got it bad.

Actually, scratch that. I already knew I had it bad. But if I hadn't, this would be a dead giveaway: the fact that I cannot glance at a colander and twelve dirty forks without seeing Liam's dark eyes as he leans against the counter, arms crossed on his chest; without hearing his stern-yet-teasing voice asking me, "Postmodern installation art? Or are we just out of soap?"

It comes right on the trail of arriving home late and noticing that he left the porch light on for me. That one . . . oh, that one always makes my heart hiccup in a half-lovely, half-wrenching way. Also heart-hiccup inducing: I remember to turn it off once I'm inside. Very unlike me, and possibly a sign that the chia seed sludge he's been making me for breakfast in the mornings when I'm late for work is actually making my brain smarter.

It's good that I've decided to move out. For the best. These heart hiccups are not sustainable in the long term, not to my mental or cardiovascular health. I'm only a humble beginner at this whole pining thing, but I can safely state that living with some guy you used to hate and somehow ended up slipping in love with is *not* a wise move. Trust me, I have a doctorate.

(In a totally unrelated field, but still.)

You know what *is* good about the pining? The constant nervous energy. It has me looking at the pile of dishes and thinking that cleaning the kitchen could be a fun activity. When Liam enters the room, I'm riding the unexpected urge to load the dishwasher as far as it will carry me. I glance up at him, notice the way he nearly fills the doorframe, and order my heart not to hiccup. It does it anyway—even adds a flip for good measure.

My heart's a jackass.

"You're probably wondering if a sniper is forcing me to do the dishes at gunpoint." I beam at Liam without really expecting him to smile back, because—Liam. He's next to impossible to read, but I've long stopped trying to *see* his amusement, and I just let myself *feel* it. It's nice, and warm, and I want to bathe in it. I want to make him shake his head, and say "Mara" in that tone of his, and laugh against his better judgment. I want to push up on my toes, reach out to fix the dark strand of hair on his forehead, burrow into his chest to smell the clean, delicious smell of his skin.

But I doubt *he* wants any of that. So I turn back to rinse a cereal bowl hiding under the colander.

"I figured you were being mind-controlled by those parasitic spores we saw on that documentary." His voice is low. Rich. I will miss it so, *so* much.

"Those were barnacles— See, I knew you fell asleep halfway."

He doesn't reply. Which is fine, because—Liam. A man of few smiles and even fewer words. "So, you know the neighbors' puppy? That French bulldog? He must have gotten away during a walk, because I just saw him run toward me in the middle of the street. Leash hanging from his neck and all." I reach out for a towel and my hand bumps into him. He's standing right behind me now. "Oops. Sorry. Anyway, I carried him back home and he was so cute . . ."

I stop. Because all of a sudden Liam is not just *standing* behind me. I'm being crowded against the sink, the edge of the counter pressed into my hip bones, and there's a tall wall of heat flat against my back.

Oh my God.

Is he . . . Did he trip? He must have tripped. This is an accident. "Liam?"

"This okay, Mara?" he asks, but he doesn't move away. He stays right where he is, front pressed against my back, hands against the counter on each side of my hips, and . . . Is this some kind of lucid dream? Is this a heart-hiccup-generated cardiovascular event? Is my brain converting my most shameful nighttime fantasies into hallucinations?

"Liam?" I whimper, because he is nuzzling my hair. Right above my temple, with his nose and maybe even his mouth, and it seems deliberate. Very much not an accident. Is he—? No. No, surely not.

But his hands spread on my belly, and that's what tips me off that this is different. This doesn't feel like one of those accidental brushing of arms in the hallway, the ones I've been telling myself to stop obsessing over. It doesn't feel like that time I tripped over my computer cord and almost stumbled into his lap, and it doesn't feel like him gently holding my wrist to check how badly I burned my thumb while cooking on the stove. This feels . . . "Liam?"

"Shh." I feel his lips at my temple, warm and reassuring. "Everything's okay, Mara."

Something hot and liquid begins to coil at the bottom of my belly.

One ⚙

Frankly, "They get on like a house on fire" is the most misleading saying in the English language. Faulty wiring? Misuse of heating equipment? Suspected arson? Not evocative of two people getting along in the least. You know what a house on fire has me picturing? Bazookas. Flamethrowers. Sirens in the distance. Because nothing is more guaranteed to start a house fire than two enemies blowtorching each other's most prized possession. Want to trigger an explosion? Being nice to your roommate is not going to do it. Lighting a match on top of their kerosene-soaked handmade quilt, on the other hand—"

"Miss?" The Uber driver turns, looking guilty about interrupting my pre-apocalyptic spiel. "Just a heads-up—we're about five minutes from your destination."

I smile an apologetic *Thank you* and glance back at my phone. My two best friends' faces take up the entire screen. Then, on the upper corner there's me: more frowny than usual (well justified), more pasty than usual (is that even possible?), more ginger than usual (must be the filter, right?).

"That's a totally fair take, Mara," Sadie says with a puzzled expression, "and I encourage you to submit your, um, very valid complaints to Madame Merriam-Webster or whoever's in charge of these matters, but . . . I literally only asked you how the funeral went."

"Yes, Mara—how'd—funeral—go—?" The quality on Hannah's end of the call is pitiful, but that's business as usual.

This, I suppose, is what happens when you meet your best friends in grad school: One minute you're happy as a clam, clutching your shiny brand-new engineering diploma, giggling your way through a fifth round of Midori sours. The next you're in tears, because you're all going separate ways. FaceTime becomes as necessary as oxygen. There are zero neon-green cocktails in sight. Your slightly deranged monologues don't happen in the privacy of the apartment you share, but in the semipublic back seat of an Uber, while you're on your way to have a very, *very* weird conversation.

See, that's the thing I hate the most about adulting: at some point, one has to start doing it. Sadie is designing fancy eco-sustainable buildings in New York City. Hannah is freezing her butt off at some Arctic research station NASA put up in Norway. And as for me . . .

I'm here. Moving to D.C. to start my dream job—scientist at the Environmental Protection Agency. On paper, I should be over the moon. But paper burns *so* fast. As fast as houses on fire.

"Helena's funeral was . . . interesting." I lean back against the seat. "I guess that's the upside of knowing that you're about to die. You get to bully people a bit. Tell them that if they don't play 'Karma Chameleon' while lowering your casket your ghost will haunt their progeny for generations."

"I'm just glad you were able to be with her in the last few days," Sadie says.

I smile wistfully. "She was the worst till the very end. She cheated in our last chess game. As if she wouldn't have beaten me anyway." I miss her. An inordinate amount. Helena Harding, my Ph.D. advisor and mentor for the past eight years, was family in a way my cold, distant blood relatives never cared to be. But she was also elderly, in a lot of pain, and, as she liked to put it, *eager to move on to bigger projects*.

"It was so lovely of her to leave you her D.C. house," Hannah says. She must have moved to a better fjord, because I can actually make out her words. "Now you'll have a place to be, no matter what."

It's true. It's all true, and I am immensely grateful. Helena's gift was as generous as it was unexpected, easily the kindest thing any-one has ever done for me. But the reading of the will was a week ago, and there's something I haven't had a chance to tell my friends. Something closely related to houses on fire. "About that . . ."

"Uh-oh." Two sets of brows furrow. "What happened?"

"It's . . . complicated."

"I *love* complicated," Sadie says. "Is it also dramatic? Let me go get tissues."

"Not sure yet." I take a fortifying breath. "The house Helena left me, as it turns out, she didn't really . . . own it."

"What?" Sadie aborts the tissue mission to frown at me.

"Well, she did own it. But only a little. Only . . . half."

"And who owns the *other* half?" Trust Hannah to zoom in on the crux of the problem.

"Originally, Helena's brother, who died and left it to his kids. Then the youngest son bought out the others, and now he's the sole owner. Well, with me." I clear my throat. "His name is Liam.

Liam Harding. He's a lawyer in his early thirties. And he currently lives in the house. Alone."

Sadie's eyes widen. "Holy shit. Did Helena know?"

"I have no clue. You'd assume, but the Hardings are such a weird family." I shrug. "Old money. Lots of it. Think Vanderbilts. Kennedys. What even goes on in rich people's brains?"

"Probably monocles," Hannah says.

I nod. "Or topiary gardens."

"Cocaine."

"Polo tournaments."

"Cuff links."

"Hang on," Sadie interrupts us. "What did Liam Vanderbilt Kennedy Harding say about this at the funeral?"

"Excellent question, but: he wasn't there."

"He didn't show up to *his aunt's funeral*?"

"He doesn't really keep in touch with his family. Lots of drama, I suspect." I tap my chin. "Maybe they're less Vanderbilts, more Kardashians?"

"Are you saying that he doesn't know that you own the other half of his house?"

"Someone gave me his number and I told him I'd be coming around." I pause before adding, "Via text. We haven't talked yet." Another pause. "And he didn't really . . . reply."

"I don't like this," Sadie and Hannah say in unison. Any other time I'd laugh about their hive mind, but there's something else I still haven't told them. Something they'll like even less.

"Fun fact about Liam Harding . . . You know how Helena was, like, the Oprah of environmental science?" I chew on my lower lip. "And she always joked that her entire family was mostly liberal-leaning academics out to save the world from the clutches of big corporations?"

"Yeah?"

"Her nephew is a corporate lawyer for FGP Corp." Just saying the words makes me want to gargle with mouthwash. And floss. My dentist will be thrilled.

"FGP Corp—the fossil fuels people?" A deep line appears in the middle of Sadie's brow. "Big oil? Supermajors?"

"Yep."

"Oh my *God*. Does he know you're an environmental scientist?"

"Well, I did give him my name. And my LinkedIn profile is just a Google search away. Do rich people use LinkedIn, you think?"

"No one uses LinkedIn, Mara." Sadie rubs her temple. "Jesus Christ, this is really bad."

"It's not that bad."

"You can't go meet with him alone."

"I'll be fine."

"He'll kill you. You'll kill him. You'll kill each other."

"I . . . maybe?" I close my eyes and lean back against the seat. I've been talking myself out of panicking for seventy-two hours—with mixed results. I can't crack now. "Believe me, he's the last person I want to co-own a house with. But Helena did leave half of it to me, and I kind of need it? I owe a billion in student loans, and D.C. is crazy expensive. Maybe I can stay there for a bit? Save on rent. It's a fiscally responsible decision, no?"

Sadie face-palms just as Hannah says combatively, "Mara, you were a grad student until ten minutes ago. You're barely above the poverty line. Do *not* let him kick you out of that house."

"Maybe he won't even mind! I'm actually very surprised he lives there. Don't get me wrong, the house is nice, but . . ." I trail off, thinking about the pictures I've seen, the hours spent on Google Street View scrolling and rescrolling through the frames, trying to get a grip on the fact that Helena cared about me enough to *leave me a house*. It's a beautiful property, certainly. But more of a family residence. Not what I'd expect from an ace lawyer who probably earns a European country's annual GDP per billable hour. "Don't high-powered attorneys live in luxury fifty-ninth-floor penthouses with golden bidets and brandy cellars and statues of themselves? For all I know he barely spends time in the house. So I'm just going to be honest with him. Explain my situation. I'm sure we can find some kind of solution that—"

"Here we are," the driver tells me with a smile. I return it, a tad weakly.

"If you don't text us within half an hour," Hannah says in a dead-serious tone, "I'm going to assume that Big Oil Liam is holding you captive in his basement and call law enforcement."

"Oh, don't worry about that. Remember that kickboxing class I took in our third year? And that time at the strawberry festival, when I kicked the butt of the guy who tried to steal your pie?"

"He was an eight-year-old boy, Mara. And you did *not* kick his butt—you gave him your own pie and a kiss on the forehead. Text in thirty, or I'm calling the cops."

I glare at her. "Assuming a polar bear hasn't mugged you in the meantime."

"Sadie's in New York, and she has the D.C. police on speed dial."

"Yup." Sadie nods. "Setting it up right now."

I start feeling nervous the moment I exit the car, and it gets worse the farther I drag my suitcase up the path—a heavy ball of anxiety slowly nestling behind my sternum. I stop about halfway to take a deep breath. I blame Hannah and Sadie, who worry way too much and are apparently contagious. I'll be fine. This will be fine. Liam Harding and I will have a nice, calm chat and figure out the best possible solution that is satisfactory to . . .

I take in the early-fall yard around me, and my trail of thought fades away.

It's a simple house. Large, but no topiary shit or rococo gaze-bos or those creepy gnomes. Just a well-kept lawn with the occasional landscaped corner, a handful of trees I don't recognize, and a large wooden patio furnished with comfortable-looking pieces. In the late-afternoon sunlight, the red bricks give the house a cozy, homey appearance. And every square inch of the place seems dusted in the warm yellow of ginkgo leaves.

I inhale the smell of grass, and bark, and sun, and when my lungs are full I let out a soft laugh. I could so easily fall in love with this place. Is it possible that I already am? My very first love at first sight?

Maybe this is why Helena left the house to me, because she knew I'd form an immediate connection. Or maybe knowing that she wanted me here has me ready to open my heart to it. Either way, it doesn't matter: this place feels like it could be home, and Helena is once again being her meddling self, this time from the afterlife. After all, she always went on and on about how she wanted me to really belong. *"You know, Mara, I can tell you're lonely,"* she'd say whenever I stopped by her office to chat. *"How do you even know?" "Because people who aren't lonely don't write fan fiction for* The Bachelor *franchise in their spare time." "It's not fan fiction. More of a metacommentary on the epistemological themes that arise in each episode and—my blog has* plenty *of readers!" "Listen, you're a brilliant young woman. And everyone loves redheads. Why don't you just date one of the nerds in your cohort? Ideally the one who doesn't smell like compost." "Because they're all dicks who keep asking when*

I'll drop out to go get a degree in home economics?" "Mmm. That is *a good reason."*

Maybe Helena finally realized that any hope of me settling down with *someone* was a lost cause, and decided to channel her efforts into me settling down *somewhere*. I can almost picture her, cackling like a satisfied hag, and it makes me miss her a million times harder.

Feeling much better, I leave my suitcase just off the porch (no one is going to steal it, not covered as it is in geeky KEEP CALM AND RECYCLE ON, and GOOD PLANETS ARE HARD TO FIND, and TRUST ME, I'M AN ENVIRONMENTAL ENGINEER stickers). I run a hand through my long curls, hoping they're not too messy (they probably are). I remind myself that Liam Harding is unlikely to be a threat—just a rich, spoiled man-boy with the depth of a surfboard who cannot intimidate me—and lift my arm to ring the bell. Except that the door swings open before I can get to it, and I find myself standing in front of . . .

A chest.

A broad, well-defined chest under a button-down. And a tie. And a dark suit jacket.

The chest is attached to other body parts, but it's so wide that for a moment it's all I can see. Then I manage to shift my gaze and finally notice the rest: Long, well-muscled legs filling what's left of the suit. Shoulders and arms stretching for miles. A square jaw and full lips. Short dark hair, and a pair of eyes barely a shade darker.

They are, I realize, fixed on me. Studying me with the same avid, confused interest I'm experiencing. The man appears to be unable to look away, as if spellbound at some base, deeply physical level. Which is a relief, because I can't look away, either. I don't want to.

It's like a punch to my solar plexus, how attractive I find him. It addles my brain and makes me forget that I'm standing right in front of a stranger. That I should probably say something. That the heat I'm feeling is probably inappropriate.

He clears his throat, looking as flustered as I feel.

I smile. "Hi," I say, a little breathless.

"Hi." He sounds the exact same. He wets his lips, as though his mouth is suddenly dry, and *wow*. That's a good look for him. "Can I . . . Can I help you?" His voice is beautiful. Deep. Rich. A little hoarse. I could marry this voice. I could roll around in this voice. I could listen to this voice forever and give up every other sound. But maybe I should first answer the question.

"Do you, um, live here?"

"I think so," he says, as though too wonderstruck to remember. Which makes me laugh.

"Great. I am here for . . ." What am I here for? Ah. Yes. "I was looking for, um, Liam. Liam Harding. Do you know where I can find him?"

"It's me. I'm he." He clears his throat again. Is he flushing? "That is, I am Liam."

"Oh." Oh no. Oh *no*. No, no. No. "I'm Mara. Mara Floyd. The . . . Helena's friend. I'm here about the house."

Liam's demeanor changes *instantly*.

He briefly closes his eyes, like one would when given a tragic, insurmountable piece of news. For a moment he looks betrayed, as though someone gave him a precious gift only to steal it from his hands the second it was unwrapped. When he says, "It's you," there is a bitter tinge to his beautiful voice.

He turns around and begins to stalk down the hallway. I hesitate for a moment, wondering what to do. He didn't close the door, so he wants me to follow him. Right? No clue. Either way, I half own the house, so I'm probably not trespassing? I shrug and hurry after him, trying to keep up with his much longer legs, taking in next to nothing of my surroundings until we reach a living area.

Which is stunning. This house is all large windows and hardwood floors—oh my God, is that a *fireplace*? I want to make s'mores in it. I want to roast an entire piglet. With an apple in its mouth.

"I'm so glad we can finally talk face-to-face," I tell Liam, a little out of breath. I'm finally recovering from . . . whatever happened at the door. I fidget with the bracelet on my wrist, watching him write something on a piece of paper. "I am so sorry for your loss. Your aunt was my favorite person in the whole world. I'm not sure why she decided to leave me the house, and I do understand that this co-owning business comes a bit out of left field, but . . ."

I trail off when he folds the paper and hands it to me. He's so tall, I have to consciously lift up my chin to meet his eyes. "What is this?" I don't wait for his answer and unfold it.

There's a number written on it. A number with zeros. Lots of them. I look up, confused. "What does this mean?"

He holds my gaze. There is no trace of the flustered, hesitant man who greeted me a few moments earlier. This version of Liam is coldly handsome and self-assured. "Money."

"Money?"

He nods.

"I don't understand."

"For your half of the house," he says impatiently, and it suddenly dawns on me: he is trying to buy me out.

I look down at the paper. This is more money than I've ever had in my life—or ever will. Environmental engineering? Not a lucrative career choice, apparently. And I don't know much about real estate, but my guess is that this sum is *way* above the actual value of the house. "I'm sorry. I think there's a misunderstanding. I'm not going to—I don't—" I take a deep breath. "I don't think I want to sell."

Liam stares, expressionless. "You don't *think*?"

"I *don't*. Want to sell, that is."

He nods once, curtly. And then asks, "How much more?"

"What?"

"How much more do you want?"

"No, I—I'm not interested in selling the house," I repeat. "I just can't. Helena—"

"Is double enough?"

"*Double*—how do you *even*—do you have *corpses* buried under the flower beds?"

His eyes are blocks of ice. "How much more?"

Is he even listening to me? Why is he being so insistent? Where has his cute, boyish blush gone? At the door, he just seemed so . . .

Whatever. I was clearly wrong. "I just can't sell. I'm sorry. But maybe we can figure out something else in the next few days? I don't have a place to stay in D.C., so I was thinking of moving in for a little while . . ."

He exhales a silent laugh. Then he realizes that I'm serious, and shakes his head. "No."

"Well." I try to be reasonable. "The house seems large, and—"

"You're not moving in."

I take a deep breath. "I understand. But my financial situation is very precarious. I'm starting my new job in two days, and it's really close by. On foot. This is a perfect place for me to live for a little while, until I get back on my feet."

"I just handed you the solution to all of your financial problems."

I wince. "It's really not that simple." Or maybe it is. I don't know, because I just can't stop remembering the ginkgo leaves settling on the hydrangeas and wondering what they would look like in the spring. Maybe Helena would have wanted me to see the yard in every season. If she'd meant for me to sell, she would have left me a chunk of cash. Right? "There are reasons why I'd prefer not to sell. But we can work out a solution. For instance, I could, um, temporarily rent you my half of the house and use the money to stay in another place?" That way, I'd still be holding on to Helena's gift. I'd be out of Liam's way and above the destitution threshold. Well, *slightly* above. And in the future, once Liam gets married to his girlfriend (who's probably a Fortune 500 CEO who can list the Dow 30 by market cap and has a favorite item in the *goop* newsletter), moves to a McMansion in Potomac, Maryland, and starts a politico-economic dynasty, I could revisit this place. Move in, like Helena seems to have wanted. If by then I've gotten a raise and can cover the water bill on my own, that is.

It's a fair proposal, right? Wrong. Because Liam's response is: "No." Boy, he loves the word.

"But why? You clearly have the money—"

"I want this settled once and for all. Who is your attorney?"

I'm about to laugh in his face and crack a joke about my "legal team" when his iPhone rings. He checks the caller ID and swears softly under his breath. "I need to take this. Stay put," he orders, way too bossy for my taste. Before he steps out of the living room he pins me with his cold, stern eyes and declares, "This is not, and will *never* be, your house."

And that, I believe, is it.

It's that very last sentence that clinches it. Well, together with the condescending, domineering, arrogant way he talked to me in the past two minutes. I walked into this house fully ready to have a productive conversation. I gave him several options, but he shut me down and now I'm getting *pissed*. I have as much legal right as he does to be here, and if he refuses to acknowledge it . . .

Well. Too bad for him.

Anger bubbling up my throat, I tear the paper Liam gave me in four pieces and drop it on the coffee table for him to find later. Then I go back to the porch, retrieve my suitcase, and start looking for an unused bedroom.

Guess what? I text Sadie and Hannah. Mara Floyd, Ph.D., just moved into her new house. And it's most definitely on fire.

Two ⚙️♥

Five months, two weeks ago

don't have time for this.

I am late for work. I have a meeting in half an hour. I have yet to brush my teeth *and* my hair.

I *really* don't have time for this.

And yet, like the fool that I have grown to be, I give in to temptation. I slam the fridge door, turn around to lean against it, cross my arms as menacingly as I can, and stare at Liam across the expanse of the open-concept kitchen.

"I know you have been using my coffee creamer."

It's wasted energy. Because Liam just stands on the side of the island, as impassible as the granite of the countertop, calmly spreading butter on a piece of toast. He doesn't fight back. He doesn't look at me. He proceeds with his buttering, unbothered, and asks, "Have I?"

"You're not as stealthy as you think, buddy." I give him my best glare. "And if this is some kind of intimidation tactic, it's not working."

He nods. Still unbothered. "Have you informed the police?"

"What?"

He shrugs his stupid, broad shoulders. He is wearing a suit, because he is *always* wearing a suit. A charcoal three-piece that fits him perfectly—and yet not at all, because he really doesn't have the evil-corporate-businessman physique. Maybe during his mandatory Kill the Earth training he interned as an oil rig driller? "This alleged theft of coffee creamer appears to distress you a lot. Have you told law enforcement?"

Deep breaths. I need to take deep breaths. In D.C., murder can be punished with up to thirty years in prison. I know, because I looked it up the day after I moved in. Then again, a jury of my peers would never convict me—not if I laid out the horrors I've been subjected to in the past few weeks. They would surely rule Liam's death as self-defense. They might even give me a trophy. "Liam, I'm trying here. *Really* trying to make this work. Do you ever stop and wonder if maybe *you* are being an asshole?"

This time he does look up. His eyes are so cold, my entire body shivers. "I did try. Once. And right when I was on the verge of a breakthrough someone started blasting the *Frozen* soundtrack at full volume."

I flush. "I was cleaning my room. I had no idea you were home."

"Mmm." He nods, and then does something I did not expect: he comes closer. He takes a few leisurely steps, making his way through the beautiful mix of ultramodern appliances and classic furniture of the kitchen until he's towering over me. Staring down as though I'm an ant problem he thought he'd long gotten rid of. He smells like shampoo and expensive fabric, and he's still holding the butter knife. Can you stab someone with that? I don't know, but Liam Harding looks like he'd be able to murder someone (i.e., me) with a beach ball. "Isn't your emotional-support creamer bad for the environment, Mara?" he asks, voice low and deep. "Think of the impact of ultraprocessed foods. The toxic ingredients. All that plastic."

He is so condescending, I could bite him. Instead I square my shoulders and step even closer. "I do something you've probably never heard of—it's called *recycling*."

"Is that so?" He sets the knife on the counter and glances next to me, at the bins I installed after I moved in. They are overflowing, but only because I've been too busy to bring them to the center. And he *knows* it.

"There's no pickup in the neighborhood. But I plan to drive to the— What are you . . ." Liam's hands close around my waist, his fingers so long, they meet both on my back *and* above my belly button. My brain stutters to a stop. What the hell is he—?

He lifts me up till I'm hovering above the floor, then effortlessly moves me a few inches to the side of the refrigerator. Like I'm as light as an Amazon delivery box, the giant ones that for some reason have only a single stick of deodorant packed inside. I sputter as indignantly as I can, but he doesn't pay any attention to me. Instead he sets me on my feet, opens the fridge, grabs a jar of raspberry compote, and murmurs, "Then you better get to it," with one last long, intense look.

He goes back to his toast, and I go back to not existing in his universe.

Lovely.

I growl my way out of the room, half flustered and all homicidal, still feeling the heels of his palms pressing into my skin. *In his sleep. I swear I'm going to kill him in his damn sleep. When he least expects it. And then I'll celebrate by throwing empty bottles of creamer at his corpse.*

Ten minutes later I am rage-sweating, walking to work while on an emergency venting-videocall (ventocall) with Sadie. There have been a lot of these in the past few weeks. *A lot.*

". . . he doesn't even drink coffee. Which means that he's either flushing creamer down the toilet to spite me or chugging it down like it's water—and I honestly don't know which scenario would be worse, because on the one hand, one serving is like six hundred and forty calories, and Liam still manages to only have three percent body fat, but on the other, taking time out of his busy schedule to deprive *me* of *my* creamer is a gesture of unprecedented cruelty that no one should ever . . ." I trail off when I notice her bemused expression. "What?"

"Nothing."

I squint. "Are you looking at me weird?"

"No! Nope." She shakes her head emphatically. "It's just . . ."

"Just?"

"You've been talking about Liam nonstop for"—she lifts one eyebrow—"eight minutes straight, Mara."

My cheeks burn. "I'm so sorry, I—"

"Don't get me wrong, I *love* this. Listening to you bitch is my jam, ten out of ten, would recommend. I just feel like I've never seen you like this, you know? We lived together for five years. You're usually all about compromise and harmony and *Imagine all the people.*"

I *try* not to live my life in a perennial state of flame-throwing anger. My parents were the kind of people who probably should not have had kids: checked out, not affectionate, impatient for me to move out so they could turn my childhood bedroom into a shoe closet. I know how to cohabitate with others and minimize conflict, because I've been doing it since I was seventeen—ten years ago. *Live and let live* is a crucial skill set in any shared living space, and I had to master it quickly. And I still have it mastered. I really do. I'm just not sure I *want* to let Liam Harding live.

"I'm trying, Sadie, but I'm not the one who keeps lowering the damn thermostat to freezing. Who doesn't bother turning off the lights before going out—our electricity bill is *insane*. Two days ago, I got home after work, and the only person in the house was some random guy sitting on my couch who offered me my own Cheez-Its. I thought he was a hitman Liam had hired to kill me!"

"Oh my God. Was he?"

"No. He was Calvin—Liam's friend, who's tragically a million times nicer than him. The point is, Liam's the kind of shit room-mate who invites people over when he's not home, without telling you. Also, why the hell can't he say hi when he sees me? And is he psychologically unable to close the cupboards? Does he have some deep-rooted trauma that drove him to decorate the house exclusively with black-and-white prints of trees? Is he aware that he doesn't have to slam the door every time he goes out? And does he absolutely need to have his stupid dudebro friends come over every weekend to play video games in the—" I finish crossing the street and look at the screen. Sadie is chewing on her bottom lip, pensive. "What's going on?"

"You were going off and didn't really seem to need me, so I did a thing."

"A thing?"

"I googled Liam."

"What? Why?"

"Because I like to put a face to people I talk about for several hours a week."

"Whatever you do, do *not* click on his page on the FGP Corp website. Do not give them the hits!"

"Too late. He actually looks . . ."

"Like global warming and capitalism had a love child who's going through a bodybuilding phase."

"Um . . . I was going to say cute."

I huff. "When I look at him all I can see are all the creamer-less cups of coffee I've been drinking since the day I moved in." And maybe sometimes, just sometimes, I remember that flustered, wonderstruck look he gave me before he knew who I was. Mourn it a little. But who am I kidding? I must have hallucinated it.

"Has he offered to buy you out again?" Sadie asks.

"He doesn't really acknowledge my existence. Well, except to occasionally stare like I'm some roach infesting his pristine living space. But his lawyer sends me emails with ridiculous buyout offers every other day." I can see my work building, a hundred feet away. "But I won't. I'll keep the one thing Helena left me. And once I'm in a better place financially I'll just move out. It shouldn't take too long, a few months at the most. And in the meantime . . ."

"Black coffee?"

I sigh. "In the meantime I drink bitter, disgusting coffee."

Three 🝰

Dear Helena,

This is weird.
    Is this weird?
    This is probably weird.
    I mean, you're dead. And I'm here, writing you a letter. When I'm not even sure I believe in the afterlife. Truth be told, I stopped pondering eschatological matters in high school because they got me anxious and made me break out in hives under my left armpit (never the right; what's up with that?). And it's not like I'm ever going to figure out a mystery that eluded great thinkers like Foucault or Derrida or that unspellable German dude with bushy sideburns and syphilis.
    But I digress.
    You've been gone for over a month, and things are same old, same old. Humanity is still in the clutches of capitalist cabals; we

have yet to figure out a way to slow down the impending catastrophe that is anthropogenic climate change; I wear my "Save the Bees & Tax the Rich" T-shirt whenever I go for a run. The usual. I do love the work I'm doing at the EPA (thank you so much for that rec letter, by the way; I'm very grateful you didn't mention that time you bailed Sadie, Hannah, and me out of jail after that anti-dam protest. The U.S. government would not have liked that one). There is the small issue that I'm the only woman in a team of six, and that the dudes I work with seem to believe that my squishy female brain is unable to grasp sophisticated concepts like . . . the sphericity of Earth, I guess? The other day Sean, my team leader, spent thirty minutes explaining the contents of my own dissertation to me. I had very vivid fantasies about clocking him in the head and tiling his cadaver under my bathtub, but you probably already know all of this. You probably just sit around on a cloud all day being omniscient. Eating Triscuits. Occasionally playing the harp. You lazy bum.

I think the reason I'm writing this letter that you will never, ever read is that I wish I could talk to you. If my life were a movie, I'd trudge to your tombstone and bare my heart while a public-domain symphony in D minor plays in the background. But you were buried in California (inconvenient, much?), which makes letter writing the only feasible option.

All of this is to say: First, I miss you. A lot. A fucking huge lot. How could you leave me here without you? Shame, Helena. Shame.

Second: I am so, so grateful you left me this home. It's the best, coziest place I've ever lived in, hands down. I've been spending my weekends reading in the sunroom. Honestly, I never thought I'd set foot in a house with a foyer without being escorted off the premises by security. I just . . . I've never had a place that was mine before. A place that's going to be there no matter what.

A safe harbor, if you will. I feel your presence when I'm home, even if the last time you set foot here was probably in the '70s on your way back from a women's liberation march. And don't worry, I fondly remember your hatred of cheesy and I can almost hear you say, Cut this shit out. So I will.

Third, and this is less of a statement and more of a question: Would you mind it if I killed your nephew? Because I am very close to it. Like—sooo close. I am basically stabbing him with a potato peeler as we speak. Though it occurs to me now that maybe it's exactly what you wanted. You never mentioned Liam in all the years I knew you, after all. And he does work for a company whose main product is greenhouse gases, so maybe you hated him? Maybe our entire friendship was a long con that you knew would end in me pouring brake fluid in the tea of your least favorite relative. In which case, well done. And I hate you.

I could give a comprehensive list of his horribleness (I curate one in my Notes app) but I like to inflict it upon Sadie and Hannah via Zoom. I just . . . I guess I wish I understood why you put me in the path of one of the asswipiest asswipes in the country. In the world. In the entire damn Milky Way. Just the way he looks at me—the way he doesn't look at me. He clearly thinks he's above me, and—

The doorbell rings. I stop midsentence and run to the entrance. Which takes me, like, two whole minutes, proving my point that this house is plenty large for two people.

I wish I could say that Liam Harding has shit taste in home decor. That he abuses inspirational-quotes decals, buys plastic fruit at Ikea, sticks neon bar lights everywhere. Sadly, either he knows how to put together a pretty nice house interior, or his FGP Corp blood money paid to hire someone who does. The place is an elegant combination of traditional and modern pieces; I'm almost certain that whoever furnished it can correctly use the word *palette* in a sentence, and that the way the deep reds, forest greens, and soft grays complement the hardwood floors is a little more than accidental. And there's the fact that everywhere looks so . . . simple. With a home as large as this one, I'd be tempted to stuff every room with tables and sideboards and rugs, but Liam somehow limited himself to bare necessities. Couches, a few comfortable chairs, shelves full of books. That's it. The house is airy, full of light, sparsely decorated in warm tones, and all the more beautiful for it. "Minimalist," Sadie told me when I gave her a video tour. "Really well done, too." I believe my response was a snarl.

And then there's the art on the walls, which is unwelcomely growing on me. Pictures of lakes at sunrise and waterfalls at sunset, thick woods and lone trees, frozen grounds and blooming fields. The occasional wild animal going about its day, always in black and white. I don't know why, but I've been catching myself staring at them. The framing is simple, the subject mundane, but there's something about them. Like whoever took those photos really connected with the settings. Like they tried to truly capture them, to take home a piece of them.

I wonder who the photographer is, but I can find no signature. It's probably some starving Georgetown MFA grad, anyway. They poured their soul into the series hoping it'd be bought by someone who appreciates art, and instead here it is. Owned by a total ass. I bet Liam didn't even choose them. I bet they were just a tax-deductible purchase for him. Maybe he figured that in the long run a nice collection is as good as stock dividends.

"I'll need a signature," the UPS guy tells me when I open the door. He's chewing bubblegum and looks about fifteen. I feel decrepit inside. "You're not William K. Harding, are you?"

William K. It's almost cute. I hate it. "Nope."

"Is he home?"

"No." Mercifully.

"Is he your husband?"

I laugh. Then I laugh some more. Then I realize that the UPS guy is squinting at me like I'm the Wicked Witch of the West. "Um, no. Sorry. He's my . . . roommate."

"Right. Can you sign for your roomie?"

"Sure." I reach for the pen, but my hand stills in midair when I notice the FGP Corp insignia on the envelope.

I hate them. Even more than I hate Liam. Not only does he make me miserable at home mowing the lawn at seven thirty A.M. on the one day of the week I can sleep in, but he adds insult to injury by working for one of my professional nemeses. FGP Corp is one of those huge conglomerates that keep on causing environmental messes—a bunch of overeducated dudes in $7K suits who disseminate biotoxins around the world with utter disregard for the brown pelicans (and the entire future of humanity, but I'm personally more attached to the pelicans, who did *nothing* to deserve this).

I glare at the thick bubble mailer. Would Liam sign for an EPA envelope on my behalf? I doubt it. Or maybe he would. Then he'd tie it to red balloons his buddy Pennywise provided and watch it disappear into the sunset. I'm already 73 percent certain that he's been hiding my socks. I'm down to four matching pairs, for crisp's sake.

"Actually." I take a step back, smiling, reveling in my own pettiness. *Helena, you'd be so proud.* "I probably shouldn't sign for him. I bet it's a federal crime or something."

The UPS guy shakes his head. "It's really not."

I shrug. "Who's to say?"

"Me. It's literally my job."

"Which you are performing admirably." I beam. "But I still won't sign for the envelope. Would you like a cup of tea? A glass of wine? Cheez-Its?"

He frowns. "You sure you won't? This is express shipping. Someone paid a lot of money for same-day delivery. It's probably really urgent shit that William K. will need as soon as he gets home."

"Right. Well, that sounds like a William K. problem."

He whistles. "That's *cold*." He sounds admiring. Or just scared. "So, what's wrong with poor William K.? Does he leave the toilet seat up?"

"We have separate bathrooms." I mull it over. "But I'm sure he does. In the very remote possibility I end up using his."

He nods. "You know, when my sister was in college she used to have a roommate she hated. I'm talking warfare. They'd yell at each other the entire time. She once wrote an entire list of everything she hated about him on her phone and it crashed her Reminders app. It was *that* long."

Uh-oh. That sounds familiar. "What happened to her?"

I cross my fingers that the answer won't be *She's serving a life-time sentence at a nearby correctional facility for shaving off his hair while he was sleeping and tattooing "I'm a bad person" on his scalp.* And yet, what UPS guy ends up saying is ten times more disturbing.

"They're getting married next June." He shakes his head and turns around with a wave of his hand. "Go figure."

✿✿✿

I'm dreaming of a concert—a bad one.

More noise than music, really. The kind of '70s German electronic crap that Liam owns in vinyl form and will sometimes play when one of his friends comes over to play first-person shooter video games. It's loud and obnoxious and irritating, and it goes on for what feels like hours. Until I wake up and realize three things:

First, I have a horrible headache.

Second, it's the middle of the night.

Third, the noise-music is actually just regular noise, and it's coming from downstairs.

Burglars, I think. *They broke in. They're not even trying to be quiet—they probably have weapons.*

I have to get out. Call 911. I have to warn Liam and make sure that he—

I sit up with a frown. "Liam." But *of course*.

I fling myself out of bed and stomp out of my room. I'm halfway down the stairs when it occurs to me: my curls are all over the place, I'm not wearing a bra, and my shorts were already too small fifteen years ago, when my middle school issued them free of charge as part of my lacrosse uniform. Well. Too bad. Liam's going to have to deal with it, and with my "There Is No Planet B" T-shirt. It might teach him something.

By the time I reach the kitchen, I am considering one-clicking on a bullhorn to sneak up on him while he's asleep every night for the next six months. "Liam, do you *know* what time it is?" I erupt. "What are you even . . ."

I'm not sure what I expected. Definitely not to find the contents of the fridge cluttering every inch of the counter; definitely not to see Liam intent on slaughtering a stalk of celery like it stole his parking spot; definitely not to see him naked, *very* naked, from the waist up. The plaid pajama bottoms he's wearing have a low waist.

Very low.

"Could you please put something on? Like a baby-seal fur coat or something?"

He doesn't stop chopping his celery. Doesn't look up at me. "No."

"No?"

"I'm not cold. And I live here."

I live here, too. And I have every right not to look at that brick wall he calls a chest in my own kitchen, which is supposed to be a soothing environment where I can digest food without having to stare at random male nipples. *Still*, I decide to let the matter go and push it to the back of my mind. By the time I'm ready to move out, I'm going to need therapy, anyway. What's one more trauma to deal with? Right now, I just want to go back to sleep. "What are you doing?" I ask.

"My tax return."

I blink. "I—what?"

"What does it look like I'm doing?"

I stiffen. "I don't know what it *looks* like, but it *sounds* like you're just banging pans together."

"The noise is an unfortunate by-product of me making dinner." He must be done with the celery, because he moves to slicing a tomato—is that *my* tomato?—and back to ignoring me.

"Oh, and that's totally normal, isn't it? Cooking a five-course meal at one twenty-seven in the morning on a weeknight?"

Liam finally lifts his eyes to mine, and there is something unsettling about his gaze. He seems calm. He looks calm, but I know he's not. *He is furious*, I tell myself. *He is really, really furious. Get out of here.* "Did you need anything?" His tone is deceptively polite, and my self-preservation is clearly still asleep in bed.

"Yes. I need you to keep it down. And that better not be my tomato."

He pops half of it in his mouth. "You know," he says evenly while chewing, managing to talk with his mouth full and yet still look like the aristocratic product of several generations of wealth, "I'm usually not in the habit of being awake at one twenty-eight in the morning."

"What a coincidence. Neither was I, before meeting *you*."

"But today—that is, yesterday—the entire legal team I run ended up having to work past midnight. Because of some very important missing documents."

I tense. He cannot mean—

"Don't worry, the documents were found. Eventually. *After* my boss tore me and my team a new one. Sounds like something went wrong when they were delivered." If he could incinerate people with eye lasers, I'd be long cremated. Clearly he knows everything about my little afternoon spite-attack.

"Listen." I take a deep breath. "It wasn't my proudest moment, but I'm not your PA. And I don't see how it justifies you banging all the pots in the house in the middle of the night. I have a long day tomorrow, so—"

"So do I. And as you can imagine, I've had a long day today. And I'm hungry. Which means that I'm not going to keep it down. At least not until I've had dinner."

Until about ten seconds ago I was angry in a cool, reasonable way. All of a sudden, I am ready to wrestle the knife out of Liam's hand and slice his jugular. Just a tiny bit. Just to make him bleed. I won't, because I don't think I'd flourish in jail, but I'm also not going to let this go. I've tried to have measured responses when he refused to let me install solar panels, when he threw away my broccoli stir-fry because it smelled "swampy," when he locked me out of the house while I was on my run. But this is the final straw.

I'm done. The back of my camel is broken in two. "Are you fucking *kidding* me?"

Liam pours olive oil in a pan, cracks an egg in it, and seems to revert to his default state: forgetting that I exist.

"Liam, whether you like it or not, I. Live. Here. You can't do whatever the hell you want!"

"Interesting. You seem to be doing exactly that."

"What are you talking about? *You* are making an omelet at *two in the damn morning*, and *I* am asking you not to."

"True. Although there *is* the fact that if you had done your dishes this week I wouldn't need to wash them so noisily—"

"Oh, shut up. It's not like you don't leave your stuff around the house all the time."

"At least I don't stack garbage on top of the trash can like it's a Dadaist sculpture."

The sound that comes out of my mouth—it almost scares me. "*God*. You are *impossible* to have around!"

"That's just too bad, since I'm here."

"Then just *move the fuck out!*"

Silence falls. An absolute, heavy, very uncomfortable silence. Just what we both need to replay my words over and over in our heads. Then Liam speaks. Slowly. Carefully. Angry in a scary, icy way. "Excuse me?"

I regret it immediately. What I said and *how* I said it. Loud. Vehement. I am many things, but cruel is not one of them. It doesn't matter that Liam Harding has displayed the emotional range of a walnut; I said something hurtful and I owe him an apology. Not that I particularly *want* to offer him one, but I should. The problem is, I just can't stop myself from continuing. "Why are you even here, Liam? People like you live in mansions with uncomfortable beige furniture and seven bathrooms and overpriced art they don't understand."

"People like *me*?"

"Yes. People like *you*. People with zero morals and way too much money!"

"Why are *you* here? I've offered to buy your half about a thousand times."

"And I said no, so you could have spared yourself about nine hundred and ninety-nine of them. Liam, there is no reason for you to want to live in this house."

"This is *my* family's house!"

"It was Helena's house as much as it's yours, and—"

"Helena is fucking *dead*."

It takes a few moments for Liam's words to fully register. He abruptly turns off the stove and then stands there, half-naked in front of the sink, hands clenched around the edge of the counter and muscles as tight as guitar strings. I can't stop staring at him, this—this *viper* who just mentioned the death of one of the most important people in my life with such angry, dismissive carelessness.

I am going to *destroy* him. I'm going to *annihilate* him. I am going to make him suffer, to spit in his stupid smoothies, to break his vinyls one by one.

Except that Liam does something that changes everything. He presses his lips together, pinches his nose, then wipes a large, exhausted hand down his face. All of a sudden something clicks inside my head: Liam Harding, standing right in front of me, is tired. And he hates this, *all of this*, just as much as I do.

Oh God. Maybe my broccoli stir-fry really did stink, and I should have put it in a Tupperware. Maybe the *Frozen* soundtrack can be a tiny bit annoying. Maybe I could have signed for that stupid envelope. Maybe I wouldn't react well to someone coming to live under my roof, either, especially if I didn't have a say in the matter.

I press the heels of my hands into my eyes. Maybe I am the asshole. Or at least one of them. God. Oh *God.*

"I . . ." I rack my brain for something to say and find nothing. Then some dam inside me breaks, and the words explode out. "Helena was my family. I know you don't get on with your family, and . . . maybe you hated her, I don't know. Granted, she could be really grumpy and nosy, but she . . . she loved me. And she was the only real home I ever had." I dare to glance at Liam, half expecting a sneer of derision. A snarky comment about Helena that will make me want to punch him again. But he's staring at me, attentive, and I force myself to look away and continue before I can change my mind. "I think she knew that. I think maybe that's why she left me this house, so that I'd have some kind of . . . of something. Even after she was gone." My voice breaks on the last word, and now I'm crying. Not full-on bawling like when I watch *The Lion King* or the first ten minutes of *Up*, but quiet, sparse, implacable tears that I have no hope of stopping. "I know you probably see me as some . . . proletarian usurper who's come to take over your family fortune, and believe me, I get it." I wipe my cheek with the back of my hand. My voice is rapidly losing heat. "But you have to understand that while you're living here because you're trying to prove some point, or for some sort of pissing contest, this pile of bricks means the world to me, and . . ."

"I didn't hate Helena."

I look up in surprise. "What?"

"I didn't hate Helena." His eyes are on his half-made omelet, still sizzling on the stove.

"Oh."

"Every summer she'd leave California for a few weeks. Where did you think she went?"

"I . . . she just said she spent her summers with family. I always assumed that . . ."

"Here, Mara. She came here. Slept in the room next to yours." Liam's voice is clipped, but his expression softens into something I've never seen before. A faint smile. "She claimed it was to check up on my world-pollution plans. Mostly, she nagged me about my life choices in between meeting with old friends. And she kicked my ass at chess a lot." He scowls. "I am positive she cheated, but I could never prove it."

"I . . ." He must be making this up. Surely. "She never mentioned you."

His eyebrow lifts. "She never mentioned *you*. And yet you were in her will."

"But . . . But, wait. Hang on a minute. At the funeral . . . I thought you didn't get along with your family?"

"Oh, I don't. They're pretentious, judgmental, performative assholes—and I'm quoting Helena, here. But she was different, and I got on with her. I cared about her. A lot." He clears his throat. "I'm not sure where you got the idea that I didn't."

"Well, you not coming to the funeral fooled me."

"Knowing Helena, do you think she'd have cared?"

I think about my second year. The one time I organized a small surprise party for Helena's birthday in the department, and she just . . . left. Literally. We yelled *Surprise!* and dropped a handful of balloons. Helena gave us a scathing look, stepped inside the room, cut a slice of her birthday cake while we stared in silence, and then went to her office to eat it alone. She *locked* herself in. "Okay. That's a good point."

Liam nods.

"Do you know why she left me the house?"

"I do not. Initially I figured it was some kind of prank. One of her chaotic power plays. Like when she'd guilt-trip you into watching old shows with her."

"God, she *always* picked—"

"*The Twilight Zone*. Even though she already knew all the twist endings." He rolls his eyes. Then his expression changes. "I didn't know her health had gotten so bad. I called her two days before she died, exactly two days, and she told me . . . I shouldn't have believed her."

My heart sinks. I was there. I know the exact conversation Liam is referring to, because I heard Helena's side of it. The way she fielded questions and minimized the concerns of the person on the other side of the line. She lied her way through an hour of chatter—it was obvious that she was happy about the call, but she wasn't honest about how bad things had gotten, and I felt uncomfortable about the deception. Then again, she did that with everyone. She'd have done the same with me if I hadn't been her ride to doctors' appointments.

"I wish she'd let me be there." Liam's tone is impersonal, but I can hear the unsaid. How painful it must have been to be kept in the dark. "But she didn't, and it was her decision. Just like leaving you the house was her decision, and . . . I'm not happy about it. I don't understand it. But I accept it. Or at least I'm trying to."

For the first time, I realize what my arrival in D.C. must have been like from Liam's perspective: Some girl he'd never even heard about, some girl who'd had the privilege to be with Helena during her last few days, suddenly showing up and forcibly wiggling her way into his home. His life. While he was trying to come to terms with his loss and mourn the only relative he felt close to.

Maybe he acted like an asshole. Maybe he never made me feel

welcome or wasn't particularly nice, but he was in pain, just like me, and . . .

What a total mess. What an obtuse idiot I've been.

"I . . . I'm sorry for what I said earlier. I didn't mean any of it. I don't know you at all, and . . ." I trail off, unsure how to continue.

Liam nods stiffly. "I'm sorry, too."

We stay there, in silence, for long beats. If I go back to my room now, Liam will order a pizza and I'll be able to fall asleep without having to hunt down my stash of earplugs. I almost leave to do just that, but something occurs to me: Things could be better. *I* could be better. "Maybe there could be a . . . a truce of sorts?"

He lifts one eyebrow. "A truce."

"Yeah. I mean . . . I could . . . I guess I could stop raising the thermostat to twenty-five degrees as soon as you turn around. Wear a sweater instead."

"Twenty-five degrees?"

"I'm a scientist. We don't really do Fahrenheit, since it's a ridiculous scale and . . ." He's looking at me with an expression that I can't quite decipher, so I quickly change the topic. "And I guess I could lay off with the Disney soundtracks?"

"Could you?"

"Yeah."

"Even *The Little Mermaid*?"

"Yes."

"What about *Moana*?"

"Liam, I'm really trying here. If you could please—" I am ready to storm out of the kitchen when I realize that he's actually smiling. Well, sort of. With his eyes. Oh my God, was that a joke? He *jokes*? "You're not as funny as you think."

He nods, and doesn't say anything for a moment or two. Then, "The Disney soundtracks are not that bad." He sounds pained.

"And I'll try to be better, too. I'll water your plants when you're out of town and they're about to die." I knew he'd let my cucumber die on purpose. I *knew* it. "And maybe I'll make a sandwich for dinner, if I get hungry past midnight."

I lift my eyebrow.

Liam sighs. "Past ten P.M.?"

"That would be perfect."

He crosses his huge arms on his equally huge, still bare chest, and then rocks a bit on his heels.

"Okay, then."

"Okay."

The silence stretches. Suddenly, this situation feels . . . tense. Sticky. A verge of some sort. A turning point.

A good time for me to leave.

"I'm going to . . ." I point toward the stairs, where my bedroom is. "Have a good night, Liam."

I don't turn around when he says, "Good night, Mara."

Four ⚙

There are plenty of things I wouldn't expect Liam Harding to do when he enters the kitchen.

For instance, he's unlikely to whip out castanets and flamenco his way around the island. To break into a Michael Bolton hit from the '80s. To sell me a leaf blower and recruit me into some gardening tools MLM venture. These are all *very* improbable events, and yet none of them would shock me as much as what he actually does. Which is to look at me and say:

"It's . . . nice outside today."

It's not that it isn't. It is, in fact, really nice. Unseasonably warm. It's because Earth is dying, of course. Rising average global temperatures are associated with widespread fluctuations in weather patterns, and that's why we're still wearing lightweight jackets, even though it's late November in D.C. and Christmas trees have been popping up for weeks now. A few years ago, Helena wrote a paper about the way human action is increasing the periodicity and intensity of extreme weather events. It got published in *Nature Climate Change* and has about a zillion citations.

I could say all of this to Liam. I could be my most obnoxious self and lecture on the topic for hours. But I don't, and the reason is that even through his clipped, hesitant tone and his currently lowered gaze, I can recognize an olive branch when it bites me in the ass.

Which, right now, it absolutely is. Biting, that is.

It's been about two weeks since I first became aware that Liam is capable of human emotions. And as it turns out, being in a truce while living together means having significantly fewer shouting matches, but still doesn't make finding topics of conversation any easier. Which is fine. Most of the time. It's a big house, after all. But on the rare occasions in which our schedules overlap and we end up in the living room or in the kitchen together . . .

Awkward.

As fuck.

"Yeah." My nod is sprain-your-neck enthusiastic—overcompensating. "It's nice. To have good weather, I mean."

Liam nods, too (stiffly, but maybe I'm just projecting), and just like that, we're back to square one: silence.

I bite my thumbnail. Apparently I did *not* stop doing that when I turned fourteen. I need something to say. What do I say? *Quick, Mara. Think.* "Um . . . So . . ."

No thoughts. Head empty.

I let my sentence dangle like an overcooked noodle and temporize by turning around to grab a . . . a what? A spatula? A toaster? A snack! Yes, I'll have a snack. I think I bought single servings of Cheez-Its. Trying to cut back and all that. Except that I can't find them in my cupboard. There's a family box. Another. A third one, in cheddar flavor—Jesus, I have a problem. But the little bags are not . . . Ah, there they are. Highest shelf, of course. I remember throwing them up there, thinking it'd be a problem for Future Mara.

Future Mara tries, but cannot reach them. So she looks back to ask Liam to grab one for her, and her heart sinks.

He's staring at where my shirt rode up on my lower back—i.e., my ass.

Well, no. He isn't. William K. Harding would never stoop so low, and the idea that he'd voluntarily glance at my scrawny ass is laughable. But he is looking at me, *there*, his lips slightly parted and his hand forgotten in midair, which likely means that he's . . . horrified? By my eight-year-old sweatpants, I bet. Or by the explosion of freckles on my skin. Or by . . . God, what panties do I even have on? Please, let it not be the ones with Jeff Goldblum's face Hannah got me last year. And how many holes do they have? He's going to report me to the underwear police. I will be executed by the Victoria's Secret mob, and—

He clears his throat. "Here." He bravely overcomes his disgust and comes to stand behind me. He is just *massive*. So big that he completely blocks the overhead light. For a microsecond I feel warm, oddly tingly. Then he drops a bag next to my hand without me even having to ask, and says, "Should I move them to a lower shelf for you?"

His voice is a little gravelly. Maybe he's coming down with a cold. I hope I don't get it. "Um, that would be great. Thanks." It takes him about half a second. Then we're both back to our original positions, me with my coffee, Liam with his tea, and I realize that in the mildly mortifying adventures of the last minute, I forgot to think of a decent olive branch topic of conversation. *Fantastic.*

So I blurt out: "The Nationals are doing well this season." I *think*? I overheard a dude say it on the bus. Liam's always playing video games with his dude friends. He probably likes sports, too.

"Oh. That's . . . good." Liam nods.

I nod.

More awkward nodding, and then silence. Again.

Okay. This is *way* too uncomfortable. I'm going to install motion sensors in every room in the house so I can make sure our paths never cross again—

"What sport is that, again?"

I look up from the coffee I'm furiously stirring. "Mmm?"

"The Nationals. What sport?"

"Ah . . ." I glance around the kitchen, looking for clues. Find a grand total of none. "I have no idea."

Liam dunks a tea bag in his mug, a gleam of amusement in his eyes. "Me, neither."

We leave the room from opposite doors. I wonder whether he's aware that we almost smiled at each other.

Five ⚙

look out the window, trying to use my engineering degree to approximate how many meters of snow fell overnight. One? Seventeen? Sadly, there was no Ballpark How Snowbound You Are 101 in my grad school curriculum, so I give up to glance down at my phone.

There's no way I can make it to work, and my entire team at the EPA is in the same situation. Sean's car is stuck in his driveway. Alec, Josh, and Evan can't even make it *to* their driveway. Ted is on his fifth joke about extreme weather events. The Slack channel pings with a few more messages cursing all forms of precipitation, and then Sean makes the call that we all should just work from home. Accessing the secure server from our EPA-issued laptops. Which for me is a bit of a problem.

So I text Sean:

MARA: Sean, I don't have my EPA-issued laptop at home with me.

SEAN: Why?

MARA: You haven't issued me one yet.

SEAN: I see.

SEAN: Well, you can just take the day to answer emails and stuff like that, then. We're just going to try to fix the electrostatic sprayer issue today, so we don't really need you.

SEAN: And next time make sure to remind me that you don't have a laptop yet.

How passive-aggressive would it be to forward to Sean the reminder email I sent him two days ago? Very, I imagine.

I sigh, text a quick Will do, and try not to grind my teeth over the fact that I'd love to give my input on the electrostatic sprayer issue. It's actually closely related to my graduate work, but who am I kidding? Even if I were present, Sean would act like he always does: politely hum at my contributions, find a trivial reason to discard them, and fifteen minutes later paraphrase and restate them as his own ideas. Ted, my closest ally in the team, tells me not to take it too personally, because Sean's a jerk to pretty much everyone. But I know I'm not imagining that his most egregious behavior is always directed at me ("I wonder why," I muse to myself, stroking my woman-in-STEM chin). But Sean's the team leader, so . . .

Did I say that I love my new EPA job? Maybe I lied. Or maybe I do love it, but I hate Sean more. Hard to tell.

I spend the day doing what work I can without access to classified information—i.e., very little. I briefly FaceTime with Sadie,

but she's on a deadline for some hippy-dippy eco-sustainable project ("I haven't slept in thirty-eight hours. Please, tie an anvil to my
neck and drop me in the Sargasso Sea."), Hannah is unreachable
(probably frolicking with the walruses on a slab of ice), and . . .
That's it. I don't really have any other friends.

I should probably work on that.

By one P.M. I am mortally bored. I nap; I watch a YouTube
video on the plate arrangement of the stegosaurus; I paint my
nails a pretty red matte color; I write a half-assed post for my
Bachelor blog on my expectations for the next season; I practice
braiding my hair in a crown; I wonder whether I'm a workaholic,
decide that I probably am.

I can't remember the last time I was inside all day. I've always
been a bit restless, a bit too antsy. *Much too active*, my parents
would say as they tried to enroll me in every possible team sport
to keep me busy. They aren't bad people, but I doubt they wanted
a kid, and I know for sure that they weren't fans of whatever
changes my arrival brought to their lifestyle. Probably the reason
they were never huge fans. We talk maybe once or twice a year
now—and I'm always the one who calls.

Oh well.

I lean my forehead against the chilly glass of the window, feeling an odd sense of isolation, as though I'm disconnected from
the entire world, swaddled in a muffled white cocoon.

I should start dating again.

Should I start dating again?

Yeah. I should. Except that . . . men. No, thank you. I am well
aware that #NotAllMen are condescending shitlets like Sean, and
I've had my share of perfectly nice boyfriends who didn't feel the
need to *Actually* me when I tried to have a conversation. But even
at their best, all my romantic relationships felt like work. In a way

Sadie and Hannah and Helena never did. In a way *actual work* never did. And for what? Sex? Jury's still out on whether I even care about that.

Maybe I should skip the dating and just visit Sadie in NYC as soon as the weather gets better. Yeah, I'll do that. We'll make a weekend out of it. Ice-skate. Get that frozen hot chocolate thing she's been raving about, the one she insists is not just a rebranded milkshake. But in the meantime it's still snowing, and I'm still stuck in here. Alone.

Well, not *alone* alone. Liam's around. He came downstairs this morning, large hand brushing over the smooth wooden railing, looking . . . not quite disheveled. But he didn't bother with his usual suit. The faded jeans and worn T-shirt made him seem younger, a more human version of his aloof, stern self. Or maybe it was the hair, dark as usual, but sticking up just a bit in the back. If we hated each other a tad less, I'd have reached up and fixed it for him. Instead I watched him step into the roomy entrance until it didn't feel quite so roomy anymore. No high ceiling is *that* high when someone as tall as Liam stands under it, apparently. I stared at him half-mesmerized for a few moments—till I realized that he was staring right back. *Oops.* Then he looked out the window, sighed deeply, and headed back upstairs. Phone already on his ear as he gave calm, detailed instructions about a project that's probably aimed at freeing the planet from the evil clutches of photosynthesizing plants.

I haven't seen him since, but I heard him. Laughter here. Barefooted steps there. Creaking wood and the beep of the microwave. Our rooms are one and a half hallways away. I know he has a home office, but I've never been in there—a bit of a tacit Do-not-go-to-the-West-Wing, *Beauty and the Beast* situation. I've considered snooping around when he was gone, but what if he put live traps around? I picture him coming home, finding me wailing, my ankle tangled in a snare. He'd probably leave me there to starve.

Plus, he doesn't go out much. There are those couple of friends of his who come over to do surprisingly nerdy stuff (which reminds me a bit too much of me, Sadie, and Hannah making brownies for a *Parks and Rec* marathon—which in turn is vaguely painful—so I pretend it doesn't happen). His workdays seem to be sixteen hours long, even when I'm not being a petty gremlin about signing for his mail, but that's about it. I wonder if he dates. I wonder if he sneaks a different girl into the house every night and tells her *Shh, be quiet. My squatting ginger roommate will key my record player if we're too loud.* I wonder if I'm simply failing to notice the masked orgies he has in the kitchen every weekend while I'm tucked under my granny quilt, carefully composing my blog posts.

I wonder why I wonder.

When I pad downstairs for dinner, the house is dark and silent. And cold. Honestly, how is Liam not freezing? Is it the seventy pounds of muscles? Does he coat himself in baby-seal fat? I shake my head as I raise the thermostat and heat up more food than I need to eat (but, crucially: not more food than I *can* eat).

There are a few living/sitting/front/lounge/whatnot rooms on the first floor, but my favorite is the one connected to the kitchen. It has a large, comfortable couch that probably cost more than my graduate education, a soft area rug I like to stealthily caress when I'm home alone, and the pièce de résistance: a giant TV. I move my (many) food containers to the walnut coffee table and let myself plop down on the couch.

For reasons I don't understand, Liam pays for cable television and for about fifteen different streaming services that I've never seen him use. I'm in no way above exploiting FGP Corp's blood money, so I find a rerun of a season twelve episode of *The Bache-*

lorette. Not my favorite, for reasons I explained at length on my blog (don't judge me), but decent. I settle in.

Ten minutes later, an idiot with an obvious tanning-bed addiction is fist-fighting an idiot who clearly snorts protein powder, all under a delighted girl's eyes—i.e., the premise of the show. But I realize that not all noises are coming from the TV. When I mute it, I can hear another argument. From upstairs. In Liam's voice.

It's not loud enough to make out the gist of it, but I do manage to eavesdrop the occasional words. *Wrong. Unethical. Opposed,* maybe? Quite a few firm *Nos,* but that's about it. After a brief moment, the sounds are muffled again. Another minute, and a door slams; feet quickly make their way down the steps.

Crap.

I consider quickly switching to a Lars von Trier movie, but Liam arrives before I can fool him into thinking that I'm an intellectual. I look up from my egg roll and he's there, in the slice of kitchen I can see from the couch, looking like . . . murder.

That is: more than usual.

My first instinct is to flatten myself against the couch, keep watching my trashy show and eating my excellent food. But he turns, our eyes meet, and I have no choice but to hesitantly wave at him. He answers with a curt nod, and . . . he looks broody and dark, like he just had a terrible ten minutes, perhaps a terrible day. Even worse, he looks like he's ready to take it out on the first person he'll find in his path—which, given the weather conditions, is regrettably going to be me. He looks like he needs a distraction, and a very stupid idea pops into my head.

Don't do it, Mara. Don't do it. You're gonna regret it.

But Liam is visibly clenching his teeth. The way he's staring into the open fridge suggests that he'd like to strangle each and every jar of tartar sauce (for unknowable reasons, he owns three).

Maybe the ketchup, too. The line of his overbroad shoulders is so tense I could use it as a bubble level, and—

Ah. Screw it.

"So." I clear my throat. "I ordered way more food than I need." I resist the urge to cover my discomfort with nervous laughter. He can probably smell it, my abject terror. "Would you, um, like some?"

He slowly closes the fridge door and turns around. "Excuse me?" He looks at me like I just offered to go rob a bank together. To buddy-sign up for aerial yoga. To spend the rest of the night moth watching.

"Takeout. Chinese. Want some?"

He glances at the window. Yes, it's still snowing. We're officially the North Pole. "You ordered takeout." He sounds dubious.

"Not today. Two days ago. I always order too much, because leftovers taste better. Especially the lo mein, it really needs to soak into the sauce to . . ." I stop. And flush. "Anyway, would you like some?"

"We're in the middle of a snowstorm, Mara." Why am I shivering all of a sudden? Ah yes. Because it's cold. Not because he said my name. "You should be hoarding your food."

Yeah, I should. "It's about to go bad. And I'm happy to share."

It takes Liam an inordinate amount of time to answer. Ten good seconds of him staring skeptically, perhaps suspecting me to be a deranged murderess on the prowl for roommates to poison. Eventually he says: "Sure."

He sounds everything but sure. Very cautious. Looks cautious, too, as he makes his way to me. He slides his hands in the back pockets of his jeans and looks around morosely, and it's obvious that he has no idea what to do—sit on the couch, the chair, the floor. Eat standing in the middle of the living room. It occurs to me for the first time that his entire aloof, stern persona might hide a smidge of awkwardness. Could he be one of those people who are hyperconfident in professional settings and the total opposite in their social lives? Nah. Unlikely.

I pat a spot next to mine, already regretting this. We've never sat together before. So far, every interaction between us has been circumstantial. The act of sitting next to each other implies intentionality and a longer duration. A new territory.

Weird.

Liam is so heavy and tall that the cushion dips when he sits down, and I have to tense my abs and readjust to avoid sliding toward him. I hand him a plate and a pair of chopsticks, pretending there's nothing unusual about any of this. He does the same as he accepts them with a brief nod, his fingers never accidentally touching mine.

"What are you watching?" he asks.

"*The Bachelorette.*" No sign of recognition. "It's this stupid, *amazing* show. Reality. You don't have to watch with me. Save yourself while you can." Surprisingly, Liam stays put. Still looks a bit like he wouldn't mind trashing the entire house, but his expression is slightly less bloodthirsty. Progress? "So, Sheryl, the girl in the green dress—the only girl—has a few weeks to choose a husband among all the guys."

Liam squints at the TV for a moment. "Based on what? They all look the same."

"They do, don't they?" I shrug. "They take her on dates. And chat. Toward the end they might even have sex."

Is he flushing? No. It's just the light. "On-screen?"

"Hey, it's ABC, not HBO." I put a spring roll on his plate. Then I take a look at him—his arms filling his shirt, his chest, his general . . . hugeness—and add two more. How many million calories does he need a day? I should find out. In the name of science. "You see the guy wearing glasses he obviously doesn't need in the vain hope of looking less imbecilic?"

"Blue shirt?"

"Yes. We're rooting for him."

"Are we."

"Yep. Because he's from Michigan. And I went to U of M for undergrad," I explain, licking a drop of hoisin sauce off my thumb. His eyes linger on my lips for a too-long moment, then abruptly slide away.

"I see."

"It's a great place. Ever been?"

"I don't believe so, no." He's still not looking at me. Maybe he holds a profound and irrational hatred for Ann Arbor?

"Where did you go to school?"

He seems mildly surprised that I'm asking. Fair, since I haven't exactly excelled at turn taking and conversation making in the past. "Dartmouth. Then Harvard Law School."

"Right." I nod knowingly. "That sounds . . . cheap."

He has the decency to look sheepish, so I take pity on him. "Want some cashew chicken?"

"Ah . . . Yes, please."

"Here. You can finish it, I've already eaten, like, ten pounds of it."

He nods. "Thanks."

Liam Harding. Being polite. Wow. "You're welcome."

For a couple of minutes we are silent—Liam watching the TV, me sneakily watching Liam as he eats ravenously, large quick bites that are youthfully endearing. Then he turns to me.

"Mara."

"Yes?"

"You clearly are some kind of genius."

Uh? Am I? "Is this—are you—making fun of me?"

He looks dead serious and faintly offended at the idea. "You're basically a rocket scientist."

"*Basically* being the operative word."

"And Helena, who had ridiculous standards, chose you to work with her. You're obviously remarkable."

Oh God. Is this a compliment? Am I going to blush? "Um . . . thanks?"

He nods. "What I don't understand is, why is someone as smart as you watching this shit?"

I smile into my fried rice. "You'll see."

One hour later, when Sheryl says, *"I think our relationship has come a long way, but I am not convinced that it could develop any further . . ."* I slam my hand on my armrest and yell, "Oh, come *on*, Sheryl," just as Liam slaps his armrest and yells, "Sheryl. What the hell?"

We turn to each other and exchange a brief, bemused look. *Told ya*, I think at him with a smile. His mouth twitches, like he heard me loud and clear.

". . . at this point, I just know that it's not gonna work out between us. Can I walk you out?"

Liam shakes his head, horrified. "That's just a bad decision."

"I know."

"He's the best of the lot."

"Soooo stupid, right? She's gonna regret this so bad. I know it, because I've already seen the season." *Multiple times.* I reach for one of the beers Liam took out of the fridge a few minutes ago. "Want another crab rangoon?" I ask.

He nods and settles back, long legs stretched next to mine on top of the coffee table. The snow outside is still falling, and we wait for the next episode to start.

✿✿✿

He shovels snow like it's his one and only vocation.

Maybe it's the isolation-induced insanity speaking, but there's something hypnotic about it. The rhythmic rise and fall of his shoulders under the black fleece. The seemingly effortless way he's been going at it for hours, occasionally stopping to wipe the sweat off his brow with the back of his sleeve. I press my forehead to the window and just . . . stare. I can almost hear Helena's voice in my head (*Would you like to borrow my birding binoculars?*). I blithely ignore it.

Maybe that's what he majored in at Dartmouth: Snow Shoveling. Nicely complemented by a minor in Muscles. His honors thesis was titled *The Importance of Armceps in Ergonomic Excavating.* Then he moved to graduate school to study How-to-Make-a-Mundane-Winter-Task-Look-Attractive Law. And here I am, unable to take my eyes off a decade of overpaid-for higher education.

This is getting weird. It's giving me flashbacks to the first time I saw him, when his dark eyes and those (frankly ridiculous) shoulders hit me like a brick in the head. It's not a memory I want to revisit, so I look away and head downstairs to make lunch, blaming my temporary lunacy on skipping breakfast. This is what I get for falling asleep late last night, halfway through the finale, in the middle of explaining to Liam between yawns that *Bachelor* and *Bachelorette* contestants get mandatory STD screenings. What I get for waking up this morning on the couch, a soft, heavenly smelling blanket laid over me. I wonder where it came from, anyway. Not from the living room. I'm positive that there wasn't one around.

It's not that Liam and I are friends now. I don't know him any better than I did yesterday—except, I guess, that he has some surprisingly valid opinions when it comes to reality TV. But for some unparsable reason, when I start working on my soup I find myself making enough for two.

See, this is why humans are not meant to be sequestered at home. Boredom and loneliness turn their minds to mushy oatmeal, and they start imposing their poorly cooked food on unsuspecting Snow Lawyers. And I'm apparently embracing my weird, because when Liam comes in, dark hair damp and curling from the melting snowflakes, cheeks glowing from the exercise, I tell him, "I made lunch."

He stares, arms dangling at his sides, as though unsure how to answer. So I add, "For both of us. As a thank-you. For doing that. The shoveling, I mean." He stares some more. "If you want. It's not mandatory."

"No. No, I . . ." He doesn't finish. But when he notices me reaching toward a high shelf to the bowls, he comes up behind me and sets two on the counter.

"Thank you."

"No problem." I might be imagining this, but I think I hear him inhale slowly before he moves away. Does my hair smell bad? I washed it yesterday. Has Garnier Fructis finally failed me after years of faithful service? I'm wondering whether it's time to switch to Pantene by the time we're politely eating at the kitchen table, in front of each other, like we're a young family in a Campbell's commercial.

Problem: without the TV on, it's pretty conspicuous that we have nothing to talk about. Liam glances at me every few seconds, as though me stuffing my face is either something he likes to look at, or something totally hideous—who's to say? As the silence stretches, I am once again regretting every choice I've ever made. And when his phone rings, I'm so relieved I could fist-pump.

Except that he doesn't pick up. He checks caller ID (*FGP Corp—Mitch*), rolls his eyes, and then turns the phone around in a dismissive movement that has me chuckling.

Liam gives me a puzzled look.

"Sorry. I didn't mean to . . . Just . . ." I shrug. "It's nice to know that you hate your colleagues, too."

He lifts one eyebrow. "You hate your colleagues?"

"Well, no. I don't hate them. I mean, I *sometimes* hate them, but . . ." Why is this about *me*? "Anyway, do you think the snow is over for good?"

"Why do you sometimes hate your colleagues?"

"I don't. I misspoke. It's just . . ." Liam has stopped eating and is looking at me like he's actually interested. *Ugh.* "They're all men. All engineers. And men engineers can be . . . yeah. And I'm the newest arrival, and they're all kind of chummy already. And I'm pretty sure that Sean, my boss, thinks that I'm some sort of pity diversity hire. Which I'm not. I'm actually a really good engineer. I have to be, or Helena would have butchered me in my sleep."

He nods as though he understands. "She'd have butchered you awake."

"Right? She wasn't exactly forgiving. And I'm not complaining—I owe her so much. She truly helped me become a better scientist, but everyone in my team treats me as though I'm some infant engineer who doesn't know what an ohm is, and—" Why am I *still talking*? "Well, everyone except for Ted, but I'm not sure whether he actually respects me or is just trying to get laid, since he's already asked me out, like, three times, which makes things kind of awkward . . ."

Liam's face instantly hardens. His spoon sets in the bowl with a loud clink. "This is sexual harassment."

"Oh, no."

"At the very least, it's highly inappropriate."

"No, it's not like that—"

"I can talk to him."

I blink. "What?"

"What's his last name?" Liam asks, like it's a totally normal question. "I can talk to him. Explain that he has made you uncomfortable and he should stop—"

"What?" I let out a laugh. "Liam, I'm not going to tell you his last name. What are you gonna do, pour a barrel of oil on his house?"

He looks away. Like it was an option.

"No, I . . . I actually like Ted. He's nice. I mean, I've even considered saying yes. Why not, right?" *Why not?* is what Helena would say, but Liam's expression darkens at that. Or maybe it's just my entire soul, darkening at the idea of putting on eyeliner to go out with a guy who's perfectly fine and excites me as much as boiled spinach. "It's just that . . ." I shrug. How to explain that I am forever uninspired by the men I meet? I won't even bother. It's not like he cares. "Thank you, though," I add.

He looks like he'd like to insist, but just says, "Let me know if you change your mind."

"Um. Okay." I guess I have a six-foot-three mountain of muscles in my corner now? It's kinda nice. I should make soup more often. "So, since I have you here," *and to avoid dropping into awkward silence again*, "what's up with the pictures?"

"The pictures?"

"The black-and-white pictures of trees and lakes and stuff. Hanging on literally every single wall."

"I just like to take them."

"Wait. You took the pictures yourself?"

"Yeah."

"Does that mean that you've actually been to all those places?"

He swallows a spoonful of soup, nodding. "It's mostly national parks. A few state ones. Canada, too."

I'm a little shocked. Not only are the pictures good, professional-level good, but . . . "Okay"—I point at the frame behind the table, an image of a mobius arc in what looks like Sierra Nevada—"this is not the work of someone who hates the environment."

He gives me a puzzled look. "And I hate the environment?"

"Yes!" I blink. "No?"

He shrugs. "I might not compost my own feces or hold my breath to avoid emitting CO_2, but I do like nature."

I'm a little dumbfounded. "Liam? Can I ask you a question that will possibly make you want to throw the bowl at me?"

"It won't."

"You haven't heard the question."

"But the soup is really good."

I beam. And then I immediately feel self-conscious at the surge of warmth that comes from knowing he likes my cooking. Who cares if he does? He's a random dude. He's Liam Harding. On paper, I hate him.

"You said you really respected Helena's work. And that she was your favorite aunt. And that you were close. But you work at FGP Corp, and I've been wondering . . ."

"How I'm still alive?"

I laugh. "Pretty much."

"I'm not quite sure why she spared me."

"A bit out of character, isn't it?"

"I hid the sharp knives every time she visited. But she mostly focused on sending me daily texts about all the evil FGP Corp is doing in the world. Maybe she was going for a slow grind?"

"I just . . . I don't understand how you love Helena and nature *and* working at a company that lobbies to eliminate carbon taxes like its aim is to plunge civilization into fiery darkness."

He huffs out a laugh. "You think I *enjoy* working there?"

"I assumed you did. Because you seem to work all the time." I flush—okay, fine, I noticed his hours, sue me—but he doesn't seem to care. "You . . . don't?"

"No. It's a shitty company and I hate everything it stands for."

"Oh. Then why . . ." I scratch my nose. Oh. I did *not* expect that. "You're a lawyer. Can't you, um, lawyer elsewhere?"

"It's complicated."

"Complicated?"

The spoon scrapes the bottom of the bowl for a moment. "My mentor recruited me."

"Your mentor?"

"He was one of my professors. I owe him a lot—he helped me get all my internships lined up, advised me during law school. When he asked me to take this job, I didn't feel like I could say no. He's my boss now, and . . ." He leans back in his chair and runs a hand through his hair. Tired. He looks very tired. "I have a lot of complicated feelings about what FGP Corp does. And I don't like the company, or its mission. But in the end, it's a good thing that I'm around. If it weren't me, someone else would do my job just as well. And at least I can be there for the team I lead. And run interference between them and my boss when it's necessary."

I think about the words I overheard last night. *Unethical. Wrong.* "Is he the one you were arguing with? On the phone?" He lifts one eyebrow, and my cheeks warm. "I promise I wasn't eavesdropping!" But Liam shrugs as though he doesn't mind. So I smile, leaning forward across the table. "Okay, maybe I was. Just a bit. So, what's his name?"

"Whose name?"

"Your boss. Maybe *I* can talk to *him* while *you* talk to *Ted*? Some good old reciprocal proxy bullying? Mutual warn-off? Leave-My-Friend-Alone Sixty-Nine?"

He smiles at me then—a full, real smile. His first in my presence, I think, and it makes breathing that much harder, the temperature of the room that much hotter. How—*why* is he so handsome? I stare at him, speechless, unable to do anything but notice the clear brown of his eyes, the lopsided way his lips stretch, the fact that he seems to be studying me with a warm, kind expression, and—

Our eyes dart to his phone. Which is ringing again.

"Work?" I ask. My voice is hoarse.

"No. It's . . ." He stands from the table and clears his throat. "Excuse me. I'll be right back."

As he walks out, I hear him chuckle. On the other side of the phone, a female voice is saying his name.

Six ⚙️

take a careful step out of the shower, letting my toes dig deep into the thick, soft mat. It turns out to be a lethally poor choice, because I do it in the same exact moment Liam opens the bathroom door to take a step inside.

It leads to me jumping. And flailing. And yelling:

"Aaaaaaaaah!"

"Mara? What—"

"Aaah!"

"Sorry—I didn't—"

My entire body is slippery and frantic—not a good combination. I almost lose my balance trying to wrap the shower curtain around me. Then I *do* lose my balance, and I'm positive Liam can see everything.

The outie belly button Hannah always teases me about.

The sickle-shaped lacrosse scar above my right boob.

Said right boob, *and* the left one.

For a fraction of a second we both stand motionless. Staring at each other. Unable to react. Then I say, "Can you—could you, um, hand me that towel over there?"

"Ah—sure. Here you go. I . . ."

He extends his arm and turns the other way while I wrap the towel (his towel; Liam's towel) around myself. It's fluffy and clean and it smells good and—who uses black towels, anyway? Who produces them? Where does he even buy them, Bloodbath and Beyond?

"Mara?" He is standing under the doorframe, pointedly looking away from me.

"Yes?"

"Why are you in my bathroom?"

Crap. "Sorry. I'm *so* sorry. My shower isn't working, and . . . I think there's something wrong with a pipe, and . . . I don't know, but I called Bob."

"Bob?"

"The plumber. Well, *a* plumber. He's coming out tomorrow morning."

"Oh."

"But I went for a run earlier, and I was all sweaty and smelly, so . . ."

"I see."

"Sorry. I should have asked before. You can turn now, by the way. I'm decent."

Liam does turn. But only after about ten seconds of what looks like a pretty intense internal debate. His expressions are never the easiest to read, but he seems a little flustered.

A lot, actually. As in, even more than I am.

Which is odd. I'm the one who got boobsposed, and Liam is probably very used to being with naked women. That is, *actually* naked women. Way more naked than I currently am. Let's be real—his ex is likely a Victoria's Secret Angel who recently quit modeling to finish a doctorate in art history and become a junior curator at the Smithsonian. She has an impeccable belly button and knows what PlayStation button to press to throw a grenade. Did I say *his ex*? They're still dating, for all I know. Having a very athletic sex life. I'm talking role play and toys. Butt action. Lots of oral, which they both excel at. Okay, this train of thought needs to crash right now.

Maybe he's just embarrassed for me? Not that he should be. I'm pretty. I mean, I *think* I'm pretty. Cute, in a befreckled, wish-I-was-two-inches-taller, slightly-self-conscious-about-that-hump-on-my-nose way. Sometimes, usually after Sadie has put eyeliner on me, I even think I'm beautiful. But I'll never be as attractive as Liam. Is that why he's doing this weird thing—staring while obviously trying his best not to stare?

"I'm so sorry I didn't warn you. I thought you were out of town or something. Because you didn't come home last night, and . . ." I feel a bit embarrassed that I noticed. But how could I not? Ever since the snowstorm, we've gotten into this weird rhythm. Dinner together at seven. Not that there's an acknowledged agreement or anything, but I know from before that he used to eat a little later, and I know from my whole life that I used to eat a little earlier, and somehow we converged on a time that works for both of us . . . Maybe I was close to texting him last night. But decided not to, because it seemed like crossing some kind of unspoken line.

"No, I just . . . I had to be at work. Because of a deadline. I was going to warn you, but . . ." *You didn't want to cross some kind of unspoken line?* I want to ask. But one does not speak of unspoken things, so I just go with:

"Of course." I clear my throat. "I'll go to my room. Get dressed."

"Right."

I make to leave. Except that Liam's still standing there, blocking the exit. The only exit, if one doesn't count the window, which I briefly consider before acknowledging that it's not a feasible option. Not in my current state of dishevelment. "You are . . ." He doesn't seem to understand *where* he is. I'd gesticulate and point it out, but I have to clutch my towel with both hands to avoid flashing him, and—

"Oh. Oh, right, I . . ." He takes a large step to the side. Too large—he's basically plastered against the sink now.

"Okay. Thanks again for letting me use your bathroom."

"No problem."

I really should leave now. "And I borrowed a bit of your shampoo. Well, stole. It's not as if I'm ever going to return it. But, you know."

"It's okay."

"I love Old Spice, by the way. Solid choice."

"Oh." Liam looks everywhere but at me. "I just grab the first one I see at the store."

I know in that moment, I simply know, that Old Spice is William K. Harding's favorite brand of personal hygiene products, and that he suffers deep shame because of it. "Right. Of course." He can be adorable, sometimes. "Hey, just FYI, I'm not embarrassed. So you shouldn't be, either."

"What?"

"I don't care that you saw me naked. Because I know you don't care. Just saying, we don't need to be weird about it. Believe me"—I laugh—"I know you're not going to use your annoying ginger roomie's tiny freckled boobs as spank bank material."

I expect him to reply with a joke, like he usually does, but he doesn't. He doesn't reply at all, in fact. Just presses his lips together, nods once, and all of a sudden things feel even more awkward. *Crap.*

"Anyway. Thanks again."

"You're welcome."

I step out with a small wave and notice two things: he's staring hard at his feet, and his left hand is a tight fist at his side.

Seven

There's nothing wrong with the waveguide. That, I know for sure. The transformer and the stirrer seem fine, too, which has me thinking that the problem is in the magnetron. Now, I'm not really an expert, but I'm hoping that if I tinker with the filament the assembly will fix itself and—

"Is this because last night we watched *Transformers*?"

I look up. Liam, a soft smile on his face, is standing on the other side of the kitchen island, taking in the microwave oven parts I meticulously laid out over the marble countertop.

I might have made a mess.

"It was either this or writing Optimus Prime fan fiction."

He nods. "Good choice, then."

"But also, your microwave isn't working. I'm trying to fix it."

"I can just buy a new one." His head tilts. He studies the components with a slight frown. "Is this safe?"

I stiffen. "Are you asking because I'm a woman and therefore unable to do anything remotely scientific without causing radio-active pollution? Because if so, I—"

"I'm asking because *I* wouldn't know where to start, and because *I* am so ignorant about anything remotely scientific that you could be building an atomic bomb and I wouldn't be able to tell," he says calmly. As though he doesn't even need to be defensive, because the idea that me being a puny-brained girl never even entered his mind. "But you clearly can." A pause. "Please don't build an atomic bomb."

"Don't tell me what to do."

He sighs. "I'll make room for the plutonium in the cheese drawer."

I laugh, and realize that it's the first time I've done it in hours. Which, in turn, makes me sigh. "It's just . . . Sean is being a total dick. Again."

His expression darkens with understanding. "What'd he do?"

"The usual. That deco project I told you about? I was explaining this really cool idea about how to fix it, but he only let me talk for half a minute before telling me why it wouldn't work." I fiddle with the magnetron, then start reassembling the oven. The second both my hands are occupied, a strand of hair decides to fall into my left eye. I blow it away. "Thing is, I'd already considered all of his objections and found solutions. But did he let me continue? Nope. So now we're going with a much-less-elegant method, and . . ." I trail off. At this point, Liam gets two to four Sean-related rants a week from me. The least I can do is keep them short. "Anyway. Sorry for being defensive."

"Mara. You should report him."

"I know. It's just . . . this constantly belittling behavior is so hard to prove, and . . ." I shrug—bad idea, since my hair is now back in my eyes. I feel a little stuck. A lot stuck.

"So, what's Sean's last name?" Liam asks.

"Why?"

"Just curious." He tries to sound casual, but he's so bad at it. He's clearly the worst liar in the world—how did he get through law school? It makes me smile every time.

"You need to practice," I say, pointing my screwdriver at him.

"Practice?"

"Practice telling . . ."

My voice trails off. Because Liam is reaching up to brush his fingers against my cheekbone, a faint smile on his lips. My brain short-circuits. What—? Did he—?

Oh. *Oh*. My hair. My lost, wayward strand of hair. He tucked it behind my ear. He's just being nice and helping his ginger klutz roommate, who in turn is having a major brain fart. *Classy, Mara. Very classy.*

"Practice telling what?" he asks, still staring at the shell of my ear. It's probably misshapen, and I never even knew it.

"Nothing. Lies. I . . ." I clear my throat. *Get it together, Floyd.* "Hey, you know what?" I try to keep my tone light. Change the topic. "The beginning of this cohabitation was an absolute night-mare, but I like this a lot."

"This?"

"This thing." I begin to screw in the back plate of the micro-wave. "Where we chat without throwing chairs at each other and you offhandedly ask for the last names of dudes who are mean to me with the obvious idea of committing unsanctioned acts of vig-ilante justice against them."

"That's not what I—"

I lift my eyebrow. He blushes and looks away.

"Anyway, I like this much better. Being friends, I guess."

He glares at me. "I'm *not* your friend."

"Oh." I almost recoil. Almost. "Oh. I—I'm sorry. I didn't mean to imply that—"

"The other night Eileen gave Bernie a rose, and you said that it was a good move. That's not something I can accept from a friend."

I burst out laughing. "Come on, he's cute. He is a dog trainer. He likes K-pop!"

"See, this? The reason you're my sworn enemy." He shakes his head at me, and I laugh harder, and then my laughter dies down and for a second we're just smiling at each other and an unfamiliar liquid warmth spills inside me.

"I am *positive* Helena would have rooted for Bernie."

He snorts. "You say it like it's an endorsement. Like she didn't constantly try to set me up with random people I cared nothing for."

"She did the same with me!"

"And when I was a teenager she dated this guy who had been on a four-month shower strike."

"Oh God. Why?"

"Not sure. The environment?"

"No—why was she dating him?"

Liam winces. "Apparently—and I quote—'astounding carnal chemistry.'"

I morbidly contemplate Helena's sex life until Liam breaks the quiet and asks, "Do you ever think about switching jobs?"

I shake my head. "It's the EPA. Where I always wanted to be. Seriously, fifteen-year-old Mara would travel through time to shank me if I were to quit." I think I picked up on an odd note in his question, though. "Why did you ask? Do *you* ever think about switching jobs?"

He shakes his head, too. "I couldn't," he says. But I'm starting to know him, a little bit. I'm more attuned to his moods, his thoughts, the way he turns inward whenever he considers something serious. There is a wall of sorts that he builds between himself and everyone who tries to know him. Sometimes I wish it weren't there. So I push gently against it and ask, "How are things at work?"

He is silent for a while, hands pressed wide against the island, watching me quietly as I finish screwing the pieces back together. My hair remains safely tucked behind my ear. "He asked me to fire someone today."

"Oh." I already know who *he* is. Mitch. Liam's boss. Whom I privately hate with the intensity of a thousand microwave ovens. Who's the reason Liam feels like he cannot pack up his black-market-organ-priced graduate degrees and his years of experience being a corporate meanie and find another job. "Why?"

"Someone on my team made a really stupid mistake. But fixable. And still . . . it's just a mistake. We all fuck up—I know *I* do." He absentmindedly rubs the back of his hand against his lips. "I really thought I could talk him out of it." He shakes his head, and I frown. And press my lips together. And order myself to count to five before I say anything, just to avoid being intrusive or aggressive. Five, four, three—

"Honestly, your boss is a shit nugget and he doesn't deserve you and you should quit and leave him to stir in his shit broth!"

Liam looks up, surprised. And amused, I think. "A shit nugget?"

I flush. "A valuable but underrated insult. But Liam, really, you deserve to have a better job. And before you point out that it's hypocritical of me to tell you to switch jobs while I won't do it myself, let me say that it's a totally different situation. I *love* my job—I just hate the people I have to do it with. Including Sean. Especially Sean. Really, mostly Sean." Oh, how I'd love to boil my post-run socks, make soup out of them, and then feed it to Sean.

"You could ask for a transfer."

"I plan to. But it won't help." I shrug and plug the microwave back in. "The EPA's opening a new unit. I'm applying to be transferred, but Sean the Asshole is, too." I roll my eyes. "He's impossible to shake off. Like a parasitic toenail fungus."

"So you'll be competing with him for the position?"

"Well, no. He's applying to lead. I'd be among the plebs—a lowly team member."

"You can't lead because you don't have enough seniority?"

"Oh, I don't think there are seniority requirements."

"Then why are you not applying to lead it?"

"Because—" I snap my mouth shut and look down at my screwdriver. Yes. Why? Why *wouldn't* I apply for a leader position? What is wrong with me? It's not like Sean is smarter than I am. He just loves to impose the sound of his own voice on unsuspecting passersby. And maybe I don't have enough leadership experience to know that I'll be a good boss, but I do have enough Sean experience to know that *he* won't be. He keeps calling me Lara, for fuck's sake. In *emails*. That he writes to my email address, marafloyd@ epa.gov. Dude, you can literally *copy* and *paste*?

I look up. Liam is staring at me with a calm expression, as though patiently waiting for me to reach this very exact conclusion: I am better than Sean. Because *everyone* is better than Sean, and that includes me.

I feel a shiver of something warm run down my spine, as

though I'm being held. Which is weird, since I haven't hugged someone in . . . God, months. Not since Helena.

"Tell you what." I put my hands on my hips, suddenly determined. "I'm going to apply for the leader position."

"That's exactly what you should—"

"If *you* leave your job."

He pauses, then exhales a laugh. "If I leave my job, who'll keep you in the expensive multi-ply toilet paper lifestyle you're accustomed to?"

"You will, since you're probably sitting on generational piles of old New England money. Plus, you could totally still be a lawyer for other, slightly less disgusting corporations. If there are any, that is. And if we strike this blood pact and I get the job, there's something even better in it for you."

"You let me hold Sean's head in the toilet bowl?"

"No. Well, yes. But also, if I get a team leader position, I'd be making more money. And I'll finally be able to move out." *Without needing to sell my half of the house.*

Liam's expression shifts abruptly. "Mara—"

"Think about it! You, walking around naked in a pleasantly freezing house, scratching your butt in front of a fridge full of tartar sauce, cooking tacos at three A.M. while listening to postmodern industrial pop on your gramophone. All around are giant screens, broadcasting video game playthroughs twenty-four/seven. Sounds nice, huh?"

"No," he says flatly.

"That's because I forgot to mention the best part: your pesky ex-roommate is gone, nowhere to be seen." I beam. "Now, tell me you're not going to love every second of—"

"I won't, Mara. I—" He turns away, and I can see his jaw clench like it used to before, when my presence in this house annoyed him and he considered me the bane of anything good. But his hand tightens around the edge of the counter once, and he seems to collect himself. He studies me for a long moment.

"Please," I press. "I won't apply if you won't. Do you really want to condemn me to a lifetime of Sean?"

He closes his eyes. Then he opens them and nods. Once. "I won't leave my job—"

"Oh, come on!"

"—till I have another lined up. But I will start looking around."

I smile slowly. "Wait—for real?" I did *not* think this would work.

"Only if you apply for the leader position."

"Yes!" I clap my hands. "Liam, I'll help you. Are you on LinkedIn? I bet recruiters would be all over you."

"What's LinkedIn?"

"Ugh. Do you at least have a recent headshot?"

He stares at me blankly.

"Fine, I'll take a picture of you. In the garden. When there's good natural light. Wear the charcoal three-piece suit and that blue button-down—it looks amazing on you." He cocks his eyebrow, and I instantly regret saying that, but I'm too excited at the idea of this weird professional-suicide pact to blush too hard. "This is *amazing*. We've got to shake on it."

I thrust out my hand, and he takes it immediately, his own firm and warm and large around mine, and—it might be the first time we touch on purpose, as opposed to arms brushing while we're working at the stove, or fingers grazing as he sorts out my mail. It feels . . . nice. And right. And natural. I like it, and I look up to Liam's face to see whether he likes it, too, and . . . there are a thousand different expressions passing on his face. A million different emotions.

I can't begin to parse even one.

"Deal," he says, voice deep and a little hoarse.

He uses his free hand to turn on the microwave—which, lo and behold, is working again.

Eight

Rain is my favorite kind of weather.

I am most partial to summer storms, their strong winds and hot air, the way they make me feel like I'm sitting on the humid inside of a balloon that's about to burst. As a kid, I'd run outside as soon as the rain started just to get all wet—which seemed to outrage my mother to no end.

But I'm not particular. It's barely February, early in the night, and the hard drops beating a tattoo on the plastic of my umbrella, they just make me happy. I smile when I unlock the front door. Hum, too. I walk down the hall, listening to the rain instead of what's happening inside the house, and that must be the reason I don't hear them.

Liam and a girl. No: a woman. They are in the kitchen. Together. He's leaning back against the counter. She's sitting on it, at his side, close enough to lay her cheek on his shoulder while she

shows him something on her phone that has both of them smiling. It's the most relaxed I've seen Liam with anyone. Clearly a
very intimate moment that I should *not* be interrupting, except
that I can't make myself move. I feel my stomach sink and remain
rooted to the floor, unable to retreat as the woman shakes her
head and murmurs something in Liam's ear that I cannot hear,
something that has him chuckling in low, deep tones, and—

I must gasp. Or make some sort of noise, because one moment
they're laughing, arms pressed against each other, and the next
they're both looking up. At me.

Shit.

I try really hard not to let my eyes take in how cozy and comfortable he looks, how familiar and at ease. It's nothing like what
happens when he and I accidentally bump against each other in the
hallway, like that charged, electric tension that seems to crackle
between us when we forget ourselves and our hands happen
to brush together. But that's the point, right? Any physical contact
between me and Liam is probably unwanted on his part, while
this . . .

This is mortifying. I want to get out of this room and never
come back. Buy an insulated lunch bag and a camping stove, shove
them in my bedroom, and be completely self-sufficient.

The woman, though, doesn't seem nearly as unsettled, or self-
conscious about the fact that she's currently perched on a piece of
furniture in a home that's not hers, her skirt riding up to show
long, toned legs. She smiles at me, and somehow, somewhere, I
find my voice. "Sorry. I'm so sorry, I didn't mean to interrupt . . . I
wanted to get something to drink, and I . . ." And I? *And I will now
go to my room to flush myself down the toilet. Good-bye, cruel world.*

"I thought you'd be . . ." Liam's voice seems deeper than usual.
I wonder if they were about to take whatever this is to his bed-

room. *Oh God. Oh God, I just interrupted my roommate and his girl-friend. I'm such a loser.* "Out. I thought you'd be out."

Oh. Right. I was supposed to go on a date myself. With Ted. Something I agreed to do the other day under the impetus of: meh, why not? This morning I told Liam why I'd be home late, except that I ended up canceling because . . . I didn't really feel like going.

For some reason.

That is unclear to me.

"No. I mean, yes. Yes, I was. But . . ." I gesture vaguely in the air. As good an explanation as I can come up with.

"Oh."

"Yeah. I . . ." I should really go to my room and do that self-flushing thing. But it's hard, with Liam staring at me like that. Half-curious, half-happy to see me, half–something else. It's the first time I find him with someone who's not Calvin or another one of his dude friends he's obviously known since forever, some-one who's clearly . . . Okay. He's on a date. With a woman. About to get laid, probably. And I interrupted. *Shit.*

"I'm . . . I'm gonna go now, so you guys can—"

"No need," a voice says.

A voice? Ah. Yes. Right. There is a third person in the room. A beautiful woman with long dark hair who's still sitting on the counter, glancing with captivated interest between me and Liam, and . . .

"I was *just* about to leave," she says. But it's a lie. She was defi-nitely *not* about to leave. "Right, Liam?" She and Liam exchange a silent, loaded look that I'd give half a kidney to be able to decipher.

"Oh, no. You don't have to leave," I say weakly. "I—"

"By the way, I'm going to introduce myself, since Liam here is clearly not going to." She hops down with grace that I've seen only in ballet dancers and Olympic gymnasts before, and holds out her hand. I hate myself for trying to remember if it's the same hand that was wrapped around Liam's arm while her head was on his shoulder. "I'm Emma. You must be the famous Mara?"

Why she would know my name is an absolute mystery. Unless Emma and Liam are very serious, and then Liam would have mentioned his annoying roommate once or twice, and will you look at that? It appears that I just cannot bear the thought. "Yes. Um . . . Nice to meet you."

Emma's handshake is cool and firm. She smiles briefly, nice and self-assured, then turns to pick up her jacket from a stool.

"Well. This was fun. Informative, too. Mara, I hope we'll meet a *ton* more times. And you . . ." She turns to Liam. Her voice drops lower, but I can still make out the words. "Cheer up, buddy. I don't think you're as doomed to a lifetime of pining as you think. I'll call you tomorrow." She's not very tall and has to stand on her tiptoes to kiss him on the cheek, one hand pressing against his abs for balance, and if Liam minds having her up in his space, he doesn't show it. Then there is a friendly wave, directed at me this time, a cheerful "Good night," the sound of her heels against the parquet flooring on her way to the entrance, and then—

Gone.

That noise was the front door opening and closing, which means that Liam and I are alone.

"Liam, I'm *so* sorry. I didn't mean to . . ."

"To?" He scratches the back of his neck, looking confused by my reaction. He's still leaning against the counter, and I can't make myself move away from the entrance. I can't make myself continue and apologize for interrupting his date. *I was going to leave. I promise. You guys could have continued in your room, Liam. I wouldn't have minded.*

Really.

"How did the presentation go?"

I look up from inspecting my shoes. "What?"

"Your presentation today? For the lead position?"

"Ah." Right. The presentation. The one I've been complaining about for days. The one I practiced with him yesterday. And the day before. The one he probably knows by heart. "Um, very good. Good. Well, okay. Passable."

"It's getting worse by the word."

I wince. "It was . . . I stumbled a bit."

"I see."

"But maybe I still did better than Sean?"

"Maybe?"

"Probably."

Liam smiles. "Probably?"

I smile back. "Almost certainly."

"What a speedy improvement."

I chuckle, and he pushes away from the counter and comes to stand right in front of me. Like he wants to be closer for this conversation. Closer to me.

"It's bad news for you, though," I say.

"Is it?"

"If I get this position, you're going to have to step up and find a new job, too."

"Ah. Yes."

"We made a deal."

"A deal is a deal."

"Also, after the interview they gave us information on the salary. It's a big raise. I'll definitely be able to move out."

His eyes harden, then switch back to a neutral mask. "Right."

"What?" I tease him. "You afraid you can't afford to buy your own creamer?" *What does he even use it for? I still don't know.*

"Just concerned I'll have to watch Eileen make terrible life choices on my own."

"Eileen knows what she's doing. As I explained in my last blog post."

"Which I have, of course, read."

He's not funny. He's not *that* funny. I'm not half in love with his weird sense of humor. "I can't believe you commented 'delete your account.' It's cyberbullying, Liam."

He is now smiling, and there is something warm unfurling in my chest now. Which really shouldn't be there, because . . . Because. "Are you and your friend . . . ?" I ask.

"My friend?"

"Emma."

"Ah."

Silence. I wring my hands, realizing that I haven't really formulated a question. *Is she your* . . . No. Too direct. *Are you two dating?* And what is this hiccup in my heart as I contemplate the thought? Maybe Liam has never mentioned a girlfriend. Or any girl. But what did I think? That he was living in celibacy? It's not my business, anyway. We're just friends. Good friends. But friends.

"What?" He gives me a long look, like I just asked a preposterous question that's not grounded in reality. The reality that I just walked in on him PDAing her.

"I thought you two . . . ?"

"No." He shakes his head once. Then he shakes it again. "No, Emma is . . . We were in kindergarten together. And she . . . No. We're friends, good friends, but nothing like that."

"Oh." Oh? Really? No way. Way?

"We're just friends," he repeats again. Like he wants to make sure I know it. Like he's afraid that I don't believe him. Which, to be fair, I don't. Look at her. Look at *him*. "She's actually . . . She knows that I . . ." He wipes a hand down his face, like he always does when he's overwhelmed or tired. It's a gesture I'm seeing more of lately. Because Liam has been letting me see more of him. They're not all bad, the sharp edges and deep grooves of this man's personality. Unexpected, but not bad at all.

"Knows that you?"

"That I don't usually . . . I never . . . Well, *almost* never, apparently . . ." Liam shakes his head, as if to say *Never mind*, and I remain unsure as to what he almost never does, because he doesn't continue and I'm not certain that I want to probe. Plus, he's looking at me in a way I can't understand, and I'm suddenly feeling like it's time to skedaddle. "I'm gonna go to sleep, okay?" I smile. "I have an early morning tomorrow."

He nods. "Okay. Sure." But when I'm almost out of the room, he calls after me. "Mara?"

I pause. Don't turn around. "Yeah?"

"I . . . Have a good night."

It doesn't sound like what he originally meant to say. But I answer, "You, too," and run back to my room anyway.

Nine ⚙

had lots of fun tonight."

"Good. Thank you. I mean . . ." I clear my throat. "So did I."

Ted is nothing if not predictable. He took me to the Ethiopian restaurant I told him I'd been wanting to try (excellent); he raised topics of conversation I know enough about to feel comfortable, but not so familiar that I got bored within a few minutes; and now, now that he's walked me to my door, he's going to lean in and kiss me, just like I could have anticipated when he picked me up exactly three hours ago.

It is, predictably, a good kiss. A solid kiss. It could probably lead into good sex if I decided to invite him inside for a drink. Solid sex. Long-time-no-have sex. We're talking years, here. Helena would pop the champagne and remind me to dust off the cobwebs.

And yet.

I have no intention of asking him to come in. It's truly been ages, but this thing with Ted is just . . . no.

He's a nice guy, but this is not going to work, for a variety of reasons. Which, I tell myself, have nothing to do with how long Liam stared at me earlier today, before Ted pulled up our driveway. Or with the way he instantly averted his gaze when I caught him. Or with the hoarse quality of his voice when he took in my dress and said, "I . . . You look beautiful."

He sounded like he wanted to say something else. A little wistful. Almost apologetic. It made me regret spending thirty minutes putting on makeup to go out with someone else, some poor guy I don't even want to impress for the simple reason that he isn't . . .

Yeah.

"I . . ." I take a deep breath and take a step back from Ted, whose only fault is . . . not being another guy. I cannot picture him watching *The Bachelor* with me, which is apparently a deal breaker. The more you know, huh? "I'm gonna go inside now. But thanks for everything. I had a lovely evening."

If Ted is disappointed, I can't tell. To his credit, he hesitates only briefly. Then he smiles and retreats to his car without any *I'll call you* or *See you next time* that we both know would be nothing more than lies of politeness. I silently thank the EPA gods for transferring him to another team last week, and make my way inside.

I'm surprised to find Liam in the living room, sitting on the couch with a beer in one hand, a stack of papers in another, ridiculously cute reading glasses perched on his nose. Or maybe I'm not. It's Saturday night, after all. We usually spend our Saturday nights on that very couch, watching TV, talking about everything and nothing. It makes sense that he's here, even though I was gone.

For the life of me, I can't remember a better activity than staying at home in my pj's and hanging out with my roommate.

"What are you reading?"

Liam glances up at me, takes in my short-but-not-too-short

dress, my loose hair, my red lips, then immediately looks back to his papers. "Just a guideline document for work."

"How to achieve your very own oil spill in ten easy steps?"

His lips quirk upward. "I think you only need the one."

"Listen, we've been over this. It's okay if you don't want to quit just yet, but the very least you can do is *not* work on weekends. Come on, Liam. Do it for the environment."

He sighs, but he takes off his glasses and puts away the papers. I smile and reach forward to grab his beer and take a sip without bothering to ask. Liam studies me in silence, but doesn't start reading again. When I lift one eyebrow—*what?*—he caves, and asks: "Isn't he coming in?"

"Who?"

Liam looks toward the entrance.

"Ah." Right. Other men exist, too. Hard to remember sometimes. "No. Ted's not . . . He went home."

"Oh."

"I'm not . . . We're not . . ." How to put it? "We haven't . . ."

Liam nods, though he cannot possibly have made sense of what I just mumbled. And then he says nothing. And then things seem to get a bit weird. There is an odd tension in the room. Like we're both holding back something. I'd rather not search inside myself to figure out what.

"I should go to bed."

"Okay." He swallows. "Good night."

It might be that two fuzzy navels were too many, or maybe I just never really got the hang of high heels. The fact remains that I lose my balance and stumble just as I try to walk past him. His hands, large and solid and warm even through my dress, close around my hips until I'm stable again. I'm standing, and he's sitting down, and like this I'm several inches taller than him, and . . .

It's new, seeing him from this perspective. He looks younger, almost softer, and my first drunken instinct is to cup his face, trace the line of his nose, run my thumb over his lower lip.

I stop myself, but my slow, misfiring brain doesn't. It feeds me an odd image: Liam smiling and pulling me down into his lap. Pushing between my knees. His hands skimming up my thighs, under my dress, tickling my skin, making me laugh. He reaches my lower back and his grip tightens, long fingers sliding under the elastic of my panties, cupping my ass to press me to . . . *Oh.* He is hard. Big. Insistent. He arranges me exactly how he wants me and I exhale just as he groans in my ear, "Careful, Mara."

Wait. What?

I blink out of whatever the hell *that* was, just as Liam lets go of me. He says, "Careful, Mara," and I take a step back before I can humiliate myself with something moronic and utterly embarrassing.

"Thanks." Our eyes hold for what feels like too long. I clear my throat. "Are you going to bed, too?"

"Not yet."

"You are not allowed to read more oil spill stuff, Liam."

"Then maybe I'll just play a bit."

"Without Calvin?" I cock my head. "Didn't you say Calvin would come over?"

"He was supposed to."

"You know what?" I run a hand through my hair. It's a split-second decision. "I'm actually not that sleepy, either. Should I play with you?"

He laughs. "Really?"

"Yes. What?" I take off my shoes, grab a blanket—the one he put on me that first night, the one that's been in this room ever since—and let myself fall onto the couch, right next to him. A little too close, maybe, but Liam doesn't complain. "I have a Ph.D. I can pretend to kill bad guys using a . . . joystick?"

"Controller." He shakes his head, but he looks . . . happy, I think. "Have you ever played a video game?"

"Nope. Full disclosure, they look awful and I'm not sure why an obviously smart person with a bunch of Ivy League degrees that cost more than my internal organs would be so into this pew-pew crap, but I run a *Bachelor* blog, so I have no leg to stand on." I shrug. "So, what happened to Calvin?"

"Couldn't make it."

"Playing with someone else?"

"A date."

I hum. "Maybe you should have joined him. Was Emma busy?"

He gives me a look that I cannot quite decipher. As though there's something catastrophically wrong about what I said. "I told you, Emma doesn't want to date me any more than I want to date her."

I doubt it. Who wouldn't? Also, how freaked out would you be if I told you that the other night I dreamt of you and Emma, sitting side by side in the kitchen, and I was sad? But only for a little. Because after a while it wasn't you and Emma. It was you and me and you were standing between my legs and you put your hands on my inner thighs and you pushed them open, wider, to make room for yourself and— "You could date someone else, then," I blurt out. To put a halt to what's going on in my head.

"I don't think I want to, Mara."

"Right." My heart hiccups. "You wouldn't enjoy good food and pleasant conversation and getting laid."

"Is that how your date went?" he asks softly, not looking at me anymore.

"I just meant—" I'm flustered. "You might enjoy dating the right person."

"Stop channeling Helena."

I laugh. "Gotta keep up the household tradition of being nosy about people's personal lives." Something occurs to me, and I gasp. "You know what's *really* shocking?"

"What?"

"That Helena never tried to set us up. Like, you and me. Together."

"Yeah, that's—" Liam falls silent abruptly, as though something occurred to him, too. He stares into the middle distance for a moment and then lets out a low, deep laugh. "Helena."

"What?" He doesn't answer me. So I repeat, "Liam? What?"

"I just realized that . . ." He shakes his head, amused. "Nothing, Mara." I want to insist till he explains what revelation he appears to have reached, but he puts a controller in my hand and says, "Let's play."

"Okay. Who am I supposed to kill, and how do I do it?"

He smiles at me, and a million little sparks crackle down my spine. "I thought you'd never ask."

Ten ⚙

Three weeks ago

When Liam arrives home, I can barely feel my toes, my teeth are chattering, and I am more blanket than human. He studies me from the entrance of the living room while pulling off his tie, lips pressed together in what looks a lot like amusement.

Asshole.

He observes me for long moments before coming closer. Then he crouches in front of me, widens the gap between the layers of blankets to better see my eyes, and says, "I'm afraid to ask."

"Th-th-the heat isn't working. I already looked into it—I think a fuse has b-blown. I called the guy who fixed it last t-time, he should b-be here in half an hour."

Liam cocks his head. "You're under three Snuggies. Why are your lips blue?"

"It's freezing! I can't get warm."

"It's not that cold."

"Maybe it's not that cold when you have six hundred pounds of muscles to insulate you, but I'm gonna d-d-die."

"Are you."

"Of hypothermia."

He is *definitely* pressing his lips together to avoid smiling. "Would you like to borrow my baby-seal fur coat?"

I hesitate. "Do you really have one?"

"Would you want it, if I did?"

"I'm scared to find out."

He shakes his head and sits next to me on the couch. "Come here."

"What?"

"Come here."

"No. Why? Are you planning to steal my seat? Back off. It took me ages to warm it up—"

I don't get to finish the sentence. Because he picks me up, Snuggies and all, and lifts me across his lap until my ass is resting on his thighs. Which . . .

Oh.

This is new.

For a moment, my spine stiffens and my muscles tense in surprise. But it's very brief, because he's so deliciously *toasty*. Way cozier than my stupid spot on the couch, and his skin . . . it smells familiar and good. So, so good. "You're so warm." I let my forehead fall against his cheek. "It's like you generate heat."

"I think all humans do." His nose touches the icy tip of my ear. "It's physics, or something."

"First law of th-thermodynamics. Energy can be neither created nor destroyed."

His hand travels up my spine to cup my nape, and the temperature is suddenly five, ten degrees higher. Heat licks down my spine and spreads around my torso. My breasts. My belly. I almost whimper. "Except by you, apparently," he says.

"It's so unfair." Liam's thumb is tracing patterns on the skin of my throat, and I have no choice but to sigh. I'm already feeling better. I'm *glowing*.

"That you are where the heat goes to die?"

"Yeah." I burrow closer into his chest. "Maybe my parents are secretly shark shapeshifters. Of the cold-blooded, poikilothermic variety. They forgot to warn me that I inherited zero thermoregulation skills and should never live on dry land."

"It's the only possible explanation." His breath chuffs against my temples, a fine, pleasant itch.

"For my pathological inability to maintain thermal homeostasis?"

"For how little they appreciate you." He's suddenly holding me a little tighter. A little closer. "Also, for how rare you like your steak."

"I . . . Medium rare." My voice shakes. I tell myself that it's because of the cold and not the fact that he remembers the things I told him about my family.

"Please. Basically raw."

"Humph." No point in arguing with him, not when he's right. Not when his hand is running up and down my arm—a warming, calming gesture, even through the blankets. "Do you think he'll be able to fix the fuse tonight?"

"I hope so. If not, I'll run to the store and get you a heater."

"You would do that?"

He shrugs. There are about ten layers between us (Liam vastly underestimated the number of Snuggies I can put on at once), but he feels so warm and solid. A few months ago, I thought him cold, in every possible way. Back when I used to believe that I hated him. "It feels like less work than driving you to the ER for frostbite treatment." His cheek curves against my brow.

"You're not as heartless as you think, Liam."

"I'm not as heartless as *you* think."

I laugh and lean back to take a look at him, because it feels like he might be smiling, a whole wide grin, and that's a rare and wondrous phenomenon that I want to savor. He's not, though. He's staring at me, too, studying me in that weighty, serious way he sometimes does. First my eyes, and then my lips, and what is this, this moment of heavy, full silence that has my heart racing and my skin tingling?

"Mara." His throat moves as he swallows. "I—"

Loud knocking makes us startle.

"The electrician."

"Oh. Yeah." My voice is both shrill and breathless.

"I'll get the door, okay?"

Please, don't. Stay. "Okay."

"Do you think you can avoid hypothermia if I let go of you?"

"Yes. Probably." *No.* "Maybe?"

He rolls his eyes in that put-upon way that reminds me so much of Helena. But his smile, the one I was looking for earlier— here it is. Finally. "Very well, then." Without letting go, he stands and carries me all the way to the entrance.

I hide my face in his neck, humming with warmth and something else, unfamiliar and unidentifiable.

Eleven ⚙♥

I get the phone call on a Wednesday night, before dinner but after I've returned from work.

I am remarkably composed throughout: I *oh* and *ah* in all the right places; I ask pertinent, important questions; I even remember to thank the caller for sharing the news with me. But after we both hang up, I completely lose it.

I don't call Sadie. I don't text Hannah in the hope that she has reception in the belly of whatever Nordic sperm whale is her current residence. I run upstairs, almost tripping on carpets and furniture that's been in the Harding family for five generations, and once I'm in front of Liam's office I throw the door open without knocking.

Which, in hindsight, is not my most polite moment. And neither is the next, when I run to Liam (who's talking on the phone by the window), throw my arms around his waist with utter disregard for whatever he's doing, and yell:

"I got it! Liam—I got the job!"

He doesn't skip a beat. "The team leader position?"

"Yes."

His grin is blinding. Then he tells, "I'll call you back," to whoever is on the line, totally ignores the fact that their reply is "Sir, this is a time-sensitive issue—" and tosses the phone on the nearest chair.

Then he hugs me back. He lifts me up like he's too happy for me to even consider stopping himself, like this phone call I just had that changed my life changed his, too, like he's been wanting this as much and as intensely as I have. And when he spins me around the room, one single, perfect whirl of pure happiness, that's when I realize it.

How incredibly, utterly gone for this man I am.

It's been there for weeks. Months. Whispering in my ear, creeping at me, hitting me in the face like a train on an iron track. It has grown too formidable and luminous for me to ignore, but that's okay.

I don't want to ignore it.

Liam sets me on my feet. His hands linger over me before he takes a step back—one hand trailing down my arm, the other pushing a lock of hair past my temple, behind my ear. When he lets go, I want to follow him. I want to beg him not to.

"Mara, you are fantastic. Brilliant."

I feel fantastic. I feel brilliant, when I'm with you. And I want you to feel the same. "I clearly deserve to choose what to watch on TV tonight."

"You choose what to watch on TV every night."

"But tonight I actually *deserve* it."

He laughs, shaking his head, holding my eyes. Time stretches. Heavy, sweet tension thickens between us. I want to kiss him. I want to kiss him so, so much. Should I ask him? Would he push me away? Or would he push right back, press me against his desk, turn me around and hold me down with a hand splayed between my shoulder blades and whisper to me *Finally*, and *Be still*, and *Let's celebrate*, and—

No. Stop.

I gasp. "Oh my God—what do you think Sean is doing right now?"

"Crying in the bathroom, I hope."

"Hopefully he's tweeting out his despair and listening to a My Chemical Romance playlist on Spotify. I *must* go stalk him on social media. Be right back." I make to skip out of Liam's office as fast as I ran in. He stops me, though, with a hand on my wrist.

"Mara?"

"Yes?"

I turn around. His happy, uncharacteristically open face has melted away into something else. Something more subdued. Opaque.

"You said . . . A few weeks ago, you said that if you got the job, you'd move out."

Oh.

Oh.

The reminder stabs like a knife between my ribs. I *did* say that. I did. But it's been weeks. Weeks of stealing food off each other's plates and texting in the middle of the day to bicker about Eileen's love life and that time he made me laugh so hard I couldn't breathe for ten minutes.

Things . . . Haven't things changed with us? Between us?

For a moment, I cannot speak. I don't know what to say to the fact that his first thought was that I'd move out— No, that's uncharitable. He was happy for me. Genuinely happy. His *second* thought was that he'd finally go back to living alone.

I try to crack a joke. "Why? Are you kicking me out?"

"No. No, Mara, that's not what I—" His phone rings, interrupting him. Liam gives it a frustrated glance, but by the time his eyes are on me again I've collected myself.

If Liam wants to live alone, that's fine. He likes me. He cares about me. He's a great guy—I know all of that. But being friends with someone doesn't equate with wanting to spend every single moment of your life with them, and . . . yeah.

I guess that's my own problem to solve. Something to work on once I move out and this part of my life is over.

"Of course I'm going to look for a new place." I try to sound cheerful. With poor results. "I cannot wait to walk around naked and gorge myself on creamer to celebrate Eileen's excellent life choices and . . ." I can't make myself continue, and my voice trails off.

Liam's eyes remain withdrawn. Absent, almost. But after a while he says, "Whatever you want, Mara," in a kind, gentle tone.

I manage one last smile and slip out of his office as the first tear hits my collarbone.

Twelve ⚙

One day ago

No dimensional plane exists in which apartment hunting (more precisely: apartment hunting while heartbroken) could ever be pleasant. I have to admit, however, that browsing Craigslist on the phone with my friends while I sip on the overpriced red wine Liam got from an FGP Corp retreat does dull the pain of the ordeal.

Sadie just spent an hour recounting in wrathful detail how she recently went on a date with some engineer who later turned out to be a total dick—a problem, given that she actually liked the guy (as in really, *really* liked the guy). Even though she's being uncharacteristically dodgy about it, I am 97 percent sure that sex happened, 98 percent sure that the sex was excellent, 99 percent sure that the sex was the best of her life. It appears to be fueling her plans to lace the guy's coffee with toad venom, which, if you know Sadie, is pretty on-brand.

Hannah is back in Houston, which is good for her Internet connection, but bad for her peace of mind. She has been butting heads with some NASA big-shot guy who has been vetoing her pet research project for no reason whatsoever. Hannah is, of course, ready for murder. I can't see her hands through FaceTime, but I'm almost positive she's sharpening a shiv.

There is something reassuring in hearing about their lives. It reminds me of grad school, when we couldn't afford therapy and we'd engage in some healthy communal bitching every other night, just to survive the madness. There were some bad moments—it was grad school: there were *a lot* of bad moments—but in the end, we were together. In the end, everything turned out to be all right.

So maybe that's what will happen this time, too. I'm on the verge of homelessness, my heart feels like a stone, and I want to be with someone way more than that someone wants to be with me. But Sadie and Hannah are (more or less) here, and therefore things will turn out to be (more or less) all right.

"Men were a mistake," Sadie says.

"Big mistake," Hannah adds.

"*Huge.*" I sink deeper into the living room couch, wondering if Liam, my personal mistake, will come home tonight. It's already past nine. Maybe he's out for dinner. Maybe, if he has something to celebrate, he'll sleep elsewhere. At Emma's, perhaps.

"Sometimes they're useful," Sadie points out. "Like that guy with a Korn T-shirt who helped me open a jar of pickled radishes in 2018."

"Oh yeah." I nod. "I remember that."

"Hands down my most profound experience with a man."

"In hindsight, you should have asked him to marry you."

"A missed opportunity."

"Could it be that we've just been exceptionally unlucky?" There is some noise on Hannah's side of the line. Maybe she *is* sharpening a shiv. "Could it be that the tides will turn and we'll finally meet dudes who don't deserve to be fed a bowl of thumbtacks?"

"It could be," I say. *Be positive*, Helena used to tell me. *Negativity is for old farts like me.* "Really, everything could be. It could be that we'll be randomly selected for a lifetime supply of Nutella."

Sadie snorts. "It could be that the surrealist slam poem I wrote in third grade will win me the Nobel Prize for literature."

"That my cactus will actually bloom this year."

"That they'll start producing Twizzlers ice cream."

"That *Firefly* will get the final season it deserves."

No one talks for a few seconds. Until Hannah says: "Mara, you broke the flow. Come up with something delightful and yet unobtainable."

"Oh, right. Uhm, it could be that Liam will come home, and ask me not to move out, and then he'll bend me over the nearest piece of furniture and fuck me hard and fast." By the time I've finished the sentence, Sadie is laughing and Hannah is whistling.

"Hard and fast, huh?"

"Yup." I shake my head. "Absolutely preposterous, though."

"Nah. Well, no more than my slam poem," Sadie concedes. "So, how goes the unrequited crush?"

"It's not *really* a crush." Plenty unrequited, though.

"I thought we had agreed that fantasizing about being bent over the kitchen sink *does*, in fact, constitute a crush?"

I huff. "Fine. It's . . . good. Barely there, really. I don't really daydream about having sex with him that often." Liar. What a liar. "Still in the larval stage." It's hitting its teenage years and is strong as an ox. "I think that some distance will be good. I have a lead on a cheap-ish apartment downtown." I'll miss this place. I'll miss feeling close to Helena. I'll miss the way Liam makes fun of me for being unable to learn the buttons of the stupid PlayStation controllers. So, so much.

"And you're sure Liam's okay with you leaving?"

"It's what he wants." Things have been a little weird in the past week. Awkward. A bit of a step back for us, but . . . I'll be fine. It'll be fine. "I think it'll go away. The crush."

"Right," Sadie agrees, without looking much like she does agree.

"Very soon," I add.

"I'm sure."

"I just need him to . . . never find out about the furniture fantasies," I explain.

"Hm."

"Because it would make things weird for us," I explain. "For him."

"Yeah."

"And he doesn't deserve it."

"No."

"He's a good friend. Also, he's in the middle of making lots of life changes. I want to be supportive. And I like hanging out with him."

"Yup."

"Basically, I don't want him to feel uncomfortable around me."

"Nope."

"Anyway." My cheeks feel warm. It must be all the wine. "We should talk about something else."

"Okay."

"Like. Literally anything else."

"Fine."

"One of you should propose a topic."

If they were here in person, Sadie and Hannah would exchange a long, loaded look. As it is, they are silent for a few moments. Then Hannah says, "Can I tell you a story?"

"Sure."

"It's about a friend of mine."

I frown. "Which friend?"

"Ah . . . Sarah."

"Sarah?"

"Sarah."

"I don't think I know her. Since when do you have friends I don't know about?"

"Not important. So, a couple of years ago my friend Sarah moved in with this guy, um . . . Will. And initially they really hated each other, but then they figured out that they were more similar than they thought, and she started talking about him more and more, in increasingly positive terms. So Sadie and I—Sadie knows her, too—well, we were like, *Jeez, is she falling for this dude?* And then one night my friend confessed to me that she had very filthy, very elaborate-sounding fantasies about Will bending her over the kitchen table and—"

"Bye, Hannah."

"Wait," Sadie says, "we haven't heard the ending!"

"You guys are shit friends and I'm not sure why I love you so much." I hang up on them, laughing despite myself. I toss my phone away and get up to refill my glass of wine, thinking that when Hannah and Sadie fall for someone I'll tease them mercilessly and make up fake stories about fake people, and then they'll know how it feels, to be—

"Mara."

Liam is standing in the entrance of the living room, necktie in one hand, looking tired and handsome and tall and—

Oh shit. "Liam?"

"Hi."

"W-when did you get here?"

"Just now."

"Oh." *Thank fuck.* "How was your . . . The interview, how did it go?"

"Good, I think."

"Oh. Good."

He just got here, he said. He can't have possibly overheard me. I haven't said anything compromising in the past few seconds. And Hannah's knockoff fairy tale used different names.

Why is he staring at me like that, then?

"When will you know if you got the job?"

He shrugs. "A few days, I assume." He cut his hair last week. Not too short, but shorter than it ever was. Sometimes—often I'll see him in a certain light, or I'll catch him making one of those faces that I'm sure he doesn't let anyone else see, and my breath will hitch from the wonder of it.

"Are you hungry? I made a stir-fry. There's leftovers."

He studies me and says nothing.

"No carrots. I promise." What will I do with all this knowledge I have of his likes and dislikes? This knowledge of *him*? Where will it go once he's not in my life anymore?

"I'm not hungry, but thanks."

"Okay." I walk around the couch, looking for something to do with myself, and lean against the doorjamb. Just a few feet away from him. "I think I've found a place. To move, I mean."

"You have?" Unreadable, his expression.

"Yeah. But I won't know till a few days from now."

Silence. And a long, thoughtful stare.

"I still won't sell my half. Sorry, I know you want to buy me out, but—"

"I don't."

I frown. "What do you mean, you don't?"

"I don't."

I laugh. "Liam, you've been offering to buy me out for a million years."

His mouth quirks. "A million years ago the house didn't exist and this place was a swamp, but it's not as if you're an environmental scientist and could possibly know—"

"Oh, shut up. All I'm saying is, for a long time . . ." Though, now that I think about it, his lawyer hasn't emailed me in . . . weeks. Months, maybe? "Oh my God. Liam, are you broke?" I lean forward. "Is it the stock market? Have you gambled away all your money? Have you bet the entirety of your savings on the U.S. male soccer team winning the World Cup and only belatedly realized that they didn't even qualify? Have you become involved in a Lu-LaRoe pyramid scheme and can't stop buying new leggings—"

"Are you drunk?"

"No. Well, I had some of your wine. A lot. Why?"

"You get annoying when you're drunk." There's a hint of a smile in his eyes. "But cute."

I stick my tongue out. "You're annoying all the time." *And cute, too.*

Liam's smile widens a little, and he looks down at his feet. Then: "Good night, Mara." He turns around and heads for his room. The yellow light of the lamp casts a warm, golden glow over the breadth of his shoulders.

"By the way," I call after him, "I bought a new creamer. It's cinnamon. You'll hate it!"

Liam doesn't answer and doesn't pause on his way out. I don't see him until the following night, and that . . .

That's when it happens.

Thirteen ♥

The weirdest part is how quickly everything changes.

One minute, I'm in the middle of cleaning up the kitchen, wondering whether the smoothie blender is dishwasher safe, thinking about my ongoing pining and my upcoming move, about how much I'll miss this—coming home after work, finding twelve forks and a colander in the sink, wondering how many of them are Liam's.

The next, he is standing behind me. Liam Harding is standing right behind me, on *purpose*, and pressing me into the counter. As though he *wants* to be here, close, touching me, as much as I want him to be. I am too stupefied to do anything about the water running in the kitchen, but he leans forward to turn it off, and all of a sudden the room is silent.

His hand closes around my hip, and I cannot think. I cannot comprehend what is happening. I'm breathing. He's breathing. We're breathing together—same rhythm, same air—and for a moment I just feel it. This. It's nice. It's good. It's what I've been wanting.

Then he shifts my hair behind my shoulder; uncovers the base of my throat. I feel something—teeth, maybe?—grazing at my skin.

"Liam?" I half moan.

"It's me." He is kissing me. There. "Is this okay?"

I'm nodding—*Yes*—to what, I don't know. *Yes, you're Liam. Yes, this is okay. Yes, I'm about to melt to the floor.*

"You smell so good, Mara."

Thank God for the kitchen sink to hold on to, because my knees are about to give out. Thank God for Liam's hands, too. Except that one is sliding under my shirt. I've never thought of myself as dainty, but it somehow manages to cover my entire torso, and his thumb . . .

It's brushing against the underside of my breast, and—

Oh.

He licks the pulse in the dip of my throat, and I'm mortified to hear myself whimper.

"You are so soft." His breath is hot in my ear, and I shiver. Exactly once. "I think I imagined you wouldn't be. You're always running, working out. You always look so strong, but . . ."

He lets go of me for a fraction of a second, and every single cell in my body revolts at once.

No.

Wait.

Stay.

But he's only adjusting me. His hand presses on my lower back, angling me just so: slightly bent forward, like . . . God, like he's about to—

He's back on me immediately. Begins to undo the zipper of my jeans, the catch of it like a drum in the silence. Air rushes out of my lungs in a sharp exhale.

"Okay?" he asks again, soft, deafening, and it *is* okay. Even if my jeans are sliding down my thighs, and I have never, ever felt less in control. I think we're about to have sex, but sex is *not* like this. Sex is awkwardly pulling off clothes, and negotiating positions, and hours of foreplay peppered with *Are you sure you shouldn't be on top?* and *Wait, that's my elbow.* Sex is not going from zero to a million this way. Not for me. It's not gripping the edge of the sink to stop myself from moaning, or needing to grind against something— anything—or feeling my knees weaken to jelly.

"Is this what you wanted, Mara?" He slides a finger under my panties and parts my folds. One single finger. "What you— *Oh.*"

For a moment, I panic. I cannot possibly be wet, not yet. But then I realize that I am, and I can feel it and hear it, the slick slide of skin against skin, my own body already beginning to flutter.

And Liam makes it clear that he likes it. "You," he grunts into my ear. "You wouldn't believe it, the things I've thought about doing."

"The . . . ?"

"Is this how you wanted it?"

"Wanted . . . what?"

"You said you wanted to be fucked. Hard and fast." Did I say that? I can't recall. I can't remember my own name, and then things get even worse: behind me, he goes on his knees. What is he—? "Off." Liam tugs at my jeans and panties until they're pooling around my ankles, then tosses them on the other side of the room once I've stepped out of them. "Good girl."

I gasp. Did he just say that? To me? But I can't ask him to repeat himself, since he clearly got a little distracted on his way up. His hand travels along my inner thigh, long fingers grip the soft skin of my backside. It occurs to me in that moment that I am now bare. Completely naked except for a flimsy T-shirt and an even flimsier bra. And that this person softly biting into the flesh of my ass as though I am a piece of ripe fruit, this person is Liam Harding.

Liam. Harding. Who touches me as though he already knows my body. Who spreads me apart like I'm a law school book and buries his face into me. Who groans into my flesh and mutters, "Sorry." He manages to sound genuinely apologetic as he pulls back to lick and suck the skin of my right buttock. "I know you want it hard and fast. Just, I think about this a lot. About you." A heartbeat, and he's on his feet again, chest pressed against my back. One hand tightens sweetly around my hip, and he pushes a knee between my legs, until most of my weight is resting on his thigh. I hear vaguely obscene sounds: something clinking, something fumbling, something being shoved aside. Then it's hot flesh pushing against mine and a murmured, "Okay?" that I must have nodded to, because—

Friction.

My vision blurs around the edges. Liam is inside me. Barely. Just the tip. He's also enormous—no room, *no room*—relentless, lovely, magnificent. *Deep.*

"Fuck, Mara. This is *unreal.*"

There's a lot of harsh breathing, and "Just a bit more," and tight muscles clenching and releasing, but he bottoms out, and it's just this side of too much. It *would* be too much, but it helps that Liam holds on to me like letting go would kill him, and that his fingers are unsteady as he pushes my hair away from my shoulder. But my body seems to be into this, unused, hidden spaces stuffed full, fluttering around . . . God.

Around Liam's cock.

"I can't think when you're around." His voice is rough. He holds still inside me, as though he's in no hurry to start, but I can feel him vibrate with tension. The heel of his palm slides down to rest against my clit. "I can't think when you're *not* around. It's been a problem. I feel like I haven't formulated a coherent thought in months. I feel like you won't stop being in my head, and—"

Just like that, it's all over. Liam hasn't even moved yet, but my mind goes blank. The world recedes and I start coming without warning, arching against him, biting into my lip to silence a scream. Pleasure sinks into me, and I'm helpless to stop it.

I don't know how long passes before I'm back to myself, his breath sharp in my ear. "Did you just—?" Liam sounds in pain. "Did you really come, just from me . . ."

I'm dazed. My nerve endings are still tingling. I shut my eyes tight and nod my embarrassment just as his teeth close around the fleshy part of my shoulder. He grunts like an animal, like he's desperate to keep whatever control he can.

"Fuck, Mara, you . . . can I take you to bed?"

His tone is unlike anything I've ever heard from him, pleading and a little raw. He's still twitching inside me; every few seconds or so he seems to lose whatever grip he has on himself and rolls his hips. It doesn't help my focus. Or his focus. *Our* focus.

Which we maybe should keep. This should stop right now, maybe. As good as it's been—and it has just redefined sex for me— I'm not quite sure why Liam wants this, and if it's just some im- promptu fucking that means nothing to him but has lots of heartbreak in store for me . . . Maybe we should stop here?

"I'll try to keep it fast." He's licking away the sting of his earlier bite. "But let me take you to bed."

The thing is, I don't want to stop. I've come once already, just from him sliding into me and stretching me too tight, from the feel of his hand clutching my hip bone—a small miracle in and of itself, because it usually takes me *forever*. But if I let him take me to bed, he's going to wreck me. He is going to ruin me for anyone else. He is going to destroy me in each and every possible way.

"Please," he murmurs.

I don't really have a choice: I want to say yes, so I nod. *Whatever you want, you can have, Liam.*

It's not pretty, when he pulls out. He gasps a breath of pure frustration and it's clear that he hates it. I hate it, too, and I'm the one who just had a life-altering orgasm. Liam's the one who gave it to me and took very little for himself—which doesn't even come as a surprise.

I wouldn't have fallen for an unkind man.

He takes my top and bra off, and I'm too stupid with aftershocks of pleasure to do anything but stand there and let him, watch him stare his fill with dark, unreadable eyes, even though I'm completely naked and my belly button is still an outie and the lacrosse scar is there, gleaming white in the dim lights of the room.

"Come here. Mara, you . . . Fuck. Come here." His jaw is tense as he picks me up and carries me to his room. My first time here, but I know this place—because I know Liam. Dark colors. Framed pictures of semihostile nature from the trips he told me about. Sparse furniture. A stack of books on his bedside table. Reading glasses, the ones I tease him about, unfolded in the middle of his desk. I want to explore every corner, but there's no time. The mattress bounces underneath my back, and then he's taking up my entire field of view.

"Can I kiss you?" His mouth is hovering a few inches above mine, so I press my hands down his nape and arch into him, kissing him myself.

It's slow, and warm, and achingly careful. He was fucking me less than a minute ago. He was so deep inside me that I felt deliciously split in two. But now there's this gentle sliding of lips and tongues, Liam nibbling on me, holding first my chin, then the back of my head, and my heart sings for him.

I am catastrophically, ruinously in love with you.

"I love kissing you," I sigh into his mouth.

"Mara." His lips. His voice. "I want to kiss you everywhere." He moves back, as if something occurs to him just then. "Can I go down on you?"

I feel my cheeks heat. Does he really want to?

"Just for a minute," he adds, and then . . . Incredible, how he's waiting for my answer. He just bent me over the kitchen sink and slid into me and made me come on his cock, but he's asking for permission to eat me out like I'd be doing *him* a favor.

"Are you sure?"

"Thirty seconds. Please."

"Yes. I mean, if . . . if you're sure that you— Oh."

He's very good at it. Not . . . Maybe not deftly skilled, but he is completely lost to it, so thorough, so noisy in his utter, amazed enjoyment of the act, of me. My hips arch and he has to hold me down, carry me through the pleasure. It lasts more than thirty seconds. It lasts more than three minutes, maybe more than ten— but my thighs are trembling and my pussy spasms and I start to come like an ocean wave, and when I think the pleasure is finally subsiding he slides two fingers inside me and my hips buck up, because it's not over. My entire world is spinning. I've officially had more orgasms in the past twenty minutes than in the last year.

Fingers still inside me, he looks up, eyes soft and earnest and swallowed by his pupils. "Thank you."

Oh. "I think . . ." I clear my throat. My voice remains scratchy. "Maybe I should be the one thanking you."

He shakes his head and lifts himself over me, balanced on one arm, and my eyes widen. He strokes himself with the other hand while staring down at my breasts with an awestruck expression. "This is so good, Mara. You are so good. Why do you want it to be fast?" He leans forward to kiss me again, licking the inside of my mouth, nibbling down my throat. "I just want to make it last," he rasps against my skin.

I have no idea what he's referring to. I don't want this to be fast. I've never said I did, but he keeps telling me that . . .

Except that I *did* say it. Shit, I did say it. Just not to *him*. "You heard me."

Liam is preoccupied. Licking one of my nipples. Biting gently. Licking again. Doing a *fantastic* job.

"You heard me," I repeat. I twine my finger in his hair to slow him down. "On the phone."

He stops, but doesn't lift his head. His breath, warm against my breast, has me shivering. "Remember when I found you in my bathroom? I haven't stopped thinking about your tits ever since—"

"Liam, you heard me tell my friends about . . ." He's currently busy sucking on the underside of my breast, but for some reason I cannot bring myself to repeat the words. "About what I wanted you to do. You heard me."

He looks up. He's flushed, turned on, and more beautiful than ever. "I can do it, Mara. I can do it for you. What you want."

"I don't—" This is mortifying. I push him away, but he barely budges. "If this is some kind of charity, I don't need a pity fuck. I am perfectly capable of—"

He takes my palm and drags it down his chest, past his abdomen, until his cock is hot in my hand. He is massive, and almost automatically my fingers close around him. Liam grimaces, biting his lower lip, and I have the sudden realization that he's been touching me in all sorts of manners, but I haven't touched him yet, not at all. It seems sad, and unfair, and unbearably stupid. Something to remedy.

"Does this feel like I'm giving you a pity fuck?"

No. No, it definitely does not. But. "I don't know."

Of its own free will, my hand starts moving up and down his length, simple strokes that have him gasping and shutting his eyes. His lips part as I circle around the damp head with my thumb. The arm he's leaning on shakes. Visibly.

"Come on, Mara." His hips are thrusting now. In and out of my fist. He's getting closer. Closer to something. "You must know."

"Know what?"

"How hard it's been, to—*fuck*—to keep my hands off you. How much I've wanted this, almost since the very beginning."

Oh.

Oh *God*.

His eyes are glazed, muscles taut. He is on the verge of coming, that much is obvious. So obvious that I'm shocked when his fingers wrap around my wrist to stop me.

"Please, let me fuck you. Let me give you what you need. Let me try, at least." He kisses a spot under my jaw. "Hard and fast."

I'm not about to tell him no. I'm not about to tell *myself* no. Instead I smile and pull him on top of me, arms twined around his neck as I silently mouth against the flesh of his shoulder how much I like him, how much I love this, and Liam adjusts us and angles himself until he's almost inside again, hot and wet and . . . the most annoying thought occurs to me. *Shit*.

"Condom! We need—do you—?"

Liam groans. "*Fuck*." His biceps are shaking, fingers white as they fist in the sheets. Then he takes a deep breath and shifts, rearranging until he can slide one finger—two—deep inside me, curling them upward so that he is thrumming exactly where I need him.

"What are you—?" God, this feels insanely good.

"I don't have any condoms." His words are a bit slurred. "I'm just going to make you come like this and then get myself off." He sounds like he's doing the single hardest thing in his life, and yet it's clear that he's absolutely fine with it. Which . . . No. No, no, no, *no*.

"Liam, are you—*Ah*—are you clean?" His thumb brushes my clit. I moan. "Because I'm on the pill, and . . ."

"I have no idea."

How does he not know? I reach down to hold his forearm still. Problem is, he can still curve his fingers. His long, beautiful fingers.

"Have you been tested, since the last time you . . . ?"

I brace for all sorts of horrifying answers, ranging from *Why, of course not, my last one-night stand was yesterday*, to *Everyone has HPV anyway*. But what comes is, "I've had a bunch of yearly physicals for work. I— Mara, it doesn't matter." He kisses me on the cheek, and a clever twist of his wrist makes my brain go blank. "I think I can make you come with my fingers. That's safe. And you don't have to be around later, when I . . ."

Yearly physicals? *Plural?* "When was the last time you had sex? Can you—*ah*, please, please stop that."

"I have no idea." Liam pulls out his fingers. For a second, the friction is distracting. Then my pussy clenches in protest. "I don't have sex, Mara."

"You . . . You what?"

He looks away. We are both breathing too hard. "I don't like sex."

I look down. He is so hard. His cock is so heavy on my thigh. There is pre-come on my skin. "You seem to . . . um, you seem to like it fine."

"Yeah. But I really don't. It's just . . ." He holds my eyes. His are a dark, beautiful brown. "I like *you* very much, Mara. I like talking to you. I like watching you do yoga. I like the way you always smell like sunscreen. I like how you manage to say pretty much whatever you want while still being unbelievably kind. I like being in this house with you, and everything we do in here." His throat bobs. "I don't think it's a surprise that I really, *really* like the idea of fucking you."

Oh my God. Oh my God oh my God oh my God—

"But I don't need to . . . I'm enjoying this"—he grimaces, as if appalled by the understatement—"maybe too much, since I almost lost it . . . a number of times, just by being near you, so I'll be more than fine if you just let me take care of you and—"

No.

I push at his shoulder, his chest, and then keep pushing through his first resigned, then confused, then shocked expression. Once his back is on the mattress, he lets me straddle his hips and groans. "What are you doing?"

I lean over and whisper in his ear, "Hard and fast, Liam."

There is a long moment in which he just stares up at me, disoriented. Then he must realize: we are perfectly lined up. I'm working to take him inside, struggling a little, because he's so *big* this way. But I'm moving now, balancing my palms on his chest, up and down and up again, and a few minutes later, on the downstroke, he's completely wedged inside me.

The angle is so deep, my vision spots. Liam's grip digs almost painfully around my waist.

"Mara." He is panting. "I'm not going to be able to pull out."

"It's fine." It's *perfect*. "Just do what feels good."

Everything does, anyway. The slide of flesh, the wet friction—even within the clumsy mess of our movements, as he slips out and has to nudge himself back in, this feels like perfection. The way he stares at my face, my breasts, the rise and fall of my hips, looking stunned; the wet, filthy sounds of us moving together; the things he says about how beautiful I am, how precious, about all the times he has imagined doing this—and there are so many.

I feel my pulse spike, and I smile at him as I lean forward. *I love you*, I think. *And I suspect that you love me, too. And I cannot wait for us to admit it to each other. I cannot wait to see what happens next.*

"I think," he grunts against my throat. "Mara, I think I'm going to come now."

I nod, too close to speak, and let him roll us over.

✿✿✿

Well. That was certainly fast." Liam hasn't caught his breath yet. His tone is mildly self-deprecating.

"Yup." Delicious. It was *delicious*.

"I can do better," he says. I'm pretty sure he has no clue that this *was* better. Best. Ever. "I think. Maybe with practice."

I'm not even sure it's over yet. My nerve endings are still twitching. My entire body is flooded with an electric sort of pleasure, wrenched out of me and then poured back in again. "It wasn't *that* fast," I say.

Liam buries his face in my neck and curls around me, dwarfing me. Yeah. It *was* fast.

"I mean," I mumble against his chest, "that it wasn't *too* fast. It was . . ." Extraordinary. Spectacular. Transcendent. "Good. Very good." He presses a kiss to my throat, and I add, "But it wasn't that hard, either."

He tenses. "I'm sorry. Do you—"

"That is to say, we should do it again." He pulls back to meet my eyes. He looks very, *very* serious. I'm feeling considerably less so. "And again. And again. Until we get it right. Perfectly hard, and perfectly fast. You know?"

His smile unfurls slowly. "Yeah?" Hopeful and happy, he looks younger than ever. I grin and pull him in for a kiss.

"Yeah, Liam."

Epilogue

Six months later

Who puts coffee creamer in their smoothies, anyway?"

"People."

"No way."

"Plenty of people."

"Name one."

"Me."

I roll my eyes. "Name two."

Silence.

"See?"

Liam sighs. "It doesn't mean anything, Mara. Normal people don't have conversations about coffee creamer."

"You and I certainly do. Hazelnut or vanilla?"

"Vanilla."

I put two bottles in the cart. Then I push up on my toes and plant a kiss on Liam's mouth, short and hard. Liam follows me for a bit when I step back, as if reluctant to let me go.

"Okay." I smile. Lately, I'm always smiling. "What else?"

Liam browses the list I wrote earlier today, sitting between his thighs while he was busy killing bad guys on the PlayStation. He squints a little at my terrible handwriting, and I try not to laugh. "I think we're done. Unless you need a few more family-size Cheez-It boxes?"

I stick my tongue out at him. My hand falls to my side, until it's brushing against his. He starts pushing the shopping cart and twines our fingers together. "Ready to go?" he asks.

"Yeah." I beam. "Let's go home."

Stuck
with You

For Marie, my fave Elizabeth Swann

One ⚙

My world comes to an end at 10:43 on a Friday night, when the elevator lurches to a stop between the eighth and seventh floors of the building that houses the engineering firm where I work. The ceiling lights flicker. Then go off completely. Then, after a stretch that lasts about five seconds but feels like several decades, come back with the slightly yellower tinge of the emergency bulb.

Crap.

Fun fact: This is actually the second time my world came to an end tonight. The first was less than a minute ago. When the elevator I'm riding stopped on the thirteenth floor, and Erik Nowak, the last person I ever wanted to see, appeared in all his blond, massive, Viking-like glory. He studied me for what felt like too long, took a step inside, and then studied me some more while I avidly inspected the tips of my shoes.

Re-crap.

It's a slightly complicated situation. I work in New York City, and my company, GreenFrame, rents a small office on the eighteenth floor of a Manhattan building. Very small. It has to be very small, because we're a baby firm, still establishing ourselves in a pretty cutthroat market, and we don't always make a ton of money. I guess that's what happens when you value things like sustainability, environmental protection, economic viability and efficiency, renewability rather than depletion, minimization of exposure to potential hazards such as toxic materials, and . . . well, I won't bore you with the Wikipedia entry on green engineering. Suffice it to say, my boss, Gianna (who coincidentally is the only other engineer working full-time at the firm), founded Green-Frame with the aim of creating great structures that actually make sense within their environment, and is delightfully, crunchily hard-core about it. Unfortunately, that doesn't always pay very well. Or well.

Or at all.

So, yeah. Like I said, a slightly complicated situation, especially when compared with more traditional engineering companies that don't focus as much on conservation and pollution control. Like ProBld. The giant firm where Erik Nowak works. The one that takes up the whole thirteenth floor. And the twelfth. Maybe the eleventh, too? I lost track.

So when the elevator began to slow down around the fourteenth floor, I felt a surge of apprehension, which I naively discarded as mere paranoia. You have nothing to worry about, Sadie, I told myself. ProBld has tons of offices. They're always expanding. Orchestrating "mergers" and eating up smaller firms. Like the Blob. They are truly the corrosive alien amoeboid entity of the business, which translates to hundreds of people working for them, which in turn means that any one out of those hundreds of people could be calling the elevator. Any one. There's no way it's Erik Nowak.

Yeah. No.

It was Erik Nowak, all right. With his massive, colossal presence. Erik Nowak, who spent the entirety of our five-floor ride staring at me with those ruthless icy-blue eyes of his. Erik Nowak, who's currently looking up at the emergency light with a slight frown.

"The power's out," he says, an obvious statement, with that stupidly deep voice of his. It hasn't changed one whit since the last time we talked. Nor since that string of messages he left on my phone before I blocked his number. The ones that I never bothered answering but also couldn't quite bring myself to delete. The ones I could not stop myself from listening to, over and over.

And over.

It's still a stupid voice. Stupid and insidious, rich and precise and clipped and low, with acoustic properties all its own. "I moved here from Denmark when I was fourteen," he told me at dinner when I asked him about his accent, slight, hard to detect, but definitely there. "My younger brothers got rid of it, but I never managed." His face was as stern as usual, but I could see his mouth soften, a slight uptick on the corner that felt like a smile. "As you can imagine, there was lots of teasing growing up."

After the night we spent together, after all that happened between us, I felt as if I couldn't get the way he pronounced words out of my head. For days I constantly squirmed, turning around because I thought I'd heard him somewhere in my proximity. Thought that maybe he was nearby, even though I was jogging at the park, alone in the office, in line at the grocery store. It just stuck to me, coated the shell of my ears and the inside of my—

"Sadie?" Erik's infamous voice cuts through my thoughts. It

has that tone, the one of someone who's repeating himself, and maybe not just for the first time. "Does it?"

"Does . . . what?" I glance up, finding him next to the control panel. In the stark shadows of the emergency light he's still so . . . God. Looking at his handsome face is a mistake. He is a mistake. "I'm sorry, I . . . What did you say?"

"Does your phone work?" he asks again, patient. Kind.

Why is he so kind? He was never supposed to be kind. After what happened between us, I decided to torture myself by asking around about him, and the word *kind* never came up. Not once. One of New York's top engineers, people would often say. Known for being as good at his job as he is surly. No-nonsense, aloof, standoffish. Though he was never any of these things with me. Until he was, of course.

"Um." I fish my phone out of the back pocket of my black tailored pants and press the home button. "No service. But this is a Faraday cage," I think out loud, "and the elevator shaft is steel. No RF signal is going to be able to make a loop and . . ." I notice the way Erik is staring at me and abruptly shut up. Right. He's an engineer, too. He already knows all of this. I clear my throat. "No signal, no."

Erik nods. "Wi-Fi should work, but it doesn't. So maybe this is—"

"—a building-wide power outage?"

"Maybe even the whole block."

Shit.

Shit, shit, shit. Shit.

Erik seems to be reading my mind, because he studies me for a moment and says reassuringly, "It might be for the best. Someone is bound to check the elevators if they know that the power's

gone." He pauses before adding, "Although it might take a while."
Painfully honest. As usual.

"How long?"

He shrugs. "A few hours?"

A few what? A few hours? In an elevator that is smaller than
my already-minuscule bathroom? With Erik Nowak, the broodi-
est of Scandinavian mountains? Erik Nowak, the man who I . . .

No. No way.

"There must be something we can do," I say, trying to sound
collected. I swear I'm not panicking. No more than a lot.

"Nothing that I can think of."

"But . . . what do we do now, then?" I ask, hating how whiny my
voice is.

Erik lets his messenger bag drop to the floor with a thump. He
leans against the wall opposite mine, which should theoretically
give me some room to breathe, even though for some physics-
defying reason he still feels too close. I watch him slide his phone
in the front pocket of his jeans and cross his arms on his chest
His eyes are cold, unreadable, but there is a faint gleam in them
that has a shiver running down my spine.

"Now," he says, gaze locked with mine, "we wait."

It's 10:45 on a Friday night. And for the third time in less than
ten minutes, my world crashes to an end.

Two ♥

There are worse things in the world.

There are, without a single doubt, giant heaps of worse things in the world. Wet socks. PMS. The *Star Wars* prequels. Oatmeal raisin cookies that masquerade as chocolate chip, slow Wi-Fi, climate change and income inequality, dandruff, traffic, the finale of *Game of Thrones*, tarantulas, food-scented soap, people who hate soccer, daylight saving time (when it moves one hour ahead, not behind), toxic masculinity, the unjustly short life span of guinea pigs—all of these, just to name a small handful, are truly terrible, dreadful, horrific things. Because such is the way of the universe: it's full of bad, sad, upsetting, unfair, enraging circumstances, and I should know better than to pout like a ten-year-old who's half an inch too short for the roller coaster when Faye tells me from behind the counter of her small coffee shop:

"Sorry, honey, we're all out of croissants."

To be clear: I don't even want a croissant. Which I know

sounds weird (everybody should *always* want a croissant; it's a law of physics, like the Fermi paradox or Einstein's field equation), but the truth is, I would gladly do without *this* specific croissant—if this were a regular Tuesday morning.

Unfortunately, today is pitch day. Which means that I'm meeting with potential future GreenFrame clients. I talk to them, tell them the hundreds of little things I can do to help them manage large-scale sustainable building projects, and hope they'll decide to hire us. It's what I've been doing for about eight months, ever since I finished my Ph.D.: I try to bring in new clients; I try to keep the ones we already have; I try to ease Gianna's workload, since she just had her first baby—who, incidentally, is three babies. Apparently, triplets do happen. And they're adorable, but they also wake one another up in the middle of the night in a never-ending spiral of sleeplessness and exhaustion. Who would have thought? But back to the clients: GreenFrame has been venturing dangerously close to not-quite-in-the-black territory, and today's pitch meeting is critical to keep the red at bay.

Enter the croissants. And that other little problem I happen to have: I am a little superstitious. Just a tad. Just a little stitious. I have developed a complex system of rituals and apotropaic gestures that need to be performed to ensure that my pitch meetings will go as planned. I have more years of science education than anyone ever needed, and should probably know better than to believe that the color of my socks is in any way predictive of my professional success. But do I?

Nope.

Back in college, it was exactly three braids in my hair for every single soccer game (plus two coats of L'Oréal mascara if we were playing away), and I had to listen to "Dancing Queen" and "My Immortal" before each and every final—strictly in that order.

Thank God I managed to graduate on time, because the emotional whiplash was starting to grind at me.

Not that this issue of mine is something I like to admit widely. Mostly just to Mara and Hannah, my supposed best friends. We met during the first year of our Ph.D.'s and have been lumbering together through the tribulations of STEM academia ever since. For the most part, having them in my life has been my one true joy, but there have been less-than-outstanding aspects of it. For instance, the fact that during the four years we lived together they oscillated between staging anti-superstition interventions and pranking me by inviting stray black cats into our apartment on every Friday the 13th. (We even ended up adopting one for a few months, JimBob, till we noticed that the kitty in the Missing flyers all over the neighborhood suspiciously resembled him; JimBob was, in fact, Mrs. Fluffpuff, and we returned her quietly, in the middle of the night. She's been dearly missed ever since.) Anyway, yes: I have horrible, amazing, superstition-unsupportive BFFs. But we don't live together anymore. We don't even live in the same city: Mara is in D.C. at the EPA, and Hannah has been working for NASA and commuting between Texas and Norway. I can throw salt over my shoulder and frantically look around for wood to knock on to my heart's content.

Why, *why* am I like this? I have no clue. Let's just blame my aggressively Italian mother.

But back to this Tuesday morning: the crux of my problem, you see, is that back in the winter, before my most successful client pitch to date, I got a bit peckish. So I popped into Faye's hole-in-the-wall coffee shop, and instead of just asking for the usual—punishingly black coffee: no sugar, no cream, just the bitter oblivion of darkness—I tacked a croissant on to my order. It was just as good as the coffee (i.e., simultaneously stale and under-cooked; taste hovering between starch and salmonella) and, to my eternal dismay, was promptly followed by me bagging the most lucrative contract GreenFrame had seen in its young history.

Gianna was over the moon. And so was I, until my half-Italian brain started forming a million little connections between the croissant from hell and my big professional win. You know where this is going: yes, I now desperately feel that I must eat one of Faye's croissants before every single pitch meeting, otherwise the un-thinkable will happen. And no, I have no idea how to react to her kind but definitive, "Sorry, honey, we're all out of croissants."

Did I say that there are worse things in the world? I lied. This is a disaster. My career is over. Are those sirens in the distance?

"I see." I bite into my lower lip, order it to un-pout itself, and force myself to smile. After all, it's not Faye's fault if my mom drilled into my baby neurons that walking under the stairs is a surefire way to a lifetime of despair. I go to therapy for that. Or I will. At some point. "Are you, um, making more?"

She looks at the display case. "I've got muffins left. Blueberry. Lemon glaze."

Oh. That actually sounds good. But. "No croissants, though?"

"And I can make you a bagel. Cinnamon? Blueberry? Plain?"

"Is that a no on the croissants?"

Faye cocks her head with a pleased expression. "You really like my croissants, don't you?"

Do I? "They're so, um." I clutch the strap of my fake-leather messenger bag. "Unique."

"Well, unfortunately I just gave the last one to Erik over there." Faye points to her left, toward the very end of the counter, but I barely glance at Erik-over-there—*tall man, broad shoulders, wears suit, boring*—too busy cursing my own timing. I should *not* have spent twenty minutes tickling the majestic beauty of Ozzy's little guinea pig tush. I am now rightfully paying for my mistakes, and Faye is giving me an assessing stare. "I'll toast you a bagel. You're too skinny to skip breakfast. Eat more and you might grow a little taller, too."

I doubt I'll manage to finally push past five feet at the ripe old age of twenty-seven, but who's to say. "Just to recap," I say, in one last pleading, whiny attempt at salvaging my professional future, "you're *not* making more croissants today?"

Faye's eyes narrow. "Honey, you might like my croissants a little *too* much—"

"Here."

The voice—not Faye's—is deep and pitched low, coming from somewhere above my head. But I barely pay it any attention because I'm too busy staring at the croissant that has miraculously appeared in front of my eyes. It's still whole, set on top of a napkin, a few stray flakes of dough slowly crumbling off its top. I've had Faye's croissants before, and I know that what they lack in taste they make up for in size. They are very, very large.

Even when delivered by a very, very large hand.

I blink at it for several seconds, wondering if this is a superstition-induced mirage. Then I slowly turn around to look at the man who deposited the croissant on the counter.

He's already gone. Half out of the door, and all I get is a brief impression of broad shoulders and light hair.

"What—?" I blink at Faye, pointing at the man. "What . . . ?"

"I guess Erik decided you should have the last croissant."

"Why?"

She shrugs. "Wouldn't look a gift croissant in the mouth if I were you."

Gift croissant.

I shrug myself out of my stupor, toss a five-dollar bill in the tip jar, and run out of the café. "Hey!" I call. The man is about twenty steps ahead of me. Well, twenty steps with my tiny legs. Might be less than five with his own. "Hey, could you wait a . . . ?"

He doesn't stop, so I clutch my croissant and hurry after him. I channel my best Former Soccer Scholarship Kid self and dodge a lady walking her dog, then her dog, then two teenagers making out on the sidewalk. I catch up right around the corner, when I come to a halt in front of him.

"Hey." I grin up. And up and up and up. He's taller than I calculated. And I'm more winded than I'd like. I need to work out more. "Thank you *so* much! You really didn't have to . . ." I fall silent. For no real reason other than because of how striking he looks. He is just so . . .

Scandinavian, maybe. Viking-like. Norse. Like his ancestors frolicked below the aurora borealis on their way to funding Ikea. He is as big as a yeti, with clear blue eyes and short, pale-blond hair, and I would bet my gift croissant that his name contains one of those cool Nordic letters. The *a* and the *e* smushed together; that weird *o* slashed through the middle; the big *b* that's actually two *s*'s stacked on top of each other. Something that requires a lot of HTML knowledge to be typed.

It takes me by surprise, that's all, and for a moment I'm not sure what to say and just stare up. The strong jaw. The deep-set eyes. The way the angular parts of his face come together into something very, very handsome.

Then I realize that he's staring back, and instantly become self-conscious. I know exactly what he's seeing: the blue button-down I tucked into my chinos; the bangs I really need to trim; the brown, shoulder-length hair I *also* need to trim; and then, of course, the croissant.

The croissant! "Thank you *so* much!" I smile. "I didn't mean to steal your food."

No reply.

"I could pay you back."

Still no reply. Just that severe North Germanic stare.

"Or I could buy you a muffin. Or a bagel. I really didn't mean to interfere with your breakfast."

Number of replies: zero. Intensity of stare: many millions. Does he even understand what I'm— Oh.

Ooooh.

"*Thank. You,*" I say, very, very slowly, like when my mom's side of the family, the one that never immigrated to the U.S., attempts to speak Italian with me. "For"—I lift the croissant in front of my face—"this. Thank"—I point at the Viking—"*you*. You are very"—I tilt my head and scrunch my nose happily—"*nice.*" He stares even longer, pensive. I don't think he got it. "You don't understand, do you?" I murmur to myself dejectedly. "Well, thank you again. You really did me a solid there." I lift the croissant one last time, like I'm toasting him. Then I turn around and begin to walk away.

"You're welcome. Although you'll find that the croissant leaves much to be desired."

I whirl back to him. Blondie the Viking is looking at me with an indecipherable expression. "D-did you just speak?"

"I did."

"In English?"

"I believe so, yes."

I feel my soul crawl outside my body to astral project itself into the burning flames of hell out of pure, sheer embarrassment. "You . . . you weren't saying anything. Before."

He shrugs. His eyes are calm and serious. The span of his shoulders could easily moonlight as a plateau in Eurasia. "You didn't ask a question." His grammar is better than mine and I am withering inside.

"I thought . . . It seemed . . . I . . ." I close my eyes, remembering the way I mimicked the word *nice* for him. I think I want to die. I want this to be over. Yes, my time has come. "I am very grateful."

"You probably won't be, once you try the croissant."

"No, I . . ." I wince. "I know it's not good."

"You do?" He crosses his arms on his chest and gives me a curious look. He's wearing a suit, like 99 percent of the men who work on this block. Except that he looks unlike any other man I've ever seen. He looks like a corporate version of Thor. Like Platinum Ragnarok. I wish he'd smile at me, instead of just observing me. I'd feel less intimidated. "Could have fooled me."

"I— The thing is, I don't really *want* to eat it. I just need it for a . . . for a thing."

His eyebrow lifts. "A thing?"

"It's a long story." I scratch my nose. "Kind of embarrassing, actually."

"I see." He presses his lips together and nods thoughtfully "More or less embarrassing than you assuming I don't speak English?"

The swift and violent death I was talking about earlier? I need it now. "I am so, so sorry about that. I really didn't—"

"Watch out."

I look around to see what he means right as some guy almost runs me over with his skateboard. It's a close call: between the precious croissant I clearly feel ambivalent about and my bag, I nearly lose my balance, and that's where Corporate Thor intervenes. He moves way quicker than anyone his size should be able to and slides between me and Skateboard Guy, straightening me with a hand around my biceps.

I glance up at him, nearly out of breath. He's as towering as a Greenlandic mountain range, pressing me a bit against the window of the corner barbershop, and I think he's saved my life. My professional life, of course. And now also my *life* life.

Oh shit. "What even *is* this morning?" I mutter to no one.

"You okay?"

"Yeah. I mean, I'm clearly on a downward spiral of struggle and mortification, but . . ."

He keeps his eyes and the angles of his handsome, aggressive, unusual face on me. His expression is grave, unsmiling, but for a fraction of a second a thought runs through my head.

He's amused. He finds me funny.

It's a fleeting impression. It lingers a brief moment and dissolves the instant he lets go of my biceps. But I don't think I imagined it. I'm almost sure I didn't, because of what happens next.

"I think," he says, his voice more delicious than Faye's croissants could ever hope to be, "that I'd like to hear that long, embarrassing story of yours."

Three ⚙

'm almost positive that the elevator is shrinking.

Nothing dramatic, really. But I estimate that every minute we spend in here, the car gets a couple of millimeters smaller. I've tucked myself into a corner, arms around my legs and forehead on my knees. Last I glanced up, Erik was in the opposite corner, looking fairly relaxed. Mile-long legs stretched out in front of him, sequoia-wide biceps crossed on his chest.

And, of course, the walls are looming over me. Pushing us closer and closer together. I shiver and curse power outages. The walls. Erik.

Myself.

"Are you cold?" he asks.

I lift my head. I'm wearing my usual work outfit of chinos and a nice blouse. Solid, neutral colors. Professional enough to be taken seriously; modest enough to convince the dudes I meet through work that my presence at any given meeting is to assess the efficacy of the biofiltration system design and *not* to provide them with "something cute to look at." Being a woman in engineering can be tons and tons of fun.

Erik, though . . . Erik looks a bit different. He's wearing jeans and a dark, soft sweater that stretches around his chest, and it seems unusual, given that in the past I've only ever seen him in a suit. Then again, I've only ever seen Erik twice before, technically on the same day.

(That is, if one doesn't count the times in the past month that I glimpsed him around the building and promptly turned away to change direction. Which I very much don't.)

Still, I cannot help but wonder if the reason he looks uncharacteristically informal is that earlier today he was working on-site. Supervising. Consulting. Maybe he was called in to give recommendations on the Milton project, and . . . Yeah. Not going there.

I straighten and square my shoulders. My resentment for Erik Nowak, the feeling I've been cradling in my pocket like a little mouse for the past three weeks, the one I've been feeding bile and scraps, stirs awake. And honestly, it feels nice. Familiar. It reminds me that Erik doesn't *really* care whether I'm cold. I bet he has ulterior motives for asking. Maybe he wants to sell my organs. Or he's planning on establishing a pee corner on my rotting corpse.

"I'm fine," I say.

"You sure? I can give you my sweater."

I briefly picture him taking it off and handing it to me. I've seen him do it before in flesh and blood, which means that I wouldn't even need to get creative. I remember well the way he grabbed the collar and pulled it up over his head, his muscles flexing and contracting, the sudden expanse of pale flesh . . .

He'd hold the sweater out to me, and it'd still be warm. Maybe even smell like his skin, or like his sheets.

Wow. Wow, wow, *wow*. What *was* that? I've been in this elevator for approximately nine minutes and my brain is already developing Swiss cheese–style holes. *Holding on strong, Sadie Grantham. Congrats on your emotional fortitude. Way to be horny for a truly horrible person.*

"No need," I say, shaking my head a little too eagerly. "Are you sure we should just wait?" I ask. "Just—do nothing and wait?"

He nods calmly, clearly broadcasting that it's not hard for him to be a good sport about this situation, that the idea of being stuck with me doesn't bother him one bit, and that, unlike some of us, he's not tempted to bury his face in his hands and cry. Show-off.

"What if we scream?" I ask.

"Scream?"

"Yes—what if we scream? This is a giant building. Someone is bound to hear us, right?"

"At eleven on a Friday night?" His reply is much kinder than my idiotic question deserves. "While the elevator is stuck between floors? *This* elevator?"

I look away because he's right. Frustratingly right. This cursed elevator we're on is in the deepest part of the building, next to a hallway no one would walk by at night. A true tragedy, overshadowed only by the fact that it also has the narrowest car I've ever seen. Guests and clients rarely use it, which is why it has the advantage of being quicker—and the disadvantage of being small.

As in: minuscule. I knew it was tiny, but there's nothing like realizing that this might be the place where I die to register *how* tiny. If I stretch my arms, I'll bump into Erik. If I stretch my legs, I'll bump into Erik. If I thrash around on the floor like I so desperately want to, I'll *also* bump into Erik. What a quandary.

"Are you okay?" he asks softly. His eyes look soft, too. A ball of something I cannot quite define knots in my chest.

"Yeah."

"Here." He rummages in his bag for a moment. Then holds something out to me. "Have some water."

I don't know why I accept his *2019 NYC Amateur Soccer League* water bottle. I don't know why my fingers brush against his for the briefest of moments. And I don't know why, as I drink small sips, he studies me with something that resembles concern.

He's not *really* concerned, because Erik Nowak is just not that kind of guy. The kind of guy he *actually* is? A backstabber. A liar. A sentient human McMansion who values only his own professional success. An F.C. Copenhagen supporter—which, it pleases me to say, is a mediocre soccer team at best. Yes, I said what I said.

"Better?"

"I told you, I'm fine. I'm totally great."

"You look pale." His head tilts, as if to observe me better. "Are you claustrophobic?"

"No. I don't think so." Am I, though? It would explain a lot. The walls closing in. This greasy, barfy feeling in my stomach. The way I'd love to claw at this place because it's so small and Erik takes up so much room inside my head and I can smell his soap and I just want to forget everything about him and maybe I thought I had but now *he's here and it's all coming back and I—*

"Sadie." Erik is looking at me like he knows exactly what kind of spiral is currently unfolding in my brain. "Take a deep breath."

"I know. I am. Taking deep breaths, that is." Or maybe I wasn't. Because now, with some air in my lungs, my brain is getting a tad quieter.

"Is it your first time?"

I blink at him. "Breathing?"

He smiles faintly. Like he doesn't mind that we're going to die in here. "Being stuck in an elevator."

"Oh. Yes." I think about it for a moment. "Wait, is it not yours?"

"Third."

"Third?"

He nods.

"Are you . . . cursed or something?"

"I see your superstitions are going strong," he says, clearly teasing, and the idea that he thinks he *knows* me, the fact that after everything that happened he'd feel allowed to *joke* with me . . .

I stiffen.

And judging by his expression, Erik notices. "Sadie—"

"I'm fine," I interrupt him. "I promise. But could we please just be quiet? For a little bit?" I hate how weak my voice sounds.

I set down the water bottle and hide my face back in my knees. I listen to his sharp exhale, to the tense, uncomfortable silence that falls between us, and try not to think about the last time I was with him.

When I never wanted to stop talking, not even for a second.

Four ⚙

Three weeks ago

have my pitch meeting in one hour, a little mountain of giga-
bytes of files to review, and I'm pretty sure that my interns are
currently eighteen floors above, trying to decide whether I aban-
doned them to join a cult or have been abducted by an urban Sas-
quatch. But I cannot help staring at Corporate Thor's mouth as he
tells me, matter-of-factly:

"Money laundering front."

"No way!"

He shrugs. We are sitting right next to each other on a bench
in a pocket park that, as it turns out, is just behind my building.
The sun is shining, the birds are chirping, I've spotted at least
three butterflies, and yet I remain vaguely intimidated by his size.
And his cheekbones. "It's the only possible explanation."

I bite my lip, trying to think it through. "Couldn't Faye just be,
you know . . . a really bad baker?"

"She certainly is. Her coffee is also questionable."

"It *is* very reminiscent of brake fluid," I concede.

"I always thought of plasma coolant. Point is, she was here ten years ago, when I started working in that building, and she'll be here long after you and I are gone. Despite that." He points at the croissant I'm still clutching. Honestly, I should just bite the bullet and choke it down. My hand sweat is not going to make it any tastier. "There is no valid entrepreneurial reason for her to still be in business."

I nod thoughtfully. He might have a point. "Aside from money laundering operations and ties to organized crime?"

"Precisely." Okay, his grammar might be perfect, but I'm starting to pick up a vague foreign accent. I want to ask a million and ten questions about it—a wish in direct competition with my desire to not come across as a weirdo. A lofty goal, as I am, in fact, a weirdo.

"I see your theory. But. Hear me out." I blow my bangs out of my eyes. Erik's expression doesn't move a nanometer, but I know he's listening. There is something about him, like his attention is something physically tangible, like he's good at seeing and hearing and *knowing.* "So, remember how I talked about my . . . problem?"

"The magical-thinking one? Where you believe that your professional success relates to the items you ate for breakfast?"

I cannot believe I *admitted* to it. God, he already knows I'm a weirdo. Though, to his credit, he seems to be taking it in stride. "Okay, listen, I know it sounds like I'm foolishly clutching the atavistic remnants of ancient times."

"Sounds?" His eyebrow lifts.

I might be flushing. "I like to think of it as . . . more of a way to bind myself and celebrate the traditions of my previous successes, you know? And less as establishing an empirical causal connection between the color of my underwear and future events."

"I see." The corner of his mouth twitches upward. Just barely, though—still not a smile. Maybe he's not capable. Maybe he has a debilitating medical condition. Smilopathy: now with its very own ICD-10 code. "So, what's the lucky color?"

"What?"

"Of underwear."

"Oh. Um . . . lavender."

He seems briefly stumped. "Purple?"

"Kind of, yeah." I forgot that most men can't name more than five colors. "A little lighter. Between purple and pink. Pastel-like."

He nods slowly, like he's trying to picture it. "Cute," he says, and his tone is as simple and straightforward as it's been in the last few minutes. There is absolutely no creepy lasciviousness, as though he's complimenting a flower or a puppy. My heart skips a beat nonetheless.

Would he . . . ? If he saw me wearing my . . . would he still think that . . . ?

Oh my *God*. What is *wrong* with me? This poor man just gave me his *croissant*.

"Anyway," I hasten to add, "maybe there're a lot of people buying good luck croissants, because I'm not alone in my . . . magical thinking—nice way to put it, by the way. For example, my friend Hannah works at NASA, and she says that the engineers there have had whole complex routines involving Planters peanuts and mission launches for the past, like, fifty years. And I'm an engineer. Basically, I'm professionally required to—"

"You're an engineer?" His eyes widen in surprise.

My heart sinks with disappointment. *Oh God. He's one of those. I can't believe he's one of those.*

I scowl and stand from the bench, looking down at him with a frown. "FYI, in the U.S., fifteen percent of the engineering work-force is made up of women. And that number has been steadily increasing, so there is no need to be so shocked that—"

"I'm not."

My frown deepens. "You sure looked like—"

"I'm an engineer myself, and it seemed like a coincidence of sorts." His mouth twitches again. "I thought your magical think-ing might be tickled."

"Oh." My cheeks burn. "Oh." Wow. *Am I the Asshole, Reddit? Why, you kind of are, Sadie.* "Sorry, I didn't mean to imply—"

"Where did you study?" he asks, unruffled, pulling at my wrist till I sit again. I end up a little closer to him than I was before, but it's fine. It's okay. *Siri, how many times can I utterly humiliate myself in the span of thirty minutes? Infinite, you say? Thank you, that's what I figured.*

"Um, Caltech. I finished my Ph.D. last year. You?"

"NYU. Got my master's . . . ten, eleven years ago?"

We stare at each other, me calculating his age, him . . . I don't know. Maybe he's calculating, too. He must be six or seven years older than me. Not that it's in any way relevant. We're just chat-ting. We're going our separate ways in twelve seconds.

"Where do you work?" he asks.

"GreenFrame. You?"

"ProBld."

I scrunch my nose, instantly recognizing the name—from both the plaques in the lobby of my office building and the New York engineering grapevine. There are lots of firms in this area, and he works at my least favorite. The big jellyfish that keeps expanding by eating the smaller jellyfish. Not that they're terrible—they're fine. But they're old-school and don't focus on sustainability nearly as much as we do. But they do have a solid rep, and some of our potential clients even choose them over us because of that. Which: bleh.

"Did you just make a repulsed face when I mentioned my company?"

"No. No! I mean, yeah. A little. But I didn't mean it in an offensive way. They just don't seem to adopt a whole-systems approach to problem-solving when dealing with environmental challenges . . ." His eyes shine. Is he teasing me? Does Corporate Thor *tease*? "I mean, I am now over twenty minutes late for work. Realistically, I'll probably be fired and end up begging you guys for a job."

He nods, lips pressed together. "Good. I have an in with the partners."

"Is that so?"

"I'm sure they'd love to have you on board. To develop a whole-systems approach to problem-solving when dealing with environmental challenges." I stick out my tongue, which he ignores. "What name should I give when I recommend you?"

"Oh. Sadie Grantham." I hold out my non-croissant hand. He looks at it for a long moment, and I am suddenly, inexplicably, tsunamingly afraid. Oh my God. What if he won't take it?

Yeah, Sadie? A wise, mean, pragmatic voice whispers in my ear. *What if a stranger won't take your hand? How will you deal with the zero-point-zero impact it'll have on your life?* But the voice is moot, because he does take it, and my heart gallops at how nice his skin feels, solid and a little rough. His hand swallows my fingers, warming my flesh and the cheap, cute rings I put on this morning.

"Nice to meet you, Dr. Grantham." My breath hitches. My heart melts. I've had my Ph.D. for less than a year, so I still relish being called doctor. Especially because no one ever does. "Erik Nowak."

Well. No one ever does except for Erik Nowak.

Erik Nowak. "Can I ask you something kind of inappropriate?"

He shakes his head, slowly, gravely. "Unfortunately, I am not wearing purple underwear."

I laugh. "No, it's . . . when you write your last name, are there cool, fancy letters in it?" I blurt the question out and instantly regret it. I'm not even sure what I'm asking. I'll just roll with it, I guess?

"It has an *n*. And a *w*. Are they considered fancy?"

Not really. Pretty boring. "Sure."

He nods. "What about the *k*? It's my favorite letter."

"Er, yeah. That's fancy, too." Still boring.

"But surely not the *a*?"

"Uh, well, I guess the *a* is . . ."

His mouth is twitching. Again. He's teasing me. *Again.* I hate him.

"Damn you," I say without heat.

He's *almost* smiling. "No umlauts. No diacritics. No Møller. Or Kiærskou. Or Adelsköld. Though I did go to school with them." I nod, vaguely disappointed. Till he asks: "Disappointed?" and then I can't help hiding behind my croissant and laughing. When I'm done he's *definitely* smiling, and he says, "You should really eat that. Or you'll lose your client and NASA's next rocket will explode."

"Right, yes." I tear a piece away. Hold it out to him. "Would you like a bite? I don't mind sharing."

"Really? You don't mind sharing my own famously disgusting croissant with me?"

"What can I say?" I grin. "I'm a generous soul."

He shakes his head. And then adds, as though it just occurred to him, "I know a really good French bistro."

My entire body perks up. "Oh?"

"They have a bakery, too."

My body perks up *and* tingles. "Yeah?"

"They make excellent croissants. I go there often."

The sun is still shining, the birds are still chirping, I've now spotted five butterflies, and . . . the noise in the background slowly recedes. I look at Erik, study the way the shade from the trees falls across his face, study him as closely as he's studying me.

In my life, I've been asked out for drinks by enough random acquaintances that I think maybe, just *maybe*, I might know what he's trying to get at. And in my life, I've wanted to say no to drinks with every single one of those random acquaintances, which is why I have learned to prevent the question from even being asked. I am good at broadcasting disinterest and unavailability. Very, very good.

And yet, here I am.

On a New York bench.

Clutching a croissant.

Holding my breath and . . . hoping?

Ask me, I think at him. *Because I want to try that French bistro that you know. With you. And talk more about money laundering and a whole-systems approach to environmental engineering and purple underwear that is actually lavender.*

Ask me, Erik Nowak. Ask me, ask me, ask me. Ask me.

There are cars in the distance, and people laughing, and emails piling up in my inbox, eighteen floors above us. But my eyes hold Erik's for a long, stretched-out moment, and when he smiles at me, I notice that his eyes are just as blue as the sky.

Five ⚙

According to the plaque above the floor-selection console (which, by the way, does not include an emergency button; I am mentally composing a strongly worded email that will likely never get sent), the elevator has a 1,400-pound capacity. The inside, I'd estimate, is about fifteen square feet, fourteen of which are inconveniently taken up by Erik. (As usual: thank you, Erik.) A stainless steel handrail is installed in the innermost side, and the walls are actually quite pretty, white baked enamel or some similar material that maybe dates the car a bit, but hey, it's better than mirrors. I hate mirrors in elevators, and I'd hate them the most in this elevator. They'd make avoiding glimpses of Erik about three times harder than it already is.

On the ceiling, between the two energy-efficient (I hope?) recessed lights that are currently off, I noticed one large metal pane. And that's what I've been staring at for the past minute or so. I am no elevator expert, but I'm almost positive that's the emergency exit.

From my five-feet vantage point, Erik is somewhere between six-three and six-six. Based on that, I approximate that the car is about seven feet tall. Too high for me to reach on my own, and too offset from the wall for me to use the handrail as a climbing point. But. *But*, I am sure that Erik could easily lift me up. I mean, he's done it before. On several occasions, in the span of the twenty-four hours we spent together. Like when we got hungry halfway through the night: he picked me up like I was a four-pound kitten, deposited me on his kitchen counter while I gasped in awe at his beautiful, overfull fridge, and then proceeded to inspect an extensive series of Chinese leftovers before sharing them with me. Not to mention that *other* time, when we were in his shower and he put one hand under my ass to push me against the wall and . . .

The point is: he could help me reach the panel. I could dislodge it, climb out of the car, and if we're close enough to the upper floor, I might be able to pry the doors open and hoist myself out. At that point, I would be free. Free to go home and feed Ozzy, who's no doubt currently whistling his little heart out like he always does when he hasn't eaten in more than two hours. He'd look at me like I'm a horrible rodent mother, but then he'd be grudgingly accept my carrot stick and snuggle in my lap. And of course, when my phone has reception, I'd call for help so that someone can come take care of Erik. But I wouldn't stick around to see him out, because I've already had plenty of—

"No."

I startle and look at Erik. He is still in the corner opposite mine, giving me a flat stare. "No, what?"

"It's not going to happen."

"You don't even know what—"

"You're not going to climb out of the emergency exit."

I nearly recoil, because despite my magical-thinking tendencies I am aware that mind reading is not really a thing that exists. Then again, I am also aware that this is not the first time Erik seems to know exactly what's going on in my head. He was pretty good at it during our dinner together. And then later, of course. In bed.

But in this house (i.e., my brain) we do not acknowledge that.

"Well," I say, "you're way bigger and way heavier. So you can't do it." Plus, I'm not sure I trust him not to leave me here. I've trusted him before and heavily regretted it.

"Neither can you, because I'm not going to let you."

I frown. "I might be able to reach the exit by myself. In which case you technically don't have to *let* me."

"If that happens, I'm going to physically prevent you from doing it."

I hate him. So much. "Listen, what if we're stuck in here for days? What if me climbing out is our only chance?"

"There is nothing to suggest that the elevator won't start up again the second the power outage is resolved. We've been in here for about thirty minutes, which is nothing, considering that the repair crew is probably working on the grid to fix a block-wide outage. Not to mention how incredibly *dangerous* what you are proposing would be."

He's right. I'm being impatient and irrational. Which flusters me. "I—only for me."

His face turns into stone. "*Only* for you?"

"You'd be safe in here. You'd just need to wait for me to call for help, and—"

"You think I would be okay with you putting yourself in danger?" At baseline, Erik is not exactly a warm, convivial guy, but I had no idea he could sound like this. Deceptively calm, but furiously, icily livid. He leans forward as if to better glare at me, and his hand reaches up to close around the handrail, knuckles stretched white. I have a brief vision of him snapping it in two.

His anger, of course, gives me anger FOMO and makes me just as angry. So I lean forward, too. "I don't see why not."

"Really, Sadie? You don't? You don't fucking see why I wouldn't be okay letting *you*, out of *all* people—" He looks away abruptly, jaw tense, a muscle ticking in his cheek. His hair, I notice, is shorter than when I touched it. And I think he might have lost a bit of weight. And I cannot, I truly *cannot* bear how handsome he is. "Would you really rather do something that idiotic and reckless than be in here with me for a few more minutes?" he asks, turning back to me, voice icy and calm again.

Of course not, I almost blurt out. I'm not some horror movie not-quite-final girl who follows the DEATH THIS WAY sign only to be flabbergasted when an ax murderer chops off her leg. I'm usually a responsible, levelheaded person—*usually* being the key word, because right now I'm kind of tempted to run into the loving, ax-wielding bosom of a serial killer. Rationally I know that Erik is right: we won't be stuck in here for long, and someone is bound to come get us. But then I remember how betrayed and disappointed I felt in the days after he did what he did. I remember crying on the phone with Mara. Crying on the phone with Hannah. Crying on the phone with Mara *and* Hannah.

Being here with him seems just as reckless as anything else, honestly. Which is how I find myself shrugging and saying, "Kind of, yeah."

I expect Erik to get angry again. To tell me that I'm being foolish.

To make one of those dry jokes of his that made me laugh every time. Instead he takes me by surprise: He looks away guiltily. Then he presses his thumb and forefinger in his eyes, like he's suddenly, overwhelmingly exhausted, and murmurs quietly, "Fuck, Sadie. I'm sorry."

Six ⚙♥

have a grand total of zero superstitious rituals centered around dating.

And I promise I'm not saying this to brag. There is a simple reason I haven't convinced myself that I need to chug down a Capri Sun or do seven jumping jacks before going out with someone, which is: I do not date. Ever. I used to, of course. Once upon a time. With Oscar, the Love of My Life.

Like Hannah often points out, it's a little misleading for me to refer to the guy who met another woman at a data science corporate bonding retreat and two weeks later called me in tears to tell me that he was falling for her as the Love of My Life. And I swear, I do get the irony. But Oscar and I go way back. He gave me my first kiss (with tongue) when we were sophomores in high school. He was my date to the senior prom, the first nonfamily person I went on vacation with, the one whose shoulder I bawled on when he got accepted to his dream school in the Midwest, exactly seven states away from me.

We actually made it work pretty well during four years of long distance for college. And we did get to spend summers together, except when I was on internships, which was . . . well, yes, every summer but junior year, and I had that coding boot camp at UCSB then, so . . . yup, every summer. So maybe there were no summers together, but I did end up with a killer CV, and that was nice. Better, even.

When we graduated college, Oscar was offered a job in Portland, and I *was* going to follow him and find something there, but I got into Caltech's Ph.D. program, which was too good an opportunity to pass up. I really thought we could do five more years of long distance, because Oscar was a great guy and so, *so* patient and understanding—till the beginning of my third year. Till the day he FaceTimed me, crying because he'd met someone else and had no choice but to break up with me.

I wept. I stalked his new girlfriend on Instagram. I ate my weight in Talenti gelato (salted caramel truffle, black raspberry vanilla parfait, and, on a particularly shameful night, mango sherbet melted into a pot of Midori sour; I am filled with regrets). I cut my hair short, to what my hairdresser dubbed *the longest bob in the history of bobs*. I couldn't bear to be alone, so I slept in Mara's bed for a week, because Hannah tosses around way too much and I'm pretty sure she changed the sheets twice in the five years we lived together. For about ten days I was utterly, soul-smashingly heartbroken. And then . . .

Then I was more or less fine.

Seriously, considering that Oscar and I had been together for almost a decade, my reaction to being one-sidedly broken up with was nothing short of miraculous. I aced all my classes and my lab work, spent the summer touring Europe by train with Mara and Hannah, and a couple of months later found myself shocked to realize that I hadn't checked Oscar's girlfriend's Twitter in weeks. *Huh.*

"Could it be that it wasn't real love?" I found myself asking my friends over Midori sours (sans mango sherbet; I had regained my dignity by then).

"I think that there are lots of kinds of love," Hannah said. She was nestled next to me at our favorite booth at Joe's, the grad student bar closest to our apartment. "Maybe yours with Oscar was closer to the sibling variety than to anything resembling a passionate affair between soul mates? And you're still in touch. You know that you still love each other as friends, so your brain knows that there's no need to mourn him."

"But initially I was really, *really* devastated."

"Well, I don't want to armchair-psychologize you . . ."

"You *totally* want to armchair-psychologize me."

Hannah smiled, pleased. "Okay, if you insist. I wonder if maybe you were more devastated at the idea of losing your safe harbor—the person who was there for you since you were kids and promised to be there for you forever—than at the idea of losing Oscar himself. Could it be that he was a crutch of sorts?"

"I don't know." I poked at my garnish cherry. "I liked being his girlfriend. He was so . . . *there*, you know? And when we were apart I missed him, but not too much. It was . . . easy, I guess."

"Could it be that it was *too* easy?" Mara asked before stealing my lime.

I've been pondering her question ever since.

But there hasn't been anyone after Oscar. Which means that he still technically retains the title of Love of My Life, even if two months ago I got an invite to his wedding—pretty glaring clue that I'm not the Love of His. I could have gotten out more, I guess, especially in grad school. I could have tried harder. "When one door shuts, another opens," Hannah and Mara would say. "Now you can date around. You missed out on so many hot dudes in the past few years—remember the guy we met in Tucson? Or the one who always asks you out at conferences? Oh my God, the guy in fluid dynamics who was clearly in love with you? You should hit him up!"

Of course, whenever the topic of my love life comes up, and because dragging is a sacrosanct part of the covenant of friendship, I never hesitate to point out that even though both Hannah and Mara have been mostly single ever since starting grad school, they barely take advantage of their amazing dating opportunities. It usually ends with Mara defensively muttering that she's busy, and Hannah rebutting that she's on a break from hooking up with people, because her last two fuck buddies were Can I Jizz in Your Hair and Human Skull on the Nightstand Girl, and they would put anyone off sex. It usually ends with us collectively deciding that no relationship could ever compete with our jobs, guinea pigs, or . . . Netflix, maybe? If the idea of staring at blueprints is more appealing to me than hitting the club (whatever that even means; what even *is* a club, really?) then maybe I should just hang out with the blueprints. Not that things cannot change, since Mara is now embarrassingly, fantastically in love with her Formerly Asshole Roommate.

Maybe the blueprints and I will common-law tie the knot. Who's to say?

Anyhoo. All of this to say: I haven't really dated a whole lot, which is the sole reason I haven't developed weird, ritualistic habits around the process. Or I *hadn't*. Till right now.

Because I am about fifteen minutes into the night, and I'm thinking that I'll have to keep these black jeans for the rest of my life. The lightweight green sweater I put on? Can't throw it away. Ever. This is now my lucky-date outfit. Because the second I sit down at the bistro, where everything smells delicious and our narrow window table has the cutest little succulent in its center, Erik's phone pings.

"Sorry. I'll mute it." He does, but not before rolling his eyes. Which is such a far cry from his usual stoic, nonplussed vibe, I cannot help but burst into laughter. "Please, do not mock my pain," he deadpans, taking the seat across from mine. I'm not sure how, but I know that he's joking. Maybe I'm developing telepathic powers.

"Work?" I ask.

"I wish." He shakes his head, resigned. "Way more important stuff."

Oh. Maybe he wasn't joking. "Is everything okay?"

"No." He slides his phone in his pocket and leans back in his seat. "My brother texted that my football team just traded one of our best players. We're never going to win a game again."

I smile into my water. I never really got into American football. It seems kind of boring —a bunch of overgrown dudes standing around in '80s shoulder pads and bashing their heads toward chronic traumatic encephalopathy—but I'm way too soccer mad to judge fans of other sports. Maybe Erik used to play. He's big enough, I guess. "Then they should really invest in lucky underwear."

He gives me a lingering look. "Purple."

"Lavender."

"Right. Yes." He glances away, and I think that this is nice. I'm sitting across from someone who's not Oscar, and I'm not feeling too nervous, or too much weirder than usual. For all that he's a blond steely mountain of muscles, Erik is surprisingly easy to be around.

"What's your team? Giants? Jets?"

He shakes his head. "It's not that kind of football."

I cock my head. "Is it, like, a minor league?"

"No, it's European football. Soccer, you'd call it. But we don't need to talk about—"

I nearly do a spit take. "You follow soccer?"

"An intervention-worthy amount, according to my family and friends. But don't worry, I do have other topics of conversation. Like pastries. Or the practical implementation of smart factory technology. Or . . . that's about it."

"No! No, I—" I don't even know where to start. "I *love* soccer. Like, *love* love. I stay up till ridiculous hours to watch games in Europe. My parents always get me fancy jerseys for my birthday because that's literally my only interest. I went to college on a soccer scholarship."

He frowns. "So did I."

"No way." We stare at each other for a long moment, a million and one words running through the eye contact. *Impossible. Amazing. Really? Really, for real?* "You used to play?"

"I still play. Tuesday nights and weekends, mostly. There are lots of amateur clubs here."

"I know! On Wednesdays I go to this gym near my place, and . . . Soccer was my first career choice. The engineering Ph.D. was definitely my plan B. I really, *really* wanted to go pro."

"But?"

"I wasn't quite good enough."

He nods. "I'd have loved to go pro, too."

"What stopped you?"

He chuckles. It sounds like a hug. "I wasn't *nearly* good enough."

I laugh. "So, what's your team and who did they trade?"

"F.C. Copenhagen. And they got rid of—"

"Don't say Halvorsen."

He closes his eyes. "Halvorsen."

I wince. "Yeah, you're never gonna win another game, not for all the purple underwear in the world. But you weren't gonna win much *with* him, anyway. You need a better coach, honestly. No offense."

"Plenty of offense." He's glaring.

"You follow women's soccer, too?" I ask.

He nods. "Proud OL Reign supporter since 2012."

"Me, too!" I beam. "So you don't *always* have terrible taste."

"What's *your* men's team?" A cute, charming vertical line has appeared between his brows.

I rest my chin on my hands. "Guess. I'll give you three tries."

"Honestly, I can accept any club except for Real Madrid."

I continue with my chin hands, unperturbed.

"It's Real Madrid, isn't it?"

"Yup."

"Outrageous."

"You're just jelly because *we* can afford to buy decent players."

"Right." He sighs and hands me one of the menus I never even noticed the waiter dropped off. "I'm going to need food for this conversation. And so will you."

We spend the rest of the night arguing, and it's . . . fantastic. The best. I suspect the food is as good as he promised, but I don't pay very much attention, because Erik has incredibly incorrect opinions on the way Orlando Pride is using Alex Morgan and on the Premier League trajectory of Liverpool, and I must dedicate all my efforts to talking him out of them.

I fail. He stands by his wrong ideas and systematically makes his way through the bread, then an appetizer, then an entrée, like a man who is used to comfortably consuming seven large meals a day. At the end, when our plates are clean and I'm too full to bicker with him over the offside-sanctions rules, we both lean back in our chairs and are silent for a moment.

I'm smiling. He's . . . not smiling, but close, and it makes me smile even more.

I think this might have been the most fun I've had in years. Okay, false: I *know* it is.

"How did it go, by the way?" he asks quietly.

"What?"

"Your pitch."

"Oh. Good, I think."

"Thanks to Faye's croissant?"

I grin. "Undoubtedly. And my lavender underwear."

He lowers his eyes and clears his throat. "Who's the client?"

"A cooperative. They're building a rec center based in New Jersey and are shopping around for consultants. It's a second location for them, so they bought an old grocery store to turn into a gym of sorts. They're looking for someone who'll help them design it."

"You?"

"And my boss, yes. Though two of her kids have been colicky, so for now mostly me."

"What did you tell them?"

"I talked them through my plans for energy independence, green building standards, smart water management, minimizing off-gas chemicals . . . that stuff. They were going for a green edge, they said."

"And what are your plans?"

I hesitate. I really don't want to bore Erik, and I've gotten feedback from . . . literally *everyone* that when I start talking about engineering stuff, I go on for way too long. But Erik seems more than a little interested, and even though I blabber about raw materials and federal limits and life-cycle assessment for over ten minutes, his attention never seems to waver. He just nods pensively, like he's filing away the information, and asks lots of clever questions.

"So you got the project?"

I shrug. "They're meeting with someone else tomorrow, so I don't know yet. But they said we're their first choice so far, so I'm optimistic."

Erik doesn't reply. Instead he just studies me, serious, intent, like I'm a particularly intriguing blueprint. Does it make me uncomfortable? I don't know. It should. I'm out with a guy. For the first time in a million years. And he's staring. Yikes, right? But . . . I kind of don't mind.

Mostly, I'm wondering whether he likes what he sees, which is a bit different. I feel, sometimes, like I've lost the habit to wonder whether I'm pretty in favor of agonizing over other qualities. Do I look professional? Smart? Organized? Someone who should be taken seriously, whatever the hell that means? I generally find the idea of men commenting on my attractiveness, favorably or otherwise, repulsive. But tonight, right now . . . the possibility that Erik might find me beautiful uncurls warmly at the base of my stomach.

And then freezes when I consider that he might be staring for the opposite reason. Could he be staring for the opposite reason? Okay. This is—no. I need to stop with the ruminating. "What are you thinking?" I ask.

He huffs a laugh. "Just wondering something."

"What?"

He drums his fingers on the table. "Whether you want a job."

"Oh, I still have one. Despite my efforts this morning, I didn't actually get fired."

"I know. And this is very inappropriate, I am aware. But I'd love to poach you."

"Ah. 1 . . ." Suddenly, I'm feeling hot and weirdly tingly. "I like my job. It pays okay. And my boss is great."

"I'll pay you more. Name a figure."

"1 . . . what?"

"And if there's anything you don't enjoy about your current job, I'd be happy to come to an agreement about your duties. I'm very open to negotiating."

"Wait—*you*?"

"ProBld," he amends.

I frown. He talks about ProBld like he has a lot of say in their administrative choices, and I wonder if he has a managerial position. It would explain the suit. And the fact that he clearly came to dinner directly from work, even though we met at eight. He's wearing the same clothes as this morning, albeit without his tie and jacket, and with the sleeves of his button-down rolled up to his forearms. Which look strong and oddly *male*, and I've been trying hard not to ogle. I'm about to ask what exactly his job description is, but I get distracted when the waiter brings the check and hands it to Erik. Who readily accepts it.

Is he paying? I guess he's paying. Should I politely insist that we split it? Should I rudely insist that we split it? Should I offer to pay for both of us? He did buy the croissant this morning. How does one dine out with company? I have no clue.

"Thank you," the waiter says before leaving. "Always nice to see you, Erik."

"You *do* come here a lot," I tell him.

He shrugs, slipping his credit card inside the book. Okay. The paying ship has sailed. *Crap.* "With big clients, mostly."

"So it's not your default date place?" The question comes out before I can turn the words in my head. Which means that I don't realize its implications until well after it's lingering between us. Erik is staring, *again*, and I'm suddenly flustered. "I don't know if . . . if you don't . . . I didn't mean to say that this is a *date*."

His eyebrow lifts.

"I mean—maybe you just wanted to . . . as friends, and . . ."

The eyebrow lifts higher.

I clear my throat. "I . . . *Is* this a date?" I ask, my voice small, suddenly insecure.

"I don't know," he says carefully, after mulling it over for a second.

"Maybe it isn't. I . . ." *I didn't want to make it weird. Maybe you just think I'm a nice girl and wanted someone to have dinner with and I totally misread the situation and I'm so, so sorry. It's just, I think I like you a lot? More than I can remember liking anyone? It's possible that I projected and—*

The waiter comes to pick up the check, which interrupts my spiraling and gives me a chance to take a deep breath. It's all good. So maybe it wasn't a date. It's fine. It was fun, anyway. Good food. Good soccer talk. I made a friend.

"Can I ask *you* a question?"

I look up from the hand-wringing currently going on in my lap. *Is it whether I'm a needy, dangerous stalker?* "Uh, sure."

"I don't know if this is a date," he says, serious, "but if it isn't, will you go on one with me?"

I smile so wide, my cheeks nearly hurt.

✿✿✿

The pistachio gelato melts down my cone while I explain why Neuer is a much better goalkeeper than he's made out to be. We walk around Tribeca side by side without touching even once, block after block after block, the night air balmy and the lights fuzzy. My shoes are not new, but I can feel a nasty blister slowly forming on my heel. It doesn't matter, because I don't want to stop.

Neither does Erik, I don't think. Every few words I bend my neck to look up at him, and he is so handsome in his shirtsleeves and slacks, so handsome when he shakes his head at something I said, so handsome when he gestures with his large hands to describe a play, so handsome when he almost smiles and little wrinkles appear at the corners of his eyes, so handsome that sometimes I *feel* it, physically, viscerally. My pulse quickens and I cannot breathe and I'm starting to think about unnerving things. Things like *after*. I listen to him explain why Neuer is an incredibly overrated goalkeeper and laugh, genuinely loving every minute of it.

At the ice cream place, he didn't order anything. Because, he says, "I don't like to eat cold things."

"Wow. That might be the most un-Danish thing I have ever heard."

It must be a sore spot, because his eyes narrow. "Remind me to never introduce you to my brothers."

"Why?"

"Wouldn't want you to form any alliances."

"Ha. So you are a notoriously bad Dane. Do you also hate ABBA?"

He looks briefly confused. Then his expression clears. "They're Swedish."

"What about tulips—do you hate tulips?"

"That would be the Netherlands."

"Damn."

"So close, though. Want to try again? Third time's the charm."

I glare, licking what's left of the sticky pistachio off my fingers. He looks at my mouth and then away, down to his feet. I want to ask him what's wrong, but the owner of the coffee shop on the corner comes out to retrieve his sidewalk sign and I realize something.

It's late.

Very late. Really late. End-of-the-night late. We're standing in front of each other on a sidewalk, over twelve hours after meeting for the first time on . . . another sidewalk; Erik probably wants to go home. And I probably want to be with him a little longer.

"What train do you take?" I ask.

"I actually drove."

I shake my head, disapproving. "Who even drives in New York?"

"People who have to visit construction sites all over the tristate. I'll take you home," he offers, and I beam.

"Geniuses. Kind, ride-giving geniuses. Where are you parked?"

He points somewhere behind me and I nod, knowing I should turn around and begin to walk by his side again. But we seem to be a little stuck in this *here* and this *now*. Standing in front of each other. Rooted to the ground.

"I had fun tonight," I say.

He doesn't answer.

"Even though we forgot to get croissants at the bistro."

Still no answer.

"And I am seriously tempted to buy you a life-size cardboard cutout of Neuer and— Erik, are you still doing that thing where you don't talk because I'm technically not asking you a question?"

He laughs silently and my breath hitches high in my chest. "Where do you live?" he asks softly.

"Farthest reaches of Staten Island," I lie.

It's supposed to be my revenge, but he just says, "Good."

"Good?"

"Good."

I frown. "It's a toll of seventeen dollars, my friend."

He shrugs.

"One-way, Erik."

"It's fine."

"How is it fine?"

He shrugs again. "At least it'll take a while to get there."

My heart skips a beat. And then another. And then they all catch up at once, a mess of overlapping thumps, a small wild animal caged in my chest, trying to escape.

I have no idea what I'm doing here. Not a clue. But Erik is standing right in front of me, the streetlight a soft glow behind his head, the warm spring breeze blowing softly between us, and something clicks within me.

Yes. Okay.

"Actually," I say, and even though my cheeks are burning, even though I cannot look him in the eye, even though I'm shifting on my toes and contemplating running away, this is the bravest moment of my life. Braver than moving here without Mara and Hannah. Braver than the time I megged that midfielder from the UCLA. Just *brave*. "Actually, if you don't mind, I'd rather skip Staten Island and just go to your place."

He studies me for a long moment, and I wonder if maybe he cannot quite believe what I just said, if his brain is also struggling to catch up, if maybe this feels as extraordinary to him as it does to me. Then he nods once, decided. "Very well," he says.

Before we start to walk, I see his throat bob.

Seven

On paper, I should be pleased.

After weeks of sometimes-murderous, often-mopey, intense rage, I finally told Erik that I'd rather take my chances and fall down an elevator shaft—*Return of the Jedi* Emperor Palpatine style—than spend one more minute with him. I told him, and from the way his lips pressed together, he really hated hearing it. Now his eyes are closed and he's leaning his head back against the wall. Which, given his reserved Nordic genes, is likely the equivalent of a regular person going on his knees and bellowing in pain.

Good. I stare at the line of his jaw and the column of his throat, forbid myself from remembering how fun it was to bite into his scratchy, unshaven skin, and think, a little savagely, *Good*. It's good that he feels bad about what he did, because what he did *was* bad.

Really, I should be pleased. And I am, except for this heavy, twisted feeling at the bottom of my stomach, which I don't immediately recognize but has me thinking back to something Mara said to me the evening after my night at Erik's. Hannah's end of the call had gone dark, presumably when a falling icicle severed whatever Internet cable connects Norway to the rest of the world, and it was just the two of us on the line.

"He tried to call me," I said. "And he texted me asking if we could get dinner tonight. Like nothing happened. Like I'm too stupid to realize what he did."

"The fucking audacity." Mara was incensed, her cheeks red with anger, almost as bright as her hair. "Do you want to talk to him?"

"I . . ." I wiped the tears off with the back of my hand. "No. I don't know."

"You could yell at him. Rip him a new asshole. Threaten him with a lawsuit, maybe? Is what he did illegal? If so, Liam's a lawyer. He'll represent you for free."

"Doesn't he do weird tax corporation stuff?"

"Eh. I'm sure the law's the law."

I laughed wetly. "Shouldn't you ask him first?"

"Don't worry, he seems to be physically incapable of saying no to me. Last week he let me hang up wind chimes on the porch. The question is, do you *want* to talk with Erik? Or would you rather forget about him and pretend he never existed?"

"I . . ." I thought about being with him the previous night. And then, later, about discovering what he'd done. *Could* I forget? *Could* I pretend? "I want to talk with the Erik I had dinner with. And breakfast. Before I knew what he was capable of."

Mara nodded, sad. "You could pick up next time he calls. And confront him. Demand an explanation."

"What if he laughs it off as something that I should have expected?"

"It's possible that he's trying to call you to own what he did and apologize," she said, pensive. "But maybe that would be even worse. Because then you'd know that he knew exactly the harm he was doing but went ahead with it anyway."

I think that's exactly it. I think that's why I hated Erik's *I'm sorry*, and why I hate that he hasn't looked at me in several minutes. It makes me wonder if he's aware that he ruined something that could have been great out of greed. And if that's the case, then I didn't imagine it: the night we spent together was as special as I remember, and he still threw it into the garbage chute—*A New Hope* Princess Leia style.

"I saw Denmark won against Germany," I say, because it's preferable to the alternative. The silence, and my very loud thoughts.

He turns to me and exhales out a laugh. "Really, Sadie?"

"Yeah. Two—no, three nights ago." I look down at my hand, chipping at what little is left of last week's nail polish. "Two-one. So maybe you *did* have a point about Neuer—"

"Really?" he repeats, harsher this time. I ignore him.

"Though, if you remember, when we had gelato I did concede that his left foot is kind of weak."

"I do remember," he says, a little impatient.

God. These nails of mine are just *embarrassing*. "Even then, it probably had more to do with Denmark playing exceptionally well—"

"Sadie."

"And if you guys can sustain this level of play for a while, then . . ."

There is some rustling from his corner of the elevator. I look up just in time to see Erik squat in front of me, knees brushing against my legs, eyes pale and serious. My heart somersaults. He *does* look thinner. And maybe a bit like he hasn't been having the best sleep of his life in the past few weeks. His hair gleams golden in the emergency light, and a brief memory resurfaces, of pulling at it when he—

"Sadie."

What? I want to scream. *What more do you want?* Instead I just look back at him, feeling like the elevator has shrunk again, this time to the pocket between my eyes and his.

"It's been weeks, and . . ." He shakes his head. "Can we please talk?"

"We are talking."

"Sadie."

"I'm saying stuff. And you're saying stuff."

"Sadie—"

"Okay, fine: you were right about Neuer. Happy?"

"Not particularly, no." He looks at me in silence for several seconds. Then he says, calm and earnest: "I'm sorry."

It's the wrong thing. I feel a surge of anger travel up my spine, bigger even than when I learned about his betrayal. There is a bitter acid flavor in my mouth when I lean forward and hiss, "I hate you."

He briefly closes his eyes, resigned. "I know."

"How *could* you do that, Erik?"

He swallows. "I had no idea."

I laugh once. "Seriously? How—how *dare* you?"

"I take full responsibility for what happened. It was my fault. I . . . I liked it, Sadie. A lot. So much so that I completely misread your signals and didn't realize that you didn't."

"Well, what you did was—" I stop abruptly. My brain screeches to a halt and finally computes Erik's words. *Liked it? Misread?* What does that even mean? "What signals?"

"That night, I . . ." He bites the inside of his cheek and seems to turn inward. "It was good. I think . . . I must have lost control."

I freeze. Something about this conversation isn't quite right. "When you said you were sorry a minute ago, what were you referring to?"

He blinks twice. "The things I did to you. In my apartment."

"No. No, that's not . . ." My cheeks are hot and my head's spinning. "Erik, why do you think I stopped picking up your calls?"

"Because of the way I had sex with you. I was on you all night. Asked for too much. You didn't enjoy it." Suddenly, he looks as confused as I feel. Like we're both in the middle of a story that doesn't quite make narrative sense. "Sadie. Isn't that the reason?"

His eyes bore into mine. I press my palm against my mouth and slowly shake my head.

Eight ⚙

We haven't touched all night.

Not at the restaurant. Not in the car. Not even in the elevator up to his Brooklyn Heights apartment, which is larger than mine but doesn't look it because Erik is standing in it. We've been chatting like we did over dinner, which is fun and great and kind of hilarious, but I'm starting to wonder whether when I fooled myself into believing that I was bravely hitting on Erik, he actually thought that I was inviting myself over to play the *FIFA* video game. He's going to say *Come, I want to show you something.* I'll follow him down the hallway jelly-kneed, and once I'm at the end he'll open the door of the Xbox room and I'll quietly die.

I stand in the entrance while Erik locks the door behind me, shifting awkwardly on my feet, contemplating my own mortality and the possibility of making a run for it, when I notice the cat. Perched on Erik's spotless living room table (which appears *not* to be a repository for mail piles and take-out flyers; *huh*). It's orange, round, and glowering at us.

"Hi there." I take a few steps, cautiously holding out my hand. The cat glowers harder. "Aren't you a nice little kitten?"

"He isn't." Erik is taking off his shoes and hanging his jacket behind me. "Nice, that is."

"What's his name?"

"Cat."

"Cat? Like . . . ?"

"Cat," he says, final. I decide not to press him.

"I'm not sure why, but I pegged you for more of a dog person."

"I am."

I turn and give him a puzzled look. "But you have a cat?"

"My brother does."

"Which one?" He has four. All younger. And it's clear from the way he talks about them, often and with that half-gruff, half-amused tone, that they're thick as thieves. My only-child, "Have this coloring book while Mommy and Daddy watch *The West Wing*" self burns with envy.

"Anders. The youngest. He graduated college and is now . . . somewhere. Wales, I believe. Discovering himself." Erik comes to stand next to me. He and Cat glare at each other. "While I temporarily watch his cat."

"What's *temporarily*?"

He presses his lips together. "So far, one year and seven months." I try to keep a straight face, I really do, but I end up smiling into my hand, and Erik's eyes narrow at me. "The beginning of our . . . relationship was rough, but we are slowly starting to come to an agreement," he says, just as Cat jumps off the table and pauses to hiss at Erik on his way to the kitchen. Erik snaps back with something that sounds very harsh and consonant based, then looks at me again. "Slowly."

"*Very* slowly."

"Yeah."

"Do you lock your bedroom door at night?"

"Religiously."

"Good."

I smile, he doesn't, and we slip into a lull of not-quite-comfortable silence. I fill it by looking around and pretending that I'm fascinated with the map of Copenhagen that hangs on the wall. Erik does it by standing next to me and asking, "Would you like something to drink? I think I have beer. And . . ." A pause. "Milk, probably."

I laugh softly. "Two percent?"

"Whole. And chocolate," he admits, a little bashful. Which has me chuckling some more, Erik finally smiling, and then . . . more silence.

We're idling between the entrance and the living room, facing each other, him studying me, me studying him studying me, and something heavy knots in my throat. I'm not sure what's going on. I'm not sure what I expected, but the entire night was so easy, and this is not. "Did I . . . Did I misunderstand?"

He doesn't pretend not to know exactly what I mean. "You didn't." He seems . . . not insecure, but cautious. Like he's a scientist about to mix two very volatile substances together. The product might be great, but he'd better be extra sure. Wear protective equipment. Take time. "I don't want to assume anything."

The knot tightens. "If you have changed your—"

"That's not it."

I bite into my lip. "I was going to say, if you don't want to—"

"It's the opposite, Sadie," he says quietly. "The exact opposite. I need to tread carefully."

Right, then. Okay. I make a split-second decision, my second act of bravery of the evening: I step closer to him, till our feet touch through our socks, and push up to the tips of my toes.

The first thing that hits me is how good he smells. Clean, masculine, warm. All-around delicious. The second: his collarbone is the farthest I can reach, which would be kind of amusing if my ability to breathe weren't shot all of a sudden. If I want this kiss to happen, I'll need his cooperation. Or rock-climbing equipment.

"Will you . . ." I laugh helplessly against the collar of his shirt. "Please?"

He won't. He doesn't. Not for the longest time, instead choosing to wrap his hand around my jaw, cup my face, stare down at me. "I think this is it," he murmurs, thumb swiping over my cheekbone, eyes pensive, like he's processing a momentous piece of information. My pulse races. I'm dizzy.

"I . . . What?"

"This." His eyes are on my lips. "I don't think I'm going anywhere from this."

"I'm not sure I . . ."

He moves so quickly I can barely keep track. His hands close around my waist, lift me up, and a second later I'm sitting on the shelf in the entrance. The height difference between us is much less dramatic and . . .

It's the best kiss of my life. No: it's the best kiss *in the world*. Because of the way he presses a hand into my shoulder blade to arch me into him. Because of the scratch of his stubble against my cheeks. Because it starts slow, just his mouth on mine, and stays like that for a long time. Even when I loop my arms around his neck, even when he leans into me and pushes my thighs open to make space for himself, even when we're flush against each other, my heart beating like a drum against his chest, it's just his lips and mine. Close, brushing, sharing air and warmth. Achingly careful.

And then I open my mouth, and it becomes something else entirely. The soft press of our tongues. His grunt. My moan. It's new, but also right. The scent of him. The way he holds my head in his hand. The delicious liquid heat spreading in my belly, rising up my nerve endings. Good. It's good, and I'm trembling, and it's really, *really* good.

"If . . ." I start when he comes up for air, but immediately stop when he buries his face in my throat.

"This okay?" he asks before inhaling deeply against my skin, as though my Target body wash is some kind of mind-addling drug.

My "Yeah" is faint, breathless. When he bites my collarbone, I wrap my arms around his shoulders and my legs around his waist, and the pleasure of being so close slices through me like the sharpest blade.

He is hard. I can feel exactly *how* hard. He wants me to feel it, I think, because his hand slides down to my ass and pulls me into him. I squirm, twisting my hips experimentally, and he groans ruggedly into my mouth. "Be good," he chides, stern, a little rough. He grips me tight, holds me still against him, and I unexpectedly shiver at the command in his words.

It escalates quickly. For me, at least. There is a stretch of seconds, maybe minutes, in which we just kiss and kiss and *kiss*, Erik leaning even closer and me following his lead, liquid heat flooding inside me. And then I start noticing them: the soft groans. The sharp hiss as his cock rubs against my inner thigh. The way his fingers dig hungrily into my hips, the nape of my neck, the small of my back. He alternates between clutching me to his body as tight as he can and avoiding touching me at all, hands white-knuckled against the edge of the shelf as he puts some distance between us. I think he might be trying to slow this down. Pace himself, maybe.

I think he's not managing to, not very well.

I pull away, and his eyes slowly blink open. They're glassy, un-focused, a nearly black blue fixed on my lips. When he tries to lean down for another kiss, I stop him with a hand on his chest. "Bedroom?" I gasp, because he looks like he could just fuck me in the hallway, and I'm afraid that I'd gladly let him. "Or if you want . . . here is . . . fine, if you—"

He cups a hand under my ass and carries me all the way down the hallway, like I'm no heavier than his cat. When he flips the light switch on, the bed is huge and unmade, and the room smells so much like him, I have to briefly close my eyes. He sets me on my feet, and I'm about to ask him if this is necessary, if we could please do this in the semi-dark, but he's already unbuttoning his shirt, eyes fixed on me. My mouth goes dry. On second thought, light's fine. Probably.

Erik is a mountain. A giant dome of flesh and muscles—not *GQ*-cut, ridiculously defined ones, but solid, oak-tree big, and I might have gotten absorbed into staring and catastrophically lost track of time because:

"Take off your clothes," he says, no, *orders*, and I shiver again. There's something about him. Something commanding. Like his first instinct is to take charge. "Sadie," he repeats. "Take them off."

I nod, shrug out of my jeans first, then my sweater. I'm franti-cally looking for the courage to continue when I hear a low, hoarse, "Not purple."

I look up. Erik stands in front of me, naked, tall, big, and like . . . like a minor deity from some Norse pantheon, a reserved one who likes to keep to himself but would still get a couple of Baltic Sea islands named after him. He is gloriously unself-conscious about his nudity. I, on the other hand, am apparently too embarrassed to take off my white tank top *or* to glance any lower than his belly button.

Not that he seems to notice. His eyes are glassy again, staring at the way my black panties stretch around my hips like he'd like them burned into his retinas. I am tempted to put my jeans back on. "What?"

"They're not purple."

"I don't . . . Oh. I went home and changed. And . . . is this considered a pitch meeting?" I still should have worn something nicer. Maybe a matching bra. Problem is, if five hours ago someone had told me I'd end up in Erik Nowak's bedroom by the end of the day, I'd have blamed a fever dream and handed them some Advil. "And it's not purple, it's—"

"Lavender," he says with the bare twitch of a smile, and then I don't have to think much anymore because one of his thighs slides between mine and he's walking me backward to his bed. There is a down comforter under my back, and a pretty intimidating erection I *still* cannot bring myself to look at against my stomach, and hundreds of pounds of Danishness above me. Erik is eager, and determined, and clearly experienced. He groans into my neck, then my sternum, muttering something that could be *fuck*, or *perfect*, or my name. The way he's been thinking about this all day during meetings, *all fucking day*. His hands slide under my top and travel up: soft kneading, more groans and a few soft *fuck, Sadie, fuck*, a light pinch on my nipple and greedy bite through the fabric, and it feels perfect, scary, exhilarating, new, filthy, right, good, wet, embarrassing, exciting, fast—*all* these things, *all* at once.

Then, in the next breath, they all dissolve. Except for one: *scary.*

Erik has hooked his fingers in the elastic of my panties, taken them off. He's kissing down my hip bones, full lips pressed into my abdomen, and I know exactly what he's planning to do, but I cannot stop thinking that he's . . .

He is really *very* big. And his forearm is laid out across my stomach, pinning me to the bed, and I met him—shit, I met this guy *this morning,* and even though I *did* briefly google him to make sure his real name wasn't Max McMurderer, I don't know *anything* about him and he is much larger and stronger than I am *and am I even good at this?* and he could do whatever he wanted with me he could make me and I feel hot I feel cold I *cannot breathe and—*

"Stop! Stop stop *stop—*"

Erik stops. Instantly. And I instantly squirm out from underneath him, dragging myself to the headboard, legs drawn up and arms around them. His eyes are on me, once again light blue, once again *seeing.* What is he going to do? What is he—

"Hey," he says, pulling back on his knees as if to give me even more space. His tone is gentle, like he's approaching skittish, injured wildlife. A good chunk of my panic melts, and . . . Oh my God. What is *wrong* with me? We were having a good time, he was being perfectly fine, and I had to go and be a fucking weirdo.

"I'm sorry. I just . . . I don't know why I'm freaking out. You're just so big, and I barely ever— I'm not used to this. Sorry."

"Hey," Erik says again. His hand reaches out to touch me. Hovers above my knee. Then he seems to think better of it and pulls it back, which makes me want to cry. I ruined this. I ruined it. "It's okay, Sadie."

"No. No, it's not. I . . . I think the problem is that I have only ever done this with my ex, and I . . ."

"I see." His face turns stony in an impersonal, scary way. "Did he hurt you?"

"No! No, Oscar would *never*. It was good. It's just he was . . . different. From you." I laugh nervously. I hope I don't burst into tears. "Not that it's bad. I mean, everybody's different. It's just that . . ."

He nods, and I think he gets it, because his expression clears up. Which in turn helps me feel a little less anxious. Like I don't need to be huddled away from him as though he's a contagious rabid animal. I take a deep breath and scoot up closer, toward the center of the bed.

"I'm sorry," I say.

"Why are you sorry?" He seems genuinely puzzled.

"I just didn't think this would feel . . . scary. I figured I'd be way cooler. Smoother, I guess."

"Sadie, you . . ." He exhales and reaches for me again. This time he doesn't stop and pushes back my hair, tucking it behind my ear like he wants to see my face in full. Like he wants me to see *him*. "You don't have to *be* any way. I didn't bring you here so you could *perform* for me."

I swallow against the lump in my throat. "Right. You brought me here because *I* propositioned you, and then—"

"I brought you here because I wanted to *be* with you. I'd have kept on walking around the city till dawn if that was what you wanted. So, here's the deal: we can spend the night fucking, and I won't lie, I'd greatly enjoy that, but we could also play Guess Who?, or you could help me give my brother's cat his flea medication, since it's a two-, maybe three-person job. Any of the above works."

I really, really don't want to tear up. Instead I let myself fall back onto the bed, my head on his one pillow. "What if I wanted to play the *FIFA* video game?"

"I would ask you to leave."

"Why?"

"Because I do not own any gaming console."

I laugh, a little watery. "I knew you were too good to be true."

"I used to have a Game Boy in the '90s," he offers. "Maybe my dad kept it."

"Partial redemption." We're both smiling now, and my fear of *him* liquefies, like snow in the sun. Only to ice all over again in another form: fear of *not having him*. "Did I fuck this up?"

"Fuck what up?"

I gesticulate in his direction, then in mine. *Us*, I want to say, but it seems premature. "This . . . this thing."

He lies down next to me, facing me. He purposefully left a few inches between us, but of their own volition, like vines twining around tree trunks, my legs travel across the sheets and tangle loosely with his. This time the contact is not scary, only right and natural. He's still big and different and a little awe-inducing, but he's not on top of me, and I feel more in control. Like I could step away whenever. And I know now that he'd let me. "Maybe I can unfuck it up?" I ask hopefully.

He sighs. "Sadie, I want to tell you something, but I'm afraid you won't like it."

Oh no. "What is it?"

A pause. "You are a brilliant engineer who knows the Premier League stats of the past three decades off the top of your head. Physically, you are the uncanny combination of every single feature I've ever found attractive—no, I will *not* expand on that. And you saved me on your phone as Corporate Thor, even after I gave you my full name."

"I wasn't sure about the spelling and—you *saw* that?"

"Yup." His hand comes up to cup my cheek. "This is it, Sadie. I don't think there's any fucking this up."

A million hopeful fireworks explode in my head. My heart squeezes in my chest, heavy and sweet. *Okay. Okay.* "So I have not turned you off sex forever?"

He huffs out a laugh. "I doubt me not wanting to have sex with you is something we'll ever need to worry about, Sadie."

"Even if I'm bad at it?"

"You're not."

"I didn't think so. I thought I was okay. I mean, average. But maybe—"

"Sadie." With a hand on my waist he pulls me a little closer. Just enough for his eyes to meet mine and for my entire world to narrow to him. "Let's take it slowly. We'll get there," he tells me, like he knows, he just *knows* that this is the first night of many.

"Are you sure?"

"Strong suspicion. Would you feel better if I put my clothes back on?"

I shake my head, and then, on an impulse, close the distance between us. The other kisses he led, which I loved, but with this one I'm in charge, and it's exactly what I need. He doesn't try to deepen it till I do. Doesn't come closer till I shift toward him. Doesn't try to touch me till I take his hand and set it on my hip, and even then it's gentle, fingers skimming up and down my thigh, tracing my rib cage ridge by ridge, my spine knob by knob.

I feel myself relax. Drift away. Expand and contract and forget. Become wet and pliant, a beautiful, delicious heat spreading into my stomach. When my thigh accidentally brushes against Erik's erection, my breath hitches and he makes a noise, deep and low in the back of his throat.

"Sorry," he rasps, starting to arrange me so that I'm turned away.

I stop him with a hand on his biceps. "I like this, actually."

"You do?"

"Yeah. You?"

He exhales. "You have no idea, do you?"

"Of what?"

He doesn't elaborate. "I'm happy to do this until sunrise."

"Really?" I let out a laugh. "You'd be happy channeling your best high school self and making out?"

He shrugs. "I'm probably going to come at some point. But I can warn you. You don't have to be part of it, and there's a bathroom across the hallway."

"No! No, I'm—" *dying of embarrassment.* "I'd like to. Be part of it, that is." I clear my throat. "I think we should try again. What we were doing before I freaked."

I see it play out on his face: a split second of eagerness, then a mask of bland skepticism. "I think we should wait for that. Take it slow. Go out a few more times until you get used to the fact that I'm . . . *so* big, apparently."

I flush. "But I was thinking . . . what if I go on top? That way I won't feel trapped?"

Erik goes still. For a moment, he stops breathing. Then he asks, "Are you sure?" His pupils are dilated.

"I think so. Would you like to?"

"That would be . . ." He swallows. His fingers are gripping my hips like he simply cannot let go. "Yeah. I'd *like* that. If that's even the word for it."

I don't immediately realize the misunderstanding. Maybe because I'm busy, first shifting on the mattress and climbing over his hips, then basking in the fact that I'm on top of him. I do feel much better this way. *Okay,* I think. *Yes.* I can do this after all. I love this, actually. I love straddling Erik, looking down at his pale skin, tracing his muscles. I love his eyes on the spots where my nipples push against my top. I love the feeling of my thighs being split wide by his torso, the hairs of his happy trail against my folds. I *can* have sex with him after all. I *want* to have sex with him. I might *die* if I don't have sex with him, because right now I want us to be as close as we humanly can.

But then his hands close around my waist, and he shifts me up. And up. And up. Until my knees are pressing into the mattress on each side of his neck, and I remember what exactly he'd been about to do when we stopped. Big light bulb energy. Oh my God. He thinks I want him to—

"Erik, I—"

He starts with a long swipe across my core, parting me with his tongue. I make an embarrassing animal sound that's half gasp, half whimper, and fall forward, catching myself on the headboard. My core flutters. My entire body shakes, electric.

"Fuck, Sadie," he says gutturally right before licking into me again, thorough and impatient in a way that redefines the word *enthusiasm*. His tongue plays with my entrance, pushing past squeezing muscles. The thumb of the hand that's not caging my ass comes up to draw circles around my clit. I'm trembling. Spasming. Clenching. All of a sudden I'm *agonizingly* empty.

"Oh my God," I whisper into the back of my hand. Then I bite it, because if I don't, I will scream. Maybe I'll scream anyway, because he grunts and arches his throat to lick up into me, pressing my pelvis against his mouth, and the noises he makes—the noises *we* make—are wet and filthy and obscene. "Oh my *God*. I—" I'm out of control. My thighs are starting to tremble. I have no idea what I'm doing, but I cannot stop rocking, rubbing myself against his mouth, his nose, and his face, squirming for more contact, more pressure, more friction, wanting to be full—

"You're doing so well, Sadie," he murmurs into my core, and the words vibrate all the way up my spine. His fingers grip my ass bruisingly tight and he's ruthless, keeping me still, angling me better, letting me know that he knows what I need—for me to let him do his job. Then he starts using his teeth on me, and I break down.

I scream.

"Can't believe you thought you were bad at this," he tells me, laughing, and I feel each and every syllable travel through me like a knife. I force myself to breathe deep, to stay upright, to look down at him. And that's when his eyes meet mine and he starts sucking hard on my clit.

I come so hard, it's nearly painful. I've always been quiet, silent in bed, but the pleasure is like a dam bursting, cutting and searing and so violent, my body has no hope to contain it. I sob and whimper into the back of my hand, powerless, confused. All through my orgasm Erik is there, holding my hips, murmuring praises and groans against my swollen folds, licking at me until it's just on the other side of too much.

Then his kisses become lighter. Gentle. He turns to suck on the inside of my left thigh, and I wonder if it's enough to leave a mark. *Erik Nowak was here.* "I've been thinking about eating you out all day," he says against my skin, which is sticky and drenched and—I cannot believe this is happening. I cannot believe this is *sex.* "All. Fucking. Day."

Somehow, he seems to know that I'm too boneless to move. He slides me back down his body, and maybe I'm imagining, but I think he's breathing as heavily as I am, and I think his hands are trembling. I want to investigate, but he wraps his arms around my torso and holds me to his chest till we're as close as we can be. The racing beat of his heart reverberates through my skin, and this, *this*, this moment couldn't be any more perfect.

Until he kisses me. And kisses me. He kisses my mouth with

the same single-mindedness he used for my core, and as my heart-beat quiets down, as my limbs slowly stop twitching with plea-sure, I begin to smile into his lips.

"Erik?"

"Yeah?" His hand curves around my ass.

"Why did you buy it?"

"Buy what?"

"Faye's croissant. If you knew it was so gross, why did you buy it?"

He smiles into the line of my shoulder. "I'm part of it."

"Of what?"

"The money laundering scheme."

I giggle and hug him tighter while it swells inside me, a surge of happiness and adoration and something hazy, something hope-ful and young that I cannot quite define yet. His cock twitches against my inner thigh. He shifts me higher to pretend it didn't happen and pulls me in for another lazy kiss. *Hmm.*

I try to wiggle and reach between us, but he stops my hand by twining his fingers against mine.

"Do you not—?"

"Ignore it," he says, nuzzling his face against my throat. He bites me, firm, playful, almost distracting. Almost.

"But you—"

"Shhh. It's fine, Sadie. We should quit while we're ahead."

I frown, propping myself up to look at him. "*We're* not ahead. *I* am ahead. It's a firm one to nothing." Probably more like twelve-blending-into-one to nothing. But.

He laughs softly. "Believe me, it did *not* feel like nothing—"

He closes his mouth so abruptly, I can hear his jaw click. Be-cause I'm sliding back, and his erection is nestled against me. First, the curve of my ass. Then, right under my core.

He inhales, harsh. Fingers dig into my waist. "Sadie—"

"I thought you said I could be in charge," I tease him, rocking on his cock like I did on his mouth. The lips of my core surround his shaft, plump and puffy. We look down at the scene at the same time. The sound he lets out is feral.

"We need to stop," he grunts out, but his hand splays on my lower back and he presses down to get better friction.

"Why?"

"Because—" The head of his cock hits my swollen clit, a sharp stab of pleasure up my spine. Erik arches up, hugs me tighter to him, and closes his eyes. "Fuck. Oh, *fuck*," he slurs. "I'm going to fuck you, am I not?" His breath catches, and we're almost aligned. Then we *are* aligned, him hard against my entrance, and I bear down because I want to, I want to feel this delicious, immense pressure that will split me at the seams, and it feels good, so good, floodingly, druggingly, overwhelmingly good—

"Condom," he gasps in my mouth. "If we're—we need a condom."

I still. *Shit.* "I—" I try to scramble off him, but Erik holds me right there. He's still kind of inside me. Just the tip. "Do you . . . Do you have one?"

"I think so. Somewhere."

Somewhere is right in the drawer of his bedside table, underneath a bottle of allergy pills, a phone charger, and two books in what I presume is Danish. He holds the condom out to me and I accept it without thinking.

The foil is golden. *Trojan*, it says. And underneath: *Magnum*. Which maybe explains a lot.

"Should I . . . ?"

He nods. We're both flushed and clumsy and out of breath, *and* I have no idea how to put on a condom. But I don't want to say,

Please, do it yourself, because my school didn't really do the banana part of sex ed, and my mom put me on birth control on my third date with Oscar. Erik is staring eagerly at the foil in my hand, like it's a gift of myrrh for the newborn king, and I think he's more than a little into the idea of me doing this for him.

I grin. I have a Ph.D. in engineering: if I can build sophisticated machinery, I can figure out how to put on a damn condom. And there's some trial and error, but Erik doesn't seem to mind, spellbound by the way my small fingers work on him. When I'm done, his breathing is shorter. More stilted.

"Come back here." He pulls me down to him.

"I— Do you want to be on top this time?"

"No."

"Are you sure? I think I'm okay with—"

"Sadie. I want to fuck you, and I need you to like me fucking you. So you're on top for now."

I have no clue what the parameters for the magnum size are, but I do get why he needs it. I'm as relaxed and turned on as I've ever been, but it still takes a while to work him in, with small increments and false starts and lots of careful maneuvering. By the time he's in as far as he'll go, I'm sweating, and Erik is drenched. He smells delicious, like salt and soap and his intense skin. So I lick the place on his jaw where the drops have been collecting.

"Can you . . . ?" He arches experimentally into me. We both let out a groan.

"What do you want?"

"I want to feel your tits."

"Oh." I'd forgotten about my top. I straighten to take it off, which involves some twisting and grinding that has Erik gasping and trying to still my hips again. *They're not much,* I almost warn him. But I remember something he said earlier. *Uncanny combination of every single feature I've ever found attractive.* "Did you mean it? When you said I'm your type, physically?"

His pupils track the progress of my hands, blown wide. "I noticed you."

"Noticed me?" I undo the clasp of my bra. He twitches inside me. His jaw ticks with restraint.

"In the building. The lobby." He closes his eyes. Then opens them. "Once in the elevator."

I take off my bra, feeling stupid to have been worried. He's staring at my body like it's somewhere between holy and utterly, deliciously pornographic. "What did you notice?"

"Sadie." His throat bobs. "A lot."

"And . . ." I push down on my knees and circle my hips twice, working him a little deeper. A fraction of an inch, but the friction, the sense of fullness—my eyes roll back in my head. I didn't know anything could be so far inside me and feel so good. Couldn't have imagined. "And what did you think?"

"Oh, *fuck*." A desperate sound comes out of Erik's throat. "This. This, and more." He swallows. "Lots of other things, and—Sadie, you're going to have to give me a minute to adjust or I'm going to—" Erik sounds just as astonished by this as I feel. His eyes are screwed shut, and his hands grip me so hard, and his teeth sink into my shoulder. "Sadie, I'm about to—"

"Don't worry," I pant against his ear, fluttering like I'm about to go under. "You're doing so well, Erik."

I come like an avalanche, and then he does, and when I squeeze my arms around his neck, I don't ever mean to let go.

✿✿✿

n the morning, I watch him shave in front of the mirror just because I can.

He uses a razor that looks like the ones I buy for my legs (i.e., cheapest at the supermarket). If he minds the bleary-eyed girl who had less than two hours of sleep and is currently sitting wrapped in a towel on his bathroom counter, he hides it well. But I'm almost sure he doesn't. Mostly because he's the one who put me here.

"You're so tall," I say, a little tired, a little stupid, leaning back against the mirror.

His mouth twitches. "You aren't."

"I know. That's what I blame the end of my soccer career on."

"Isn't Crystal Dunn pretty short?" he asks, rinsing his razor. He dries his hands on his pajama bottoms, which hang deliciously low on his hips. "Meghan Klingenberg, too. And—"

"Shut up," I say mildly, which only amuses him further. He moves closer, hands slipping inside my towel and coming to rest against the small of my back, warm and instinctive and impossibly familiar. Like it's something he's been doing every day for his entire life. Like it's something he plans to do every day for what's left of it.

I love this. The way he pulls me into him. The way he grows hard but seems to be content with this not going anywhere. The way his face nuzzles into my throat. I *love* this. But.

"I just think you might be *too* tall," I say into his clavicle. "I foresee neck problems for both of us."

"Hmm. We'll probably need surgery a few years down the line." His smile travels through my skin. "How's your insurance?"

"Meh."

"Mine's good. You should go on it when . . ." He trails off. Picks up again with, "Have lunch with me today."

"I don't usually have lunch," I tell him. "I'm more of a 'big breakfast, then forty snacks scattered throughout the day' kind of person."

"Have a big breakfast and forty snacks with me, then."

I laugh. Yes. Yes. *Yes.* "What's the closest subway stop?"

"I'll drive you into work."

"I need to go home first. Feed Ozzy. Remind him of my un-yielding love for him."

"I'll drive you home, and then I'll drive you into work. You can introduce me to the hamster."

"Guinea pig."

"Pretty sure they're the same thing."

I laugh again, exhausted and drowsy and over the moon, and I cannot help but wonder how different this morning would be if Erik hadn't been the one to buy Faye's croissant.

I cannot help but wonder if this is the first day of the rest of my life.

Nine ⚙️

don't . . . It's not that . . . It isn't even . . . If you . . ." I'm sputtering like an idiot, which . . . great. Fantastic. Empowering. I'm a role model for all jilted women in the world.

Erik is still crouching in front of me, like he's fully planning to see this conversation through. I sit up, straightening against the wall of the elevator, and take a deep breath. Collect myself.

I'm going to speak my mind. I'm going to tell him exactly how much of a dickhead he is. I'm going to unleash three weeks' worth of shower-crying on him. I'm going to chew him out for ruining pistachio gelato and orange cats for me. I'm going to *annihilate* him.

But apparently, only after I ask him the stupidest question in the history of stupid questions. "Did you really think the sex wasn't good?"

Wow, Sadie. Way to let the point of this entire chat fly over your head.

He snorts. "*I* obviously didn't."

"Then why would you say that—"

"Sadie." He studies me for a moment. "Are you for real?"

I blush. "You're the one who brought it up."

"Seriously? You know what—okay. Right. Well." His throat works. He looks . . . not quite upset, but definitely the most upset I've ever seen him. Danish-upset, maybe. "About three weeks ago I'm having my usual, fairly disgusting breakfast, and I meet this really beautiful, amazing woman. I blow off my morning meetings and ignore my phone—my team is *this* close to sending out a search party—because all I can think of is how fun it would be to sit with her on a park bench covered in bird shit and talk about . . . I don't even know. It doesn't even matter. That's how good it is with her. And because it's apparently my lucky day, I manage to convince her to come out to dinner with me, and she's not only lovely and smart and funny, it also feels like the two of us have more things in common than I thought possible, and . . . well, it's a first for me. I'm no relationship expert, but I recognize how rare this is. How utterly one of a kind. I want to take it slow because the idea of screwing this up terrifies me, but she asks to come over." He exhales a single, bitter laugh.

"I should put on the brakes, but I have zero self-control when it comes to her, so I say yes. We spend a night together, and we fuck, a lot, and *yes*, Sadie, it's really fucking phenomenal in a life-altering way I never thought I'd need to elaborate on. It's obvious that she doesn't do this often, there's some hiccups, but . . . yeah. You were there. You know." He presses his lips together and looks away. "She falls asleep and I watch her and think, *This is like nothing else. Scary, almost.*

"But then it's morning and she's still there. And when I say good-bye to her she actually runs after me, and we're at work, there's people around—we can't really kiss or do anything like that, but she reaches out and takes my hand and squeezes it hard. And I think that maybe I don't need to be scared. It's going to be all right. She's not going anywhere." He turns back to me. His eyes are cold now, dark in the yellow lights. "And then night comes. The following day. The one after. And I don't hear from her. Never again."

I stare at Erik for long moments, absorbing every single word, every little pause, every unspoken meaning. Then I lean forward, and through gritted teeth I say:

"I despise you."

"Why?" He is icily, quietly furious, but I'm not afraid of him. I just want him to hurt. To hurt as much as he hurt me.

"Because you are *a liar.*"

"Am I?"

"Of the worst kind."

"Right. Of course." Our faces are about an inch apart. I can smell his scent, and I hate him even more. "And what did I lie about?"

"Come on, Erik. You know exactly what you did."

"I thought I did, but apparently I don't. Why don't you spell it out for me?"

"Sure." I abruptly pull away, leaning back against the wall and crossing my arms on my chest. "Fine. Let's talk about how you used me to steal clients from GreenFrame."

Ten ♥

Two weeks, six days ago

Did I just see you with Erik Nowak?"

Gianna's voice startles me out of the semi-comatose state I've been in for the past five minutes, which mostly involves staring at the Megan Rapinoe Funko Pop! on my desk and . . . mooning.

I feel drugged in a sweet, delicious way. From lack of sleep, I assume. And the fluffy, syrupy waffle Erik bought me at the diner near my apartment. And the hilarious story he told me while sipping his coffee, of how two weeks ago he fell asleep on his couch and woke up to Cat licking his armpit.

I want to text him. I want to call him. I want to take the elevator and go downstairs to smell him. But I'm not going to. I'm not *that* weird. Overtly, at least.

"Glad to see you're back." I smile up at Gianna, who's leaning against my desk. She must have come into my office while I was mooning. "How's Presley?"

"Better. But now Evan and Riley have some kind of bug that involves a superfun amount of diarrhea. But I saw you in the lobby with a tall guy—was he Erik Nowak?"

"Oh. Um . . ." I think maybe I'm flushing. I don't really have a reason to—Gianna is cool and very much not the judgmental type—but what happened last night feels so . . . private. And fledgling. I haven't even told Hannah and Mara (if one doesn't count the eggplant and heart emojis I sent in response to the seventy How did it go? texts I found this morning on my phone). It feels weird to talk about it with my boss. Though lying about it would be even weirder, right? "Yes. You know him?"

"*That* Erik Nowak? ProBld's Erik Nowak?"

I cock my head. Are there any others? "Yeah?"

"Are you guys friends?"

"We only just met."

"So you're not, like, *buddies.*" She seems relieved. "Okay. Good. You were laughing together, so I just wanted to make sure."

"Why . . . Would it be a problem if we were?"

"Not quite, no. I mean, I wouldn't dream of telling you who you should and shouldn't hang out with. But the two of you seemed a bit . . . chummy, and I just wanted to make sure . . . you know." She waves a hand dismissively. "If you *were* friends and talked regularly, I'd want to remind you to be safe and very, *very* discreet when talking shop with him. But since you're just casual acquaintances, then—"

"Why would I . . ." I frown, swiveling my chair to better face her. This conversation is very odd, and I'm wondering if I should chug down another coffee before it continues. "What do you mean by *safe* and *discreet*?"

She opens her mouth. Then closes it, looks around to make

sure that none of the interns are here, and opens it again. "A while ago ProBld made me an offer. Basically, they wanted to buy Green-Frame and its client portfolio, and sort of incorporate it as a division of their company."

"Oh." I blink. Erik didn't mention it last night. Then again, neither has Gianna, ever. "I had no idea."

"Well, it was before I hired you. Two, three years ago? Before the kids. And to be honest, it wasn't the first nor the last offer I got."

"Right. I knew Innovus offered."

"And JKC. Yeah. But ProBld was kind of . . . insistent." She rolls her eyes. "The reason they wanted us on board is that they're trying really hard to expand into the ecologically sustainable market, but they haven't had much success luring in really qualified people like . . . well, like you. Since most of them would rather go to more specialized firms. Don't get me wrong, they've been hiring some promising engineers, but they don't have the expertise they need yet. So they made me a really good offer, I said no, thank you, I would rather be my own boss, and for a few months it looked like everything was going to continue as usual." She pauses. "Then it started."

I shake my head, confused. "What started?"

"A bunch of shitty little things. The worst of which was targeting some of our clients to get them to switch to ProBld. I heard that some of their people were sniffing around our sites, too. Not exactly upstanding stuff."

I stiffen. This sounds . . . bad. Real bad. "Gianna, just to be clear." I take a deep breath. "Last night I went out with Erik for dinner. So we . . . I guess we *are* chummy. But he's great, and he wouldn't do anything like what you mentioned." I say it with more certainty than I should probably feel, given that I first met him exactly twenty-four hours ago. But it's *Erik*. I trust him. "I don't know what the partners and the higher-ups are doing at ProBld, but I'm sure he'd never condone anything like that."

"Well, he *is* a partner."

I blink. "He . . . Excuse me?"

"Erik is one of the partners."

All of a sudden I'm feeling cold. And very, very nauseous. "He is a— What are you talking about?"

"You said you went to dinner with him. Are you telling me he didn't mention that he's one of the founding partners?" She must read the answer on my face, because her expression shifts to something that looks a lot like pity. "He started ProBld right out of school with two of his buddies. And the rest is history."

"I'd love to poach you . . . I'll pay you more. Name a figure . . . I'm very open to negotiating."

"Wait—you?"

"ProBld."

"Does he know you're an engineer?" Gianna is asking.

I clear my throat. "Yes. I told him I worked for GreenFrame."

"Before or after he asked you out?"

"I . . ." That wasn't the reason. It wasn't. Can't have been. "Before."

"Oh, Sadie." Same tone as before—now with more pity. "But you didn't tell him anything specific about our projects or strategies or clients, right?"

"I . . ." I massage my forehead, which suddenly feels like it's about a second from exploding. "I don't think so."

"Did he ask about anything?"

"No, he . . ."

Yes. Yes, he did.

I can clearly see him, sitting across from me at the restaurant. His almost-smile. His neat, voracious way of eating.

How did it go, by the way? . . . Your pitch.

Who's the client?

So you got the project?

"Sadie? Are you okay?"

No. No. Nope. "I think . . . I'm afraid I mentioned something. About the Milton project. It came up in conversation, and I . . . I knew he was an engineer so I went into more detail than I should have, and . . ." Gianna covers her eyes with her hand, and I want the floor to swallow me whole. The addled, blissed-out feeling from this morning has dissolved, replaced with dread and a strong desire to puke my waffle all over the floor. "Gianna, I know it seems sketchy, but I don't think Erik would ever do anything like what you mentioned. We really hit it off last night, and . . ." My voice dies down, which is just as well. I cannot bear to hear myself talking anymore.

He didn't say he was a partner. Why didn't he? Why do I feel dizzy?

"I hope you're right," Gianna says, even more of that unsettling compassion in her eyes. She pushes away from my desk, high heels clicking into her office, and doesn't look back.

I feel like I could cry. And I also feel like this is a stupid, non-sensical misunderstanding I'm going to laugh about. I have no idea which one is the right thing to do, so I try to focus on work, but I'm too tired, or preoccupied, or horrified to concentrate. At two P.M. Erik texts me: In meetings until 7. Can I take you out after? and I think about our dinner last night, in a restaurant where he usually brings clients. Am I work to him?

Two minutes later he adds, Or I could cook for you.

And then: Before you ask: no, not herring.

I stare at the messages for a long time, and then I stand to take a look at the copy machine, which has been beeping because of its usual paper jam. I ball up the offending sheet and throw it in the recycling bin, not quite seeing what's in front of me.

I answer emails. I call one architect. I smile at the interns and have them help me with research. I wait for . . . I don't know what I'm waiting for. A sign. For this weird, apocalyptic confusion to dissipate. Come on, Erik didn't go out with me as a cover for some sort of . . . corporate espionage bullshit, or whatever. This is not a John Grisham book, and what I told Gianna stands: my gut tells me that he would never, ever do anything like it. Unfortunately, I'm not positive my gut isn't lying to me. I think it might just want to make out with the most attractive man in the world during the halftime of soccer games.

The copy machine beeps three times, and then three more. Apparently, I fixed absolutely nothing.

At five thirty I hear Gianna's phone ring, and ten minutes later she walks gingerly out of her office, coming to stand in front of my desk. The interns are gone. It's just her and me in the office.

My insides are iced over. My stomach plummets.

"Guess what project we didn't get," she says. Her tone is soft. Gentle. To her credit, not a trace of I Told You So. "And guess what other firm they decided to go with."

I close my eyes. I cannot believe this. I don't want to believe this.

"The Milton people said they got another pitch today. Similar sustainability. Lower costs, though, since it's a bigger firm. They asked me if I could match their offer, and I told them I couldn't."

My eyes stay closed. I don't open them for a long, long time. Everything is spinning. I'm just trying to stay still. "I . . . I fucked up," I say, barely a whisper. I'm crying. Of course I'm crying. I'm fucking stupid and my fucking heart is broken and of fucking course I'm fucking crying.

"You couldn't have known, Sadie."

The copy machine beeps again, six times in a row. I nod at Gianna, watch her walk away, and think about broken things, broken things that sometimes cannot be fixed.

Eleven

rack my brain, trying to remember whether during our dinner Erik ever mentioned taking acting classes. I want to say no, and let's be honest, it would seem a tiny bit out of character. And yet, if I didn't know what he did, I could almost buy it. I could almost believe, from the way he's blinking confusedly at me, that he has no idea what I'm talking about.

Nice try.

"Come on, Erik."

His brow furrows. He's still crouching in front of me. "What clients?"

"You can drop it."

"What clients?"

"We both know that—"

"What. Clients."

I press my lips together. "Milton."

He shakes his head, like the name tells him nothing. If I had a knife handy I'd probably stab him. Through the muscles, right into his heart. "The rec center in New Jersey."

It takes a second, but I can see a glimmer of recognition. "The pitch? The one you were at Faye's for?"

"Yup."

"You signed that client, didn't you?"

I clench my jaw. Hard. "Fuck you, Erik."

He huffs impatiently. "Sadie, I'm really lost here, so if you don't give me a little context—"

"I *almost* signed that client. However, when they got a pitch that was almost identical to mine, they decided to go with ProBld. Ring a bell?"

It doesn't. Well, I am *positive* it must. But the acting talent is making a sudden comeback, and Erik really does look like he's completely, utterly confused. His eyes narrow, and I can almost see him try to sift through his memories.

I sigh. "This is . . . just really exhausting, Erik. Gianna told me everything. I know that ProBld tried to buy GreenFrame. I don't know if you went out with me planning to hurt the company, or you took the opportunity once you were presented with it, but I *do* know that you used what I told you at dinner to give a pitch very similar to mine, because the client—*your* client—admitted it to us."

"I didn't."

"Right. Sure."

"I *really* didn't."

"Of course." I roll my eyes.

"No, I'm serious. Are you telling me that the reason you stopped talking to me is that we coincidentally ended up getting one of your clients?"

"Two pitches that similar are *not* a coincidence—"

"They must be. I didn't even know we *had* that client until right now."

"How could you not know what projects are going in the firm *you* own?"

"Because I am *not* a junior employee." I can tell from his tone that he's starting to get frustrated with me. Which is fine because I've been frustrated with him for weeks. "I have a leadership position and manage people who manage people who manage *more* people. We're not GreenFrame, Sadie. I oversee different teams and spend my days in pretty fucking boring meetings with patent attorneys and surveyors and quality assurance managers. Unless it's a high-priority deal or an extremely lucrative project, I might not even be debriefed until it's well on its way. My job is making big-picture decisions and giving guidelines so that—"

He stops and physically recoils. One second he's leaning toward me, the next his back is straight and he's pinching the bridge of his nose between thumb and forefinger. He stays like that for long seconds, eyes closed, and then explodes in a low, heartfelt:

"*Fuck.*"

It's my turn to be confused. "What?"

"Fuck."

"What . . . Why are you doing that?"

He looks at me, not one ounce of his previous exasperation in his expression. "You're right."

"About?"

"It was me. It was my fault you didn't get the client. But not for the reason you think."

"What?"

"The day after we . . ." He runs a tired hand down his face. "That morning I had a meeting with one of the engineering managers I supervise. He told me that he was refining a pitch for a project that had specifically asked for sustainability features. He didn't go into detail and I didn't ask, but since it's not our forte he wanted to know if I had any resources. I sent him an academic article." His throat bobs. "It was the one you wrote."

I'm dizzy. I'm sitting down, but I think I might fall over. "My article? My peer-reviewed article on frameworks for sustainable engineering?"

He nods slowly. Helplessly. "I also sent your thesis out in a company-wide email and highly encouraged all team leaders to read it. Though that was a few days later, after I'd read it myself."

"My thesis?" I must have misheard him. Surely I'm in the thick of a cerebrovascular event. "My *doctoral dissertation*?"

He nods, looking apologetic. I . . . I don't think I'm even mad anymore. Or maybe I am, but it's diluted in the total, utter shock of hearing that . . . "How did you get my thesis? And my article?"

"The article was on Google Scholar. For the thesis . . ." He presses his lips together. "I had a librarian from Caltech send me a download link."

"You had a librarian send you a download link," I repeat slowly. I'm inhabiting a parallel dimension. Where atoms are made of chaos. "When?"

"The morning after. When I got to my office."

"Why?"

"Because I wanted to read it."

"But . . . why?"

He looks at me like I'm a bit slow. "Because you wrote it."

Maybe I *am* a bit slow. "So you were trying to . . . figure out GreenFrame's pitch based on my published work?"

"No." His tone drops some of the guilt and is back to three parts firm, one part indignant. "I wanted to read what you wrote because I'm interested in the topic, because at dinner it was very obvious that you're a better engineer than most people at ProBld—including myself—and because about five minutes into my work-day I realized that if I wasn't going to stop thinking about you, I might as well be productive about it. And as I read, I realized that your work is above good, and sharing it with everyone else seemed like a no-brainer. I didn't think that I was handing your pitch to my entire company, and . . . Fuck. I just didn't think." He rubs the back of his hand against his mouth. "It was my fault. It wasn't on purpose, but I take full responsibility. I'm going to talk with my engineering manager and with the client and . . . I'll figure this out. We'll find you a way to make sure you get the credit you deserve."

I stare at him, stupefied. This is . . . He's not supposed to be saying any of this. He's supposed to . . . I don't know. Double down. Defend his own shitty actions. Make me loathe him even more.

"For the future, we can probably work out an agreement. Something about not pursuing your potential clients. I don't know, but I'll talk it through with Gianna."

Excuse me? "I doubt your partners will ever agree to that."

"They will when I explain the situation to them," he says, like it's a decided matter.

"Sure, because you're one of them." My anger is back. Good. Perfect. "*Another* lie from you, by the way."

This time, he . . . Is he *blushing*? "I didn't lie."

"You just omitted. Nice loophole."

"That's not it. I . . ." For the first time since I met him, this self-possessed, severe man seems vaguely embarrassed, and I . . . I can't look away. "I wasn't sure whether you knew. Most people I meet seem to know already—yes, I know how that sounds. And then over dinner you told me about how different working for a firm was from academic life. How much you missed your friends. I figured me bragging about how I graduated and got to make that transition *with* my friends could wait a couple of days."

"That sounds really . . ." Believable, actually. Kind of thoughtful, if in an oddly misplaced way? "Sketchy."

He lets out a laugh. Like I'm being ridiculous. "Sketchy."

"I just—" I throw up my hands. "Why are we even doing this, Erik? It's obvious that you had some ulterior motive for asking me out. You even tried to offer me a job!"

"Of course I did, Sadie. I'd do it again. I will right now. Do you want to come work for me? Because that offer stands and—"

"*Stop.*" I raise my palm, put it between us like the most useless wall in the world. "Please, just . . . stop this."

"Okay." Erik takes a long, deep breath. When he talks, his voice is calm. "Okay. This is what happened, and interrupt me if I'm wrong: you thought, based on what you were told by someone you trusted, that I slept with you to steal a client and get back at Gianna for not selling, which maybe sounds a little far-fetched, but . . . I get it. It's where the clues pointed. Is that correct?"

I nod, silent. There is a prickly, heavy pressure behind my eyes.

"Okay," he continues patiently. "That's your side of what happened. But I'm asking you to consider mine. Which is that even though I absolutely fucked up by sending your work to my team, I didn't know about the consequences of it until about five minutes ago. Because I called you, but you never picked up. And when I came upstairs to talk to you, Gianna said that she was sure you didn't want to see me. And I like to think that I'm not the kind of asshole who would keep calling a woman who asked him not to, so I stopped. But I also wasn't exactly able to quit thinking about you, which had me desperately looking for the reason you pulled back, to the point that I've been replaying what happened between us that night every day—every . . . single . . . day—for the past three weeks."

"Erik—"

"I'm not exaggerating." This would be so much easier if his tone were accusatory. But no. He has to sound reasonable and logical and earnest and sincere and I want to scream. "I tore apart every minute, every second of every interaction, and after slicing all of it into pieces, the only conclusion that I could reach was that whatever I did wrong must have happened after you asked me to take you to my place, which only really left what we did there."

"That's not—"

"And I've been scared, scared like never before, that I'd hurt you." He lifts his hand. Curves it around my cheek. "That I'd left you in some—*any* kind of pain. That I couldn't make amends. Which, let me tell you, is no fun when you know in your lizard brain that you're about five minutes from falling in love with some-one." He closes his eyes. "Maybe past. Can't really tell."

They make the floor shift and shake, Erik's words. They make it fall hard and fast from under my feet, they flood my brain with a blinding flash of light, and they . . . wait.

Wait.

"The power's back," I say with a gasp, realizing that the eleva-tor is working again. Erik must have noticed, too, but he doesn't look surprised, nor does he make a move to shift away from me. He keeps holding my eyes, like he's waiting for an answer from me, for an acknowledgment of what he's said, but I can't, *won't* give it to him. I turn away from the hand on my face and grab my bag, slipping out of the corner where I wedged myself.

"Sadie." When the doors open on the first floor, I dart out of the car. Erik is right behind me. "Sadie, can you—"

"Erik!" someone calls from the other side of the lobby, the

voice echoing across the marble. There is a small group of people chatting with two men in maintenance uniforms. "You okay?" I'm almost positive (from hate-researching ProBld after our falling-out) that he's another one of the partners. A late-working bunch, clearly.

"Yeah," Erik says without moving in their direction.

"Were you stuck in the elevator?"

"In the smaller one." There is an impatient edge to Erik's tone. It shifts to something much softer when he turns to me and says, "Sadie, let's—"

"Was it just the two of you?" the man calls. "Actually, maintenance is trying to make sure that no one from ProBld is still stuck. Can you come here for a second?"

Erik's "Sure, I'll be right there" could cut diamonds.

I turn to leave, but his hand closes around my biceps, and I feel his grip travel through every single nerve ending I possess. "Stay here, okay? I just need five minutes to talk to you. Can I have five minutes? Please?" He holds my eyes until I nod.

But once he turns his back to me, I don't hesitate for even a second. I rub the spot where he just touched me until I can't feel him anymore, and then I slip out into the warm night air.

Twelve ⚙

ait. Wait wait wait wait wait. Wait wait wait. Wait." In the center of my Mac's monitor, Mara holds up both index fingers to command Hannah's and my attention. Despite the fact that she already had it. "Wait. What you're saying is that all this time we've been doing weekly summoning circles to give this guy disfiguring genital warts and toenail funguses and those giant subcutaneous pimples people get surgically removed on YouTube... but he did not, in fact, deserve any of it?"

I groan. "No. I don't know. Yes. Maybe?"

"Related question: How long were you in that elevator?" Hannah asks.

"I'm not sure. One hour? Less? Why?"

She shrugs. "Just wondering if this could be Stockholm syndrome."

I groan again, letting myself fall back on my bed. Ozzy shuffles over to sniff me, just to make sure that I haven't turned into a cucumber since the last time he checked. Then he scurries away, disappointed.

"Okay," Mara says, "let's backtrack. Is what he told you believable?"

"No. I don't know. Yes. Maybe?"

"I swear to God, Sadie, if you—"

"Yes." I straighten up. "Yes, it does make sense. I did detail my framework for sustainability proposals in my published article, and I detailed it even more in my thesis—"

"Which you maybe should have embargoed," Hannah interjects, playing with her dark hair.

"—which I *definitely* should have embargoed, so it's possible that someone who read my stuff could have used it to mimic my pitch. Of course, when it comes to actually *doing* the work, they won't have the expertise Gianna or I have, but that's a problem for later. I guess that what Erik said *is* . . . conceivable."

"So, no genital funguses?" Mara asks. "I mean, it seems only fair, considering that you *did* publish that article *and* write that thesis to encourage people to adopt your approach."

"Right. Yeah." I close my eyes, wishing for the seventeenth time in the past two hours that I could vanish into nothingness. Maybe since the last time I checked, a portal to another dimension has appeared in my closet. Maybe I can travel to Noconsequencesofmyownactionsland. "I didn't really figure it would be used by my direct competitors."

"I realize that," she says, with a tone that suggests a strong *but*. "*But*, I'm not positive that it's Erik's fault, either."

"And he did apologize," Hannah adds. "Also, the fact that he read your dissertation is kind of cute. How many of the guys I've slept with have read my stuff, do you think?"

"No clue. How many?"

"Well, as you know, I firmly believe that sex and conversation don't mix well, but I'd estimate . . . a solid zero?"

"Sounds about right," Mara says. "Plus, you said he offered to find a way to fix the situation. And that just doesn't seem like something he would do if he didn't care about you."

"Agreed." Hannah nods. "My vote is for no genital pimples."

"Same. I am dissolving the summoning circle as we speak."

"No, wait, no dissolving, I—" I scrub my eyes with the heels of my hands. "Whose side are you guys even on?"

"Yours, Sadie."

"Unlike you," Hannah adds.

"I— What does that even *mean?*"

They exchange a look. I know we're on a Zoom call and it's technically impossible for them to exchange a look, but they *are exchanging a damn look*. I can *feel* it. "Well," Hannah says, "here's the deal. You meet this guy. And you boink him. And it's really good boinking—yay. The day after, you find out that he's a dick, which sends you on a three-week downward curlicue of tears and Talenti gelato that's about twelve times more intense than the time you broke up with a dude you'd been dating for *years*. But then you find out that it was all a misunderstanding, that things might be fixable, and . . . you leave? You said he wanted to talk more, and it's obvious that you're interested in hearing what he's saying. So why *did* you leave, Sadie?"

I stare at Hannah's implacable, matter-of-fact, kind eyes, which go very well with her implacable, matter-of-fact, kind voice, and mutter: "I liked it better when you were in Lapland."

She grins. "I did, too, which is why I'm trying to get back there—but let us return to discussing your *terrible* communication skills."

"They're not that bad."

"Eh. They kind of are," Mara says.

I glare at Mara, too. I'm an equal-opportunity glarer. "You know what? I will accept that my communication skills are poor, but I refuse to be shamed by someone who's on the verge of going ring shopping with the dude she once nearly called the cops on because he left a CVS receipt in the dryer."

"Pfft, they're not going *ring shopping*." Hannah waves her hand dismissively. "I bet she's going to get some kind of family heirloom."

"Doesn't he have older brothers?" I ask. "They probably already ran out of heirlooms four weddings ago."

"Oh yeah. Maybe there will be some shopping. You think he's going to call us from some D.C. mall's Claire's asking us which ring Mara would prefer?"

"Oh my God, you know what? Last week I read somewhere that Costco sells engagement rings— Oh, hi, Liam."

Mara's boyfriend enters the screen and comes to stand right behind her. In the past few weeks he's become a sort of informal fourth in our calls—an occasional guest star, if you will, who mines for embarrassing grad school stories about Mara and kindly offers to murder our asshole male colleagues when we complain. Considering that our first introduction to him was Mara plotting to booby-trap his bathroom, it's surprisingly fun to have him around.

"Really, guys?" he asks, all frowny and dark and cross-armed. "Claire's? *Costco?*"

Hannah and I both gasp. "Costco is *amazing*."

"Yeah, Liam. What do you have against Costco?"

He shakes his head at us, presses a kiss on the crown of Mara's head, and exits the frame. I'm a fan, I must say.

"Okay," Mara says, "going back to your poor communication skills."

I roll my eyes.

"Are you still angry at Erik?" Hannah asks. "Because you spent weeks being sad, and furious, and sadly furious. Even if you now know that your reasons weren't as valid, I feel like it would still be hard to let go of that. So maybe that's the issue here?"

I think about Erik's hand closing around my arm in the lobby. About the way he kept looking at me when the elevator restarted: focused, intent, like the world could spin twice as fast as normal and he still wouldn't have cared, not if I were nearby. I don't let myself recall the words he said, but a memory resurfaces, of us laughing and standing in his kitchen and eating Chinese leftovers, and I don't push it down. For the first time in weeks, it's not soaked in resentment and betrayal. Just the achy, poignant sweetness of the night we spent together. Of Erik turning up the thermostat when I said I was cold, then wrapping his large, warm hands around the soles of my feet. That feeling of being right there, on the brink of something.

I don't think I'm angry, not anymore.

"It's not that," I say.

"Okay. So the problem is that you don't believe him?"

"I . . . No. I do. I don't think Gianna deliberately lied to me, but she didn't have all the facts."

"What is it, then?"

I swallow, trying to prod at the reason my stomach feels leaden, the reason I've been feeling sick with disappointment and fear ever since finding out the truth. And then it hits me. The one thing I have been actively trying not to verbalize hits me just as I say, "It doesn't matter, anyway."

"Why doesn't it matter?"

I close my eyes. Yes. That's it. That's why. "Because I ruined it."

"Ruined it, how?"

Now that I can name it for what it is, the horrible feeling grows, acid and bitter in my throat. "He won't be interested in me. He met me and thought that I was funny, that he had tons of things in common with me, that he really liked me, and then I . . . I acted like a totally irrational, absurd, deranged person and blocked his number and accused him of fucking *corporate espionage* and maybe he wants to set the record straight, maybe he hates the idea of me thinking that he's a horrible person, but there's no way he wants to pick up where we left off and—aaaargh." I bury my face in my hands.

I fucked up. I just . . . I fucked up. And now I have to live with the knowledge of it. I have to go on in a world in which no man will ever compare to Erik Nowak. No man will ever make me laugh, and make my body sing, and make my soul absolutely indignant with his outrageous opinions on Galatasaray—all at once.

"Oh, honey." Mara cocks her head. "You don't know that."

"I do. It's likely."

"That's not the point." Hannah leans closer to the screen till all I can see are her beautiful face and dark eyes. "Okay, so Erik now knows that you occasionally display an appalling lack of conflict-resolution initiative."

I groan. "I really wish I had the emotional fortitude to hang up on you."

"But you don't. What I'm saying is, maybe Erik will decide that you'll make for a terrible girlfriend who overreacts and is more trouble than you're worth. Maybe he'll decide that he wants to bitch about you on the relationship subreddit. But if you cut him out like you did three weeks ago, you'd just be making this decision *for* him."

I blink, confused, suddenly remembering why I went into engineering. Logarithmic derivatives are so much easier than this relationship shit. "What do you mean?"

"Sadie, I know you like this guy a lot. I know that if he does decide that he doesn't want you in his life it's going to hurt, and that you're tempted to preemptively pull back to protect yourself. But if you don't at least give him a chance to choose you, you'll lose him for sure."

I nod slowly, trying to think past the hard knot in my throat. Letting the idea—*go for it, just go for it, ask for what you want, be brave*—slowly seep through me. Remembering Erik. Remembering the breeze hanging between us on a park bench, on a deserted sidewalk. The way my stomach fluttered at the feelings it carried. Of *possibilities*. Of *maybe*.

This is my new happy place, Erik murmured into the shell of my ear the second time we had sex that night. And then he pushed my sweaty hair away from my forehead, and I looked up at him and thought, *His eyes are the exact color of the sky when the sun shines*. And I always, *always* loved the sky.

"You're right," I say. "You're so right. I should go to him."

Hannah smiles. "Well, it's actually what, one A.M. in New York? I was thinking more of a phone call tomorrow morning. Around ten."

"Yes. I should go to him *right now*."

"That's the exact opposite of—"

"I gotta go. Love you."

I hang up and bounce out of bed, looking for a jacket and my phone. I start ordering an Uber, except—shit. I know where Erik lives, but not his address. I run to the door, simultaneously looking for my keys and typing the closest landmark to his apartment that I can recall. How the hell do you spell—

"Sadie?"

I look up. Erik is standing in my open door. Erik, in all his tall, unsmiling, Corporate-Thorship splendor. Wearing the same clothes he had on when I left him plus a light jacket, his hand up in midair and clearly about to knock.

"Are you going somewhere?"

"No. Yes. No. I . . ." I take a step back. Another. Another. Erik stays right where he is, and my cheeks burn. Am I hallucinating him? Is he really here in Astoria? In my apartment? I hear a loud thunk, and my keys are on the linoleum floor. I need a nap. I need a seven-year nap.

"Here." He bends down to pick up the keys, pauses for a second to study my soccer ball key chain, and holds them out to me. "Can I come in for five minutes? Just to talk. If you feel uncomfortable, the hallway's okay, too—"

"No. No, I . . ." I clear my throat. "You can come in."

A brief hesitation. Then a nod as he steps in and closes the door behind him. But he doesn't move any farther inside, stopping in the entrance and simply saying, "Thank you."

I was coming to you, I open my mouth to say. *I was on my way to tell you many, many confusing things.* But the surprise of seeing him here has frozen my bravery, and instead of flooding him with the impassioned speech I would have typed on my Notes app in the Uber, I just stare. Silent.

For fuck's sake, what is *wrong* with me—

"Here," he says, holding out a phone. His phone.

Uh? "Why are you giving this to me?"

"Because I want you to look through it. The passcode is 1111."

I glance at his face. "1111? Are you joking?"

"Yeah, I know. Just ignore it."

I snort. "You can't ask me *that*."

He sighs. "Fine. You are allowed *one* comment."

"How about one one one one comments—"

"That's it. Your comment, you used it up. Now—"

"Come on, I have *way* more to—"

"—will you please unlock the phone?"

I pout but do as he says. Mostly out of sheer bewilderment. "Done."

He nods. "If you click on my email app, you'll find my work correspondence. Most of those messages are highly confidential, so I'm going to ask you not to read them. But I want you to search for your last name."

"Why would I do that?"

"Because it's all there. The emails. Me requesting your thesis. Me circulating it to ProBld like an asshole. A couple of instances of me generally discussing your writing. The timeline should confirm what I already told you." I stare at him. Speechless. Then he continues, and it gets worse. "This is all I can think of, but if there's anything else I can show you that will help you believe that Gianna misinterpreted things, let me know. I'm happy to leave my phone here. Take however long you want to go through it. If someone calls or texts, ignore them."

It's the calm, earnest way he's looking at me that does it. It snaps what's left of my terror of being rejected, and I'm abruptly done with whatever fearful bullshit my brain is trying to feed me.

A new knowledge uncurls inside me, and I instantly *know* what to do. I *know* how to do it. And it starts with clutching his phone tight, stepping closer, and sliding it into the pocket of his jacket. I let my hand linger inside for a second, feeling the warmth from Erik's body. The clean cotton. No lint or candy wrappers or empty ChapStick tubes.

I adore it. I love it. My hand wants to slip inside this pocket on rainy fall afternoons and chilly spring mornings. My hand wants to move in and just *live* here, right next to Erik's.

But for now, there's something else I need to do. Which is holding out my own phone to him. He looks at it skeptically, until I say, "My passcode is 1930."

His mouth twitches. "Year of the first FIFA World Cup?"

I laugh, because . . . yeah. Out of everyone, *he* would know. And then I feel myself starting to cry, because of course, out of everyone in the entire world, *he* would know.

"Unlock it, please," I say between sniffles. Erik is wide-eyed, alarmed by the tears, trying to come closer and to pull me to him, but I don't let him. "Unlock my phone, Erik. Please."

He quickly punches in the numbers. "Done. Sadie, are you—"

"Go to my contacts. Find yours. It's . . . I changed it. To your actual name." *It's hard to sustain high and prolonged levels of hatred for someone who's saved on your phone with a cutesy nickname,* I don't add, but the thought has me chuckling, wet, watery.

"Done." He sounds impatient. "Can I—"

"Okay." I take a deep breath. "Now, please, unblock your number."

A pause. Then: "What?"

"I blocked your number. Because I . . ." I wipe my cheek with the back of my hand, but there're more tears coming. "Because I couldn't bear to . . . Because. But I think you should unblock it." I sniffle again. Loudly. "So if you decided that you don't mind the fact that sometimes I can be a total lunatic, and if you want to give me a call and give the . . . the thing we were doing another chance, then I'd be happy to pick up and—"

I find myself pulled into his body, hugged tight against his chest, and I should probably insist on apologizing properly and offer an in-depth debriefing of everything that has occurred, but I just let myself sink into him. Smell his familiar scent. When he smooths my hair back, I bury my face into his shirt and melt, soaking in the silence and the relief.

"I think I just really suck at one-night stands," I say, muffled into the soft fabric.

"We didn't have a one-night stand, Sadie."

"Okay. I mean, I don't know. I've never . . ."

"I've had enough for both of us, and then some." He pulls back to look at me, and repeats, "We did *not* have a one-night stand."

I don't make the conscious decision to kiss him. It just happens. One second we're looking at each other, the next we're not. Erik tastes like himself and a late-spring night in New York. He holds my head in his palm, presses me into him; he groans, bends down to push me into the wall, and licks the inside of my mouth.

"So we're good?" he asks, coming up for air. I want to nod, but I forget when he bends down for another kiss, just as deep as the one that came before. Then he remembers his question and repeats, "Sadie? Are we good?"

I close my eyes and bite into his bottom lip. It's soft, and plump, and I remember the patient way he worked between my legs. I remember coming over and over, the pleasure so strong I couldn't comprehend it—

"Sadie." He's not breathing normally. He takes a step back, like he needs a moment to get himself under control. "Are we good? Because if you think *this* is a one-night stand, then—"

"No. I . . ." I reach up to his face. This time, when I bring his mouth down to mine, my kiss is slow and gentle. "No. We're good."

"Promise?" he asks against my lips.

I nod. And then, because it seems important: "I promise."

It's like flipping a switch. One moment he's looking at me questioningly, the next our hands are on each other, me unzipping his jeans, him unbuttoning my blouse. There is a heat growing between us, a heat that has us work frenziedly, clumsy and too eager. When I tug down his jeans and briefs, his cock springs out, straining and leaking and so hard, it has to hurt. I wrap my hand around him, pump up and down a couple of times, and he groans, a soft, guttural sound. Then he pulls me away, pins my wrist to the wall, and attacks my pants.

His fingers brush under the elastic of my underwear, and when his knuckles graze the damp cloth of my panties it's all I can do not to spread my legs as far as they'll go. "Purple," he rasps out when my slacks are pooled around my ankles. "Finally."

"Pitch today. Yesterday," I amend, helping him get rid of my top.

"By the way," he says, voice scratchy, "last time you left your bra at my place." He traces the line of the one I have on but doesn't take it off. Instead, he lowers the lace cups, tucks them under the curve of my breasts. When my exposed nipples harden to points, we both make choked, breathy noises.

"Y-you can keep it."

"Good."

"Good?"

His thumb moves back and forth across my nipple. "It's not exactly in a . . . pristine state."

I laugh, breathless. "Why? Have you been using it?"

He doesn't reply. Instead he lifts me up until my legs are

wrapped around his hips, pinning me against the wall next to the door even though there's a bed, a couch, a dozen pieces of furniture just a handful of feet away—and then stops abruptly. "Do you— Are you feeling trapped? Is this—"

"No, it's good. Perfect. Please, just—"

He hooks his fingers in the crotch of my panties, haphazardly shoves them to the side, and he tries one, two angles that can't possibly work, but then he adjusts me, he tilts me like I'm no larger than a doll, and on the third try he just . . .

Slips inside. The pressure is enormous, stretching and burning and familiar and inexorable and lovely, and all I can think of is how much I missed this, the sharp feeling of something too big that's somehow meant to fit inside me, the way he mutters *sorry, please, more, almost there.*

"I missed you," he breathes against my temple when he's reached a full seat, sounding like he's under great strain. "I only knew you for twenty-four hours, but I've never missed anyone so much."

I moan. An embarrassing, mewling sound that cannot possibly come from my mouth. "For the record." I feel so full, I can barely speak. "I thought the sex was good." It's an understatement. It's as much as I am physically able to say right now.

"Yeah?" He bites me on the flesh between my neck and my shoulder—not hard enough to break my skin, enough to suggest that he's not fully in control. It reminds me of our night together, the way he kept me still for his thrusts, the way he made me feel at once powerful and powerless. "That's good. Because I can't think of anything else." He moves inside me. Once, twice. Once more, a little too forceful, but perfect. My forehead leans against his, and he pants into my mouth. "Three weeks, and I could only think of you."

It lasts less than a dozen thrusts. His mouth is by my ear as he tells me how beautiful I am, how he wants to feel all of me, how he could fuck me every second of every hour of every day. The spasms bloom inside me, drive me mindless, and I cling to his shoulders as my orgasm explodes through my body, wiping my mind clean. *Erik*, I mouth against his hair. *Erik, Erik, Erik.* He stays still while I ride it out, a near-silent growl in his throat, the tension in his arms nearly vibrating. Then, when I'm almost done, he asks,

"Should I— Fuck, should I pull out?"

"No," I exhale. "I'm—we're good. Pill."

He comes inside me before I'm done talking, burying the sounds of his pleasure into the skin of my throat.

We stay like that, after. He holds me up, like he knows that I would wobble on my legs if he were to let go of me, and kisses me for long moments. Chaste pecks wherever he can reach, long licks up my sweaty neck, soft hickeys that have me squirming and giggling in his arms. I never, ever want this moment to end. I want to paint it and frame it and hang it on the wall—*this* wall—and treasure it and make a million more and—

"Sadie?" Erik's voice is even deeper than usual. I am happy and pliant and relaxed.

"Yeah?"

"Do you still have your hamster?"

"Guinea pig."

"Same thing. Do you still have it?"

"Yeah." I pause. "Why?"

"Just making sure that a giant rat isn't trying to eat my jeans."

I look down over his shoulder and burst into laughter for the first time in weeks.

Epilogue ⚙

Okay," I say, determined. I stare first at my masterpiece and at the remnants of my hard work, and then I repeat, louder, "Okay, I'm ready! Prepare to be blown away!"

Erik appears at the entrance of his kitchen about five seconds later, looking sleepy and relaxed and handsome in his Hanes T-shirt and plaid pajama pants. "You have dough on your nose," he says, before leaning forward to kiss it away. Then he sits across from me, on the other side of the island.

"Okay. Moment of truth." I slide a small porcelain plate toward him. On top there is a croissant—the fruit of my many, *many* labors.

So. Many. Labors.

"Looks good."

"Thank you." I beam. "Made from scratch."

"I can tell." With a small smile, he glances at how three quarters of his kitchen is coated in flour.

"My culinary genius is apparently a bit chaotic. Come on, try it."

He picks up the croissant in his huge hands and takes a bite. He chews for one, two, three, four, five seconds, and I should probably give him a little more time, but I just can't wait to ask, "You like it? Is it good?"

He chews some more.

"Amazing? Fantastic? Delicious?"

More chewing.

"Edible?"

The chewing stops. Erik sets the croissant back on the table and swallows once. With noticeable difficulty. Then washes it all down with a sip of coffee.

"Well?" I ask.

"It's . . ."

"It cannot be *bad*."

Silence.

"Right?"

He tilts his head, pensive. "Is it possible that you mixed up salt and sugar?"

"No! I . . . Is it worse than Faye's?" He thinks about it. Which is all the answer I need. "I hate you."

"There is a bit of a . . . vinegary aftertaste? Did you maybe add that instead of water?"

"What?" I scowl. "I think *you* are the problem. I think you just don't like croissants."

He shrugs. "Yeah, maybe it's me."

Cat jumps on the island. He gingerly sidesteps our mugs and with a curious expression sniffs Erik's croissant. "Oh, buddy, no," Erik whispers. "You don't want to do that." Cat takes a delicate lick. Then he turns to me to stare with a horrified, betrayed expression.

Erik doesn't even *try* not to laugh.

"I hate you." I close my eyes, quietly planning murder and mayhem and lots of truculent revenge scenarios. I will deface his jerseys. I will pour soy sauce in his chocolate milk. I will hoard the down comforter for the next ten nights. "I hate you," I repeat. "I hate you so, so much."

"Nah." When I open my eyes, Erik's smile is warm and soft. "I don't think you do, Sadie."

Below
Zero

For Shep and Celia.
Still with no polar bears, but with lots of love.

Prologue ⚙️

I dream of an ocean.

Not the Arctic, though. Not the one right here in Norway, with its close-packed, frothy waves constantly crashing against the coasts of the Svalbard archipelago. It's perhaps a bit unfair of me: the Barents Sea is perfectly worth dreaming of. So are its floating icebergs and inhospitable permafrost shores. All around me there is nothing but stark, cerulean beauty, and if this is the place where I die, alone and shivering and bruised and pretty damn hungry . . . well, I have no reason to bitch.

After all, blue was always my favorite color.

And yet, the dreams seem to disagree. I lie here, in my half-awake, half-unconscious state. I feel my body yield precious degrees of heat. I watch the ultraviolet morning light reach inside the crevasse that trapped me hours ago, and the only ocean I can dream of is the one on Mars.

"Dr. Arroyo? Can you hear me?"

I mean, this entire thing is almost laughable. I am a NASA scientist. I have a doctorate in aerospace engineering and several publications in the field of planetary geology. At any given time, my brain is a jumbled maelstrom of stray thoughts on massive volcanism, crystal fluid dynamics, and the exact kind of anti-radiation equipment one would need to start a medium-size human colony on Kepler-452b. I promise I'm not being conceited when I say that I know pretty much all there is to know about Mars. Including the fact that there are no oceans on it, and the idea that there ever were is highly controversial among scientists.

So, yeah. My near-death dreams are ridiculous *and* scientifically inaccurate. I would laugh about it, but I have a sprained ankle and I'm approximately ten feet below the ground. It seems better to just save my energy for what's to come. I never really believed in an afterlife, but who knows? Better hedge my bets.

"Dr. Arroyo, do you copy?"

The problem is, it calls to me, this nonexistent ocean on Mars. I feel the pull of it deep inside my belly, and it warms me even here, at the icy tip of the world. Its turquoise waters and rust-tinted coastlines are approximately 200 million kilometers from the place where I'll die and rot, but I cannot shake the feeling that they want me closer. There is an ocean, a network of gullies, an entire giant planet full of iron oxide, and they're all calling to me. Asking me to give up. Lean in. Let go.

"Dr. Arroyo."

And then there are the voices. Random, improbable voices from my past. Well, okay: *a* voice. It's always the same, deep and rumbling, with no discernible accent and well-pronounced consonants. I don't really mind it, I must say. I'm not sure why my brain has decided to impose it on me just now, considering that it belongs to someone who doesn't like me much—someone I might like even less—but it's a pretty good voice. A+. Worth listening to in a death's door situation. Even though Ian Floyd was the one who never wanted me to come here to Svalbard in the first place. Even though the last time we were together he was stubborn, and un-kind, and unreasonable, and now he seems to sound only . . .

"*Hannah.*"

Close. Is this really Ian Floyd? Sounding *close*?

Impossible. My brain has frozen into stupidity. It must really be all over for me. My time has come, the end is nigh, and—

"*Hannah. I'm coming for you.*"

My eyes spring open. I'm not dreaming anymore.

One ⚙

On my very first day at NASA, at some point between the HR intake and a tour of the Electromagnetic Compliance Studies building, some overzealous newly hired engineer turns to the rest of us and asks, "Don't you feel like your entire life has led you to this moment? Like you were meant to be here?"

Aside from Eager Beaver, there are fourteen of us starting today. Fourteen of us fresh out of top-five graduate programs, and prestigious internships, and CV-beefing industry jobs accepted exclusively to look more attractive during NASA's next round of recruitment. There're fourteen of us, and the thirteen that aren't me are all nodding enthusiastically.

"Always knew I'd end up at NASA, ever since I was, like, five," says a shy-looking girl. She's been sticking by my side for the entire morning, I assume because we're the only two non-dudes in the group. I must say, I don't mind it too much. Perhaps it's because she's a computer engineer while I'm aerospace, which means there's a good chance that I won't see much of her after today. Her name is Alexis, and she's wearing a NASA necklace on top of a NASA T-shirt that only barely covers the NASA tattoo on her upper arm. "I bet it's the same for you, Hannah," she adds, and I smile at her, because Sadie and Mara insisted that I shouldn't be my resting-bitch self now that we live in different time zones. They are convinced that I need to make new friends, and I have reluctantly agreed to put in a solid effort just to get them to shut up. So I nod at Alexis like I know exactly what she means, while privately I think: *Not really.*

When people find out that I have a Ph.D., they tend to assume that I was always an academically driven child. That I cruised through school my entire life in a constant effort to overachieve. That I did so well as a student, I decided to remain one long after I could have booked it and freed myself from the shackles of homework and nights spent cramming for never-ending tests. People assume, and for the most part I let them believe what they want. Caring what others think is a lot of work, and—with a handful of exceptions—I'm not a huge fan of work.

The truth, though, is quite the opposite. I hated school at first sight—with the direct consequence that school hated the sullen, listless child that I was right back. In the first grade, I refused to learn how to write my name, even though *Hannah* is only three letters repeated twice. In junior high, I set a school record for the highest number of consecutive detention days—what happens when you decide to take a stand and not do homework for any of your classes because they are too boring, too difficult, too useless, or all of the above. Until the end of my sophomore year, I couldn't wait to graduate and leave all of school behind: the books, the teachers, the grades, the cliques. Everything. I didn't really have a plan for *after*, except for leaving *now* behind.

I had this feeling, my entire life, that I was never going to be *enough*. I internalized pretty early that I was never going to be as good, as smart, as lovable, as wanted as my perfect older brother and my flawless older sister, and after several failed attempts at measuring up, I just decided to stop trying. Stop caring, too. By the time I was in my teens, I just wanted . . .

Well. To this day, I'm not sure what I wanted at fifteen. For my parents to stop fretting about my inadequacies, maybe. For my peers to stop asking me how I could be the sibling of two former all-star valedictorians. I wanted to stop feeling as though I were rotting in my own aimlessness, and I wanted my head to stop spinning all the time. I was confused, contradictory, and, looking back, probably a shitty teenager to be around. Sorry, Mom and Dad and the rest of the world. No hard feelings, eh?

Anyhow, I was a pretty lost kid. Until Brian McDonald, a junior, decided that asking me to homecoming by opening with "Your eyes are as blue as a sunset on Mars" might get me to say yes.

For the record, it's a horrifying pickup line. Do not recommend. Use sparingly. Use not at all, especially if—like me—the person you're trying to pick up has brown eyes and is fully aware of it. But what was an undeniable low point in the history of flirting ended up serving, if you'll forgive a very self-indulgent metaphor, as a meteorite of sorts: it crashed into my life and changed its trajectory.

In the following years, I would find out that all of my colleagues at NASA have their own origin story. Their very own space rock that altered the course of their existence and pushed them to become engineers, physicists, biologists, astronauts. It's usually an elementary school trip to the Kennedy Space Center. A Carl Sagan book under the Christmas tree. A particularly inspiring science teacher at summer camp. My encounter with Brian McDonald falls under that umbrella. It just happens to involve a guy who (allegedly) went on to moderate incel message boards on Reddit, which makes it just a tad lamer.

People obsessed with space are split into two distinct camps. The ones who want to *go* to space and crave the zero gravity, the space suits, drinking their own recycled urine. And the ones like me: what we want—oftentimes what we've wanted since our frontal lobes were still undeveloped enough to have us thinking that toe shoes are a good fashion statement—is to *know* about space. At the beginning it's simple stuff: What's it made of? Where does it end? Why do the stars not fall and crash onto our heads? Then, once we've read enough, the big topics come in: Dark matter. Multiverse. Black holes. That's when we realize how little we understand about this giant thing we're part of. When we start thinking about whether we can help produce some new knowledge.

And that's how we end up at NASA.

So, back to Brian McDonald. I didn't go to homecoming with him. (I didn't go to homecoming at all, because it wasn't really my scene, and even if it had been, I was grounded for failing an English midterm, and even if I hadn't been, fuck Brian McDonald and his poorly researched pickup lines.) However, something about the whole thing stuck with me. Why would a sunset be blue? And on a red planet, no less? It seemed like something worth knowing. So I spent the night in my room, googling dust particles in the Martian atmosphere. By the end of the week, I'd signed up for a library card and devoured three books. By the end of the month, I was studying calculus to understand concepts like thrust over time and harmonic series. By the end of the year, I had a goal. Hazy, confused, not yet fully defined, but a goal nonetheless.

For the first time in my life.

I'll spare you most of the grueling details, but I spent the rest of high school busting ass to make up for the ass I hadn't busted for the previous decade. Just picture an '80s training montage, but instead of running in the snow and doing pull-ups with a repurposed broomstick, I was hard at work on books and YouTube lectures. And it was *hard* work: wanting to understand concepts like H-R diagrams or synodic periods or syzygy did not make them any easier to grasp. Before, I'd never really *tried*. But at the tender age of sixteen, I was confronted with the unbearable turmoil that comes with trying your best and realizing that sometimes it simply isn't enough. As much as it pains me to say it, I don't have an IQ of 130. To really understand the books I wanted to read, I had to review the same concepts over, and over, and fucking *over* again. Initially I coasted on the high of finding out! new! things!, but after a while my motivation began to wane, and I started to wonder what I was even doing. I was studying a bunch of really basic science stuff, to be able to graduate to more advanced science stuff, so that one day I'd actually know all the science stuff about Mars and . . . and what then? Go on *Jeopardy!* and pick Space for 500? Didn't really seem worth it.

Then August of 2012 happened.

When the *Curiosity* rover approached the Martian atmosphere, I stayed up until one A.M. I chugged down two bottles of Diet Coke, ate peanuts for good luck, and when the landing maneuver began, I bit into my lip until it bled. The moment it safely touched the ground I screamed, I laughed, I cried, and then got grounded for a week for waking up the entire household the night before my brother left for his Peace Corps trip, but I didn't care.

In the following months I devoured every little piece of news NASA issued on *Curiosity*'s mission, and as I wondered about who was behind the images of the Gale Crater, the interpretation of the raw data, the reports on the molecular composition of the Aeolis Palus, my hazy, undefinable goal began to solidify.

NASA.

NASA was the place to be.

The summer between junior and senior years, I found a ranking of the hundred best engineering programs in the U.S. and decided to apply to the top twenty. "You should probably extend your reach. Add a few safety schools," my guidance counselor told me. "I mean, your SATs are really good and your GPA has improved a lot, but you have a bunch of"—long pause for throat clearing—"academic red flags on your permanent record."

I thought about it for a minute. Who would have figured that being a little shit for the first one and a half decades of my life would bring lasting consequences? Not me. "Okay. Fine. Let's do the top thirty-five."

As it turns out, I didn't need to. I got accepted to a whopping (drumroll, please) . . . one top-twenty school. A real winner, huh? I don't know if they misfiled my application, misplaced half of my transcripts, or had a brain fart in which the entire admissions office temporarily forgot what a promising student is supposed to look like. I put down my deposit and approximately forty-five seconds after getting my letter told Georgia Tech that I'd be attending.

No backsies.

So I moved to Atlanta, and I gave it my all. I chose the majors and the minors I knew NASA would want to see on a CV. I got the federal internships. I studied hard enough to ace the tests, did the fieldwork, applied to grad school, wrote the thesis. When I look back at the last ten years, school and work and schoolwork are pretty much all that stand out—with the notable exception of meeting Sadie and Mara, and of begrudgingly watching them carve spots for themselves in my heart. God, they take up *so much room.*

"It's like space is your whole personality," the girl I casually hooked up with during most of my sophomore year of undergrad told me. It was after I explained that no, thank you, I wasn't interested in going out for coffee to meet her friends because of a lecture on Kalpana Chawla I was planning to attend. "Do you have any other interests?" she asked. I threw her a quick "Nope," waved good-bye, and wasn't too surprised when, the following week, she didn't reply to my offer to meet up. After all, I clearly couldn't give her what she wanted.

"Is this really enough for you? Just having sex with me when you feel like it and ignoring me the rest of the time?" the guy I slept with during the last semester of my Ph.D. asked. "You just seem . . . I don't know. *Extremely* emotionally unavailable." I think maybe he was right, because it's barely been a year and I can't quite recall his face.

Exactly a decade after Brian McDonald miscolored my eyes, I applied for a NASA position. I got an interview, then a job offer, and now I'm here. But unlike the other new hires, I don't feel like Mars and I were always meant to be. There was no guarantee, no invisible string of destiny tethering me to this job, and I'm positive that I made my way here through sheer brute force, but does it matter?

Nope. Not even a little bit.

So I turn to look at Alexis. This time, her NASA necklace, her T-shirt, her tattoo—they pull a sincere smile out of me. It's been a long journey here. The destination was never a sure thing, but I have arrived, and I'm uncharacteristically, sincerely, satisfyingly happy. "Feels like home," I say, and the enthusiastic way she nods reverberates deep down inside my chest.

At one point in history, every single member of the Mars Exploration Program had their first day at NASA, too. They stood in the very spot where I'm standing right now. Gave their banking information for direct deposit, had an unflattering picture taken for their badges, shook hands with the HR reps. Complained about Houston's weather, bought terrible coffee from the cafeteria, rolled their eyes at visitors doing touristy things, let the Saturn V rocket take their breath away. Every single member of the Mars Exploration Program did this, just like I will.

I step into the conference room where some fancy NASA big shot is scheduled to talk to us, take in the window view of the Johnson Space Center and the remnants of objects that were once launched across the stars, and feel like every single inch of this place is thrilling, fascinating, electrifying, intoxicating.

Perfect.

Then I turn around. And, of course, find the very last person I wanted to see.

Two ⚙

'm finishing my initial semester of grad school when I first meet Ian Floyd, and it's Helena Harding's fault.

Dr. Harding is a lot of things: my friend Mara's Ph.D. mentor; one of the most celebrated environmental scientists of the twenty-first century; a generally crabby human being; and, last but not least, my Water Resources Engineering professor.

It is, quite honestly, an all-around shitty class: mandatory; irrelevant to my academic, professional, or personal interests; and highly focused on the intersection of the hydrologic cycle and the design of urban storm-sewer systems. For the most part, I spend the lectures wishing I were anywhere else: in line at the DMV, at the market buying magic beans, taking Analytical Transonic and Supersonic Aerodynamics. I do the least I can to pull a low B— which, in the unjust scam of graduate school, is the minimum passing grade—until week three or four of classes, when Dr. Harding introduces a new, cruel assignment that has fuck all to do with water.

"Find someone who has the engineering job you want at the end of your Ph.D. and do an informational interview with them," she tells us. "Then write a report about it. Due by the end of the semester. Don't come to me bitching about it during office hours, because I *will* call security to escort you out." I have a feeling that she's looking at me while saying it. It's probably just my guilty conscience.

"Honestly, I'm just going to ask Helena if I can interview *her*. But if you want, I think I have a cousin or something at NASA's Jet Propulsion Lab," Mara says offhandedly later that day, while we're sitting on the steps outside the Beckman Auditorium having a quick lunch before heading back to our labs.

I wouldn't say that we're close, but I've decided that I like her. A lot. At this point, my grad school attitude is some mild variant of *I did not come here to make friends*: I don't feel in competition with the rest of the program, but neither am I particularly invested in anything that isn't my work in the aeronautics lab, including getting acquainted with other students, or, you know . . . learning their names. I'm fairly sure that my lack of interest is strongly broadcasted, but either Mara didn't pick up the transmission, or she's gleefully ignoring it. She and Sadie found each other in the first couple of days, and then, for reasons I don't fully understand, decided to find me.

Hence Mara sitting next to me, telling me about her JPL contacts.

"A cousin or something?" I ask, curious. It seems a bit sketchy. "You *think*?"

"Yeah, I'm not sure." She shrugs and continues to make her way through a Tupperware of broccoli, an apple, and approximately two fucktons of Cheez-Its. "I don't really know much about him. His parents divorced, then people in my family had arguments and stopped talking to each other. There was a lot of prime Floyd dysfunction happening, so I haven't actually spoken to him in years. But I heard from one of my other cousins that he was working on that thing that landed on Mars back when we were in high school. It was called something like . . . *Contingency*, or *Carpentry*, or *Crudity*—"

"The *Curiosity* rover?"

"Yes! Maybe?"

I put my sandwich down. Swallow my bite. Clear my throat. "Your cousin *or something* was on the *Curiosity* rover team."

"I think so. Do the dates add up? Maybe it was some kind of summer internship? But honestly, it might just be Floyd family lore. I have an aunt who insists that we're related to the Finnish royals, and according to Wikipedia there are no Finnish royals. So." She shrugs and pops another handful of Cheez-Its in her mouth. "Would you like me to ask around, though? For the assignment?"

I nod. And I don't think much about it until a month or so later. By then, through means that I am still unable to divine, Mara and Sadie have managed to worm their way into my heart, causing me to amend my previous *I did not come here to make friends* stance to a slightly altered *I did not come here to make friends, but hurt my weird Cheez-It friend or my other weird soccer friend and I will beat you up with a lead pipe till you piss blood for the rest of your life.* Truculent? Perhaps. I feel little, but surprisingly deeply.

"By the way, I sent you my cousin-or-something's contact info a while ago," Mara tells me one night. We're at the cheapest grad bar we've been able to find. She's on her second Midori sour of the night. "Did you get it?"

I raise my eyebrow. "Is that the random string of numbers you emailed me three days ago? With no subject line, no text, no explanations? The one I figured was just you tracking your lottery dream numbers?"

"Sounds like it, yeah."

Sadie and I exchange a long look.

"Hey, you ungrateful goblin, I had to call about fifteen people I'd sworn never to talk to again to get Ian's number. *And* I had to have my evil great-aunt Delphina promise to blackmail him into saying yes once you reach out to ask for a meeting. So you better use that number, and you better play the Mega Millions."

"If you win," Sadie added, "we split three ways."

"Of course." I hide my smile in my glass. "What's he like, anyway?"

"Who?"

"The cousin-or-something. Ian, you said?"

"Yup. Ian Floyd." Mara thinks about it for a second. "Can't really say, because I've met him at, like, two Thanksgivings fifteen years ago, before his parents split. Then his mom moved him to Canada and . . . I don't even know, honestly. The only thing I remember is that he was tall. But he was also a few years older than me? So maybe he's actually three feet. Oh, also, his hair is more brown? Which is kind of rare for a Floyd. I know it's scientifically unsound, but our brand of ginger is *not* recessive."

Great-Aunt Delphina's emotional manipulation game is clearly on point, because when my assignment's deadline approaches and I text Ian Floyd in a panic, asking for an informational interview—whatever the hell *that* is—he replies within hours with an enthusiastic:

IAN: Sure.

HANNAH: Thanks. I'm assuming you're in Houston. Should
we do virtual? Skype? Zoom? FaceTime?

IAN: I'm in Pasadena at JPL for the next three days, but
virtual works.

The Jet Propulsion Lab. Hmm.

I drum my fingers on my mattress, pondering. Virtual would
be so much easier. And it would be shorter. But as much as I hate
the idea of writing a report for Helena's class, I do want to ask this
guy a million questions about *Curiosity*. Plus, he's Mara's mysterious relative, and my curiosity is piqued.

No pun intended.

HANNAH: Let's meet in person. The least I can do is buy
you coffee. Sound good?

No reply for a few minutes. And then, a very succinct That
works. For some reason, it makes me smile.

✿✿✿

My first thought upon entering the coffee shop is that Mara
is full of shit.

To the brim.

The second: I should really double-check the text Ian sent me.
Make sure that he really said I'll be wearing jeans and a gray t-shirt
like I seem to remember. Of course, it would be a little redundant,
especially considering that the coffee shop where he asked to meet

is currently populated by only three people: a barista, busy doing a pen-and-paper sudoku like it's 2007; me, standing in the entrance and looking around, confused; and a man, sitting at the table closest to the entrance, gazing pensively through the glass windows.

He's wearing jeans and a gray T-shirt, which would suggest: Ian. The problem . . .

His hair is the problem. Because, despite what Mara said, it's most definitely *not* brown. Maybe a fraction of a shade darker than her bright, carroty orange, but . . . really *not* brown. I'm ready to dial her number and demand to know what ridiculous ginger scale the Floyds operate on when the man slowly stands and asks, "Hannah?"

I have no idea how tall Ian is, but he's much closer to eight feet than to three. And I find it very interesting that Mara claims to barely know him, considering that they look like they could be siblings, not just because of the aggressively red hair, but also because of the dark-blue eyes, and the dusting of freckles over pale skin, and . . .

I blink. Then I blink again. If three seconds ago someone had asked me whether I'm the type to multiple blink at the sight of some guy, I'd have laughed in their face. *This* guy, though . . .

I guess I stand corrected.

"Ian?" I smile, recovering from the surprise. "Mara's cousin?"

He frowns, as if momentarily blanking on Mara's name. "Ah, yes." He nods. Only once. "Apparently," he adds, which makes me laugh. He waits for me to take a seat across from him before folding back into his chair. I notice that he doesn't hold out his hand, nor does he smile. Interesting. "Thank you for agreeing to meet with me."

"No problem." His voice is low-pitched but clear. Deep timbre.

Confident; polite but not too friendly. I'm usually fairly good at reading people, and my guess for him is that he's not quite enthused to be here. He'd probably rather be doing whatever it is that he came to California to do, but he's a nice guy, and he's planning to make a valiant effort to avoid letting me know.

He just doesn't seem to be particularly good at faking it, which is . . . kinda cute.

"I hope I didn't mess up your day."

He shakes his head—an obvious lie—and I take the opportunity to study him. He seems . . . quiet. The silent type, aloof, a little stiff. Big, more lumberjack than engineer. I briefly wonder if he's military personnel, but the day-old stubble on his face tells me it's unlikely.

And such an intriguing, handsome face it is. His nose looks like it was broken at some point, maybe in a fight or a sports injury, and never bothered to heal back quite perfectly. His hair—*red*—is short and a little mussed, more *I've been up working since six* A.M. than artful styling. I watch him scratch his—*big*—neck, then cross his—*wide*—biceps on his—*broad*—chest. He gives me a patient, expectant look, like he's fully committed to answering all my questions.

He is, physically, the opposite of me. Of my small bones and tanned complexion. My hair, eyes, sometimes even my *soul*, are black-hole dark. And here he is, Martian red and ocean blue.

"What can I get you?" a voice asks. I turn and find Sudoku Boy standing right next to our table. Right. Coffee place. Where people consume beverages.

"Iced tea, please."

He walks away without a word and I look at Ian once again. I'm itching to text Mara. Your cousin looks like a slightly jacked version of Prince Harry. Maybe you should have kept in touch?

"So." I cross my hands and lean my elbows on the table. "What does she have on you?"

He tilts his head. "She?"

"Great-Aunt Delphina." He blinks twice. I smile and continue, "I mean, it's a Thursday afternoon. You're in California for a handful of days. I'm sure you have something better to do than meet up with your long-lost cousin's friend."

His eyes widen for a split second. Then his expression levels back to neutral. "It's fine."

"Is it an embarrassing baby pic?"

He shakes his head. "I don't mind helping out."

"I see. A baby *video*, then?"

He's silent for a moment before saying, "As I said, it's not a problem." He looks like he isn't used to people pushing him, which is unsurprising. There is something subtly removed about him. Vaguely distant and intimidating. Like he's not *quite* reachable. It makes me want to get closer and poke.

"A baby video of you . . . running around in the kiddie pool? Picking your nose? Rummaging around the back of your diaper?"

"I—"

Sudoku Boy drops off my iced tea in a plastic cup. Ian's eyes follow him for a few seconds, then return to mine with an interesting mix of stoic resignation. "It was more of a toddler video," he says cautiously, like he's surprising even himself.

"Ah." I grin into my tea. It's both too sweet and too sour. With a subtle aftertaste of gross. "Do tell."

"You don't want to know."

"Oh, I'm positive I do."

"It's bad."

"You're really selling it to me."

The left corner of his mouth curves upward, a small hint of

amusement that's not quite fully there yet. I have an odd stray thought: *I bet his smile is lopsided. Beautiful, too.* "The video was taken at a Lowe's. With my older brother's new camcorder, sometime in the late '90s," he tells me.

"At a Lowe's? Can't be *that* bad, then."

He sighs, impassive. "I was around three or four. And they had one of those bathroom displays. The ones with model sinks and showers and vanities. And toilets, naturally."

I press my lips together. This is going to be fun. "Naturally."

"I don't really remember what happened, but apparently I needed to use the restroom. And when I saw the display I was . . . inspired."

"No way."

"In my defense, I was very young."

He scratches his nose, and I laugh. "Oh my God."

"With no concept of sewage systems."

"Right. Sure. Honest mistake." I cannot stop laughing. "How did Great-Aunt Delphina get a copy of the video?"

"Officially: unclear. But I'm fairly sure my brother made CDs of it. Sent them to local TV stations and whatnot." He gestures vaguely, and his forearm is dusted with freckles and pale-red hair. I want to grab his wrist, hold it in front of my eyes, study it at my leisure. Trace, smell, touch. "I haven't spent a holiday with the Floyd side of the family in twenty years, but I'm told that the video is a source of great entertainment for all age groups at Thanksgiving."

"I bet it's the pièce de résistance. I bet they press play right after the turducken comes out."

"Yeah. You'd probably win." He seems quietly resigned. A big man with a put-upon-but-enduring air. In an utterly charming way.

"But how do you blackmail someone from this? How much worse can it get?"

He sighs again. His broad shoulders lift, then fall. "When my aunt called, she briefly mentioned uploading it on Facebook. Tagging the NASA official page."

I gasp into my hand. I shouldn't laugh. This is horrible. But. "Are you serious?"

"It's not a healthy family."

"No shit."

He shrugs, like he's past caring. "At least they're not trying to extort money out of me yet."

"Right." I nod solemnly and collect my features into what hopefully passes for a compassionate, respectful expression. "The assignment I told you about is for my Water Resources class, so this is surprisingly on topic. And I am truly sorry that you got stuck with meeting your little cousin's friend because you publicly urinated in a Lowe's when you barely knew how to talk."

Ian's eyes settle on me, as if to size me up. I thought I had his full attention from the moment I sat down, but I realize that I was wrong. For the first time, he's looking at me like he's interested in actually *seeing* me. He studies me, assesses me, and my first impression of him—*detached, distant*—instantly evaporates. There is something nearly palpable about his presence: a warm, tingling sensation climbing up my spine.

"I don't mind," he says again. I smile, because I know that this time he means it.

"Good." I push my tea to the side. "So, what would you be doing right now, if three-year-old you had known about sanitary sewers?"

This time his smile is a tad more defined. I'm winning him over, which is good, very good, because I'm rapidly developing a thing for the contrast between his eyelashes (*red!*) and his deep-set eyes (*blue!*). "I'd probably be running a bunch of tests."

"At the Jet Propulsion Lab?"

He nods.

"Tests on . . . ?"

"A rover."

"Oh." My heart skips three beats. "For space exploration?"

"Mars."

I lean closer, not even bothering to play it like I'm not avidly interested. "Is that your current project?"

"One of them, yeah."

"And what are the tests for?"

"Mostly attitude, figuring out where the ship is positioned in three-dimensional space. Pointing, too."

"You work on a gyroscope?"

"Yes. My team is perfecting the gyroscope so that once the rover is on Mars, it knows where it is, what it's looking at. Informs the other systems about its coordinates and movements, too."

My heart is now fully pitter-pattering. This sounds . . . wow. Pornographic, almost. Exactly my jam. "And you do this in Houston? At the Space Center?"

"Usually. But I come up here when there are issues. I've been struggling with the imagery, and the feed update keeps lagging even though it shouldn't, and—" He shakes his head, as if catching himself halfway through a rant that's been playing over and over in his mind. But I finally know what he'd rather be doing.

And I sure can't blame him.

"Did they send your entire team here?" I ask.

He tilts his head, like he has no idea where I'm going with this. "Just me."

"So your team leader is not around."

"My team leader?"

"Yeah. Is your boss around?"

He is silent for a second. Two. Three. Four? What the— Ah.

"You *are* the team leader," I say.

He nods once. A little stiff. Almost apologetic.

"How old are you?" I ask.

"Twenty-five." A pause. "Next month."

Whoa. I'm twenty-two. "Isn't that early to be a team leader?"

"I'm . . . not sure," he says, even though I can tell that he *is* sure, and that he *is* exceptional, and that even though he knows it, the thought makes him more than a little uncomfortable. I picture myself saying something flirtatious and inappropriate back—*Wow, handsome* and *smart*—and wonder how he'd react. Probably not well.

Not that I'm going to hit on my informational interviewee. Even *I* know better. Plus, he's not really my type.

"Okay, what's the security like at JPL?" I've never been. I know it's loosely connected with Caltech, but that's about it.

"Depends," he says cautiously, like he still cannot follow my train of thought.

"What about your office? Is it a restricted area?"

"No. Why—"

"Awesome, then." I stand, dig into my pockets for a few dollars to leave next to my unfinished tea, and then close my fingers around Ian's wrist. His skin glows with warmth and taut muscles as I pull him up from the table, and even though he's probably twice as big and ten times stronger than me, he lets me lead him away from the table. I let go of him the second we're out of the coffee shop, but he keeps following me.

"Hannah? What—where . . . ?"

"I don't see why we can't do this weird informational interview thing, get some work done, *and* have fun."

"What?"

With a grin, I look at him over my shoulder. "Think of it as sticking it to evil Great-Aunt Delphina."

I doubt he fully understands, but the corner of his mouth lifts again, and that's good enough for me.

✿✿✿

See this thread right here? It's mostly about the behavior of one of the rover's sensors, the LN-200. We combine its information with the one provided by the encoders on the wheels to figure out positioning."

"Huh. So the sensor *doesn't* run constantly?"

Ian turns to me, away from the chunk of programming code he's been showing me. We're sitting in front of his triple-monitor computer, side by side at his desk, which is a giant, pristine expanse with a stunning view of the floodplain JPL was built on. When I mentioned how clean his workspace was, he pointed out that it's only because it's a guest office. But when I asked him if his usual desk back in Houston is any messier, he glanced away before the corner of his lip twitched.

I am almost certain he's starting to think that I'm not a total waste of time.

"No, it doesn't run constantly. How can you tell?"

I gesture toward the lines of code, and the back of my hand brushes against something hard and warm: Ian's shoulder. We're sitting closer than we were at the coffee shop, but no closer than I'd feel comfortable being with one of the—always unpleasant, often offensive—guys in my Ph.D. cohort. I guess my crossed knees kind of pressed against his leg earlier, but that's it. No big deal. "It's in there, no?"

The section is in C++. Which happens to be the very first language I taught myself back in high school, when every single Google search for "Skills + Necessary + NASA" led to the sad result of "Programming." Python came after. Then SQL. Then HAL/S. For each language, I started out convinced that chewing on glass would surely be preferable. Then, at some point along the way, I began thinking in terms of functions, variables, conditional loops. A little after that, reading code became a bit like inspecting the label on the back of the conditioner bottle while showering: not particularly fun, but overall easy. I do have *some* talents, apparently.

"Yeah." He's still looking at me. Not surprised, precisely. Not impressed, either. Intrigued, maybe? "Yes, it is."

I rest my chin on my palm and chew on my lower lip, considering the code. "Is it because of the limited amount of solar power?"

"Yes."

"And I bet it prevents gyro drift errors during the stationary period?"

"Correct." He nods, and I'm momentarily distracted by his jawline. Or maybe it's the cheekbones. They're defined, angular in a way that makes me wish I had a protractor in my pocket.

"It's not all automated, right? Earth-based personnel can direct tools?"

"They can, depending on the attitude."

"Does the onboard flight software have specific requirements?"

"The pointing of the antenna relative to Earth, and . . ." He stops. His eyes fall on my chewed-on lip, then quickly move away. "You ask a lot of questions."

I tilt my head. "*Bad* questions?"

Silence. "No." More silence as he studies me. "Remarkably good questions."

"Can I ask a few more, then?" I grin at him, aiming for cheeky, curious to see where it'll take us.

He hesitates before nodding. "Can I ask you some, too?"

I laugh. "Like what? Would you like me to list the specs of the maze-solving bot I built for my Intro to Robotics class back in college?"

"You built a maze-solving robot?"

"Yup. Four-wheel, all-terrain, Bluetooth module. Solar powered. Her name was Ruthie, and when I set her free at a corn maze somewhere near Atlanta, she got out in about three minutes. Scared the crap out of the children, too."

He is fully smiling now. He has a heart-stopping dimple on his left cheek, and . . . Okay, fine: he's *aggressively* hot. Despite the red hair, or because of it. "You still have her?"

"Nope. To celebrate, I got wasted at a bar that didn't bother to check IDs and ended up leaving her at some University of Georgia frat house. I didn't want to go back, because those places are *scary*, so I gave up on Ruthie and just built an electronic arm for my Robotics final." I sigh and look into the mid-distance. "I'll need a lot of therapy before I can become a mother."

He chuckles. The sound is low, warm, maybe even shiver-inducing. I need a second to regroup.

I've settled—at some point on our five-minute walk here, probably when he pulled out a pretty effortless scowl to intimidate the security guard into letting me in despite my lack of ID—on the reason I can't quite pin Ian down. He is, very simply, a never-before-experienced mix of cute and overwhelmingly masculine. With a complex, layered air about him. It spells simultaneously

Do not piss me off because I don't fuck around and *Ma'am, let me carry those groceries for you.*

Not my usual fare, not at all. I like flirting, and I like sex, and I like hooking up with people, but I'm really, *really* picky about my partners. It doesn't take a lot to turn me off someone, and I almost exclusively gravitate toward the cheerful, spontaneous, fun-loving type. I'm into extroverts who love banter and are easy to talk to, the less intense the better. Ian seems to be the diametrical opposite of that, and yet . . . And yet, even *I* can see how there is something fundamentally attractive about him. Would I try to pick him up at a bar? Hm. Unclear.

Will I try to pick him up after the end of this informational interview? Hm. *Also* unclear. I know I say I wouldn't, but . . . things change.

"Okay. My question now. Mara—Mara Floyd, your cousin or something—said that you were working directly on the *Curiosity* team?" He nods. "But you were, what? Eighteen?"

"Around that age, yeah."

"Were you an intern?"

He pauses before shaking his head but doesn't elaborate.

"So you just . . . happened to be hanging out with mission control? Chilling with your space bros while they landed their remote-control rover on Mars?"

His lips twitch. "I was a team member."

"A team member at eighteen?" My eyebrow lifts, and he looks away.

"I . . . graduated early."

"High school? Or college?"

Silence. "Both."

"I see."

He briefly scratches the side of his neck, and there again is this feeling that he's not quite used to being asked questions about himself. That most people take a look at him, decide that he's just a touch too aloof and detached, and give up on figuring him out.

I study him, more curious than ever. "So . . . were you one of those kids who was really advanced for their age and skipped half a dozen grades? And then ended up joining the workforce while still ridiculously young?" *And maybe your psychosocial development was still kind of ongoing, but you were never really sharing professional or academic settings with people in your age group, just much older ones who likely avoided you and were a little intimidated by your intelligence and success, which meant being the odd man out for the entirety of your formative years and having a 401(k) before your first date?*

His eyes widen. "I . . . Yeah. Were you one, too?"

I laugh. "Oh no. I was a total dumbass. Still am, for the most part. I just thought it might be a good guess." It fits the persona, too. He doesn't come across as insecure, not quite, but he's cautious. Withdrawn.

I lean back in my chair, feeling the thrill of having puzzled him out a little better. I'm usually not this dedicated to figuring out the backstory of everyone I meet, but Ian is just interesting.

No. He's *fascinating.*

"So, how was it?"

He blinks. "How was what?"

"Being there with mission control when *Curiosity* landed. How was it?"

His expression instantly transforms. "It was . . ." He's staring down at his feet, as if remembering. He looks awestruck.

"*That* good?"

"Yeah. It was . . . Yeah." He chuckles again. God, it really does sound great.

"It looked like it. From TV, I mean."

"You watched it?"

"Yup. I was on the East Coast, so I stayed up late and all that. Looked up at the sky out of my bedroom window and cried a little bit."

He nods, and suddenly *he* is studying *me*. "Is that why you're in grad school? You want to work on future rovers?"

"That would be amazing. But anything that's space exploration will do."

"NASA can put your maze-solving skills to great use." His dimple is back, and I laugh.

"Hey, I can do other things. For instance . . ." I point at the third monitor on the desk, the one farthest away from me. It displays a piece of code Ian hasn't walked me through yet. "Want me to help you debug that?" He gives me a confused look. "What? It's code. It's always nice to have a second pair of eyes."

"You don't have to—"

"There's an error on the fifth line."

He frowns. Then he scans the code for a second. Then he turns to me, to the monitor, to me again with an even bigger frown. I brace, half expecting him to lash out defensively and deny the error. I'm familiar with the crumbling egos of men, and I'm pretty sure it's what any of the guys in my Ph.D. class would do. But Ian surprises me: he nods, fixes the mistake I pointed out, and looks nothing but grateful.

Wow. A male engineer who's *not* an asshole. The bar is pretty low, but I'm nevertheless impressed.

"Would you really be up for going through the rest of the code with me?" he asks cautiously, surprising me even more. The contrast between his gentle tone and how . . . how *big* and *guarded* he is almost has me smiling. "It's the work-around to fix the two-second delay in the pointing issue. I was going to ask one of my engineers in Houston to debug, but . . ."

"I got you." I roll my chair closer to Ian's. My knee presses against his, and I nearly move it away automatically, but in a split-second decision I decide to leave it there.

An experiment of sorts. Testing the waters. Taking the temperature.

I wait for him to shift back, but instead he studies me and says, "It's a few hundred lines. I'm supposed to be helping *you*. Are you sure—"

"It's fine. When I write my report, I'll just pretend I asked you a bunch of questions about your journey and make up the answers." Just to mess with him, I add, "Don't worry, I'll mention how having the clap did *not* set you back on your road to NASA." He scowls, which has me laughing, and then I'm going over the code with him for five, ten minutes. Fifteen. The light softens to late-afternoon hues, and over an hour goes by while we're side by side, blinking at the monitors.

Honestly, it's pretty basic rubber duck debugging: he's explaining out loud what he's trying to do, which helps him work through critical chunks, and also figuring out better ways to go about it. But I'm a pretty happy rubber duck. I like listening to his low, even voice. I like that he seems to consider every single thing I say and never dismisses anything outright. I like that when he's thinking hard, he closes his eyes, and his lashes are crimson half-moons against his skin. I like that he builds meticulously pristine code with no memory leakage, and I like that when his biceps brushes against my shoulder all I feel is solid warmth. I like his short, crisp functions, and the way he smells clean and masculine and a bit dark.

Okay. So he's *not* my type.

I do like him, though.

Would Mara mind it if I shamelessly offered myself to her kin at the informational interview she kindly set up? I would normally just go for it, but this friendship business can be a bit of a burden. That said, maybe I can safely assume that she won't care, considering that she doesn't seem to know how exactly she and Ian are related.

Plus, she's a generous soul. She'd want her friend and her cousin-or-something to get laid.

"Did you get randomly assigned to the Attitude and Position Estimation team?" I ask him when we get to the last few lines of code.

"No." He lets out a small laugh. His profile is a work of near perfection, even with the broken nose. "Clawed my way there, actually."

"Oh?"

He saves and closes our work with a few rapid keystrokes. "For *Curiosity,* I joined the team pretty late into the development stage, and I mostly focused on launch."

"Did you like it?"

"A lot." He angles his chair to face me. Our knees, elbows, shoulders have been brushing so much, the closeness feels familiar by now. So does the liquid warmth under my belly button. "But after that I began working on *Perseverance* and I asked for a change. Something actually related to the rover being on Mars as opposed to three hours in Cape Canaveral."

"So they put you on A & PE?"

"First, I joined the NASA expedition to Norway's Mars Analog site."

I inhale audibly. "AMASE?" The Arctic Mars Analog Svalbard Expedition (AMASE, for friends) is what happens when a bunch of nerds travel to Norway, in the Bockfjorden area of Svalbard. One might think that the North Pole has nothing to do with space, but because of all the volcanic activity and glaciers it's actually the place on Earth most similar to Mars. It even has one-of-a-kind carbonate spherules that are almost identical to the ones we found on meteorites of Martian origin. NASA researchers like to use it as a location to test the functionality of equipment they plan to send on space exploration missions, collect samples, examine fun science questions that can prepare astronauts for future space missions.

I want to be part of it so bad, a shiver runs down my spine.

"Yup. When I came back I asked for an A & PE placement, which apparently *everyone* wanted. To the point that the mission leader sent out a NASA-wide email asking whether we thought we'd get double pay and free beer."

"Did you?"

I laugh at the look he gives me. He is just so hilariously, deliciously *teasable*. "Why did everyone want to be part of that team, anyway?"

He shrugs. "I'm not sure why everyone else did. I assume because it's challenging. Lots of high-risk, high-reward projects. But for me it was . . ." He glances out the window, at a maple tree on the JPL campus. Actually, no: I think he might be looking up. At the sky. "It just felt like . . ." He trails off, as though not sure how to continue.

"Like it was as close as possible to actually being on Mars? With the rover?" I ask him.

His eyes return to me. "Yeah." He seems surprised. Like I managed to put something elusive into words. "Yeah, that's exactly it."

I nod, because I get it. The idea of helping build something that will explore Mars, the idea of being able to control where it goes and what it does . . . that does it for me, too.

Ian and I study each other for a few seconds in silence, both of us smiling faintly. Long enough for the idea that's been bouncing in my head to solidify once and for all.

Yeah. I'm gonna go for it. *Sorry, Mara. I like your cousin-or-something a little too much to pass this up.*

"Okay, I do have a career question for you. To save our informational interview appearances."

"Shoot."

"So, I graduate with my Ph.D. Which should take me about four more years."

"That's a while," he says, his tone a bit unreadable.

Yes, it feels like forever. "Not *that* long. So, I graduate, and I decide that I want to work at NASA and not for some weirdo billionaire who treats space exploration like it's his own homemade penis-enlargement remedy."

Ian's nod is pained. "Wise."

"What would make me look like a strong candidate? What does a great application package look like?"

He mulls it over. "I'm not sure. For my team, I would usually hire internally. But I'm almost certain I still have my application materials on my old laptop. I could send them to you."

Okay. Perfect. Great.

The opening I was waiting for.

My heart rate picks up. Warmth twists in my lower stomach. I lean forward with a smile, feeling like I'm finally in my element. This, *this*, is what I know best. Depending on how busy I am with school, or work, or binge-watching K-dramas, I do this about once a week. Which amounts to quite a bit of practice. "Maybe I could come to your place?" I say, finding the sweet spot between comically suggestive and *Let's get together to play Cards Against Humanity*. "And you could show me?"

"I meant—in Houston. My laptop's in Houston."

"So you *didn't* bring your 2010 laptop to Pasadena?"

He smiles. "Knew I'd forgotten something."

"Sure did." I meet his eyes squarely. Lean half an inch closer. "Then maybe I can still come to your place, and we could do something else?"

He gives me a half-puzzled look. "Do what?"

I press my lips together. *Okay. Maybe I overestimated my flirting skills. Have I, though? I don't think so.* "Really?" I ask, amused. "Am I *that* bad at it?"

"I'm sorry, I don't follow." Ian's expression is all arrested confusion, like I just suddenly started talking in an Australian accent. "Bad at what?"

"At hitting on you, Ian."

I can pinpoint the precise, exact moment the meaning of my words sinks into the language part of his brain. He blinks a few times. Then his big body goes still in a tight, impossible, *vibrating* way, like his internal software is buffering through an unpredictable set of updates.

He looks absolutely, almost *charmingly* mystified, and something occurs to me: I've struck up flirtatious conversations with dozens of guys and girls at parties, bars, laundromats, gyms, bookstores, seminars, muddy obstacle courses, greenhouses— even, on one memorable occasion, in the waiting room of a Planned Parenthood—and . . . *no one* has ever been this clueless. No one. So maybe he was just *pretending* not to get it. Maybe he was hoping I'd back off.

Shit.

"I'm sorry." I straighten and roll my chair back, giving him a few inches of space. "I'm making you uncomfortable."

"No. No, I—" He's finally rebooting. Shaking his head. "No, you aren't, I'm just—"

"A bit freaked out?" I smile reassuringly, trying to signal that it's okay. I can take a no. I'm a big girl. "It's fine. Let's forget I said anything. But do email me your application package once you're back home, please. I promise I won't reply with unsolicited nudes."

"No, it's not that . . ." He closes his eyes and pinches the bridge of his nose. His cheekbones look rosier than before. His lips move, trying to form words for a few seconds, until he settles on: "It's just . . . unexpected."

Oh. I tilt my head. "Why?" I thought I'd been laying it on pretty thick.

"Because." His large hand gestures in my direction. He swallows, and I watch his throat work. "Just . . . look at you."

I actually do it. I look down at myself, taking in my crossed legs, my khaki shorts, my plain black tee. My body is in its usual condition: Tall. Wiry. A bit scrawny. Olive-skinned. I even shaved this morning. Maybe. I can't remember. Point is, I look okay.

So I say it—"I look okay"—which should sound confident but comes out a bit petulant. It's not that I think I'm hot shit, but I refuse to be insecure about my appearance. I like myself. Historically, the people I've wanted to sleep with have liked me, too. My body does its job as a means to an end. It manages to let me kayak around California lakes without muscle aches the following day, and it digests lactose like it's an Olympic discipline. That's all that matters.

But his reply is: "You don't look okay," and . . . no.

"Really." My tone is icy. Is Ian Floyd trying to imply that he's out of my reach? Because if so, I *will* slap him. "How do I look, then?"

"Just . . ." He swallows again. "I . . . Women like you don't usually . . ."

"Women *like me*." Wow. Sounds like I'll actually have to slap him. "What's that? Because—"

"Beautiful. You are very, *very* beautiful. Probably the most . . . And you're obviously smart and funny, so . . ." He gives me a helpless look, suddenly looking less like a genius NASA team leader built like a cedar tree and more . . . boyish. Young. "Is this some kind of joke?"

I study him through squinting eyes, revising my earlier assessment. Perhaps my conclusions were premature, and it's not quite correct that no one can be this clueless. Perhaps *someone* can.

Ian, for instance. Ian, who could probably make good money as a stock-photo model, tags: Hot Guy, Ginger, Massive. I saw about four people check him out on our way here, but he apparently has no idea that he could be fancast to play the hot Weasley brother. Absolutely zero awareness of how glorious he is.

I grin, suddenly charmed. "Can I ask you a question?" I roll myself closer, and I'm not sure when that happened, but he angled his chair so that my knees end up slotted between his. Nice. "It's a bit forward."

He looks down at our touching legs and nods. As usual, only once.

"Can I kiss you? Like, right now?"

"I . . ." He stares. Then blinks. Then mouths something that's not a word.

My grin widens. "That's not no, is it?"

"No." He shakes his head. His eyes are fixed on my lips, the black of his pupils swallowing the blue. "It's not."

"Okay, then."

It's pretty simple, standing from my chair and leaning forward on his. My palms find the armrests and press against them, and for a long moment I stay right there, caging this bear-size man who could flick me away with his little finger but doesn't. Instead he looks up at me like I'm wondrous and beautiful and awe-inspiring, like I'm a gift, like he's a bit dumbstruck.

Like he *really* wants me to kiss him. So I close that last inch and I do. And it's . . .

Kind of awkward, to be honest. Not bad. Just a little hesitant. His lips part in a gasp when they touch mine, and for a split second, a terrifying thought occurs to me.

It's his first kiss. Is it? Oh my God, it's his first kiss. Am I really giving someone their first—

Ian angles his head, pushes his mouth against mine, and it destroys my train of thought. I'm not sure how he manages, but whatever he's doing with his lips and teeth feels massively, aggressively right. I whimper when his tongue meets mine. He growls in response, something rumbly and deep in his throat.

Okay. This is no first kiss. This is a fucking *masterpiece.*

He's probably two hundred pounds of muscles and I have no clue whether the chair can hold us both, but I decide to live dangerously: I straddle Ian's lap, feeling his sharp inhale vibrate through my body. For a suspended second our lips part and his eyes hold mine, like we're both waiting for every piece of furniture in the room to collapse. But JPL must be investing in sturdy decor.

"*That* was high-risk, high-reward," I say, and I'm surprised at how short my breath is already. The room is silent, bathed in warm light. I let out a single, shaky laugh, and I realize where Ian's hand is: hovering half an inch above my waist. Warm. Eager. Ready to snap.

"Can I—?" he asks.

"Yes." I laugh into his mouth. "You *can* touch me. It's the whole point of—"

I don't get to finish, because the second he has permission his hands are everywhere, one on my nape, pulling my lips into his, the other on the small of my back. The moment my chest presses against his, he does another of those low, rough sounds—but ten times deeper, like it comes from his very core. He's all scratchy stubble, warm unwieldy flesh, and out of the corner of my eye I see only red, red, *so much red*.

"I'm *in love* with your freckles," I say, right before nipping at one on his jaw. "I thought about licking them the moment I saw you." I make my way to the hollow of his ear. He exhales, sharp.

"When I saw you, I—" I suck on the skin of his throat, and he stutters. "I thought you were a little too beautiful," he finishes, breathless. His hands are traveling under my shirt, up my spine, cautiously tracing the edges of my bra. He smells magnificent, clean and serious and warm.

"Too beautiful for what?"

"For everything. Too beautiful to look at, even." His grip on my waist tightens. "Hannah, you—"

I am grinding my groin against his. Which is probably the reason we both sound like we're running a marathon. And in my defense, I really only meant for this to be a kiss, but yeah. No. I'm not stopping, and judging from the way his fingers dip into the back of my shorts to cup my ass cheek and press me tighter into his hard cock, he's not planning to, either.

"Does anyone else use this office?" I ask. I'm not shy, but this is . . . good. No-interruptions-please good. I-don't-want-to-wait-till-we-get-home good. I'm-going-to-come-in-about-two-minutes good.

He shakes his head, and I could cry with happiness, but I don't have time. It's like we were playing before, and now we're in earnest. We're barely kissing, uncoordinated, unfocused, just grinding against each other, and I chase the feeling of his body against mine, the high of being so close, his erection between my legs as we both make hushed, grunting, obscene noises, as we both try to get closer, to get more contact, skin, heat, friction, friction, friction, I need *more friction—*

"*Shit.*" I cannot get *enough.* It's not a good position, and I hate this stupid chair, and this is driving me *insane.* I let out a loud, infuriated groan and sink my teeth deep into his neck, like I am made of heat and frustration, and—

Somehow, Ian knows exactly what I need. Because he stands from the cursed chair with a muted, "It's okay, it's okay, I've got you." He takes me right with him and does something that could technically qualify as destroying NASA property to make enough room for us. A moment later I'm sitting on the desk, and all of a sudden we can both move like we want to. He opens my legs with his palms and slots his own right between them, and—

Finally. The friction is—this is precisely what I asked for, precisely what I *needed—*

"Yes," I breathe out.

"Yeah?" I don't even need to move my hips. His hand slides down to grip my ass, and he somehow knows exactly how to angle me, how the hem of my shorts can brush against my clit. "Like this?" I feel his cock iron-hard on my hip and I make mewling, embarrassing, pleading sounds into the hollow of his throat, murmuring incomprehensibly about how good this is, how grateful I am, how

I'm going to do the same for him when we finally fuck, how I'm going to do *whatever he wants*—

"Stop," he pants into my mouth, urgent, a little desperate. "You need to be quiet, or I'm going to—I just want to—"

I laugh against his cheek, reedy, hushed. My thighs are starting to shake. There is a liquid, pressing heat swelling in my abdomen. "Want to—*ah*—want to what?"

"I just want to make you come."

It sends me right over the edge. Into something that's nothing like my usual, run-of-the-mill orgasm. Those tend to start like small fractures and then slowly, gradually deepen into something lovely and relaxing. Those are fun, good fun, but this . . . This pleasure is sudden and violent. It splinters into me like a wonderful, terrible explosion, new and frightening and fantastic, and it goes on and on, as though every heart-stopping, delicious second of it is being squeezed out of me. I screw my eyes shut, clutch Ian's shoulders, and whimper into his throat, listening to the hushed "Fuck. *Fuck*," he mouths into my collarbone. I was so sure I knew what my body was capable of, but this feels somewhere well beyond it.

And somehow, on top of knowing exactly how to get me there, Ian also knows when to stop. The very moment it all becomes unbearable, his arms tighten around me, and his thigh becomes a solid, still weight between mine. I twine my arms around his neck, hide my face in his throat, and wait for my body to recover.

"Well," I say. My voice is raspier than I ever remember hearing it. There's a wireless keyboard on the floor, cables dangling by my thigh, and if I move even half an inch back, I'll destroy one, maybe two monitors. "Well," I repeat. I let out a peal of winded laughter against his skin.

"You okay?" he asks, pulling back to meet my eyes. His hands are trembling slightly against my back. Because, I assume, I came.

And he didn't. Which is very unfair. I just had a life-defining or-gasm and can't really remember my own name, but even in this state I can grasp the injustice of it all.

"I'm . . . great." I laugh again. "You?"

He smiles. "I'm pretty great, to be—" I drag my hand down be-tween us, palm flush against the front of his jeans, and his mouth snaps shut.

Okay. So he has a big cock. To exactly no one's surprise. This man is going to be fantastic in bed. Phenomenal. The best sex I've ever had with a dude. And I've had *a lot*.

"What do you want?" I ask. His eyes are dark, unseeing. I cup my hand around the outline of his erection, rub the heel of my palm against the length, arch up to whisper in the curve of his ear, "Can I go down on you?"

The noise Ian makes is rough and guttural, and it takes me about three seconds to realize that he's already coming, groaning into my skin, trapping my hand between our bodies. I feel him shudder, and this big man coming apart against me, utterly lost and helpless in front of his own pleasure, is by far the most erotic experience of my entire life.

I want to get him into a bed. I want hours, *days* with him. I want to make him feel the way he's feeling right now, but a hun-dredfold stronger, a hundred million more times.

"I'm sorry," he slurs.

"What?" I lean back to look at his face. "Why?"

"That was . . . pitiful." He pulls me back to bury his face in my throat. It's followed by a lick, and a bite, and oh my God, the sex is going to be off the charts. Earth-shattering.

"It was amazing. Let's do it again. Let's go to my place. Or let's just lock the door."

He laughs and kisses me, different from before, deep but gentle and meandering, and . . . it's not really, in my experience, the type of kiss people share *after* sex. In my experience, after sex people wash up, put their clothes back on, then wave good-bye and go to the nearest Starbucks to get a cake pop. But this is nice, because Ian is an excellent kisser, and he *smells* good, he *tastes* good, he *feels* good, and—

"Can I buy you dinner?" he asks against my lips. "Before we . . ."

I shake my head. The tips of our noses brush against each other. "No need."

"I . . . I'd like to, Hannah."

"Nah." I kiss him again. Once. Deep. Glorious. "I don't do that."

"You don't do"—another kiss—"what?"

"Dinner." Kiss. Again. "Well," I amend, "I do eat. But I don't do dinner dates."

Ian pulls back, his expression curious. "Why no dinner dates?"

"I just . . ." I shrug, wishing we were still kissing. "I don't date, in general."

"You don't date . . . at all?"

"Nope." His expression is suddenly withdrawn again, so I smile and add, "But I'm very happy to come to your place anyway. No need to be dating for that, right?"

He takes a step back—a large one, like he wants to put some physical space between us. The front of his jeans is . . . a mess. I want to clean him up. "Why . . . why don't you date?"

"Really?" I laugh. "You want to hear about my socio-emotional trauma after we did"—I gesture between us—"*this?*"

He nods, serious and a little stiff, and I sober up.

Seriously? He really wants that? He wants me to explain to him that I don't really have the time or the emotional availability for any kind of romantic entanglement? That I can't really imagine anyone sticking around for something that's not sex once they really get to know me? That I've long since realized that the longer people are with me, the more likely they are to find out that I'm not as smart as they think, as pretty, as funny? Honestly, I *know* that my best bet is to keep people at arm's length, so that they never find out what I'm actually like. Which is, incidentally: a bit of a bitch. I'm just not good at *caring* about . . . anything, really. It took me about one and a half decades to find something I was truly passionate about. This friendship experiment I'm doing with Mara and Sadie is still very much that, an experiment, and . . .

Oh God. Does Ian want to *date*? He doesn't even *live* here. "So you're saying . . ." I scratch my temples, coming down fast from my post-orgasm high. "You're saying you're not interested in having sex?"

He closes his eyes in something that *really* doesn't look like a no. *Definitely* doesn't look like a lack of interest. But what he says is, "I like you."

I laugh. "I noticed."

"It's . . . uncommon. For me. To like someone this much."

"I like you, too." I shrug. "Shouldn't we hang out, then? Isn't that good enough?"

He looks away. Down, to his shoes. "If I spend more time with you, I'm only going to like you more."

"Nah." I snort. "That's not the way it usually works."

"It does. It will, for me." He sounds so solidly, irrefutably sure, I cannot do anything but stare at him. His lips are bee-stung, and everything about him is beautiful, and he looks so quietly, stoically devastated at the idea of fucking me with no strings attached that I should probably find this comical, but the truth is that I can't remember ever being this attracted to someone else, and my body is *vibrating* for his, and . . .

Maybe you could go out with him. Just this once. An exception. Maybe you could try it out. Maybe it could work. Maybe you two will—

What? No. *No.* What the fuck? Just the fact that I'm contemplating it scares the shit out of me. No. I don't—I'm not like that. These things are a waste of time and energy. I'm busy. I'm not cut out for this stuff.

"I'm sorry," I force myself to say. It's not even a lie. I'm pretty fucking sorry right now. "I don't think it's a good idea."

"Okay," he says after a long moment. Accepting. A bit sad. "Okay. If . . . if you change your mind. About dinner, that is. Let me know."

"Okay." I nod. "When are you leaving? What's my deadline?" I add, attempting some lightheartedness.

"It doesn't matter. I can . . . I travel here a lot, and . . ." He shakes his head. "You can change your mind whenever. No deadline."

Oh. "Well, if *you* change your mind about fucking . . ."

He exhales a laugh, which sounds a little like a pained groan, and for a moment I feel the compulsion to explain myself. I want to tell him, *It's not you. It's me.* But I know how that would sound, and I know better than to put the words out there. So we regard each other for a few seconds, and then . . . then there's nothing left to say, is there? My body goes through the motions automatically. I slide off the desk, take a moment to straighten the monitors behind me, the mouse, the keyboards, the cable, and when I walk past Ian through the door he follows me with his solemn, sad eyes, running his palm over his jaw.

The last words I hear from him are, "It was really good to meet you, Hannah." I think I should say it back, but there's an unfamiliar weight in my chest, and I can't quite bring myself to do it. So I make do with a small smile and a halfhearted wave. I stuff my hands in my pockets while my body is still thrumming with what I left behind, and wander slowly back to the Caltech campus, thinking about red hair and missed opportunities.

He'll make for a great boyfriend, I tell myself, leaning back in my bed and staring up at the ceiling. There is a weird green thing in one corner that I suspect might be mold. Mara keeps telling me I should just move out of this shithole and find a place with her and Sadie, but I don't know. Seems like we'd get *too* close. A big commitment. It might get messy. *He'll make for a great boyfriend. For someone who deserves to have one.*

The following day, when Mara asks me about my meeting with her cousin-or-something, I say only "Uneventful," and I don't even know why. I don't like lying, and I like lying to someone who's rapidly becoming a friend even less, but I can't make myself say any more than that.

A couple days later, when I get an email from IanFloyd@nasa.gov, my heart stumbles all over itself. But it's just an empty email, no text, not even an automatic signature. Just an attachment with his NASA application from a few years ago, together with a handful of other people's. More recent ones that he must have gotten from his friends and colleagues, a few more examples to send me.

Well.

Two weeks later, I turn in a reflection paper as part of my Water Resources class requirements.

I must admit, Dr. Harding, that I initially thought this assignment would be a total waste of time. I've known I wanted to end up at NASA for years, and I've known that I wanted to work with robotics and space exploration for just as long. However, after meeting with Ian Floyd, I have realized that

I'd love to work, specifically, on Attitude and Position Estimation of Mars rovers. In conclusion: not a waste of time, or at least not a total one.

I get an A- for the class. And in the following years, I don't let myself think about Ian too much. But whenever I rewatch video recordings of mission control celebrating *Curiosity*'s landing, I cannot help but look for the tall, red-haired man in the back of the room. And whenever I find him, I feel the ghost of something squeeze tight inside my chest.

Three ⚙

T hey said they couldn't send first responders!"

My breath, dry and white, fogs the black shell of my satellite phone. Because Svalbard in February is well into the negative Celsius. Disturbingly close to the negative Fahrenheit, too, and this morning is no exception.

"They said it was too dangerous," I continue, "that the winds are too extreme." As if to prove my point, a half-hissing, half-howling sound weaves through what I've begun to think of as *my crevasse.*

And as far as crevasses go, it's a good one to get stuck in. Relatively shallow. The western wall is nicely angled, just enough to allow the sunlight to filter in, which is probably the only reason I have yet to freeze to death or get horrible frostbite. The downside, though, is that at this time of the year there are only about five hours of light per day. And they're just about to run out.

"Avalanche danger is set at the highest level, and it's not safe for anyone to come out to get me," I add, speaking right into the sat-phone's mic. Repeating what Dr. Merel, my team leader, told me a few hours ago, during my last communication with AMASE, NASA's home base here in Norway. It was right before he reminded me that I'd been the one to choose this. That I'd known what the risks of my mission were, and I still decided to undertake it. That the path to space exploration is full of pain and self-sacrifice. That it was my fault for falling in an icy hole in the ground and spraining my fucking ankle.

Well, he did not say that. *Fucking*, or *fault*. He did, however, make sure that I was aware that no one would be able to come help me until tomorrow, and that I needed to be strong. Even though, of course, we both knew what the results of a match between me and an overnight snowstorm would be.

Storm: 100. Hannah Arroyo: dead.

"The weather's not that bad." A wave of static almost drains the voice on the other side of the line.

Ian Floyd's voice.

Because, for some reason, he's here. Coming. For me.

"It's a—it's a storm, Ian. Are you—please, tell me you're not just strolling outdoors when the worst storm of the year is just hours from starting."

"I'm not." A pause. "It's more of a brisk walk."

I close my eyes. "In a *storm*. A blizzard. Winds of at least thirty-five miles per hour. Heavy snowfall and no visibility."

"You might be wasted in engineering."

"What?"

"You're really good at meteorology stuff."

I cannot feel my legs; my teeth are chattering; every time I breathe, my skin feels like it's been chewed on by a horde of piranhas. And yet, I find the strength to roll my eyes. At least the cranky bitch inside my heart is holding strong. "You'd love it, wouldn't you? If I were busy giving the weather on local news instead of at NASA with you."

The winds are blowing holes through my eardrums. I honestly have no idea how I can hear a smile in his "Nah."

He's insane. He cannot be here in Norway. He isn't even supposed to be in Europe. "Did AMASE change their mind on sending help?" I ask. "Have the storm forecasts changed?"

"They haven't." Whenever the static dips, I hear a low, oddly familiar noise through the satphone. Ian's breathing, I suspect, heavy and loud and faster than normal. Like he's grunting his way through hazardous ground. "You're approximately thirty minutes from my current location. Once I get to you, we'll have a sixty-minute trek to safety. Which means that we should be able to just barely avoid the storm."

The second he says the word *trek*, my stupid brain decides to attempt to rotate my ankle. Which leads to me biting my chapped, frozen lips to swallow a whimper. A *terrible* idea, as it turns out. "Ian, nothing of what you just said makes sense."

"Really?" He sounds amused. How? *Why?* "Nothing?"

"How do you even know where I am?"

"GPS tracker. On your Iridium phone."

"It's impossible. AMASE said they couldn't activate the tracker. The sensors aren't working."

"AMASE isn't within range, and the coming storm was probably interfering." A strong gust of wind lifts, and for a painfully gelid moment it's everywhere: whooshing around me, piercing inside my lungs, making its way into my ears. I try to curl my body away, but it does nothing to stop the freezing air. I dig myself only deeper into the snow and jostle my stupid ankle.

Fuck.

"AMASE is over three hours from my creva—location. If you really *do* get here in thirty minutes, we're not going to make it there in time to avoid the storm. *You* are not going to make it back in time, and I'm not going to let something terrible happen to you just because I—"

"I'm not coming from AMASE," he says. "And that's not where we're going."

"But how did you even access my GPS tracker if you're not at AMASE?"

A pause. "I'm good with computers."

"You're— Are you saying you *hacked* your way into—"

"They mentioned you're injured. How bad is it?"

I glance at my boots. Ice crystals have begun to crust around the soles. "Just a few scrapes. And a sprain. I think I could *maybe* walk, but—I don't know about sixty minutes." I don't know about sixty seconds. "And on this terrain—"

"You won't have to walk at all."

I frown, even though my brow is almost frozen. "How will I get to wherever we're going if—"

"Do you have ascenders?"

"Yes. But again, I don't know if I can climb . . ."

"No problem. I'll just haul you out."

"You . . . It's too dangerous. The terrain around the edge might collapse and you'd fall in, too." I let out a choppy breath. "Ian, I *cannot* let you."

"Don't worry, I'm not in the habit of falling inside crevasses."

"Neither am I."

"You sure about that?"

Okay. Fine. I walked right into this one. "Ian, I cannot let you do this. If it's . . ." I take a shuddering, frigid breath. "If it's because you feel responsible for this. If you're risking your life because you think it's somehow your fault I ended up here, then you really shouldn't. You know that I have no one to blame but me, and—"

"I am about to start climbing," he interrupts distractedly, like I wasn't in the dead middle of an impassioned speech.

"Climbing? What are you climbing?"

"I'll put away my phone, but get in touch if anything happens."

"Ian, I *really* don't think you should—"

"Hannah."

The shock of hearing my name—in Ian's voice, cocooned by the whistle of the wind, and through the metallic line of my satphone, no less—has me instantly shutting up. Until he continues.

"Just relax and think of Mars, okay? I'll be there soon."

Four ⚙

I t's not that I'm shocked to see him.

That would be, honestly, pretty idiotic. Too idiotic even for me: a well-known occasional idiot. I might not have seen Ian Floyd in over four years—yup, since the day I had the best sex-and-it-wasn't-even-really-sex-God-what-a-waste-of-my-life and then barely forced myself to wave good-bye at him while the mahogany of his office door closed in my face. It might have been a while, but I've kept up with his whereabouts through the use of highly sophisticated technology and cutting-edge research tools.

I.e., Google.

As it turns out, when you're one of NASA's top engineers, people write shit about you. I swear I don't look up "Ian + Floyd" twice a week or anything like that, but I do get curious every once in a while, and the Internet offers so much information in exchange for so little effort. That's how I found out that when the former chief resigned for health reasons, Ian was chosen as head of engineering for *Tenacity*, the rover that landed safely in the de Vaucouleurs Crater just last year. He even gave *60 Minutes* an interview, in which he mostly came across as serious, competent, handsome, humble, reserved.

For some reason, it made me think of the way he'd groaned into my skin. His viselike grip on my hips, his thigh moving between my legs. It made me remember that he'd wanted to take me to dinner, and that I'd actually—appallingly, unfathomably—been tempted to say yes. I watched the entire thing on YouTube. Then I scrolled down to read the comments and realized that a good two thirds were from users who'd noticed exactly how serious, competent, handsome, humble, reserved, and likely well-endowed Ian was. I hastened to click out, feeling caught with my entire torso in the cookie jar.

Whatever.

I think I expected my Google search to lead to more personal stuff, too. Maybe a Facebook account with pictures of adorable ginger toddlers. Or one of those wedding websites with overproduced pictures and the story of how the couple met. But no. The closest was a triathlon he did about two years ago near Houston. He didn't place particularly well, but he did finish it. As far as Google is concerned, that's the only non-work-related activity Ian has partaken in during the last four years.

But that's really beside the point, which is: I know quite a bit about Ian Floyd's career accomplishments, and I am well aware that he's still at NASA. Therefore, it makes no sense for me to be shocked to see him. And I'm not. I'm really not.

It's just that with over three thousand people working at the Johnson Space Center, I figured I'd run into him around my third week on the job. Maybe even during my third month. I definitely did *not* expect to see him on my first day, in the middle of the freaking new-employee orientation. And I definitely didn't anticipate that he'd spot me immediately and stare for a long, long time, as though remembering exactly who I am, as though not wondering why I look familiar or struggling to place me.

Which . . . he isn't. He clearly isn't. Ian appears at the entrance of the conference room where the new hires have been parked to wait for the next speaker; with a slightly aggravated expression he looks around for someone, notices *me*, chatting with Alexis, about a millisecond after I notice *him*.

He pauses for a moment, wide-eyed. Then weaves through the clusters of people chatting around the table, marching toward me with long strides. His eyes stay fixed on mine and he looks confident and pleasantly surprised, like a guy picking up his girlfriend at the airport after she spent four months abroad studying the courtship habits of the humpback whale. But it has nothing to do with me. It's not because of me.

It *cannot* be because of me, right?

But Ian stops just a couple of feet away from Alexis, studies me with a small smile for a couple of seconds longer than is customary, and then says: "Hannah."

That's it. That's all he says. My name. And I *really* didn't want to see him. I *really* figured it would be weird to be with him again, after our not-quite-orgasmless first and only meeting. But . . .

It's not. Not at all. It just feels natural, nearly irresistible to smile at him, push away from the table and up on my toes for a hug, fill my nostrils with his clean scent, and say against his shoulder, "Hey, you."

His hands press briefly into my spine, and we fit together just like four years ago. Then, a second later, we both pull back. I don't do blushing, not ever, but my heart is beating fast and there's a curious heat creeping up my chest.

Maybe it's because this *should* be weird. Right? Four years ago, I came on to him. Then I came *on* him. Then I turned him down when he asked me to spend orgasmless, space-explorationless time with him. That's what I wanted to avoid: the male, awkward, ego-wounded reaction I was sure Ian would have.

But now he's here, disarmingly pleased to see me, and I just feel happy to be in his presence, like I did back when we coded our afternoon away. He looks a bit older; the day-old stubble is about one week old now, and maybe he's gotten even bigger. For the rest, though, he's just *himself.* Hair is red, eyes are blue, freckles are everywhere. I'm being forcibly reminded of his uniform initialization in C++—and of his teeth on my skin.

"You made it," he says, like I really did just get off a jet plane. "You're here."

He's smiling. I smile, too, and furrow my brow. "What? You didn't think I'd actually graduate?"

"Wasn't sure you'd ever pass your Water Resources class."

I burst out laughing. "What? Just because you saw me, with your own eyes, put zero effort into my assignment?"

"That *did* play a role, yeah."

"You should read the stuff I BS'd about you in that report."

"Ah, yes. What STDs did I have to battle to get to where I am today?"

"What STDs did you *not*?"

He sighs. A throat clears and we both turn— Oh, right. Alexis is *also* here. Looking between us, for some reason with saucer eyes.

"Oh, Ian, this is Alexis. She's starting today, too. Alexis, this is—"

"Ian Floyd," she says, sounding vaguely breathless. "I'm a fan."

Ian seems vaguely alarmed, as though the idea of having fans befuddles him. Alexis doesn't seem to notice and asks me, "You two know each other?"

"Ah . . . yeah, we do. We had a . . ." I gesture vaguely. "A thing. Years ago."

"A *thing*?" Alexis's eyes widen even more.

"Oh no, I didn't mean *that* kind of thing. We did some kind of—one of those—what are they called . . . ?"

"An informational interview," Ian patiently provides.

"An informational interview?" Alexis sounds skeptical. She stares at Ian, who is still staring at me.

"Yeah. Kind of. It devolved into a . . ." *Into what? Us almost fucking on NASA property? You wish, Hannah.*

"A debugging session," Ian says. Then clears his throat.

I let out a laugh. "Right. That."

"Debugging session?" Alexis sounds even *more* skeptical. "That doesn't sound fun."

"Oh, it was," Ian says. He's still staring at me. Like he's found his long-missing house keys and is afraid he'll lose them again if he looks away.

"Yeah." I cannot help making my smile just a tad suggestive. An experiment. I seem to do lots of those when he's around. "Lots of fun."

"Right." Ian finally looks away, smiling the same way. "Lots."

"How did you guys meet?" Alexis asks, more suspicious by the second.

"Oh, my best friend is Ian's cousin-or-something."

Ian nods. "How is . . ." He briefly stumbles on the name. "I want to say Melissa?"

"Mara. Your cousin's name is *Mara*. Keep up, will you?" I fail to sound stern. "Have you not talked to her since she put us in touch?"

"I don't believe we talked back then, either. Everything happened through—"

"—Great-Aunt Delphina, right. How's the Home Depot video?"

"Lowe's. I hear it's making a resurgence since Uncle Mitch started hosting Thanksgiving."

I laugh. "Well, Mara is great. She also graduated with her Ph.D. and recently moved to D.C. to work for the EPA. No interest in space stuff. Just, you know . . . saving Earth."

"Oh." He doesn't seem too impressed. "It's a good fight."

"But you're glad someone else is shouldering it while you and I spend our days launching cool gadgets into space?"

He chuckles. "More or less."

"Okay, this is very . . ." Alexis, again. We both turn to her: her eyes are narrow, and she sounds shrill. Honestly, I keep forgetting she's here. "I've never seen two people . . ." She gestures between us. "You guys are *clearly* . . ." Ian and I exchange a baffled glance. "I'm going to leave you to it," she says inscrutably. Then she turns on her heel, and Ian and I are alone.

Kind of. We're in a room full of people, but . . . alone.

"Well . . . hi," I say.

"Hey." The pitch is lower. More intimate.

"I kind of expected this would be unpleasant."

"This?"

"This." I point back and forth between us. "Seeing you again. After the way we left off."

He cocks his head. "Why?"

"Just . . ." I'm not sure how to articulate it, that my experience is that men who have been rejected by women can often be scary in a million different ways. It doesn't matter anyway. It sounds like he put what happened between us behind him the second I stepped out of his office. "Doesn't matter. Since it's not. Unpleasant, that is."

Ian nods once. Like I remember from years ago. "What team have you been assigned to?"

"A & PE."

"You don't say." He sounds pleased. Which is . . . new, mostly. My parents reacted to the news that I was hired by NASA in their usual way: showing disappointment that I did not go into medicine like my siblings. Sadie and Mara were always supportive and happy for me when I got my dream job, but they don't care enough about space exploration to fully grasp the significance of where I ended up. Ian, though, Ian knows. And even though he's now a big shot, and A & PE is not his team anymore, it still makes me feel warm and tingly.

"Yeah—this random guy I once met told me it was the best team."

"Wise words."

"But I'm not going to start with the team right away, because . . . I've managed to get them to pick me for AMASE."

His smile is so unabashedly, genuinely happy for me, my heart leaps in my throat. "AMASE."

"Yup."

"Hannah, that's fantastic."

It is. AMASE is the shit, and the selection process to take part in an expedition was brutal, to the point that I'm not quite sure how I made it in. Probably sheer luck: Dr. Merel, one of the expedition leaders, was looking for someone with experience in gas chromatography–mass spectrometry. Which I happen to have, due to some side projects my Ph.D. advisor foisted upon me. At the time, I aggressively bitched and moaned my way through them. In hindsight, I feel a bit guilty.

"Have you been there?" I ask Ian, even though I already know the answer, because he mentioned AMASE when we met. Plus, I've seen his CV, and some pictures from past expeditions. In one, taken over the summer of 2019, he's wearing a dark thermal shirt and kneeling in front of a rover, squinting at its robotic arm. There is a young, pretty woman standing right behind him, elbows propped on his shoulders, smiling in the direction of the camera.

I've thought about that picture more than just a couple of times. Imagined Ian asking the woman to dinner. Wondered if, unlike me, she was able to say yes.

"I've been there twice, winter and summer. Both great. Winter was considerably more miserable, but—" He stops. "Wait, isn't the next expedition leaving . . ."

"In three days. For five months." I watch him nod and digest the information. He still looks happy for me, but it's a little . . . subdued. A split second of disappointment, maybe? "What?" I ask.

"Nothing." He shakes his head. "It would have been nice to catch up."

"We still can," I say, maybe a bit too fast. "I'm not leaving till Thursday. Want to go out and—"

"Not get dinner, surely?" His smile is teasing. "I remember you don't . . . eat with other people."

"Right." The truth is that things have changed. Not that I now go out for dates—I very much still don't. And not that I've magically become an emotionally available person—I'm still very much *not*. But somewhere in the last couple of years, the whole Tinder game got . . . first a bit old; then a bit tiresome; then, eventually, a bit lonely. These days, I either focus on work or on Mara and Sadie.

"I do drink coffee, though," I say on impulse. Even though I find coffee disgusting.

"Iced tea," Ian says, somehow remembering my four-year-old order. "I can't, though."

My heart sinks. "You can't?" Is he seeing someone? Not interested? "It doesn't have to—" *be a date*, I hasten to say, but we're interrupted.

"Ian, you're here." The HR rep who's been showing the new hires around appears at his side. "Thank you for making time— I know you need to be at JPL by tonight. Everyone." She claps her hands. "Please, take a seat. Ian Floyd, the current chief of engineering on the Mars Exploration Program, is going to tell you about some of NASA's ongoing projects."

Oh. *Oh.*

Ian and I exchange one long glance. For just a moment, he looks like he wants to tell me one last thing. But the HR rep leads him to the head of the conference table, and there's either not enough time or it's not something that's important enough to be said.

Half a minute later, I sit and listen to his clear, calm voice as he talks about the many projects he's overseeing, heart tight and heavy in my chest for reasons I cannot figure out.

Twenty minutes later, I lock eyes with him for the last time just as someone knocks to remind him that his plane will board in less than two hours.

And a little over six months later, when I finally meet him again, I hate him.

I hate him, I hate him, I hate him, and I don't hesitate to let him know.

Five ⚙

The next time my satphone vibrates, the winds have picked up even more. It's snowing, too. I've somehow managed to nestle myself in a small nook in the wall of my crevasse, but large flurries are starting to happily stick to the mini-rover I brought with me.

Which is, I must admit, ironic in a cosmic kind of way. The very reason I ventured out here was to test how the mini-rover I designed would work in highly stressful, low-sunlight, low-command-input situations. Of course, it was not supposed to storm. I was going to drop off the gear and then immediately return to headquarters, which . . . well. It didn't quite work out like that, obviously.

But the gear *is* being covered by a layer of snow. And the sun *is* going to set soon. The mini-rover *is* in a highly stressful, low-sunlight, low-command-input situation, and from a scientific standpoint, this mission wasn't a total clusterfuck. At some point in the next few days, someone at AMASE (likely Dr. Merel, that *asshole*) will try to activate it, and then we'll know whether my work was actually solid. Well, *they* will know. By then, I'll probably just be a Popsicle with a very pissed-off expression, like Jack Torrance at the end of *The Shining*.

"Are you still doing okay?"

Ian's voice jostles me from my preapocalyptic whining. My heart flutters like a hummingbird—a sickly, freezing one who forgot to migrate south with her buddies. I don't bother answering, instead instantly ask: "Why are you here?" I know I sound like an ungrateful bitch, and while I've never concerned myself with coming across as the latter, I do not mean to be the former. The problem is his presence makes no damn sense. I've had twenty minutes to think about it, and it just *doesn't*. And if this is the place and time where I finally croak . . . well, I don't want to die confused.

"Just out on a promenade." He sounds a little out of breath, which means that the climb must have been a tough one. Ian is lots of things, but out of shape is not one of them. "Taking in the scenery. What about you? What brings you here?"

"I'm serious. Why are you in Norway?"

"You know"—the sound briefly cuts, then bounces back with a generous helping of white noise—"not everyone vacations in South Padre. Some of us enjoy cooler destinations." The huffing and puffing through the tenuous satellite line is almost . . . intimate. We're exposed to the same elements, on the same heavily glaciated terrain, while the rest of the world has taken shelter. We're out here, alone.

And it doesn't make any sense.

"When did you fly into Svalbard?" It couldn't have been any time in the last three days, because there were no incoming flights. Svalbard is well connected to Oslo and Tromsø in the peak season, but that won't start until mid-March.

So . . . Ian must have been here for a handful of days. But why? He is chief of engineering on several rover projects, and the *Serendipity* team is approaching crunch time. It makes no sense for one of their key personnel to be in another country right now. Plus, the engineering component of this AMASE is minimal. Only Dr. Merel and me, really. All other members are geologists and astrobiologists, and—

Why the hell is Ian here? Why the hell would NASA send a senior engineer on a rescue mission that wasn't even supposed to happen?

"Are you still doing okay?" he asks again. When I don't reply, he continues: "I'm close. A few minutes away."

I brush snowflakes from my eyelashes. "When did AMASE change its mind on sending relief efforts?"

A brief hesitation. "Actually, it might be more than a few minutes. The storm's intensifying and I can't see very well—"

"Ian, why did they send *you*?"

A deep breath. Or a sigh. Or a puff, louder than the others. "You ask a lot of questions," he says. Not for the first time.

"Yeah. But they're pretty good questions, so I'm going to keep on asking more. For instance, how the—"

"As long as I can ask some, too."

I nearly groan. "What do you want to know? Best concert? Favorite concert? An overview of the amenities of the crevasse? It offers very little in terms of nightlife—"

"I need to know, Hannah, if you are doing okay."

I close my eyes. The bite of the cold is like a million needles wedged under my skin. "Yes. I . . . I'm fine."

Suddenly, the call drops. The static, the noise, they all disappear, and I can't hear Ian anymore. I glance at my satphone and find it still on. *Shit.* The problem is on his end. The snow's getting thicker, it'll be pitch-black in minutes, and on top of that I'm almost sure that Ian has been attacked by a polar bear. If something happens to him, I'll never be able to forgive myse—

I hear steps cracking the snow and look up to the rim of the crevasse. The light is dimming by the second, but I make out the tall, broad outline of a man in a ski mask. He is looking down at me.

Oh God. Is he really . . . ?

"See?" Ian's deep voice says, just a little out of breath. He lowers his neck warmer before adding, "That wasn't so hard, was it?"

Six ⚙

am surprised by how much the email hurts, because it's a lot.

Not that I expected to be happy about it. It's a well-established fact that hearing that your project has been denied funding is as pleasant as plunging a toilet. But rejections are the bread and butter of all academic journeys, and since starting my Ph.D. I've had approximately twelve hundred fantabillions of them. In the past five years, I've been denied publications, conference presentations, fellowships, scholarships, memberships. I even failed at getting into Bruegger's unlimited-drinks program—a devastating setback, considering my love for iced tea.

The good thing is, the more rejections you get, the easier they are to swallow. What had me punching pillows and plotting murder in the first year of my Ph.D. barely fazed me in the last. *Progress in Aerospace Sciences* saying that my dissertation wasn't worthy of gracing their pages? Fine. National Science Foundation declining to sponsor my postdoctoral studies? Okay. Mara insisting that the Rice Krispies Treats I made for her birthday tasted like toilet paper? Eh. I'll live.

This specific rejection, though, cuts deep. Because I really, really need the grant money for what I'm planning to do.

Most of NASA funding is tied to specific projects, but every year there is a discretionary pot that's up for grabs, usually for junior scientists who come up with research ideas that seem worth exploring. And mine, I think, is pretty worthy. I've been at NASA for over six months. I spent nearly all of them in Norway, at the best Mars analogue on Earth, knee-deep in intense fieldwork, equipment testing, sampling exercises. For the past couple of weeks, ever since returning to Houston, I've taken my place with the A & PE team, and it's been really, really cool. Ian was right: best team ever.

But. Every break. Every free second. Every weekend. Every scrap of time I could find, I focused on finalizing the proposal for my project, believing that it was a fucking *great* idea. And now that proposal has been rejected. Which feels like being stabbed with a santoku knife.

"Did something happen?" Karl, my office mate, asks from across the desk. "You look like you're about to cry. Or maybe throw something out the window, I can't tell."

I don't bother to glance at him. "Haven't made up my mind, but I'll keep you updated." I stare at the monitor of my computer, skimming the feedback letters from the internal reviewers.

As we all know, in early 2010, the rover *Spirit* became stuck in a sand trap, was unable to reorient its solar panels toward the sun, and froze to death as a consequence of its lack of power. Something very similar happened eight years later to *Opportunity*, which went into hibernation when a maelstrom blocked sunlight and prevented it from recharging its batteries. Obviously, the risk of losing control of rovers because of extreme weather events is high. To address this, Dr. Arroyo has designed a promising internal system that is less likely to fail in the case of unpredictable meteorological situations. She proposes to build a model and test its efficacy on the next expedition at the Arctic Mars Analog in Svalbard (AMASE)—

Dr. Arroyo's project is a brilliant addition to NASA's current roster, and it should be approved for further study. Dr. Arroyo's vitae is impressive, and she has accumulated enough experience to carry out the proposed work—

If successful, this proposal will do something critical for NASA's space exploration program: decrease the experience of low-power faults, mission clock faults, and up-loss timer faults in future Mars Exploration missions—

Here is the issue: the reviews are . . . positive. Overwhelmingly positive. Even from a crowd of scientists that, I am well aware, feeds on being mean and scathing. The science doesn't seem to be a problem, the relevance to NASA's mission is there, my CV is good enough, and . . . it doesn't add up. Which is why I'm not going to sit here and take this bullshit.

I slam my laptop closed, aggressively stand from my desk, and march right out of my office.

"Hannah? Where are you—"

I ignore Karl and make my way through the hallways till I find the office I'm looking for.

"Come in," a voice says after my knock.

I met Dr. Merel because he was my direct superior during AMASE, and he is . . . an odd duck, honestly. Very stiff. Very hardcore. NASA is full of ambitious people, but he seems to be almost obsessed with results, publications, the kind of sexy science that makes big splashy news. Initially I wasn't a fan, but I must admit that as a supervisor he's been nothing but supportive. He's the one who selected me for the expedition to begin with, and he encouraged me to apply for funding once I went to him with my project idea.

"Hannah. How nice to see you."

"Do you have a minute to talk?" He's probably in his forties, but there is something old-school about him. Maybe the sweatervests, or the fact that he's literally the only person I've met at NASA who doesn't go by his first name. He takes off his metal-rimmed glasses, sets them on his desk, then he steeples his fingers to give me a long look. "It's about your proposal, isn't it?"

He doesn't offer me a seat, and I don't take one. But I do close the door behind me. I lean my shoulder against the doorframe and cross my arms on my chest, hoping I won't sound the way I feel, i.e., homicidal. "I just got the rejection email, and I was wondering if you have any . . . insight. The reviews didn't highlight areas needing improvement, so—"

"I wouldn't worry about it," he says dismissively.

I frown. "What do you mean?"

"It's inconsequential."

"I . . . Is it?"

"Yes. Of course it would have been convenient if you'd had those funds at your disposal, but I've already discussed it with two of my colleagues who agree that your work is meritorious. They are in control of other funds that Floyd won't be able to veto, so—"

"Floyd?" I raise my finger. I must have misheard. "Hold up, did you say Floyd? Ian Floyd?" I try to recall if I've heard of other Floyds working here. It's a common last name, but . . .

Merel's face doesn't hide much. It's obvious that he was referring to Ian, and it's obvious that he wasn't supposed to bring him up, fucked up by doing it anyway, and now has no choice but to explain to me what he hinted at.

I have exactly zero intention of letting him off the hook.

"This is, of course, confidential," he says after a brief hesitation.

"Okay," I agree hurriedly.

"The review process should remain anonymous. Floyd cannot know."

"He won't," I lie. I have no plan at the moment, but part of me already knows that I'm lying. I'm not exactly the nonconfrontational type.

"Very well." Merel nods. "Floyd was part of the committee that screened your application, and he was the one who decided to veto your project."

He . . . what?

He what?

No way.

"This doesn't sound right. Ian isn't even here in Houston." I know this because a couple of days after coming back from Norway, I went looking for him. Looked him up on the NASA directory, bought a cup of coffee and one of tea from the cafeteria, then went to his office with only vague ideas of what I'd say, feeling *almost* nervous, and . . .

I found it locked. "He's at JPL," someone with a South African accent told me when they noticed me idling in the hallway.

"Oh. Okay." I turned around. Took two steps away. Then turned back to ask, "When will he be back?"

"Hard to tell. He's been there for a month or so to work on the sampling tool for *Serendipity*."

"I see." I thanked the woman, and this time I left for real.

It's been a little over a week since then, and I've been to his office . . . in a number of instances. I'm not even sure why. And it doesn't really matter, because the door was closed every single time. Which is how I know that: "Ian is at JPL. He's not here."

"You are mistaken," Merel says. "He's back."

I stiffen. "As of when?"

"That, I could not tell you, but he was present when the committee met to discuss your proposal. And like I said, he was the one who vetoed it."

This is impossible. Nonsensical. "Are you sure it was him?"

Merel gives me an annoyed look and I swallow, feeling oddly . . . exposed, standing the way I am in this office while being told that Ian—Ian? *Really?*—is the reason I didn't get my funding. It seems like a lie. But would Merel lie? He's way too straitlaced for that. I doubt he has the imagination.

"Can he do that? Veto a project that's otherwise well received?"

"Considering his position and seniority, yes."

"Why, though?"

He sighs. "It could be anything. Perhaps he is jealous of a brilliant proposal, or he'd rather the funding go to someone else.

Some of his close collaborators have applied, I hear." A pause. "Something he said made me suspect that . . ."

"What?"

"That he didn't believe you capable of doing the work."

I stiffen. "Excuse me?"

"He didn't seem to find faults in the proposal. But he did talk about *your* role in it in less-than-flattering tones. Of course, I tried to push back."

I close my eyes, suddenly nauseous. I cannot believe Ian would do this. I cannot believe he'd be such a backstabbing, miserable dick. Maybe we're not close friends, but after our last meeting, I thought he . . . I don't know. I have no idea. I think maybe I had expectations of *something*, but this puts a swift end to them. "I'm going to appeal."

"There is no reason to do that, Hannah."

"There are plenty of reasons. If Ian thinks that I'm not good enough *despite* my CV, I—"

"Do you know him?" Merel interrupts me.

"What?"

"I was wondering if you two know each other?"

"No. No, I . . ." *Once humped his leg. It was fantastic.* "Barely. Just in passing."

"I see. I was just curious. It would explain why he was so determined about denying your project. I'd never seen him quite so . . . adamant that a proposal not get accepted." He waves his hand, like this is not important. "But you shouldn't concern yourself with this, because I have already secured alternative funding for your project."

Oh. Now *this* I did not expect. "Alternative funding?"

"I reached out to a few team leaders who owed me favors. I

asked them if they had any budget surplus they might want to dedicate to your project, and I was able to put together enough to send you back to Norway."

I half gasp, half laugh. "Really?"

"Indeed."

"On the next AMASE?"

"The one that leaves in February of next year, yes."

"What about the help I asked for? I will need one other person to help me build the mini-rover and to be in the field. And I'll have to travel quite a way from home base, which might be dangerous on my own."

"I don't think we'll be able to finance another expedition member."

I press my lips together and think about it. I can probably do most of the prep work on my own. If I don't sleep for the next few months, which . . . I've done it before. I'll be fine. The problem would be when I get to Svalbard. It's too risky to—

"I'll be there, out in the field with you, of course," Dr. Merel says. I'm a little surprised. In the months we were in Norway, I saw him do very little sample collecting and snow plodding. I've always thought of him as more of a coordinator. But if he offered, he must mean it, and . . . I smile. "Perfect, then. Thank you."

I slip out of the room, and for about two weeks I'm high enough on the knowledge that my project will be happening that I manage to do just that: not let anyone know. I don't even tell Mara and Sadie when we FaceTime, because . . . because to explain the degree of Ian's betrayal, I'd have to admit to the lie I told them years ago. Because I feel like a total idiot for trusting someone who deserves nothing from me. Because being honest with them would first require me to be honest with myself, and I'm too an-gry, tired, disappointed for that. In my rants, Ian becomes a faceless, anonymous figure, and there is something freeing in that. In not letting myself remember that I used to think of him fondly, and by name.

Then, exactly seventeen days later, I meet Ian Floyd in the stairwell. And that's when everything goes to shit.

✿✿✿

spot him before he sees me—because of the red, and the general largeness, and the fact that he's climbing up while I'm going down. There are about five elevators here, and I'm not sure why anyone would willingly choose to subject their bodies to the stress of upward stairs, but I'm not too shocked that Ian is the one doing it. It's the kind of glory-less overachieving I've come to expect from him.

My first instinct is to push him and watch him fall to his death. Except I'm almost sure it's a felony. Plus, Ian is considerably stronger than me, which means it might not be feasible. *Abort mission,* I tell myself. *Just squeeze by. Ignore him. Not worth your time.*

The problems start when he looks up and notices me. He stops exactly two steps below, which should put him at a disadvantage but, depressingly, unfairly, *tragically,* doesn't. We are at eye level when his eyes widen and his lips curve in a pleased smile. He says, "Hannah," a touch of something in his voice that I recognize but instantly reject, and I have no choice but to acknowledge him.

The staircase is deserted, and sound carries far. His "I came looking for you" is deep and low and vibrates right through me. "Last week. Some guy in your office said you don't work there much, but—"

"Fuck off."

The words crash out of me. My temper has always been reckless, one hundred miles per hour, and . . . well. Still is, I guess.

Ian's reaction is too baffled to be confused. He stares at me like he's not sure what he just heard, and it's the perfect chance for me to walk away before I say something I regret. But seeing his face makes me remember Merel's words, and that . . . that is really not good.

He didn't believe you capable of doing the work.

The worst part, the one that actually *hurts*, is how thoroughly I misjudged Ian. I actually thought he was a good guy. I liked him a *lot*, when I never let myself like anyone, and . . . how *dare* he? How dare he stab me in the back and then address me as though he's my friend?

"What exactly is it that you have a problem with, Ian?" I square my shoulders to make myself bigger. I want him to look at me and think of a cruiser tank. I want him to be scared I'm going to pillage him. "Is it that you hate good science? Or is it purely personal?"

He frowns. He has the audacity to *frown*. "I have no idea what you're talking about."

"You can cut it. I know about the proposal."

For a second he is absolutely still. Then his gaze hardens, and he asks, "Who told you?"

At least he's not pretending not to know what I'm referring to. "Really?" I snort. "Who told me? That's what seems relevant?"

His expression is stony. "Proceedings regarding the disbursement of internal funding are not public. An anonymous internal peer review is necessary to guarantee—"

"—to guarantee your ability to allocate funding to your close collaborators and fuck up the careers of the ones you have no use for. Right?" He jerks back. Not the reaction I expected, but it fills me with joy nonetheless. "Unless the reason *was* personal. And you vetoed my proposal because I didn't sleep with you, what, five years ago."

He doesn't deny it, doesn't defend himself, doesn't scream that I'm insane. His eyes narrow to blue slits and he asks, "It was Merel, wasn't it?"

"Why do you care? You *did* veto my project, so—"

"Did he also tell you *why* I vetoed it?"

"I never said that it was Merel who—"

"Because he was there when I explained my objections, at length and in detail. Did he omit that?" I press my lips together. Which he seems to interpret as an opening. "Hannah." He leans closer. We're nose to nose, I smell his skin and his aftershave, and I hate every second of this. "Your project is too dangerous. It specifically asks that you travel to a remote location to drop off equipment at a time of the year in which the weather is volatile and often totally unpredictable. I've been in Longyearbyen in February, and avalanches develop out of the blue. It's only gotten worse in the last few—"

"How many times?"

He blinks at me. "What?"

"How many times have you been to Longyearbyen?"

"I've been on two expeditions—"

"Then you'll understand why I take the opinion of someone who has been on a dozen missions over yours. Plus, we both know what the *real* reason of the veto was."

Ian opens, then closes his mouth. His jaw hardens, and I'm finally sure of it: he's mad. Pissed. I see it in the way he clenches his fist. The flare of his nostrils. His big body is just inches from mine, glowing with anger. "Hannah, Merel is not always trustworthy. There have been incidents under his watch that—"

"What incidents?"

A pause. "It's not my information to disclose. But you shouldn't trust him with your—"

"Right." I scoff. "Of course I should take the word of the guy who went behind my back over the word of the guy who went to bat for me and made sure my project was funded anyway. *Very* hard choice to make."

His hand lifts to close around my upper arm, at once gentle and urgent. I refuse to care enough to pull away from his touch. "What did you just say?"

I roll my eyes. "I said a bunch of things, Ian, but the gist of it was *fuck off*. Now, if you'll excuse me—"

"What do you mean, Merel made sure that your project was funded anyway?" His grip tightens.

"I mean exactly what I said." I lean in, eyes locked with his, and for a split second the familiar feeling of being *close, here, near* him crashes over me like a wave. But it washes away just as quickly, and all that is left is an odd combination of vengeful sadness. I have my project, which means that I won. But I also . . . Yeah. I *did* like him. And while he was always just in the periphery of my life, I think maybe I'd hoped . . .

Well. No matter now. "He found an alternative, Ian," I tell him. "Me and my *inability to carry out the project* are going to Norway, and there is nothing you can do about it."

He closes his eyes. Then he opens them and mutters something under his breath that sounds a lot like *fuck*, followed by my name and other hurried explanations that I don't care to listen to. I free my arm from his fingers, meet his eyes one last time, and walk away swearing to myself that this is it.

I will never think of Ian Floyd again.

Seven

He's not wearing NASA gear.

By now it's nearly dark, the snow falls steadily, and whenever I look up to the edge of the crevasse, huge snowflakes hurl straight into my eyes. But even then, I can tell: Ian is *not* wearing the gear NASA usually issues to AMASE scientists.

His hat and coat are the North Face, a dull black dusted with white, interrupted only by the red of his goggles and ski mask. His phone, when he takes it out to communicate with me from the edge of the crevasse, is not the standard-issue Iridium one, but a model I don't recognize. He stares down for a long moment, as if assessing the shitfuck of a situation I managed to put myself in. Flurries circle around him, but never quite touch. His shoulders rise and fall. One, two, several times. Then, finally, he lifts his goggles and brings the phone to his mouth.

"I'll send down the rope," he says, in lieu of a greeting.

To say that I'm in a bit of a predicament at the moment, or that I have a few problems on my hands, would be a *vast* understatement. And yet, staring up from the place where I was positive I'd bite it until about five minutes ago, all I can think about is that the last time I talked with this man, I . . .

I told him to fuck off.

Repeatedly.

And he did deserve it, at least for saying that I wasn't good enough to carry out the project. But at the time he also mentioned that my mission was going to be too dangerous. And now he's shown up to the Arctic Circle, with his deep-set blue eyes and even deeper voice, to pull me away from certain death.

I always knew I was an asshole, but I'd never quite realized the extent of it.

"Is this the most massive I Told You So in history?" I ask, attempting a joke.

Ian ignores me. "Once you have the rope, I'll build an anchor," he says, tone calm and matter-of-fact, not a trace of panic. It's like he's teaching a kid how to tie their shoelaces. No urgency here, no doubt that this will go as planned and we'll both be fine. "I'll prepare the lip and haul you up over my shoulder. Make sure everything is clipped to your belay loop. Can you pull on the fixed side?"

I just stare up at him. I feel . . . I'm not sure what. Confused. Scared. Hungry. Guilty. Cold. After what's probably way too long, I manage to nod.

He smiles a little before throwing down the rope. I watch it uncoil, slither down toward me, and come to rest a couple of inches from where I'm huddled. Then I reach out and close my gloved hand around its end.

I'm still confused, scared, hungry, and guilty. But when I glance up at Ian, maybe I feel a little less cold.

✿✿✿

I t's just a sprain, I'm pretty sure. But as far as sprains go, this is a bad one.

Ian is true to his promises and manages to get me out of the crevasse in barely a couple of minutes, but the instant I'm on the surface, I try to limp around, and . . . it's not looking good. My foot touches the ground and pain spears through my entire body like lightning.

"*Fu—*" I press a hand against my lips, trying to hide my gasp in the fabric of my gloves, struggling to keep upright. I'm pretty sure that the loud swishing of the wind swallows my whimper, but there isn't much I can do to help the tears flooding my eyes.

Thankfully, Ian is too busy collecting the rope to notice. "I'll just need a second," he says, and I welcome the reprieve. He might have just rescued me from becoming a polar bear's dessert, but for some reason I hate the idea of him seeing me all weepy and weak. Okay, fine: I needed saving, and maybe I don't look like much at the moment. But my pain threshold is usually pretty high, and I've never been a whiner. I don't want to give Ian any reason to believe otherwise.

Except.

Except that those two lonely tears have opened the floodgates. Behind me, Ian loads his climbing gear into his backpack, his movements practiced and economical, and I . . . I cannot bring myself to offer any help. I just stand awkwardly, trying to spare my throbbing ankle, on one foot, like a flamingo. My cheeks are hot and wet in the falling snow, and I look down at my stupid crevasse thinking that until a minute ago—until Ian Fucking Floyd—it was going to be the last place I saw. The last slice of sky.

And just like that, a rushing terror punches through me. It

knocks out the fabricated quiet of my Martian ocean, and the sheer magnitude of what nearly happened, of all the things I love that I would have missed out on if Ian hadn't come for me, sweeps through my brain like a rake.

Dogs. Three A.M. in the summer. Sadie and Mara being absolute idiots, and me laughing at them. Hiking trips, kiwi iced tea, that Greek restaurant I never got around to trying, elegant code, the next season of *Stranger Things*, really good sex, a *Nature* publication, seeing humans on Mars, the ending of *A Song of Ice and Fire*—

"We need to be on our way before the storm gets worse," Ian says. "Are you—"

Ian looks at me, and I don't even try to hide my face. I'm well past that. When he comes closer, a dark frown on his face, I let him hold my eyes, lift my chin with his fingers, inspect my cheeks. His expression shifts from urgent, to worried, to understanding. I draw in a breath that turns into a gulp. The gulp, to my horror, morphs into a sob. Two. Three. Five. And then . . .

Then I'm just a fucking mess. Blubbering pitifully, like a child, and when a warm, heavy body wraps around me and grips me tightly, I offer no resistance.

"I'm sorry," I murmur into the nylon of Ian's jacket. "I'm sorry, I'm sorry, I'm sorry. I— I have no clue what's wrong with me, I—" It's just that I hadn't known. Down in the crevasse, I was able to pretend it wasn't happening. But now that I'm out, and I don't feel numb anymore, it's all flooding back, and I cannot stop seeing them, all the things, *all the things* that I almost—

"Shh." Ian's hands feel impossibly large as they move up and down my back, cupping my head, stroking my snow-damp hair where it spills from under the hat. We are in the icy middle of a storm, but this close to him, I feel almost peaceful. "Shh. It's okay."

I cling to him. He lets me sob for long moments we cannot afford, pressing me against him with no air between us, until I can feel his heartbeat through the thick layers of our clothes. Then he mumbles "Fucking Merel" with barely restrained fury, and I think that it would be so easy to blame things on Merel, but the truth is, it's all my fault.

When I lean back to tell him, he cups my face. "We really need to go. I'll carry you to the coast. I have a light brace for your ankle, just to avoid messing it up even more."

"The coast?"

"My boat is less than an hour away."

"*Your* boat?"

"Come on. We have to get going before more snow falls."

"I—maybe I can walk. I can at least try—"

He smiles, and the thought that I could have died—I could have *died*—without being smiled at like this, by *this man*, has my lips trembling. "I don't mind carrying you." A dimple appears. "Do try to contain your love for crevasses, please."

I glare at him through the tears. As it turns out, it's exactly what he wants from me.

☼☼☼

an carries me almost all the way.

To say that he does it without breaking a sweat, in the white-out of a thickening snowstorm, in negative-ten-degree-Celsius weather, would probably be a bit of an exaggeration. He smells salty and warm as he deposits me on one of the bunks on the lower deck of the boat, a small expedition ship named M/S *Sjøveien*. I do spot little droplets of perspiration here and there, and they make his forehead and upper lip shine before he wipes them with the sleeves of his coat.

Still, I can't quite get over the relative ease with which he made his way through glaciated plateaus for over an hour, wading through old and fresh snow, sidestepping rocky formations and ice algae, never once complaining about my arms coiled tight around his neck.

He almost slipped twice. Both times, I felt the steel of his muscles as they tensed to avoid the fall, his large body solid and reliable as it balanced and reoriented before picking up the pace again. Both times, I felt bizarrely, incomprehensibly safe.

"I need you to let AMASE know that you're safe," he tells me the second we're on the boat. I look around, noticing for the first time that there are no other passengers on board. "And that you don't need responders to come out once the storm lets up."

I frown. "Wouldn't they know that you already—"

"Right now. Please." He stares pointedly until I compose and send a message to the entire AMASE group, in a way that reminds me that he is very much a leader. Used to people doing as he says. "We have a space heater, but it's not going to do a whole lot in this temperature." He takes off his jacket, revealing a black thermal underneath. His hair is messy, and bright, and beautiful. Not nearly as disgustingly hat-squished as mine, an inexplicable phenomenon that should be the object of several research studies. Maybe I'll apply for a grant to investigate it. Then Ian will veto me, and we'll be back to Mutual Hate square one. "The winds are more severe than I'd like, but on board is still a safer option than ashore. We're anchored, but the waves might get nasty. There's anti-seasickness meds next to your bunk, and—"

"Ian."

He falls quiet.

"Why are you not wearing a NASA survival suit?"

He doesn't look at me. Instead he drops to his knees in front of me and begins to work on my brace. His large hands are firm but delicate on my calf. "Are you sure it's not broken? Is it painful?"

"Yes. And yes, but getting better." The heat, or at least the lack of freezing winds, is helping. Ian's grip, comforting and warm around my swollen ankle, doesn't hurt, either. "This isn't a NASA boat, either." Not that I expected it to be. I think I know what's going on here.

"It's what we had at our disposal."

"We?"

He still doesn't meet my eyes. Instead he tightens the brace and pulls a thick woolen sock over my foot. I think I feel the ghosts of fingertips trailing briefly across my toe, but maybe it's my impression. It must be.

"You should drink. And eat." He straightens. "I'll get you—"

"Ian," I interrupt softly. He pauses, and we both seem simultaneously taken aback at my tone. It's just . . . pleading. Tired. I'm usually not one for displays of vulnerability, but . . . Ian has come for me, in a small rocking boat, across the fjords. We are alone in the Arctic Basin, surrounded by twenty-thousand-year-old glaciers and shrieking winds. There is *nothing* usual about this. "Why are you here?"

He lifts one eyebrow. "What? You miss your crevasse? I can take you back if—"

"No, really—why are you here? On this boat? You're not part of this year's AMASE. You shouldn't even be in Norway. Don't they need you at JPL?"

"They'll be fine. Plus, sailing is a passion of mine." He's obviously being evasive, but the cold must have frozen my brain cells, because all I want right now is to find out more about Ian Floyd's passions. True or made up.

"Is it really?"

He shrugs, noncommittal. "We used to sail a lot when I was a kid."

"We?"

"My dad and I." He stands and turns away from me, starting to rummage in the little compartments in the hull. "He'd bring me along when he had to work."

"Oh. Was he a fisherman?"

I hear a fond snort. "He smuggled drugs."

"He *what*?"

"He smuggled drugs. Weed, for the most—"

"No, I heard you the first time, but . . . seriously?"

"Yup."

I frown. "Are you . . . Are you okay? Is that even . . . Is that a thing, smuggling weed on boats?"

He's tinkering with something, giving me his back, but he turns just enough for me to catch the curve of his smile. "Yeah. Illegal, but a thing."

"And your father would take you?"

"Sometimes." He turns around, holding a small tray. He always looks big, but hunched in the too-low deck he feels like the Great Barrier Reef. "It would drive my mom crazy."

I laugh. "She didn't like her son being part of the family criminal enterprise?"

"Go figure." His dimple disappears. "They'd yell about it for hours. No wonder Mars began sounding so attractive."

I cock my head and study his expression. "Is that why you grew up not knowing Mara?"

"Who is M— Oh. Yeah. For the most part. Mom isn't very fond of the Floyd side of the family. Though I'm sure he's the black sheep by their standards, too. I wasn't really allowed to spend time with him, so . . ." He shakes his head, as if to change the topic. "Here. It's not much, but you should eat."

I have to force myself to look away from his face, but when I notice the peanut butter and jelly sandwiches he made, my stomach cramps with happiness. I wiggle in the bunk until I'm sitting straighter, take off my jacket, and then immediately attack the food. My relationship with eating is much less complicated than the one with Ian Floyd, after all, and I lose myself in the straightforward, soothing act of chewing for . . . for a long time, probably.

When I swallow the last bite, I remember that I'm not alone and notice him staring at me with an amused expression.

"Sorry." My cheeks warm. I brush the crumbs from my thermal shirt and lick some jam off the corner of my mouth. "I'm a fan of peanut butter."

"I know."

He does? "You do?"

"Wasn't your graduation cake just a giant Reese's cup?"

I bite the inside of my cheek, taken aback. It was the one Mara and Sadie got me after I defended my thesis. They got tired of me licking frosting and peanut butter filling off the Costco sheet cakes they usually bought and just ordered me a giant cup. But I have no recollection of ever telling Ian. I barely think of it, honestly. I remember about it only when I log into my barely used Instagram, because the picture of the three of us digging in is the last thing I ever posted—

"You should rest while you can," Ian tells me. "The storm should ease up by early tomorrow morning and we'll sail out. I'll need your help in this shit visibility."

"Okay," I agree. "Yeah. But I still don't understand how you can be here alone if—"

"I'll go check that everything is all right. I'll be back in a minute." He disappears before I can ask exactly what he needs to check on. And he's not back in a minute—or even before I lean back in the bunk, decide to rest my eyes for just a couple of minutes, and fall asleep, dead to the world.

✿✿✿

The bark of the wind and the rhythmic rocking of the boat rouse me, but what keeps me awake is the chill.

I look around in the blue glow of the emergency lamp and find Ian a few feet away from me, sleeping on the other bunk. It's too short, and barely wide enough to accommodate him, but he seems to make do. His hands are folded neatly on his stomach, and the covers are kicked to his feet, which tells me that the cabin is probably not as cold as I currently feel.

Not that it matters: it's as if the hours spent outside have seeped into my bones to keep on icing me from the inside. I try to huddle under the covers for a few minutes, but the shivering only gets worse. Perhaps strong enough to dislodge some kind of important cerebral pathway, because without really knowing why, I get out of my bunk, wrap the blanket around myself, and limp across the rolling floor in Ian's direction.

When I lie down next to him, he blinks, groggy and mildly startled. And yet his first reaction is not to throw me in the sea but to push toward the bulkhead to make room for me.

He's a way better person than I'll ever be.

"Hannah?"

"I just . . ." My teeth are chattering. Again. "I can't get warm."

He doesn't hesitate. Or maybe he does, but just a fraction of a second. He opens his arms and pulls me to his chest, and . . . I fit inside them so perfectly, it's as though there was a spot ready for me all along. A five-year-old spot, familiar and cozy. A delicious, warm nook that smells of soap and sleep, freckles and pale, sweaty skin.

It makes me want to cry again. Or laugh. I cannot remember the last time I felt this fragile and confused.

"Ian?"

"Hm?" His voice is rough, all chest. This is what he sounds like when he wakes up. What he would have sounded like the morning after if I'd agreed to go to dinner with him.

"How long have you been in Svalbard?"

He sighs, a warm chuff on the crown of my hair. I must be catching him off guard, because this time he answers the question. "Six days."

Six days. That's one day before *I* arrived. "Why?"

"Vacation." He nuzzles my head with his chin.

"Vacation," I repeat. His thermal is soft under my lips.

"Yeah. I had"—he yawns against my scalp "lots of time left over."

"And you decided to spend it in Norway?"

"Why do you sound incredulous? Norway's a good place. It has fjords and ski resorts and museums."

Except that's not where he is. Not at a ski resort, and most definitely not at a museum. "Ian." It feels so intimate, to say his name so close to him. To press it into his chest as my fingers curve into his shirt. "How did you know?"

"Know what?"

"That my project was going to be such a shitshow. That I . . . That I wasn't going to be able to finish my project." I am going to start crying again. Possibly. Likely. "Was it—was it that obvious?

Am I just this total, giant, incompetent asshole who decided to do whatever the fuck she wanted despite everyone else telling her that she was going to—"

"No, no, shh." His arms tighten around me, and I realize that I am, in fact, crying. "You are not an asshole, Hannah. And you are *the opposite* of incompetent."

"But you vetoed me because I—"

"Because of the intrinsic danger of a project like yours. For the past few months, I tried to get this project stopped in about ten different ways. Personal meetings, emails, appeals—I tried it all. And even the people who agreed with me that it was too dangerous would not step in to prevent it. So no, you're not the asshole, Hannah. They are."

"What?" I shift on my elbow to hold his eyes. The blue is pitchblack in the night. "Why?"

"Because it's a great project. It's absolutely brilliant, and it has the potential to revolutionize future space exploration missions. High risk, high reward." His fingers push a strand behind my ear, then run down my hair. "*Too* high risk."

"But Merel said that—"

"Merel is a fucking idiot."

My eyes widen. Ian's tone is exasperated and furious and not at all what I'd expect from his usually calm, aloof self. "Well, Dr. Merel has a doctorate from Oxford and I believe is a Mensa member, so—"

"He's a moron." I shouldn't laugh, or burrow even closer to Ian, but I cannot help myself. "He was at AMASE when I was here, too. There were two serious injuries during my second expedition, and both of them happened because he pushed scientists to finish fieldwork when conditions weren't optimal."

"Wait, seriously?" He nods curtly. "Why is he still at NASA?"

"Because his negligence was hard to prove, and because AMASE members sign waivers. Like you did." He takes a deep breath, trying to calm down. "Why were you out there alone?"

"I needed to drop off the equipment. The storm wasn't forecasted. But then there was an avalanche nearby, I got scared that my mini-rover would get damaged, started running away without looking, and—"

"No—why were you *alone*, Hannah? You were supposed to have someone else with you. That's what the proposal said."

"Oh." I swallow. "Merel was supposed to come for backup. But he wasn't feeling well. I offered to wait for him, but he said we'd be losing valuable days of data and that I should just go alone, and I . . ." I squeeze my fingers around the material of Ian's shirt. "I went. And then, when I called in for help, he told me that the weather was turning, and . . ."

"Fuck," he mutters. His arms tighten around me, nearly painful. "Fuck."

I wince. "I know you're mad at me. And you have every right "

"I'm not mad at *you*," he says, sounding mad at me. "I'm mad at fucking—" I study him, skeptical, as he inhales deeply. Exhales. Inhales again. He seems to cycle through a few emotions that I'm not sure I understand, and ends with: "I'm sorry. I apologize. I usually don't . . ."

"Get mad?"

He nods. "I'm usually better at . . ."

"Caring less?" I finish for him, and he closes his eyes and nods again.

Okay. This is starting to make sense.

"AMASE didn't send you," I say. It's not a question. Ian won't admit it to me, but in this bunk, next to him, it's so obvious what happened. He came to Norway to keep me safe. Every step of the way, all he did was to keep me safe. "How did you know that I was going to need you?"

"I didn't, Hannah." His chest rises and falls in a deep sigh. Another man would be gloating by now. Ian . . . I think he just wishes he could have spared me this. "I was just afraid that something might happen to you. And I don't trust Merel. Not with you." He says it—*you*—like I am a remarkable and important thing. The most precious data point; his favorite town; the loveliest, starkest Martian landscape. Even though I pushed him away, over and over, he still came in a rocking boat in the middle of the coldest ocean on planet Earth, just to get me warm.

I try to lift my head and look up at him, but he presses on it gently and keeps stroking my hair. "You really should rest."

He's right. We both should. So I push a leg between his, and he lets me. Like his body is a thing of mine. "I am sorry. About what I said to you back in Houston."

"Shh."

"And that I've put you in danger—"

"Shh, it's okay." He kisses my temple. It's wet from the slide of my tears. "It's okay."

"It's not. You could be working with your team, or asleep in your own bed, but you're here because of me, and—"

"Hannah, there is nowhere else I'd rather be."

I laugh, watery. "Not even—not even literally *anywhere* else?"

I hear him chuckle just before I fall asleep.

Eight

Before we can leave for Houston, we spend one night in a hotel in Longyearbyen, Svalbard's main settlement. It offers a bottomless breakfast buffet and keeps the rooms' temperature about ten degrees higher than needed for comfortable inside dwelling—truly the stuff of post-crevasse-Hannah's dreams. I'm not sure whether Ian shares my bliss, as he disappears as soon as I'm settled in. It's fine, though, because I have stuff to do. Mostly writing a detailed report updating NASA on what happened, which doesn't mention Ian (at his request) but ends in a formal complaint against Merel. After that, I stumble upon a rare moment of grace: I manage to connect to the mini-rover out in the field. I let out a squeal of delight when I realize that it's collecting the precise type of data I needed. I stare at the incoming feed, remember what Ian said on the boat about how valuable my project would be for future missions, and nearly tear up.

I don't know. I must still be shaken up.

We leave the following day. I've done what I came to AMASE

for (surprisingly successfully), and Ian needs to be at JPL in three days. The first plane ride is from Svalbard to Oslo, on one of those minuscule aircraft that take off from minuscule airports with their minuscule seats and minuscule complimentary snacks. Ian and I don't get to sit next to each other, nor do we from Oslo to Frankfurt. I pass the time staring out the window and watching *JAG* reruns with Norwegian subtitles. By the end of the third episode, I strongly suspect *skyldig* means "guilty."

"I guess *ikke* means 'not,' then," Ian tells me as he wheels my still-injured self through the Frankfurt airport. I turn back to look up at him, puzzled. "What? I was watching *JAG*, too. It's a good show. Reminds me of my childhood."

"Really? You used to watch a show about military lawyers with your weird smuggler dad?"

He gives me a sheepish look, and I burst into laughter.

"Do Harm and Mac end up together in the end?" I ask him.

He half smiles. "No spoilers."

"Oh, come on."

"You'll have to watch to find out."

"Or I could look it up on Wikipedia."

He keeps on smiling, like he thinks that I won't. He's right.

We are together for the last leg of the trip. Ian lets me have the window seat without me having to ask, and settles by my side after putting away our bags and wedging a pillow under my brace. He is broad and solid, his legs cramped and too long for the little space he has, and once we're both buckled in, it feels like he's blocking away the rest of the world. A wall, keeping me safe from the noise and the action. I've been restless ever since the boat and haven't managed more than very brief naps, but a few minutes after we take off, I feel myself starting to doze, exhausted. The last thing I do before falling asleep is lean my head against Ian's shoulder. The last thing I remember him doing is shifting a little lower, to make sure that I'm as comfortable as I can be.

I wake up somewhere over the Atlantic and stay exactly where I am for several minutes, my temple against his arm, the clean smell of his clothes and his skin in my nostrils. He's looking at his tablet, reading an article on plasma propulsion. I skim a few lines in the methods section before saying: "I'm usually not like this."

He doesn't seem surprised that I'm awake. "Like how?"

I think about it. "Needy." I think some more. "Clingy."

"I know." I can't see his face, but his voice is low and kind.

"How do you know?"

"I know you."

My first instinct is to bristle and push back. Something within me rejects being known, because being known means being rejected. Doesn't it? "You don't, though. Really know me. I mean, we never even fucked."

"True." He nods, and his jaw brushes against my hair. "Would you have let me get to know you if we had fucked?"

"Nah." I yawn and straighten, arching to stretch my sore back. "Do you ever think about it?"

"About what?"

"Five years ago. That afternoon."

"I think about it a lot," he says immediately, without hesitating. His expression is undecipherable to me. Utterly unreadable.

"Is that why you came to rescue me?" I tease. "Because you were thinking about it? Because you have been secretly pining for years?"

He meets my eyes squarely. "I don't know that there was anything secret about that."

He goes back to his tablet, still calm, still relaxed. Then, after several minutes and a couple of yawns, he closes his eyes and tips his head back against the seat. This time he's the one to fall asleep, and I'm left awake, staring at the strong line of his throat, unable to stop my head from spinning in a million different directions.

✿✿✿

When we step out of the TSA area of the Houston airport, there is a sign in the crowd, similar to the ones limo drivers hold up in movies when they're picking up important clients they're afraid they won't recognize.

HANNAH ARROYO, it says. And underneath: WHO ALMOST DIED AND DIDN'T EVEN TELL US. ALSO, SHE ALWAYS FORGETS TO REPLACE THE TOILET PAPER ROLL. WHAT A LITTLE SHIT.

It's a pretty big sign. All the more because it's held by two not-very-tall girls, a redhead and a brunette, who are very obviously glaring at me.

I turn around to Ian. He slept on and off for the past four hours and still looks groggy, his face soft and relaxed. *Cute*, I think. And immediately after: *Delicious. Handsome. Want.* I say none of it and instead ask, "What are my idiot friends doing here?"

He shrugs. "I figured you might want to talk through your near-death experience with someone, so I decided to tell Mara what happened. I did not expect her to come in person."

"Bold of you to assume I didn't tell her myself."

His eyebrow lifts. "Did you?"

"I was *going to*. Once I felt less *whiny*. And—whatever." I roll my eyes. Wow, I'm mature. "How did you go from not remembering Mara's name to having her number?"

"I had to do unspeakable things."

I gasp. "Not Great-Aunt Delphina."

He presses his lips together and nods, slowly, wretchedly.

"Ian, I am so sor—"

I cannot finish the sentence, because I'm being tackled by two small but surprisingly strong goblins. I wobble on my one functioning ankle, nearly choking when their arms squeeze tight around my neck.

"Why are you guys here?"

"Because," Mara says against my shoulder. They are both full-on crying—so weak, so tenderhearted. God, I love them.

"Guys. Get it together. I didn't even *die*."

"What about frostbite?" Sadie murmurs into my armpit. I'd forgotten how fantastically short she is.

"Not much."

"How many toes amputated?"

"Three."

"That's not bad," Mara says with a sniffle. "Cheaper pedis."

I laugh and inhale deeply. They smell wonderful, a mix of mundane and familiar, like airport terminals and their favorite shampoos I used to steal and our cramped Pasadena apartment. "Seriously, guys, what are you doing here? Don't you have, like, work to do?"

"We took two days off, and my neighbor is watching Ozzy, you *ingrate hag*," Sadie tells me before starting to cry harder. I pull her even closer and pat her on the back.

A few feet from us, two tall men are talking quietly to each other. I recognize Liam and Erik from their guest appearances on our late-night FaceTime hangouts, and wave at them with my best *These two, amirite?* expression. They wave back and answer with fond nods that tell me they 500 percent agree.

"Oh—Ian? You're Ian, right?" Mara detaches from our hug-lump. "Thank you so much for calling us, this moron would have never told us the extent of what happened. And, um, I'm sorry I haven't been in touch for the past . . . fifteen years?"

"Don't apologize," I tell her. "He thought your name was Melissa till twenty minutes ago."

She frowns. "What? For real?"

Ian blinks from my side, looking slightly abashed.

"Well, still." She shrugs. "I promise I don't have anything against you personally. I'm just not generally a fan of the Floyd family."

"Neither am I."

Mara's eyes lit up. "They're horrible people, right?"

"The worst."

"*Thank you.* Hey, we should secede! Form our own official branch of the family. That video of you peeing in a Lowe's that they forced me to watch over and over? I'd never mention it again."

Ian smiles. "Sounds great."

Mara smiles back, but then she leans back in to hug me once again and whisper in my ear, "I'm not even sure he's really a Floyd. His hair is *barely* red."

I burst into laughter. I think I'm home for real.

✿✿✿

I want to stay awake and bask in the joy of having Sadie and Mara in my living space again, but I fail and conk out the second we get to my place. I wake up in the middle of the night, Sadie and Mara on either side of me in my queen-size bed, and my heart is so full, I'm afraid it'll overflow. Apparently this is what I am now, a unicorn rainbow marshmallow kitten creature. Bah. I wonder groggily where their boyfriends went, promptly fall back asleep, and find out the answer only several hours later, when the sun shines bright into my kitchen and we're sitting at my cluttered table.

"They were going to stay in a hotel," Mara says. She is having

Cheez-Its for breakfast without even bothering to look ashamed. "But Ian told them they could bunk with him."

"He did?" My fridge is full, even though I unplugged it before leaving for Norway. There are several new boxes of cereal on top of it, and fresh fruit in a basket that I didn't know I owned. I wonder which one of the dependable adults in my life is responsible for this. "Does he have the space?"

"He said he has a big place."

"Hmm." I can't believe Sadie's Viking boyfriend gets to see Ian's apartment before I do. Oh well.

"So," she says, "this seems like the perfect opening to grill you and find out whether you're boinking Mara's relative. But it's obvious that you are. Plus, you just almost Popsicled yourself at the North Pole. So we'll go easy on you."

"That is very considerate." I pluck a grape from the mysterious bowl. "I'm not, though."

"Bullshit."

"No, really. We fooled around five years ago, when we met up for Helena's interview. Then we had a huge argument six months ago, when I told him to fuck off after he vetoed my expedition because it was too dangerous—not because he thought I was an idiot, like someone told me. *Then* he came to save my life when I almost died on said expedition." I don't mention our night together on the boat, because . . . there's nothing to say, really. Technically, nothing happened.

"As far as Told You Sos go, this is an excellent one," Mara says.

"Right? That's what I thought!"

"Hang on," Sadie interjects. "Did we know that he was the one who vetoed your proposal? And did we know about the fooling-around-five-years-ago bit? Did we *forget*?"

"We did not," Mara says. "We would *not* have forgotten. Thank you for keeping us updated on your life, Hannah."

"Would you have cared to know?"

Their *Hell, yeah*s are simultaneous.

Right. Of course. "Okay, let's see. We kind of made out at JPL. Then he asked me out for dinner. I said that I didn't date, but I'd fuck him anyway. He wasn't interested, and we went our separate ways." I shrug. "Now you know."

Mara glares at me. "Wow. So timely."

I blow her a kiss.

"But things have changed, right?" Sadie asks. "I mean . . . last night he carried you upstairs for seven floors because the elevator was broken. It's obvious that he has a thing for you."

"Yes," Mara agrees. "Are you going to break my blood relative's heart? Don't get me wrong, I'd still side with you. Hos before bros."

"He's not your bro in any sense of the word," I point out.

"Hey, he's my cousin-or-something."

Sadie pats her on the shoulder. "It's the *or something* that gets me every time. You can really feel the unbreakable family ties."

"We seceded last night. We're the founders of the Floyds 2.0. And you"—she points at me—"could be one of us."

"Could I?"

"Yes. If you gave Ian a chance."

"I . . . I don't know." I think about how he squeezed my hand while the plane landed. About the way he asked for cookies instead of pretzels, because I told him that they're my favorite. About his arm around my shoulders back in Norway while the concierge checked us into our rooms. About him falling asleep next to me, and me realizing how taxing, how physically demanding, it must have been to come extract me from the idiotic situation I put myself into—no matter that he didn't so much as roll his eyes at the burden of it.

I don't like the word *dating*. I don't like the *idea* of it. But with Ian . . . I don't know. It seems different with him.

"I guess we'll see. I'm not sure *he* would want to date," I say, staring at Sadie's Froot Loops. The ensuing silence drags on so long, I'm forced to look up. She and Mara are staring at me like I just announced that I'm quitting my job to take up macramé full-time. "What?"

"Did she really just use the word *date*?" Mara asks Sadie, pretending I'm not sitting *right here*.

"I think so. And *without* referring to the disgusting fruit?"

Mara frowns. "Dude, dates are amazing."

"No, they're not."

"Yes. Try wrapping them in bacon."

"Okay," Sadie acknowledges, "*anything* is amazing if you wrap it in bacon, but—"

I clear my throat. They turn to me.

"So, you're gonna go out with him?"

I shrug. Think about it. The idea is so foreign, my brain catches on it for a moment. But remembering the way Ian smiled at me back in Svalbard helps me push right through it. "I think I'll ask. If he wants to."

"Considering that he saved your life, contacted Great-Aunt Delphina, and put up two dudes he's never seen before so their girlfriends could hang out with you . . . I think maybe he does."

I nod, my eyes fixed into the mid-distance. "You know, when I fell, my expedition leader said that no one was coming to rescue me. But . . . he came. Ian came. Even though he wasn't even supposed to be there."

Sadie frowns. "Are you saying that you feel like you *have to* date him because of that?"

"Nah." I grin at her. "As you know, it's pretty impossible to get me to do something I don't want to."

Sadie bats her eyes at me. "I always manage."

"Not true."

"Yes, I do. For instance, in ten minutes I'm going to take you to the NASA doctor Ian wrote down the address for, and we're going to get your foot checked out."

I scowl. "No way."

"I am."

"Sadie, I'm fine."

"You really think you're going to win this?"

"Fuck yeah."

She leans forward over her bowl of cereal with a small smile. "It's *on*, baby. Let the best bitch win."

✿✿✿

Sadie, naturally, wins.

After the doctor tells me stuff I already knew—high sprain, yada yada—and gives me a better brace I can walk on, I take Sadie and Mara to my favorite coffee shop. Their planes are leaving late tonight, and we squeeze as much as we possibly can out of the day. When we get to Ian's apartment, I expect . . .

I don't know, actually. Based on what I know of the guys' personalities, I figured we'd find them brooding in silence, checking their work emails. Occasionally clearing their throats, maybe. But Ian buzzes us into his place, and when we walk into the wide living room, we discover all three of them sprawled on the huge sectional, each holding a PlayStation controller as they yell in the direction of the TV. Further inspection reveals that Liam's and Ian's avatars are shooting at some gelatinous monster, while Erik's huddles in the far corner of the screen. He's yelling something that could be Danish. Or Klingon.

None of them look like they've bothered to shower or change out of their pajamas. There are two empty pizza boxes on the wooden coffee table, beer cans scattered all over the floor, and I'm pretty sure I just stepped on a Cheeto. We stop in our tracks at the entrance, but if the guys notice our arrival, they don't show it. They keep on playing until Liam gets hit by a stray bullet and grunts like a wounded animal.

"I hate that I love him," Mara mutters under her breath.

Sadie sighs. "At least yours isn't running against the wall because he can't use the controller."

"Guys," I tell them, shaking my head, "maybe I was wrong in approving of your relationships. Maybe you can do better."

Mara snorts. "Excuse me? Is that a slice of pepperoni on Ian's shirt?"

Sure is. "Touché."

Sadie clears her throat. "Hey, guys, it's great that you're having fun, but we should really get going if we want to make our flights—"

They groan in a chorus. Like ten-year-olds asked to clean their rooms.

"I just . . . can't believe they actually *like* each other," Mara says, befuddled.

Sadie nods. "I don't know how I feel about this. Seems . . . dangerous?"

I cover my mouth to muffle my laughter.

Nine ⚙♥

an drives me home after we drop everybody off at the airport,
following a disturbing phone number exchange among the guys
and a few tears from Mara and Sadie. I'm definitely feeling more
like myself, because I send them through TSA with a stern "Stop
whining" and gentle slaps on their butts.

"Try not to fall into a glacier for at least six months, okay?"
Sadie yells at me from within the roped area.

I flip her off and limp back to Ian's car.

"I see why you love them so much," he tells me while driving
back to my place.

"I don't. Love them, that is. I just pretend to avoid hurting their
feelings."

He smiles like he knows how full of bullshit I am to the very
milligram, and we're quiet for the rest of the ride. The oldies radio
station plays pop songs that I remember from the early 2000s, and
I stare at the yellow glow of the streetlights, wondering if I, too,

am an oldie. Then Ian slows down to park at my place, and that relaxed, happy feeling wanes as my heart picks up speed.

I told Sadie and Mara that I'd see if he's interested in going out with me, but it's easier said than done. I've propositioned plenty of people, but this . . . it feels different. I'm not going to be good at it. I'm going to be total, utter shit. And Ian will realize it immediately.

"You could . . ." I start. Then stop. My knees suddenly look incredibly interesting. Works of art that require my most dedicated inspection. "I was thinking that . . ."

"Don't worry, I'll carry you upstairs," he says. He's wearing jeans and an ocean-blue shirt that matches his eyes and contrasts with his hair and—

It's scary, how attractive I find him. The depth of this crush of mine. I liked him since the very start, but my feelings for him have been growing steadily, then exponentially, and . . . what do I even *do* with them? It's like being handed an instrument I never learned how to play. Being asked to step onstage at a concert hall utterly unprepared.

I take a deep breath.

"Actually, they fixed the elevator. And this new brace is easy to walk on. So, no need. But you . . ." *You can do this, Hannah. Come on. You just survived polar bears thanks to this guy. You can say the words.* "You could come up anyway."

A long silence follows, in which I feel my heartbeat in every inch of my body. It draws out till it gets unbearable, and when I cannot help but glance up, I find Ian looking at me with an expression that can be described only as . . . sorry. Like he knows very well that he's going to have to let me down.

Shit.

"Hannah," he says, apologetic. "I don't think it's a good idea."

"Right." I swallow and nod. Push the weight in my chest to the side for an unspecified *later*. God, that later is going to be *bad*. "Okay."

He nods, too, relieved at my understanding. My heart breaks a little. "But if you need anything, anything at all—"

"—you'll be there. Right." I smile, and . . . maybe I'm not 100 percent yet, because I'm starting to feel teary all over again. "Thank you, Ian. For everything. Absolutely everything. I still cannot believe you came for me."

He cocks his head. "Why?"

"I don't know. I just . . ." I could bullshit an answer for him. But it seems unfair. He's earned more from me. "I just can't believe that *anyone* would do that for me."

"Right." He sighs and bites into his lower lip. "Hannah, if that changes. If you ever find yourself able to believe that someone could care about you that much. And if you wanted to actually . . . *have dinner* with that someone." He lets out a laugh. "Well . . . Please, consider me. You know where to find me."

"Oh. Oh, I . . ." I feel heat creep up my face. Am I blushing? I didn't even know my body was capable of it. "I actually wasn't asking you to come up just for . . . I mean, maybe that, too, but mostly . . ." I screw my eyes shut. "I expressed myself poorly. I was inviting you up because I would love to *have dinner*. With *you*," I blurt out.

When I find the guts to open my eyes, Ian's expression is stunned.

"Are you . . ." I think he forgot how to breathe. He clears his throat, coughs once, swallows, coughs again. "Are you serious?"

"Yes. I mean," I hurry to add, "I still think you won't like it. I'm just . . . really *not* that kind of person."

"What kind of person?"

"The kind that people enjoy being with for anything that isn't . . . well, sex. Or sex related. Or directly leading up to sex."

"Hannah." He gives me a skeptical look. "You have two friends who dropped everything to be with you. And I assume sex wasn't involved."

"It wasn't. And I—I would drop everything for them, but they're different. They're my people, and—" Shit, I really *am* about to tear up. What the hell, you almost die once and your mental stability gets all fucked up? "There are plenty of people who would disagree. Like my family. And you . . . You'll probably end up not liking me."

He smiles. "Seems improbable, since I already like you."

"Then you'll stop. You—" I run a hand through my hair, wishing he understood. "You'll change your mind."

He looks at me like I'm just a bit crazy. "In the span of one dinner?"

"Yes. You'll think I'm a waste of your time. Boring."

He's starting to just look . . . amused. Like I'm ridiculous. Which . . . I don't know. Maybe I am. "If that happens, I'll just put you to work. Have you debug some of my code."

I laugh a little and look out the window. There are no cars at this time of night, no one walking their dog or taking a stroll. It's just Ian and me on the street. I love it and hate it. "I still think you'd get the most out of this if we fucked," I mutter.

"I agree."

I turn to him, surprised. "You do?"

"Of course. You think I *don't* want to fuck you?"

"I . . . Kind of?"

"Hannah." He unbuckles his seat belt and angles himself toward me, so that I have no choice but to look him in the eyes. He looks earnest and nearly offended. "I have thought about what happened in my office every day for the past five years. You offered to go down on me, and I just . . . embarrassed myself, and it should be the most mortifying memory I have, but for some reason it's turned into the axis every fantasy of mine spins around, and"—he reaches up to pinch the bridge of his nose—"I want to fuck you. Obviously. Always have. I just don't want to fuck you *once*. I want to do it a lot. For a long time. I want you to come to me for sex, but I also want you to come to me when you need help with your taxes and moving your furniture. I want fucking to be only one of the million things I do for you, and I want to be—" He stops. Seems to collect himself and straightens, as if to give me space. To give *us* space. "I'm sorry. I don't want to crowd you. You can . . ."

He pulls back a few inches, and all I can do is look at him openmouthed. Shocked. Speechless. Absolutely . . . yeah. Did this really happen? Is it really happening? And the worst part is, I'm almost positive that his words have dislodged something in my brain, because the only thing I can think of saying in response to all he said is: "Is that a yes on dinner?"

He laughs, low and beautiful and a little rueful. And after looking at me like no one else ever has before, what he says is, "Yes, Hannah. It is a yes on dinner."

✿✿✿

Um, I could make us a . . ." I scratch my head, studying the contents of my open fridge. Okay, so it's full. The problem is, it's full exclusively of stuff that needs to be cooked, chopped, baked, prepared. Stuff that's healthy and doesn't taste particularly good. I am now 93 percent sure that Mara was the one who went shopping, because no one else would dare to impose broccoli on me. "How does one even . . . I could boil the broccoli, I guess? In a pot? With water?"

Ian is standing behind me, his chin on top of my head, chest hovering right behind my back. "Boil them in a pot with water," he repeats.

"I would *salt* them afterward, of course."

"You want to eat broccoli?" He sounds skeptical. Should I be offended?

No, Ian. I don't want to eat broccoli. I'm not even hungry, to be honest. But I have committed to this. I am a person who is capable of having dinner with another human. And I will prove it to you. "I could make a sandwich, then. There's lunch meat over there."

"I think those are tortilla wraps."

"No, they're— Shit. You're right."

I sigh, slam the door shut, and turn around. Ian does *not* take a step back. I have to lean against the fridge to be able to look up at him. "How do you feel about Froot Loops?"

"The cereal?"

"Yeah. Breakfast for dinner. *If* I still have milk. Let me check—"

He does not. Let me check, that is. Instead he envelops my face with his hands and leans over to me.

Our first kiss, five years ago, was all me. Me reaching out. Me initiating. Me guiding him. This one, though . . . Ian sets everything. The rhythm, the tempo, the way his tongue licks into my mouth—*everything*. It lasts for a minute, then two, then an uncountable length of time that blurs into a mess of liquid heat and trembling hands and soft, filthy noises. My arms loop around his neck. One of his legs slides between mine. I realize that this is going to end exactly like our afternoon at JPL. Both of us completely out of control, and . . .

"Stop," I say, barely breathing.

He pulls back. "Stop?" He's not breathing *at all*.

"Dinner first."

He exhales. "Really? *Now* you want dinner?"

"I promised."

"Did you?"

"Yes. I'm trying to—to show you that—"

"Hannah." His forehead touches mine. He laughs against my mouth. "Dinner is . . . it's symbolic. A metaphor. If you tell me that you're willing to see where things go, I believe you, and we can—"

"No," I say stubbornly. The urge to touch him is nearly painful. I can't remember the last time I was this turned on. "We're having our symbolic dinner. I'm going to show you that— What are you doing?"

He is, I believe, turning around to pluck two grapes from the same cluster I half ate this morning. He presses one against my lips till I bite into it, pops the other in his mouth. We both chew for a while, eyes locked. Though he finishes before I do, he starts kissing me again, and—a mess.

We're a *mess.*

"Done eating your dinner?" he asks against my lips. I nod. "You still hungry?" I shake my head and he picks me up and carries me to the—

"Wrong door!" I say when he tries to enter the bathroom, then the closet where I keep the vacuum cleaner I never use and the one pair of spare sheets I own, and by the time we're on my bed we're both laughing. Our teeth clack together when we try and fail to keep kissing as we undress each other, and I don't think that anything has ever been like this before, intimate and sweet and so much fun at the same time.

"Just—let me—" I finish taking off his shirt and stare at his torso, mesmerized. It's pale and broad, full of freckles and large muscles. I want to bite him and lick all over. "You're so . . ."

He has undone my brace. He sets it aside, next to the pajama bottoms that I threw on the floor this morning, then helps me wiggle out of my jeans. "Red? And spotty?"

I laugh a little harder. "Yup."

"That's what I—"

I press him down till he's lying on the bed. Then I straddle him and peel off my top, ignoring the slight sting in my ankle. This should be familiar ground for me: bodies against bodies, flesh against flesh. Just seeing what feels good and then doing more of it. It should be familiar, but I'm not sure it is. Being here with Ian is more like hearing a song I've listened to millions of times, this time with a new arrangement.

"*God*, you look so— What works best for you?" he asks between breaths. "For your ankle?"

"Don't worry, it doesn't really hu—" I stop myself as something occurs to me. "You're right. I *am* injured."

His eyes widen. "We don't have to—"

"Which means that I should probably be in charge."

He nods. "But we don't have to—"

He shuts up the moment my hand reaches the zipper of his jeans. And he stays silent, breathing sharply, staring mesmerized at the way I undo it, slow, methodical, determined. His boxers are tented. He is hard, big. I remember touching him for the first time and thinking how good the sex was going to be.

I just didn't think it would take us five years to get there.

"Hannah," he says.

I reach inside the slit of his boxers to cup him. The second my fingers close around him, his nostrils flare. "Yes?"

"I don't think you understand how— Fuck."

He is hot and huge. Closing his eyes, arching his neck before looking at me again with a half-warning, half-pleading expression. He finds me sitting on his knees, his cock spasming in my grip as

I lean over. "Hannah," he says, even deeper than usual. "What are you . . ."

I start by licking the head, thoroughly, delicately. But he feels smooth and warm against my tongue, and I immediately get impatient. I flip my hair so it's not in the way and seal my lips around him, suck gently once, twice, and then . . .

I hear a growl. Then the sound of something ripping. With the corner of my eye, I notice Ian's large hand fisting the sheet. Did he just tear my—

"Stop," he says, pleads, orders me.

My brow furrows. "You don't like it?"

"It's not—" I tighten my grip around his length, and I can almost hear his teeth grind. His cheeks are bright red. Mars Red. "We can't. Not the first time. We need to do it in a way that won't make me . . ."

I press a soft, lingering kiss at the base. He inhales once, audibly, from his nose. "So what you're saying is . . . you don't want to come?"

"It's more—*shit*—about keeping my dignity," he rushes out.

"Dignity is overrated," I say before running my teeth up his length to take the head in my mouth again. This time, he seems to just give in. His hand slides through my hair, cups the back of my skull, and for a second he keeps me there. Pulls me closer. Presses me against him until I feel the tip of his cock hitting the back of my throat. I yield to Ian, enjoying the feeling of him losing control, the salty flavor, his trembling thighs, the helpless way he tugs at my hair to get me to take more, deeper, better—

Suddenly, it's all upside down. I'm being dragged up his body, flipped on my back, pinned to the bed. One of his hands can hold both my wrists above my head, and when I look up I find him caging me. I first notice the panic in his eyes, then how close he was to coming, then the sheer relief that he managed to stave it off.

"Hannah," he says. His tone is laced with command.

"What?"

His cock twitches against my abdomen. "I think I'll be in charge now."

I pout. "But I—"

"I'm sorry, but—it's happening. I'm going to fuck you. I'm not going to come in your—" He doesn't finish the sentence. Just leans forward to kiss me, and by the time he's done, I'm nodding, breathless.

"Do you have condoms?"

"No. But I'm on the pill. We can do it without anything if you're not giving me gross STDs. But I trust that you wouldn't save me from the walruses just to have me die of chlamydia, so—"

I think he likes the idea of us doing it without anything. I think he loves the idea, because first he kisses me breathless, then he gets to work on taking everything—every last layer—off both of us.

The truth is, I can't remember the last time I was fully naked with someone. When I'm having sex—the type of sex I usually go for—there always tends to be the odd irremovable layer. A bra, a tank top. Not-quite-all-the-way-off panties. My partners have been the same, with boxers twisted at their ankles, skirts pulled up, still-cuffed open shirts.

I've never dwelled too much on the thought, but the lack of intimacy behind the encounters is crystal clear now. Now that Ian is draped over me, sucking at my breasts as if they are ripe fruits, his tongue sweet and rough against the pliant underside, alternating between too much and not enough.

He spreads my legs open with his knee, positions himself right between them, and I expect him to slide in in one smooth move. I'm certainly wet enough, and the way he grips my waist betrays his eagerness. But for long moments he just seems satisfied to nibble on my tits. Even though I can feel his erection, hot and a little wet, rubbing against the inside of my thigh whenever he shifts. It leads to me gasping and him groaning, something deep and rich rising from the pit of his chest.

"I thought you said you wanted to fuck?" I breathe out.

"I do," he rumbles. "But this . . . this is good, too."

"You can't"—a sharp intake of breath—"you can't like my tits this much, Ian."

A soft bite, right around the hard point of my nipple. My spine shoots up from the bed. "Why?"

"Because—they're . . . No one ever has." I don't want to mention that my breasts are nothing to write home about—he probably already knows, since they have been in his mouth for the better part of the last ten minutes. He seems to get it, anyway.

"You have the most perfect little tits. I always thought so. Since the first time I met you. Especially the first time I met you." He sucks on one while pinching the other. He is—precise. Good. Enthusiastic. Filthy. "They're as pretty as the Columbia Hills."

A choked laugh bubbles out of me. It's stupidly nice to have someone compare my body to a topographical feature of Mars. Or maybe it's just nice to have someone who knows the Columbia Hills tugging at my nipples and staring at them like they're the eighth and ninth wonders of the universe.

"This," he murmurs into the skin trailing up to my sternum, "this is the Medusae Fossae. It even has these pretty little freckles." His teeth close around my right collarbone. It would be hot even if the head of his cock weren't starting to brush against my pussy. It's wetness meeting wetness, a lot of mutual eagerness, a mess waiting to happen. I band my arms around Ian's neck and pull his huge shoulders into my body, like he's the sun of my very own star system.

"Hannah. I didn't think I could want you more, but last year, when I saw you at NASA, I . . ." He is slurring his words. Ian Floyd, always calm, levelheaded, articulate. "I thought I'd die if I couldn't fuck you."

"You can fuck me now," I whine, impatient, pulling his hair as he moves lower. "You can fuck me however and wherever you want."

"I know. I know, you're going to let me do it all." He exhales a ticklish trail along my rib cage. "But maybe I want to play with the Herschel crater first." His tongue dips inside my belly button, tasting and probing; but when I begin to squirm and pull him up, he follows meekly, as if aware that I can't take much more. Maybe he can't take much more, either: his finger parts my swollen labia to slip around my clit, a slow circle with a little too much pressure. Except that it might be just the right amount. I'm dissolving now, in a pool of coiled muscles and sticky pleasure.

Okay. So sex can be . . this. Good to know.

"This one," Ian pants against my mouth, no pretense of kissing now. My mouth is slack with pleasure and he's just stealing air from me, sucking bee stings into my lips and groaning his approval into my cheekbone. "This one right here is the Solis Lacus. The Eye of Mars. Getting all worked up during dust storms."

He has perfect hands. Perfect touch. I will explode and scatter everywhere, a meteorite shower all over the bed.

"And the Olympus Mons." It's his palm massaging my clit now. His fingers slip into me wherever they find an opening, until the tension inside me is so sweet, I'll go insane. "I really want to come inside you. Can I?"

I shut my eyes and moan. It's a yes, and he must be able to tell.

Because he grunts just as soon as the head of his cock begins to nudge inside me, a little too large for comfort, but very determined to make space for itself. I order myself to relax. And then, when he hits a perfect spot inside me, I order myself not to come immediately.

"Or maybe it's the Vastitas Borealis." He's barely intelligible. Doing those little thrusts that are designed more to open me up than to fuck me properly, and yet we're both this close to orgasm. It's a little scary. "The oceans that used to fill it, Hannah."

"There is no—" I try to ground myself. To find a place inside of me that is safe from the pleasure. I end up only digging my good heel into his thigh, trying to comprehend how such spectacular friction can exist. "We don't know that there ever really was an ocean. On Mars."

Ian's eyes lose focus. They widen and hold mine, unseeing. And then he smiles and begins to move for real, with a little whisper in my ear.

"I bet there was."

The pleasure crashes over me like a tidal wave. I close my eyes, hold on to him as tight as I can, and let the ocean wash over me.

Epilogue ⚙

The control room is silent. Unmoving. A sea of people in dark-blue polo shirts and red JPL lanyards who somehow manage to breathe in unison. Until about five minutes ago, the handful of journalists invited to document this historical event were clearing their throats, shuffling their equipment, asking the occasional whispered question. But that, too, has stopped.

Now we all wait. Silent.

"... *expect only intermittent contact at this time. A dropout as the vehicle switches antennas* ..."

I glance at Ian, who sits in the chair next to mine. He hasn't bothered to turn on his monitor. Instead, he's been watching the progress of the rover on mine, his frown deep and worried. This morning, when I straightened the collar of his shirt and told him how good he looked in blue, he didn't reply. Honestly, I don't think he even heard me. He's been very, *very* preoccupied for the past week. Which I happen to find . . . kind of cute.

"*Heading directly for the target. The rover is about fifteen meters off the surface, and . . . we're getting some signals from MRO. The UHF looks good.*"

I reach out to brush my fingers against his under the table. It's meant to be just a fleeting, reassuring touch, but his hand closes around mine, and I decide to stay.

With Ian, I always decide to stay.

"*Touchdown confirmed!* Serendipity *has safely landed on the surface of Mars!*"

The room erupts into cheers. Everyone explodes out of their seats, cheering, clapping, laughing, jumping, hugging. And within the delightful, triumphant, radiant chaos of mission control, I turn to Ian, and he turns to me with the widest, most brilliant of smiles.

The following day, our kiss is on the front page of the *New York Times*.

Bonus
Chapter

LIAM

f Liam were asked to compile a list of the most momentous days of his life—the ones that'll surely flash before his eyes when he's death adjacent, even though in the meantime he'll have to stash them in a corner of his heart, hidden and secure, because dwelling on the feelings they elicit is overwhelming, unmanageable, and just plain dangerous—today would make it to the very top.

Not number five, like that Tuesday two years ago when he tried to propose and Mara didn't quite let him, bursting out with a "Yes, yes, yes!" after he barely managed a "Will you m—" (It allowed him to spend the following week pretending that he'd only wanted to ask her to mail out the census form: amusing for him; less so for her.)

And not number three, like the day Mara announced that she

was planning to move into his bedroom, and to convert her own into a "*The Bachelor* blogging studio." Approximately twenty minutes later, Liam's walls were full of pictures of two girls he'd never even met in person yet, and his serviceable gray comforter had been replaced with a chevron rainbow quilt that should have given him a headache but instead had him craving cake pops for the first time in his life.

Today . . . today is number one. The most perfect day of his life. Mara in his arms, the words she just said in the air between them, and the promise of what's to come.

It could be a boy. Or a girl. Or both, or neither. It doesn't matter. Liam couldn't care less. All he hopes for is carrot-red, curly hair and freckles. The baby should have Mara's looks. And her understanding of numbers. And her temperament. Her love for broccoli, her ability to fix things, and Liam's . . .

Okay. Ideally, the baby will take exclusively after Mara. Liam would be perfectly okay if none of his alleles made it into its karyotype. Liam is taller, which *is* useful when it comes to reaching for higher shelves, but legroom on planes is a bitch and a half, and he really wouldn't wish the cramps on anyone, let alone his progeny—

"Hannah was right."

He pulls back to look at Mara. Her legs are wrapped around his waist, because he picked her up the second he got home and she used the p-word. There's something lodged in Liam's fist—ah, yes. The test.

She showed him the second he got home, wagging it under his nose. There's *probably* pee on it, and he should *probably* find it disgusting, but . . .

Yeah. No.

"Hannah? About what?"

"About *your* reaction." Mara presses a kiss to Liam's cheek, then grins, then disentangles herself from his arms. A steady, nimble descent. "She said you were going to buffer for fifteen minutes once I told you."

"When you told me . . . ?"

"About this." Her fingers splay against her abdomen, and for a split second his brain short-circuits in the best possible way. It's happening. This is going to happen. This is his life. He doesn't deserve it, but somehow this is his life, and—

"Wait." He shakes his head, chasing the other, less pleasant train of thought. "How can Hannah know about the baby?"

"I told her, of course." Mara smiles again and grabs his hand, pulling him into the kitchen. She also takes the test from him and drops it into the hallway trash bin. It's not something Liam's ready for, saying good bye to the one piece of evidence that *yes*, this is happening, so he makes a mental note to retrieve it later. In the meantime . . .

"When did you tell her?"

"Earlier this morning. When I found out."

Earlier this . . .

Liam frowns. Then he scowls. Then a sound comes out of him, and Mara stops in her tracks to look back at him. She's beautiful and still happy-looking, but also narrow eyed all of a sudden.

"Did you just . . . growl?" she asks.

"No." Yes. "Did you tell *your friends* about the baby before telling *me*?"

"Yeah." She shrugs. "I had to tell someone."

"Did you consider . . . me?"

"You were in court. All day."

"You could have called me."

"I couldn't tell you *on the phone*." Her hands come to her hips— usually Liam's cue to let go of an argument.

He does *not* let go. "You told your friends on the phone." He sounds sullen.

"It's totally different. And anyway, Hannah and Sadie have been asking for updates every day since I told them we'd been trying, so."

"They knew we—" The sound chokes somewhere in his trachea. Liam clears his throat. Twice. "They knew we were trying?"

"Yeah." Mara blushes a little, and Liam takes a step closer.

This time, it's *his* hands on *his* hips. "What did you tell them?"

"Just . . . you know . . ." The way she hand-waves is very suspicious and reveals something:

Her friends know everything about their sex lives for the last two months.

Every. Single. Thing.

"What about Ian and Erik? Do they know *I'm* having a baby?"

"I'm not sure," Mara says, evasive.

Too evasive.

"Mara."

"Well, Erik sent over celebratory croissants. They were *really* good. I left you one, by the way. Well, half. And Ian texted me to ask if we're going to call the baby X Æ A-Xii. It's an Elon Musk joke. And Elon Musk is an engineer, so it's kinda funny—"

"I know who Elon Musk is."

For maybe half a second, Mara looks contrite. It all melts when her arms slide into the loops of his and she hugs herself to his chest. "They're really happy for us," she murmurs against his shirt. "*I'm* really happy for us."

Okay. Fine. Who cares? So everyone knows about their sex schedule. Big deal. What's some reproductive life talk among friends, after all?

"I'm happier," he murmurs against the crown of her hair. "I'm happiest."

But while Mara brings him dinner (half a croissant that looks more like one third), he checks his phone, scrolls past the group chat he shares with Mara's friends and their partners, and zeroes in on the text thread with Ian and Erik. It was pinging today while he was busy in court. Ian, trying to convince Erik to buy a PS5 to play the FIFA 22 game. As if.

> First of all, you assholes could have mentioned I'm having a baby.

> Liam's just too happy to be mad.

> But more importantly: FIFA 19 is a million times better.

ERIK

The phone buzzes in Erik's pocket, but he doesn't check what for.

He doesn't move. Doesn't take his eyes off Sadie. Doesn't step away from his strategic position—leaning against the fridge—which allows him a full view of the kitchen, and, above all, of his wife.

It's not because she's pretty, or mesmerizing, or his happy place—even though she *is* all of these things. It's not because he's in love with her, or interested in what she's doing, or enthralled by the way she moves—even though he *is* all of these things.

The reason he won't look away from his beloved spouse on this beautiful April night is a bit more basic, and vaguely embarrassing:

Abject fear.

Not quite of *Sadie*, but of what she might do to his brother. His poor, unsuspecting, clearly terrified brother.

Anders has been "finding himself" all over the world for the past several years, and has therefore never met Erik's wife before today. Maybe if he'd showed up to their wedding in Copenhagen... but he was too busy picking plums in Australia. Which means that his knowledge of Sadie is undoubtedly secondhand, most likely through Erik's parents. And, oh, Erik can just imagine his mom's review. *What a kind, radiant, lovely bride. A brilliant, gentle young woman. A bit superstitious—she forbade anyone to gift knives and she put six pennies in her shoe, which fell out while she was walking to the altar—but so lovely. The football-shaped wedding cake she insisted on—unusual, but delightful. She's perfect for your brother.*

Yup. Erik can just imagine. Just like he can imagine Anders shitting himself as Sadie leans over the kitchen table to hiss at him: "Who the hell do you think you are?"

"I'm— I—" He points at Erik. To no one's surprise, his finger is shaking. "His younger brother—"

"I know who you are." Sadie's eyes narrow. "What I asked is: Who do you *think* you are, to come into *my* house and steal *my* cat?"

"Um, technically, Garfield is my—"

"His name is Cat."

Anders blinks. "Pretty sure I named him Garfield."

"You *named* him Garfield. Past tense. Then Erik took him in because you were *Eat Pray Lov*ing your way through Europe. Erik opened his home and his heart, and renamed him Cat. And Cat likes it much better than Garfield. Don't you, babe?"

On the windowsill, Cat licks his orange paw in what almost looks like a nod. *Mmm.*

"Knowing Erik, I seriously doubt he opened his heart to—"

"Things have changed around here, Anders." Sadie's tone is so sharp, Erik's six-foot-something, two-hundred-pound brother presses himself deeper into his chair. *Yeah*, Erik thinks, watching little wisps of hair come undone from her bun and frame her face. *She's terrifying. And cute.* "Especially between Erik and Cat. They are bonded now."

They are not. Cat hates Erik, and Erik hates Cat, especially after watching him scoot his asshole against Erik's toothbrush less than twelve hours ago. However, they are both very fond of Sadie, and have therefore established a truce of sorts.

To facilitate peaceful cohabitation, Erik has disseminated decoy toothbrushes all around the house.

"Okay, listen . . ." Anders scratches his neck. "Don't you guys have a budding engineering firm to run? Do you even have time to take care of Garf— Cat?"

"We have nothing but time," Sadie cuts in, as though Grantham & Nowak is not growing exponentially, as though they haven't been busier than ever. Erik fondly remembers how anxious Sadie was when they both left their previous jobs. *What if, with working and living together, you get tired of me?* It sounded so unlikely, he could only laugh. "And as you know, the house we're building upstate is almost finished. Cat could come up with us on weekends. In fact, we've been thinking about getting a dog—and I think we can all agree that Cat would love to torment a puppy. Wouldn't you, Cat?"

"Meow."

Erik's phone buzzes again. This time he takes his eyes off Sadie to check his texts.

Clearly, Mara told Liam about the baby. Clearly, she told him last.

ERIK: Congrats, man.

ERIK: Unrelated question: Are you guys ever scared of your wives?

The replies are instantaneous.

LIAM: 100%.

IAN: Hannah's still not my wife, but yeah. Shitless.

Erik sighs, slides his phone back into his pocket, and decides to intervene. He goes to Sadie, wrapping his arm around her shoulders. Her slight weight settles into his side. *Sorry*, Erik tells his brother with a look. *But she's very cute and very terrifying.* "What about joint custody?" he proposes.

Anders glares at him, and then nods, defeated.

Sadie smiles, triumphant.

Cat is nowhere to be seen. *Must be in the bathroom*, Erik thinks. *Looking for toothbrushes.*

IAN

The words come out of Ian's mouth before he's fully processed them. By the time he notices Hannah's raised eyebrows and her dubious expression, it's just too late to take them back.

She stops in the middle of the hallway.

Ian stops, too.

She looks at him, skeptical.

Ian tries not to avert his eyes.

It's not easy: The Jet Propulsion Lab is crawling with interns, students, engineers. They're all at the end of their workday, and they're all trying to exit the building from that door over there. The one that's maybe ten feet away.

And, apparently, Ian and Hannah are about to have this conversation right in front of it. Perfect.

"Excuse me?"

"Nothing." He shakes his head. "Let's just go home. Forget that I—"

"Did you just ask me why we are *not* married?"

"No. Well, yes, but . . ."

"In response to me asking you if we should get Thai tonight?"

Ian scratches his temple and looks at his feet. "Perhaps not my best segue." His hand lifts to her back, and he tries to nudge her toward the parking lot. "Let's go home."

Hannah stays put. "Where's this coming from?" she asks, just as NASA's deputy administrator strolls in and out of Ian's field of view, waving cheerfully. Hannah's eyes fall on the phone in his hand. "Aah."

"Aah?"

"Aah." She nods knowingly. "You've been talking with Erik and Liam."

Ian frowns. "What does that have to do with it?"

"You get like this when you talk to them." She grins and grabs his sleeve, pulling him into the parking lot.

"I get like what?"

"Homey. Marriagey."

"I don't."

"Yeah, you do."

"I'm pretty sure I've never mentioned marriage before." In fact, he's been very careful not to mention anything that's even remotely connected. Everyone knows that Ian and Hannah are together, but when Ian's manager asked him if he'd be taking his "wife" to her barbecue—*Dr. Arroyo, right, who leads the A & PE team?*—he made sure to say, *Yes, I'll bring my* partner. When Sadie pushed her bridal bouquet of Danish lilies into Hannah's very unreceptive, mostly slack hands, he made sure to nod while Hannah listed the reasons marriage is an archaic institution grounded in a capitalistic landscape.

It's not that he doesn't want to get married. It's more that he knows her, and her issues with commitment. She's already come so far, and it's not like Ian doesn't feel how much she loves him every minute of every day. Which means that he can accept the way she is, and the fact that she'd laugh in his face if he bought a ring, went on one knee, and proposed.

"You never mentioned marriage, and yet here you are." Hannah's eyes are inscrutable as they walk to his car. "Thinking of proposing because my best friend is having a little ginger baby."

"The baby might not be ginger—"

"It will be."

"Okay, it will be. But it was an unrelated question. I was just wondering if . . ."

"If?" Ian's car is . . . well, Ian's car. But Hannah plucks the keys from his fingers and slides in on the driver's side.

"Hypothetically," he continues, settling for the passenger seat.

"Hypothetically?"

He looks straight ahead. Swallows. Swallows again. "If I were to ask. Hypothetically. What would you say?"

There is a thick, suspicious silence on the driver's side of the car. Not at all auspicious. And when it pulls his gaze in Hannah's direction, her expression isn't serious, or annoyed, or anything else that he can discern.

"I guess you'll have to try and see," is all she says.

Ian presses his lips together and smiles. "I guess I'll have to try and see."

But her free hand slides into his immediately as they drive away, and he thinks that maybe, maybe, he knows what the answer will be. And maybe, maybe, he should ask soon.

So they pick up Thai that night. And Ian doesn't look at his phone again.

Acknowledgments

Like 99.9 percent of my writing output, these novellas originated as fan fiction, and their journey to what they have become involved approximately 999 wonderful people. First of all, each novella started out as a gift for a friend: thank you to Becca for the perfect roommates prompt, to Marie for liking small spaces, and to Celia and Sheppy for being into . . . polar bears? Yes, polar bears. Also, infinite thanks to Celia, Kate, and Jen for beta reading the original fics—and to Jen for slogging through the expanded versions. Guys, I do not deserve you and I know it.

My unparalleled agent, Thao Le, had the idea to adapt the fics into a series and guided me through the process; my brilliant editor, Sarah Blumenstock, made them as good as they could be; my beloved friend Lilith created not one, not two, but three perfect covers. And on top of my amazing Berkley team (Tina Joell, Tara O'Connor, Bridget O'Toole, Liz Sellers, and Jess Brock . . . ILY GUYS), I had a fantastic team at PRH audio (Laura Wilson, Karen Dziekonski, Katherine Punia, Heather Dalton, Brisa Robinson, and Becca Stumpf). And and aaaand, I cannot forget my film agents,

Jasmine Lake and Mirabel Michelson, or Cindy Hwang, Tawanna Sullivan, Penguin Creative, and the entire production team at Berkley, who constantly work behind the scenes to make everything better. Like I said: 999 wonderful people, and that's before getting to Andrea, Jess, and Jenn at SDLA, who are consistently The Best, and, of course, all the friends who tirelessly listen to me whine: my Grems, my Berkletes, my fellow 2021 debuts, my Reylos, my Edgy Ladies, and every single person who has taken the time to read, listen to, and spread the word about my books. I am, let's be honest, shockingly lucky to be surrounded with such amazing and talented people, and incredibly privileged that they put up with me.

Last, and also least, I would NOT like to thank my cat. (See? This is what happens when you pee on the books I write, Hux.)

Photo courtesy of the author

ALI HAZELWOOD is the *New York Times* bestselling author of *The Love Hypothesis*, as well as a writer of peer-reviewed articles about brain science, in which no one makes out and the ever after is not always happy. Originally from Italy, she lived in Germany and Japan before moving to the U.S. to pursue a Ph.D. in neuroscience. She recently became a professor, which absolutely terrifies her. When Ali is not at work, she can be found running, eating cake pops, or watching sci-fi movies with her two feline overlords (and her slightly-less-feline husband).

CONNECT ONLINE

AliHazelwood.com

🐦 EverSoAli

📷 AliHazelwood

♪ AliHazelwood

Ready to find
your next great read?

Let us help.

Visit prh.com/nextread